The Door to The Captain's Table Was Where Captain Kirk Remembered It . . .

. . . looking as always like the entrance to a supply cabinet rather than to the cozy tavern he knew lay within. Plain, nearly flush with the Martian stone of this ill-lit subterranean passageway, it was set apart from the other more ostentatious establishments on either side by nothing except a neatly painted sign just to the right of a hand-operated doorknob.

Captain Sulu cocked his head with a thoughtful wrinkling of his brow, and Kirk knew he was trying to remember why he'd never noticed the little entrance before. "This must be new," the younger captain decided at last.

Kirk hid his smile by stepping forward to take hold of the door. "I found it the first year I commanded the *Enterprise,* but some captains I know claim it had been around for dozens of years before that."

Sulu gave a little grunt of surprise, then moved back to let the door swing wide. "Sounds like the Federation's best kept secret."

A gentle swell of warmth, and sound, and scent rolled over them like a familiar blanket. "More like the galaxy's most exclusive club." With that, Kirk pulled on the doorknob and, just like a dozen times before, found himself inside The Captain's Table without specifically remembering stepping through the doorway. . . .

STAR TREK®
THE CAPTAIN'S TABLE
BOOK ONE OF SIX

WAR DRAGONS

JAMES T.
KIRK
A N D
HIKARU
SULU

AS RECORDED BY
L.A. GRAF

THE CAPTAIN'S TABLE CONCEPT BY
JOHN J. ORDOVER AND DEAN WESLEY SMITH

POCKET BOOKS
New York   London   Toronto   Sydney   Tokyo   Singapore

This book is a work of fiction. Names, characters, places and incidents are products of the author's imagination or are used fictitiously. Any resemblance to actual events or locales or persons, living or dead, is entirely coincidental.

An *Original* Publication of POCKET BOOKS

POCKET BOOKS, a division of Simon & Schuster Inc.
1230 Avenue of the Americas, New York, NY 10020

STAR TREK is a Registered Trademark of Paramount Pictures.

A VIACOM COMPANY

ISBN: 0-671-01463-3

First Pocket Books printing June 1998

10 9 8 7 6 5 4 3 2 1

Printed in the U.S.A.

WAR DRAGONS

Chapter One

KIRK

TRANSPARENT ALUMINUM spun a delicate membrane between the spindly green of transplanted Martian foliage and the blue-black Martian sky. As he watched one of the shipyard's many crew transports crawl patiently starward along a sparkling length of duranium filament, it occurred to James Kirk that man-made atmospheres were always the most fragile. Mars's chilly surface, although no longer the frigid wasteland of just a few centuries before, still clung to the planet only through the heroic efforts of her tenants. Outside the tame habitat of interlinked domes and tunnels, carefully tended flora transplanted from Earth's highest mountains and harshest tundras braved Mars' seasonal extremes, while the excess carbon dioxide from captured comets and a few million adventurous humans preserved just enough water on the surface to reward the plants with the occasional rain shower. The end result was a certain defiant beauty—spidery junipers and upright bracken reaching toward the teal spark of a homeworld their ancestors had left generations ago.

Not unlike humanity. Granted, humans pampered themselves with heaters, oxygen cogenerators, and pressurized suits and homes. But they still survived where nothing larger than a dust mote had survived before them, and Kirk liked the view they'd created.

Utopia Planitia's shipyards stretched from the skirt of the colony's main dome to beyond the horizon, arcing magically upward in the guise of shuttle-bees and crew elevators. The twinkling strings of force and fiber bound the orbiting ships only temporarily. Some nearly finished, others bare skeletons of the great leviathans they would become, they'd all turn outward soon enough. Darkened engine rooms would thunder with the pulse of great dilithium hearts, and the blood and muscle organs in the chests of her eager crew would leap up in answer, until that combined symphony of animal and mineral, creature and machine finally ignited her sleeping warp core. It was a song that kept an officer's heart beating long after no other passion could. *Old captains never die* . . .

Kirk stepped off the moving walkway in the northernmost Agridome, the one dedicated to the sparse rock gardens and dark succulents of a Terran gulf environment whose name Kirk no longer remembered. It wasn't crowded the way so many of the lux-enhanced Agridomes always were. Everyone wanted to watch the crews ship out while surrounded by bright Colombian parrots or Hawaiian orchids, as though they'd never really dared to leave Earth at all. But here the lack of tall plant life offered an unobstructed view through the sides and top of the dome, and the foliage reflected the reddish moonslight in silver washes, as though leaves and stems were spun from raw pewter. Kirk remembered coming here as a freshly minted ensign the night before he rode a crowded elevator up to his first assignment on board the *U.S.S. Farragut*. He'd stayed here until dawn, trying to count the multitude of stars he could see in the single patch of sky surrounding the ship that was to be his home, his life, his family for the next five years. That was more than forty years ago, but it felt like only yesterday. He could still hear the reverent hush of the leaves against his trousers as he picked a path through the foliage, and he still remembered the cool surface of the rock that served as his perch at the foot of the dome's widest panel. Best seat in the house.

He found the man he was looking for seated in exactly the same spot, shoulders square, head high, hands folded neatly in his lap. Beyond him and a thousand miles above, the brilliant glow of a refurbished starship dwarfed the dimmer signatures drifting around her.

Kirk smiled, and paused what he hoped was a respectful distance away. "Quite a view, isn't it?"

The younger captain rose, turning with an alert smoothness born of courtesy rather than surprise. That was something Kirk would always associate with Hikaru Sulu—the politeness which came to him apparently as naturally as breathing, with no taint of impatience or condescension. That, and an endless capacity for brilliance.

Sulu mirrored Kirk's smile, looking only a little embarrassed as he stole one last look at the magnificent ship hanging over his shoulder. "All the way into forever." He kept one hand cradled close to his waist, and extended the other as he stepped away from his now vacated stone seat. "Captain."

His grip was firm and even, as befitted a man of his position. Kirk returned the warm handshake in kind. "Captain."

"I didn't realize you were in-system," Sulu told him. "If I'd known, I would have stopped by to give my regards." It might have just been politeness, but Kirk could tell from his former helmsman's voice that the sentiment was sincere.

"Just passing through on my way to finalize the Khitomer negotiations," Kirk assured him. "I heard at the commodore's office that you were laid over to take on your new executive officer." A movement from the vicinity of Sulu's cupped hand caught Kirk's attention, and he found himself suddenly eye-to-eye with the small, spotted lizard that had clambered up onto Sulu's thumb for a better view. "He's shorter than I remember."

Sulu glanced fondly down at his stubby-tailed companion, tickling it under the curve of its bemused little smile until it blinked. "Actually, we're not scheduled to rendezvous for another two hours. This is just one of the friendly locals." Or as local as any living thing on Mars. It's anteriorly bilateral eyes and five-toed little feet hinted at a Terran origin, but it was the nearly identical gold-and-brown speckled relatives Kirk could now see lounging among the thick-leafed shrubs that gave its ancestry away. The Martian Parks Service didn't like mixing one planet's flora with another planet's fauna. Therefore, Terran landscaping equaled Terran lizards.

Each chubby little eublepharid had staked out its own rock or branch or hummock, blunt little noses lifted skyward, hindfeet splayed out behind them as though they were laconically bodysurfing on their own bliss. Kirk envied their abandon.

"Anything on your agenda for those next two hours?" he asked Sulu.

The younger captain shrugged one shoulder, startling his small passenger to abort its scrabble partway up his wrist. It paused there, as though forgetting where it meant to go, and Kirk noticed that unlike its lounging neighbors, this lizard's tail looked recently broken. Its curiosity and boldness must have gotten it in trouble recently. "I've got nothing in particular to do," Sulu admitted. "Just some long overdue relaxation while I have the chance." Kirk wondered if he'd been watching the meditating lizards instead of his own starship after all. "Did you have something in mind?"

"Some*place*." Kirk caught the politely questioning cock of Sulu's head, and smiled. "The perfect spot for overdue relaxation, as a matter of fact."

"Sounds good." Sulu glanced down as the lizard squirmed determinedly under the cuff of his uniform jacket. Before he could stop it, all that was left was a sausage-shaped bulge and an exposed nubbin where its brown-banded tail should have been. "Are they friendly toward nonhumanoids?"

"I've never known that to be a problem before," Kirk assured him. "And I'm sure that in the lizard world, that little guy was the captain of his very own rock somewhere. He'll be welcome in the Captain's Table."

He led a willing Sulu back out of the Agridomes and down the stately, curving avenues that led eventually to the spaceport proper. The door to the bar was where Kirk remembered it, looking as always like the entrance to a supply cabinet rather than to the cozy tavern he knew lay within. Plain, nearly flush with the Martian stone of this ill-lit subterranean passageway, it was set apart from the other, more ostentatious establishments on either side by nothing except a neatly painted sign just to the right of a hand-operated doorknob: The Captain's Table.

Sulu cocked his head with a thoughtful wrinkling of his brow, and Kirk knew he was trying to remember why he'd never noticed the little entrance before. "This must be new," the younger captain decided at last. He still held his arm balanced across his midsection in deference to the small passenger up his sleeve.

Kirk hid his smile by stepping forward to take hold of the door. "I found it the first year I commanded the *Enterprise,* but some captains claim it had been around for dozens of years before that."

Sulu gave a little grunt of surprise, then moved back to let the door swing wide. "Sounds like the Federation's best kept secret."

A gentle swell of warmth, and sound, and scent rolled over them like a familiar blanket. "More like the galaxy's most exclusive club." And, just like a dozen times before, Kirk found himself inside without specifically remembering stepping through the doorway.

The Captain's Table had never been a large establishment, and that didn't appear to have changed over the years. A brief, narrow entry hall spilled them abruptly into the bar's jumble of tables and chairs, and Kirk found himself veering sideways to avoid tripping over the tall alien seated directly in his path. Slitted eyes shifted almost imperceptibly within an almost featureless skull; one long, taloned finger dipped into a fluted glass half-full of viscous red liquid. It was a dance they'd performed the first time Kirk came into the Captain's Table, thirty years ago, not to mention every other time he'd stumbled onto the place on Argelius, Rukbat, or Vega. He stopped himself from laughing, not sure the lizardine patron would appreciate his humor, and instead nodded a terse apology before turning to join Sulu in the search for a table.

"Jimmee!"

It seemed everyone was here tonight.

Kirk spun around just in time to catch Prrghh at the

height of her leap. It wasn't one of her more spectacular jumps—Kirk would never forget watching her pounce from the second-floor bannister to land on her feet amid a particularly rousing discussion—but she still contacted him almost chest-high and entwined legs and arms around his torso in lithe, feline abandon. Kirk felt himself blush with pleasure when she stroked her own sleekly furred cheek against his. Acutely aware of all the other eyes in the bar, he resisted an impulse to wind his hands in her long primrose mane.

"James!" The bartender's roar collided with the low ceiling and ricocheted all over the room. "How in hell are you? Long time gone, boy-o!"

At least seven years, Kirk admitted to himself. But not a damned thing about the place had changed. Not so much as a dust mote.

"Don't be silly, Cap!" Prrghh squirmed around in Kirk's arms to look back over her shoulder, a position that would certainly have dislocated the spine of any anthropoid species. "Jimmy is always here!"

"Everyone is always here," a gruff voice behind them snarled. "Especially tonight." The female Klingon pushed past Kirk as though she had somewhere to go, then stopped abruptly and crouched to thrust her nose into Prrghh's pretty face. "If you're staying, sit down. If not, get out of the way and take your *mris* with you."

Prrghh's hiss was dry, but rich with hatred. Kirk turned them away from the Klingon, already knowing where things could lead once Prrghh's ruff had gotten up. "Why don't we find a seat, then?" he suggested smoothly. The Klingon grunted, but made no move to follow.

Kirk swung Prrghh to the floor as though he were twenty years younger or she twenty kilograms lighter. He let her fold her hand inside his, though, basketing his fingers with lightly extended claws. Her palm felt soft and familiar despite the years that had passed since it had last been fitted into his. Beside him, he noticed Sulu's failed efforts to hide a knowing grin by pretending to check on the lizard now peering curiously from beneath his cuff. Kirk wondered briefly what sorts of tales Sulu might tell out of school, considering his former commander's reputation. This time the heat in Kirk's cheeks had a little bit more to do with embarrassment.

It might have been a Saturday night, the place was so packed with bodies and voices and laughing. But, then, Kirk's memory said that it *always* looked like Saturday night, no matter what the day or time. Never too crowded to find a seat, thank God, but always just threatening to burst at the seams and overflow into the rest of the world. Kirk snagged Sulu by the hem of his jacket when the captain started toward the bar along the long end of the crowded room.

"A seat," Sulu said by way of explanation, lifting a lizard-filled hand to indicate his objective. Kirk glanced where the captain pointed and shook his head. The empty seats in question surrounded a grossly fat Caxtonian freighter pilot who appeared to have congealed around a tankard of milky brown fluid.

"He's Caxtonian," Kirk said. "By this time of night—"

Prrghh wrinkled her delicate nose. "He stinks fiercely!" Her long, supple tail snaked up between the men to twitch their attention toward the foot of the stairs. "This other human is looking at you."

The captain Prrghh pointed out looked human enough, at least. Salt-and-pepper beard, with hair a matching color that hung just a little longer than the current civilian standard. Kirk liked the well-worn look of his leather jacket, with its rainbow shoulder patch and anomalously fleece-trimmed collar. He was lean and wiry, with an earnest smile and tired but friendly eyes. Two other seats at his table were already filled by a rapier-thin dandy with black hair pulled back into a neat queue, and a broad bear of a man with a wild white beard and a curl of pipe smoke covering most of his head. When their leather-jacketed comrade waved again, Kirk acknowledged his gesture by slipping between a knot of standing patrons to blaze a path to the table.

"Gentlemen. Welcome to the Captain's Table." The salt-and-pepper haired human took Kirk's hand in a firm, somewhat eager shake. "Humans?" he asked, with just the slightest bit of hopefulness in his tone.

7

Kirk glanced at the freighter designation stenciled beneath the ship name on the leather jacket's patch, and recognized the wearer for a fellow captain. Of course. "The genuine article." He stole a chair from an adjacent table and offered it to Prrghh as Sulu conscientiously offered the freighter captain his left hand for shaking to avoid disturbing the reptilian passenger sprawled happily across his right palm.

The freighter captain pumped Sulu's hand without seeming to notice either the deviation from convention or the little passenger. "I'm sure pleased to see you," he grinned. "We were feeling a bit outnumbered tonight." He tipped a cordial nod to Prrghh as she slipped into her seat. "No offense, Captain. I just sometimes get real tired of aliens."

Her ears pricked up and green eyes narrowed on the other captain's lean face. Kirk recognized the expression—she liked a challenge. "Perhaps you have not met the right aliens."

The freighter captain lifted an eyebrow, and Kirk suspected he enjoyed his share of challenges, too. "Perhaps not," he admitted with a smile. "Maybe you can educate me."

"A surprisingly trusting lot, all points considered." The black-haired dandy tipped the tankard in his hand and squinted down its throat to verify it was empty. He hadn't interrupted his story for Kirk and Sulu's arrival, and didn't interrupt it now as he waved the tankard over his head to catch a server's attention. "They brought us neatly upside, lashed our hulls together, and came aboard with every thought of liberating our hold of its treasures. Alas, our only cargo was a crew of well-armed men and the good old Union Jack. By the time we'd taken our due, that was one Jolly Roger which never flew again."

"A clever story." The white-haired captain bit down on his meerschaum pipe and nodded wisely. "You're a cunning man, Captain, using that pirate crew's own expectations against them."

"The best judge of a pirate is one of his own," the Englishman admitted. His tankard still waggled above one shoulder. "My duties may seal me now to the queen, but I'm loathe to believe that any man who never ran with pirates can ever be their match."

Kirk straightened in his seat, stung by the remark. "Oh, I don't know about that."

The table's patrons turned to him almost as a unit, and he found himself momentarily startled by the frank challenge in their stares.

"Do you mean to disavow my own experience?" There was steel in the dark-haired Englishman's voice despite his friendly countenance.

The white-haired bear lifted one big hand in an obvious gesture of placation. "Easy, my friend. He sounds like a man with experience of his own."

"Some." Kirk settled back as a wiry serving boy scampered up to their table with a tray full of drinks. He gave the others first pick from the offerings, knowing what he wanted would still be there when they were done. "Pirates were never my primary business, but I've run across my share." He wrapped his hands around the mug of warm rum the boy placed in front of him, well familiar with the price every captain had to pay for the first round of drinks after his arrival. "Let me tell you about a time when I rescued the victims of some pirates, only to find out they weren't exactly what I'd expected. . . ."

I told myself it wasn't resentment. I didn't have the right to resent him. He hadn't killed my helmsman; he'd never placed my ship and crew in danger; he hadn't forced my chief medical officer to retire. He hadn't even murdered my best friend. He had never been anything but responsible, conscientious, and reliable. In these last few weeks, he'd stepped into a position made vacant by my own actions—not because he wanted it or because he hoped to prove anything to anybody, just because it was necessary. He was that kind of officer; service without complaint. Duty called, and he answered.

Still, I hadn't quite figured out how to separate him from everything that had come before. So while he stood there in the gym doorway, waiting for my answer with his damned impenetrable patience, my first instinct was to tell him to go to hell. Instead, I asked in the mildest tone I could muster, "Mr. Spock, can't this wait until later?"

I must not have sounded as patient as I'd hoped. He lifted one eyebrow a few micrometers, and peered at me with the same keen interest he probably applied to alien mathematics problems. Subtle emotions often had that effect on him, I'd noticed. It was as though he couldn't decide what informational value to assign such a random variable, and it annoyed him to settle for an imperfect interpretation.

Except, of course, that annoyance was a human emotion.

"Regulations stipulate that a starship's captain and executive officer shall meet once every seven days to coordinate duties and exchange pertinent crew and mission information." He didn't fidget. He just folded his hands around the data pad at his waist and settled in as though there was no place else he needed to be. "Our last such meeting was eleven days ago."

I turned back to my interrupted workout, leaving him to recognize the implied dismissal. "Then a few more hours won't make any difference." I aimed a high sweep-kick at the sparring drone, and earned a flash of approving lights for smashing into the upper-right-quadrant target.

Spock was silent for what seemed a long time, watching me with his usual cool fascination, no doubt, as I did my best to sweat out my personal demons at the expense of a supposedly indestructible robot.

In the end, they both managed to outlast me. I stopped before I started to stumble, but not before I was forced to suck in air by the lungful, or before I raised dark welts on the edges of both hands. I still secretly believed that if I could push myself just a little further, a little longer, I'd finally beat out the last of my uncertainty and guilt. But I'd entertained this secret belief for at least three weeks and hadn't yet found the magic distance. And now I refused to fall down in front of my new executive officer while I still struggled to find it.

He gave me what was probably a carefully calculated amount of time to catch my breath, then said to my still-turned back, "May I remind the captain that when he is not eating, sleeping, or engaging in some necessary physical activity, he is on duty. As senior science officer, my duty shift is concurrent with the captain's. As acting executive officer, my second duty shift coincides with when the captain is off-duty. Logic therefore suggests that rather than disrupt the necessary human sleep function, the most efficient time period during which to conduct our required conferencing would be during the one-hour fifteen-minute interval between the termination of my secondary duty shift and the beginning of your regular tour." He paused as though giving my slower human mind a moment to process his argument, then added blandly, "Which is now."

I swiped a hand over my eyes to flick away the worst of the sweat, and heaved an extra-deep breath to even out my panting. "Is this your way of telling me you're working a few too many hours, Mr. Spock?"

Both eyebrows were nearly to his hairline; I could almost feel the lightning flicker of his thoughts behind those dark Vulcan eyes. "No, Captain." He was as deadly serious as if I'd asked him to contemplate the course of Klingon politics over the next hundred years. "My current schedule allows ample time for research, personal hygiene, and the intake of food. Since Vulcans are not limited by the same stringent sleep requirements as humans, I find the hours between my shifts more than sufficient for meditation and physical renewal."

I tried not to sigh out loud. My entire Starfleet career would be a success if I could teach even one Vulcan to have a sense of humor. "What would you like to discuss, Mr. Spock?" I asked wearily.

Where anyone else—anyone human—would have promptly flipped up the pad to consult its readout, Spock announced, apparently from memory, "According to the first officer's log, there are currently eight hundred fifty-four individual crew evaluations which are late or incomplete."

I paused in the action of scooping up my towel to frown at him. "There are only four hundred and thirty crew on board the *Enterprise*."

Spock acknowledged my point with a microscopic tilt of his head. "Four hundred twenty-four evaluations are still outstanding from the quarter ending stardate ten thirteen

11

point four. The other four hundred thirty were due at the end of the most recent quarter, which ended on stardate twelve ninety-eight point nine."

And Gary—perpetually behind when it came to such mundane administrative duties—died before he had the chance to turn in even one from the most recent batch. I tried to disguise a fresh swell of frustration by scrubbing at my face and scalp with the towel, and began to dictate, for the record: "Since last quarter, Lt. Lee Kelso was killed in the line of duty. Dr. Elizabeth Dehner—killed in the line of duty. Lt. Commander Gary Mitchell—" I hid a bitter scowl by turning and banning the sparring drone back to its storage locker. "Killed." The word still tasted like cold gunmetal in my mouth. "I've ordered the lateral transfer of Lt. Hikaru Sulu and Ensign David Bailey from astrosciences to cover the vacant bridge positions, and have accepted Lt. Commander Spock's application for temporary assignment as ship's first officer." Snatching up my tunic and boots with a brusqueness that surprised even me, I came to a stop just shy of touching Spock, knowing full well how discomforting such proximity tended to be for Vulcans. "On a brighter note, Chief Medical Officer Mark Piper has retired to a safe, well-paying civilian position at Johns Hopkins University on Earth, and his replacement, Leonard McCoy, seems to be adapting nicely." That last was half a lie, since I hadn't actually spoken to my old friend McCoy since the day he first came aboard. I hadn't managed to say much even then, thanks to the doctor's colorful tirade against the ship's transporter. I hadn't remembered him being quite so technophobic, and found myself wondering if this was going to be a problem. "Why don't you put all that in Gary's files and call them done?"

Spock said nothing as I pushed past him on my way to the showers, merely stepping neatly to one side to avoid any unseemly physical contact. These were the kinds of little skills he must practice daily, I realized. Memorized patterns of behavior, movement, and response based on the thousands—perhaps millions—of social interactions he'd endured with a species whose conduct must seem positively arcane to him. I doubted he even understood much of the social data he mentally collected about his crewmates—he simply noted which interactions produced what results, and adjusted his model accordingly. If there was a difference between that and how a soulless machine would make use of the same information, at that particular moment I couldn't see what it was.

He followed me into the showers at what was no doubt a carefully calculated distance. Why did his patient silences always make me feel so guilty about whatever random bitterness popped into my head? Probably just another side-effect of his conversational style. I made a note to read up on Vulcan social customs, naively believing that I might find some understanding of Spock in their workings.

"The completion of Commander Mitchell's reports should pose no undue difficulty. I calculate that, by committing only forty-two point three percent of my on-duty time, I can deliver the reports to you within sixty-eight hours."

I hoped he didn't expect me to vet them quite so quickly. Eating and sleeping aside, I still had too much shoring up to do with the ship's new crew assignments to catch up on nearly 900 reports over the next three days.

"I must confess, however . . ."

Reluctance? I paused with the water crashing over my head to stare at him.

He all but rushed on before I could say a word. "I find the guidelines as laid out by Starfleet . . . baffling."

That admission of near-weakness surprised me more than almost anything else he could have said. I turned off the water and leaned out to study him. "How so?"

If he was human, I almost think he might have blushed. Not in embarrassment, but from the stone-faced frustration young children sometimes display when confronted with an impenetrable question they secretly suspect is a joke at their expense. I wondered if Vulcan children ever teased each other, or if the Vulcan Science Academy practiced hazing.

"The precise goal of such record keeping in the format specified is unclear," he said, quite formally, yet somehow without actually meeting my eyes. "There are no statistical data to be compiled, no discrete procedures to be followed. The desired end result is entirely inadequately conveyed."

I felt a strange warmth when I realized what he was saying. Sympathy, almost. "The desired end result is insight," I told him. He looked at me, and I smiled gently, explaining, "It's the first officer's job to be liaison to the crew. As captain, I depend on your observations—your instincts and feelings about the crew's state of mind."

Any emotion I might have imagined in his features evaporated with the infinitesimal straightening of his shoulders. "I am Vulcan. I have no instincts or feelings, only logic."

But the crew is human, I wanted to tell him, *just bubbling over with emotion.* Who in God's name had ever thought a Vulcan could serve as a human crew's XO?

The chirrup of my communicator saved us from pursuing a discussion neither of us was sure how to follow. I ducked out of the shower, careless of the water I dripped as I scooped up the communicator and flipped back the grid. "Kirk here. Go ahead."

The communications officer's honey-rich voice seemed strangely out of place in the conflicting Vulcan-human landscape of our interrupted conversation. "Sir, sensors have detected a disabled ship two point two kilometers to our starboard. There're some shipboard functions, but they don't respond to our hails."

A real problem. Not overdue reports, Vulcan emotional illiteracy, or misplaced captain's angst. A way to avoid feelings of helplessness by directing all my energy toward something I could change. "Plot a course to intercept, and scan the ship for survivors. I'm on my way to the bridge." I was already shaking my tunic free from the rest of my clothing by the time I snapped the communicator shut and tossed it to the bench. "I'm afraid you're on your own with those reports, Mr. Spock." As we left for the bridge, I flashed him a grin over the collar of my shirt, one that was probably as reassuring as it was strictly sincere. "Just do the best you can."

The bridge felt alien and strangely quiet when the turbolift deposited us on its margins. I missed Gary's laughter. It had been omnipresent—sometimes irritatingly so—and I found myself missing the sudden guilty hush that meant Gary had been sharing some particularly bawdy story with the rest of the crew. I missed his liar's smile, and his all-too-innocent, "Captain on the bridge" to announce my arrival.

Instead, the smoothly deep voice of my new helmsman made the call, and nobody abruptly ceased what they were doing or ducked their heads to hide a sudden onset of blushing. Decorum reigned, and I felt like I'd stumbled onto some other captain's vessel.

Still, I made that first step beyond the turbolift's doors without any outward sign of hesitation, briskly taking the steps down to my chair as Spock rounded behind me to head for his own station at the science console. "Mr. Sulu, report."

The helmsman—*my* helmsman, I reminded myself firmly—half turned in his seat, one hand still hovering possessively over his controls. "Sensors detect life on the vessel, but still no response to our hails. Their power exchange is in bad shape—the distress call might be on automatic."

Meaning the crew either couldn't use ship's systems to respond, or were too badly injured to make the attempt. I drummed my fingers on the arm of my command chair, thinking. On the viewscreen, the flat, elongated vessel drifted lazily clockwise, passing into a long silhouette, presenting us her nose, wafting lengthwise again. Her engines had been burned down to nubs, and the characteristic shatter of disruptor fire carved jagged stripes down her sides. It looked like at least half the ship was in vacuum, and the other half looked too dark to be getting anywhere near normal power. If there was anything or anyone still alive on board, they wouldn't stay that way forever.

"Spock, do we have any idea what kind of ship that is?"

He was silent for a moment. I gave him that—I'd figured out early on that he didn't like giving answers until he'd looked at all the data.

"Sixty-three percent of the identifiable ship's components strongly resemble an Orion Suga-class transport," Spock said at last, still scanning the computer's library screens. "Eleven point six percent are from an Orion-manufactured slaving facility. Four point two percent still bear the registration codes for a Klingon unmanned science probe. The remaining twenty-two point two percent resemble nothing currently on record."

I rubbed thoughtfully at my chin. "Could they be Orions?" I asked after adding up those bits and pieces. "Or maybe Orion allies?"

"Starfleet has reported no recent Orion pirating activity in this sector." While it wasn't exactly an answer to my question, it still led me a few steps closer to something that was. Spock swivelled in his chair to lift an eyebrow at the screen. "To my knowledge, the Orions have no allies."

Which told you everything you needed to know about the Orions. Still . . . "Just because we don't know about any allies doesn't mean there are none." I resisted an urge to toss Spock a puckish grin he wouldn't appreciate. "After all, even the Devil had friends."

He tipped his head in grave acknowledgment of my point, and I felt for one startled moment as though he were teasing me. *He's a Vulcan, not Gary Mitchell. Vulcans don't tease.* I turned forward again to hide my chagrin, and tapped my chair intercom with the side of my hand. "Bridge to transporter room."

"Transporter room. Scott here."

It worried me sometimes that my chief engineer spent so much time with the transporter. I tried to reassure myself that it was a fascinating piece of equipment, with all manner of systems to explore. But sometimes I just couldn't shake the suspicion that there was more to Scott's constant tending than mere affection. Probably not something I should mention around Dr. McCoy. "Scotty, can you get a fix on the life-forms inside that alien vessel?"

"Fifteen to twenty of them," he reported, managing to sound pleased with himself and a little frustrated all at the same time. "Maybe as many as twenty-four—the numbers are hopping all over the place."

"See if you can isolate them with a wide-angle beam." I muted the channel and glanced aside at Spock. "What sort of environment does that ship hold?"

He opened his mouth, took a small breath as though to say something, then seemed to change his mind at the last minute. Without having to reconsult his equipment, he informed me, "Slightly higher in oxygen and nitrogen than Earth normal, and at a slightly greater atmospheric pressure. Fluctuations in their gravitational equipment average at just a little less than one Earth gravity." Then he continued on without pausing, saying what I suspected had been the first thing to cross his mind. "May I infer from your questions that you intend to bring any survivors on board?"

"Indeed you may." I sent an automated request to security for a small reception committee, and a similar request to sickbay for an emergency medical team. "I've never ignored another ship's distress signal, and I don't intend to start now."

Spock stood smoothly as I jumped up from my chair, his own quiet way of announcing that he was following me down to the transporter room. "And if the captain who initiated this distress call is an Orion ally, as you speculate?"

I looked up at the viewscreen, quickly refreshing my image of its crumpled superstructure and ruptured sides. "Then they still need rescuing." We certainly couldn't tow them anywhere—I doubted their ship would stand up to the grasp of the tractor beam, much less to having its tumble forcibly stilled and its whole mass accelerated along a single vector. Besides, towing wouldn't take care of their wounded. I wouldn't put any captain in the position of being helplessly dragged along while his crew died around him. Not if I could help it.

"Don't worry, Mr. Spock," I continued as I circled my command chair and took the stairs to the second level in a single step. "We can isolate our guests in rec hall three until arrangements are made to drop them off with whatever allies they're willing to claim." The turbolift doors whisked aside for me, and I slipped inside with one hand on the sensor to hold them open as Spock caught up. "No one's going to get free run of the ship just because we're giving them a ride."

He stepped in neatly beside me, pivoting to face the front of the 'lift with a precision that seemed to be just a part of his movement, not something he planned. "Worry is a human emotion," he stated, as though correcting me on some particularly salient fact.

I stepped back from the doors and let them flash closed on us, taking up my own place on the opposite side of the turbolift. "Of course it is," I said, rather flatly. I kept my eyes trained on the deck indicator to avoid having to look at him. "How could I have forgotten?"

Chapter Two

SULU

THE RESOUNDING CRASH of furniture interrupted Captain Kirk's story. Hikaru Sulu swung around to see what kind of trouble might be brewing in the shadowy depths of the Captain's Table. All he saw was the female Klingon heading for the bar with an empty tankard swinging in one large fist. Apparently, kicking over her chair with a booted foot was her method of politely disengaging herself from a conversation when she wanted more blood wine. There was something a little odd about the Klingon, something that nagged at the edge of Sulu's usually reliable memory, but he couldn't pin down exactly what it was. Did the Imperial medals of honor on her chest look just a bit outdated, or were they slightly futuristic? He felt as he often did back in the old days, when he and Chekov would spend their shore leaves in cheap spaceport flight simulator games that hadn't been reprogrammed or updated in years. Nothing looked quite right, and yet none of it seemed quite serious enough to worry about either.

"Relax," Kirk said softly, when Sulu turned back to their table and his unfinished drink. "That's what you came here to do, remember? And this is the one place in the galaxy

19

where you don't have to feel responsible for everything that happens."

Sulu gave him a quizzical look. "Because I'm not the only captain in the room, you mean?"

"Because there is no one in the room who is *not* a captain." The felinoid alien on Sulu's other side wrapped a slender hand around his biceps, flexing her pearly claws at his involuntary look of surprise. Sulu was grateful that Kirk had caught him only a few steps out of the station commander's office, so that he still wore the tough red synthetic wool of his Starfleet jacket. "Yes, silly. Even me. Captains come in many shapes and sexes." She aimed a wicked look across the table at the freighter captain in his worn leather jacket. "And *species*," she added meaningfully.

The human's salt-and-pepper beard split with a rueful wince. "Very true, *Captain.*"

"About all we have in common are the headaches," said the massive, white-maned man next to him. He took his meerschaum pipe from his mouth and made an old-fashioned gesture of respect toward the felinoid. "Or whatever part of your anatomy responds to having too few hours in the day to solve too many problems."

"Spine," she said and curled herself into a cat-smooth stretch that would have put her into traction if she were a human. "Ahh! That last run to Andor was a killer. The only good thing about it was—" She paused and glanced across the table at the English dandy, then lowered her voice to a hiss, "the Orion pirates left us alone, *this* time."

The freighter captain watched her with appreciative eyes. "Pirates are the one thing I've never had to deal with, knock on wood." He wrapped his knuckles on the table, startling the stub-tailed lizard into a short skittle from where it had been basking in the light from their table's lamp. The passing bartender promptly dropped another bottle of Martian Red Ice Ale onto the space the lizard had vacated. Since his own mug was still full, the bearded human offered it to the felinoid, who accepted with a flirtatious flick of her long eyelashes. "As bad as it must be to hunt them, I bet it's even worse to be the one they're hunting."

"Not if you keep your hull clean and your sails mended," said the Englishman. With his thigh-high boots and cutlass, he could have walked straight from the pages of a swash-buckling Rafael Sabatini adventure novel. Whatever costume party he was attending later that night, he'd probably win a prize for best historical accuracy. Even his boots were a perfect reconstruction from the days when shoemakers hadn't bothered to make different shoes for right and left feet. "Trust me, there's not a pirate in the world who ever bothered to scrape all the barnacles off his belly."

"Very true," agreed the man with the meerschaum pipe, with a look of grudging respect. "If you have a good steady wind behind you, you can loft your canvas and leave them wallowing like garbage scows."

The felinoid captain shook her caramel-colored mane of hair. "I theenk thees pirates are not sso eezee to run from, or to fyght," she said definitively. "I haf heard thiss story, how thees Nykusss mersenries almost start a war wiss the Klingons." She wrinkled her nose in the direction of the loud female Klingon who was just returning to her own table with a fresh drink. "Who can blame them?"

"That was later," Kirk told her. "The Anjiri and the Nykkus were on the run when I met them. But a few years after that, when they came after *us*—that was when things really got interesting." He gave Sulu a sidelong look, his hazel eyes gleaming with laughter. "Of course, you really should hear that part of the story from the man who got attacked by them on his first cruise with a brand-new ship—"

Sulu winced at the reminder of his initial botched mission on the *Excelsior,* but he couldn't help smiling as well. As soon as he recognized the story Captain Kirk was spinning he should have guessed that he wasn't going to escape without telling his part of it. And considering who he was waiting for here at Utopia Planitia, recounting that particular encounter with pirates did seem like an appropriate way to pass the time. Sulu glanced around at the circle of waiting faces and took a fortifying sip of Red Ice ale.

"It all started back on Deep Space Three," he said. He tickled the lizard under its chin until it wiggled up onto his hand, feeling strangely reassured by its cool presence against his skin. "Of course, we didn't know then that Captain Kirk's story was just the beginning of ours. Or

21

that ours was the finish of his, I guess. All we knew was that we had a delivery to make, and a brand-new starship crew to make it with. . . ."

This really should be more nerve-wracking, I thought, watching the coordinated array of industrial-sized transporter beams play over the sleek, gull-winged shape of an FL-70 Falcon. After all, this unusual procedure—beaming a fleet of small reconnaissance ships directly into a starship's shuttle bay—wasn't just being tested for the first time, it was being tested on a newly designed and newly commissioned starship. *My* starship, the *U.S.S. Excelsior.* I know you'll say I'm prejudiced, but I had come to be extremely fond of the *Excelsior* in the short time since I'd been promoted to be her captain. She was a big muscular ship, built for maximum self-sufficiency and self-defense rather than speed and sleekness. The result was a workhorse, not anywhere as pretty to look at as the *Enterprise,* but the working model for a future line of long-range Starfleet cruisers.

Right now, however, the *Excelsior* was the only one of her kind and thus the only starship in the fleet whose main shuttle bay was big enough to carry all twelve Falcons. With the current level of diplomatic tension that existed between the Klingons and the Federation, that meant she was the only way those reconnaissance ships could get transferred to the Neutral Zone without making the Empire suspect they were being invaded. So, despite the fact that her shuttle bay doors were precisely one meter too small for the Falcons to fly through, this critical assignment had fallen to me, my ship, and my newly trained crew. You can see why I should have been shaking in my boots.

But as I watched the first FL-70 begin to glitter and fade out of existence, all I felt was the sweet relief of finally being done with testing and shakedown cruises and getting down to actual work. We'd spent months putting the *Excelsior* and her crew through every torturous test and trial that Starfleet's Corps of Astronomical Engineers could devise. In theory, our goal was to locate and correct any mechanical or computer flaws before we actually took the big ship out on her first mission, but I'd come to suspect that there was another, more subtle reason for shakedown cruises. By the time they were done, your entire crew was so hardened to crisis—and impatient for action—that any potential for nervous human error had been entirely burned away.

It took a surprisingly long time for the first Falcon to vanish from Deep Space Three's huge docking hanger. Its edges sparkled with transport effect long moments before the center did, and it vanished the same way, with a gleaming curve of cockpit windows lingering to the end like the Cheshire Cat's smile. The power drain created by the transport generators made the hangar lights dim, and the catwalk on which I was standing shook with subsonic vibrations as inertial dampeners cut in to compensate for the sudden shift in mass from the old-fashioned revolving station to the *Excelsior*. There was a lengthy pause after the Falcon was gone, then the slim communicator on my wrist chirped a request for attention.

"Sulu here."

"First Falcon's in the nest, sir," said Tim Henry gruffly. My chief engineer didn't have Montgomery Scott's rolling brogue or his tendency to prophesy disaster any time the ship's systems were stressed, but Henry had his own idiosyncracies. He spent all his off-duty hours building molecular model cities out of nano-machinery, creating what his xeno-biologist wife Sandi affectionately called "quantum flea circuses." This quirk was more than outweighed, however, by his superb trouble-shooting intuition. While all the engineers around him were scratching their heads and reaching for their computer models to determine which of the *Excelsior*'s many newly designed systems could be causing a ship malfunction, Henry already had panels off and was testing circuits. Ninety percent of the time, his first guess turned out to be the right one. If there was one thing my years on the *Enterprise* had taught me, it was that you could forgive a lot of eccentricity in a good engineer.

"Any problems with inertial compensation?" I craned my head to glance over the transporter tech's shoulder at the monitor which showed the *Excelsior*, docked high on the station's outer ring. It was an irrational thing to do, of course, since I couldn't possibly tell from the outside if the transport of this enormous and unwieldy piece of cargo had damaged my starship's delicate link to Deep Space Three. But the unlikely vision of my ugly metal behemoth floating like a swan against the background swirl of stars always made me smile.

"Barely a flicker on the readouts, sir," Henry reported. "If anything, we started to compensate for the mass a few milliseconds too soon. I'm going to synchronize our inertial dampeners with the transporter power surge next time. Clear for number two."

"Acknowledged." I nodded at the station's transporter chief and she punched in the coordinates of the second FL-70. This time I watched the power gauges instead of the glittering sweep of the beam, and whistled at the energy consumption they recorded. If we had been anywhere near an inhabited planet, that much diversion of sunlight might have caused a noticeable climate change. However, the massive red giant that Deep Space Three orbited had long ago engulfed and charred any planets it once had. The space station was free to drain off as much radiant energy as it needed.

"We've got the highest capacity cargo transporters in the sector, Captain." The station commander had seen the direction of my gaze and interpreted my whistle correctly. Wendell Barstow was an older man, brisk and businesslike as befitted someone who oversaw both Starfleet and mercantile operations on his watch. "And we've handled bigger packages than those FL-70s of yours. Don't worry, we'll get them all into your shuttle bay without burning out any power circuits."

"But will the Neutral Zone outpost we're heading for have the transporter capacity to get them out again?" asked a grim voice from beside me. "If not, the *Excelsior*'s shuttle bay doors aren't going to fit anymore."

I glanced over at my executive officer, a little surprised that this long-awaited call to action hadn't ignited the same cheerfulness in him that it had in me. "Our orders are to deliver the Falcons to Elaphe Vulpina Nine," I said. "Last time I checked, that was the Neutral Zone outpost set up specifically to guard the Vulcans' main transporter research station. Don't worry, Mr. Chekov, those patrol ships won't have to blast their way out of the *Excelsior*'s belly."

"Assuming the Klingons haven't recently blasted Elaphe Vulpina," Chekov reminded me. "You know we've been on the brink of war with them ever since we butted heads on the Genesis planet. If they decided to attack—"

"A dozen little reconnaissance ships built for stealth and speed won't be any help to us. They can stay right inside our cargo bay while we stop any Klingon incursion." I eyed my second-in-command with more attention than I'd paid to him since the day he'd first reported to his new post on the *Excelsior*. He looked older than in the days when we'd manned the helm of the *Enterprise*, of course, but then so did I. Less muscle and more bone showing in our faces, less rashness and more wisdom in our eyes. But the lines carved between his dark eyebrows seemed sharper than usual today, and his eyes met mine reluctantly. I frowned, and took a few steps away from the station commander and his transporter chief, trusting that the rumble of the big inertial compensators would cover our lowered voices.

"Pavel, what's the matter? I told you when you came aboard, if there's some part of a mission you don't like, it's your job as my executive officer to say so." That was another thing I'd learned from serving with Captain Kirk and Commander Spock back on the *Enterprise*. "Are you worried the Klingons will find out we're delivering a fleet of military ships to the border and attack us?"

Chekov shook his head, but remained silent. I held my tongue as the second Falcon slowly began to vanish. Ten years of serving together, and nearly twenty years of friendship, let me know when to push this man and when to let him be. At length, he made a face. I don't think it was the stale smell of Deep Space Three's regenerated air that inspired it.

"I think this all just reminds me a little too much of the *Kobayashi Maru,*" my executive officer admitted. "Why did Starfleet Command have to make our very first mission one that involves the Klingons and the Neutral Zone?"

"Our mission parameters don't have us coming within fifty kilometers of the Neutral Zone itself," I reminded him. "Unless they happen to be patrolling near Elaphe Vulpina, the Klingons should never even know we were there."

"Right." I couldn't tell from his clipped-off voice if

Chekov was being sardonic or just serious. He watched in silence as the second Falcon disappeared. This time, it was the sensor-deflecting nose array that lingered until last. "Just promise me you won't answer any mysterious distress calls from the other side of the Klingon border."

"Don't worry," I said dryly. "I got that out of my system back at the academy." My wrist communicator chirped again, and I tapped the channel open. "Sulu here."

I was expecting Tim Henry's confirmation that the second small patrol ship had arrived intact, but what I got instead was the younger voice of Nino Orsini, my chief security officer. "Captain, we just got a call from the ship's resupply team. They've gotten delayed down on level eight because of a little alien trouble."

I frowned. "What kind of alien trouble?"

"A confrontation with some—er—revenue agents from the local dilithium supplier. The station quartermaster insists their tax claim on Deep Space Three's dilithium stock isn't valid, but they're refusing to let our supply team take it without paying a tariff. Should I take a detail from the *Excelsior* down to deal with it or call in station security?"

I glanced over at Chekov and got an answering nod without even needing to ask the question. "Neither, Lieutenant. Commander Chekov is going to straighten out the situation."

"Aye, sir. And by the way, Chief Henry says to tell you that the second Falcon came in just fine with the modified inertial dampening procedure."

"Acknowledged. Sulu out."

By the time I'd lifted my thumb off the communicator controls, Chekov had already vanished into the nearest turbolift. I sighed, and turned back to the glitter of transporter beams scything through the station's cargo hold. The third Falcon was beginning to vanish, leaving nine more to go. If the truth be told I was already bored, but being a starship captain meant more than just making all the hard decisions in times of crisis. It also meant being present at all of your ship's momentous occasions, from major events like the signing of peace treaties to small ones like the arrival of new crew members and the first-ever transport of ships into shuttle bays.

It also meant delegating authority, something I was still trying to accustom myself to. I knew better than to try dealing with every problem and crisis in person, but part of my brain was still down in that turbolift with Chekov, trying to foresee and solve the problems he'd encounter on deck eight. Was that the right way to delegate, or was I supposed to just hand the problem over to a competent member of my crew and then forget about it? It was something I still wasn't clear on, and in this case it was no use asking myself what my mentor, Captain Kirk, would have done. Delegating authority was the one thing he was notoriously bad at.

"Problem, Captain Sulu?"

"A minor one." I joined Wendell Barstow back at the transporter desk in time to see the third Falcon dissolve into glitter. "How long has your local dilithium supplier been trying to levy a tariff on Starfleet requisitions?"

"What?" The station commander looked as blank as if I'd told him that the Klingons had just signed a peace treaty with the Federation. "Who says they are?"

"My resupply team. They've been asked to pay a surcharge to top off the *Excelsior*'s stocks."

Barstow snorted at that and pressed his wrist communicator on. "Barstow to Operations Room. How many non-Starfleet ships do we have in port now, Rebovich?"

"Four, sir," said the voice of his second-in-command. "An Andorian luxury liner, an Earth courier, a Tellerite merchant ship, and an Orion private yacht."

"Thanks. Barstow out." The station commander gave me a tolerant look. "Sounds to me like your resupply team is getting itself caught in a classic Orion swindle. You did say this was the *Excelsior*'s first full-fledged mission, didn't you, Captain Sulu? You should have warned your greenhorns never to pay a toll to the trolls."

I felt my cheeks tighten with embarrassment, and it wasn't just at the stationmaster's blunt frontier slang. It was hard enough to be a brand-new captain without the additional burden of shepherding a brand-new crew through all the pitfalls that unscrupulous aliens could throw at them. "I'll warn my XO not to fall for it," I managed to say calmly enough, but I tapped my communicator channel open with more force than it needed. Fortunately, Starfleet built its equipment to sustain worse things than a captain's irritability.

"Sulu to Chekov."

"Chekov here." From the slowing pitch of the turbolift whistle in the background, I could tell he had almost arrived at his destination. It made his disgruntled tone understandable. "Change of orders, Captain?"

"No, just a change of context. Commander Barstow thinks our 'dilithium revenue agents' are probably Orion swindlers. I thought you'd want to be prepared—"

"To rescue the supply team from their clutches," Chekov finished for me, the irritation in his voice replaced by a veteran space-traveler's amusement. "Understood. Chekov out."

I released the communicator button and stood watching a fourth Falcon fade into glimmers beneath the scouring of the station's immense transporter beams. It looked like pure magic, as any sufficiently advanced technology does, but I knew that billions of complex computer functions were being carried out during each second of that transfer, accompanied by an input of solar power so vast that magnetically confined power conduits were required to supply it. And the net result of all this technological wizardry? Twelve little two-man reconnaissance ships were moved a distance they could easily have coasted to on the strength of their own warp exhaust, if the engineers who designed the *Excelsior*'s shuttle bay doors had only foreseen the need to admit them.

My communicator chirped again, but this time it didn't wait for me to announce myself. "Captain, you and the station commander need to hear this," said my security chief's voice. Before I could respond, the crackle of a poor-quality or very distant subspace transmission burst from the speaker on my wrist.

"Ships converge Deep Space Three attack wait explosion capture ships converge Deep Space Three attack wait explosion capture ships converge—"

Orsini's voice replaced the ominous babble. "We picked it up on a routine scan of subspace frequencies, sir," he said before I could ask. "About a minute ago."

"Klingons?" I demanded. Deep Space Three was the major restocking point for the entire length of the Klingon Neutral Zone, although it wasn't anywhere near the boundary itself. If it was under attack by the Klingon Empire, a major incursion was in progress and Chekov's gloom regarding our mission had been well-justified.

"No, Captain. The transmission signature isn't Klingon, and the language was barely decipherable." That was my chief communications officer, Janice Rand. Her composed voice, the result of long years of deep space experience, contrasted noticeably with Orsini's youthful urgency. "Our universal translator found a comparable alien language sampled twenty years ago in a sector near here, but the translation you just heard only has a forty-five percent confidence interval. We're not even sure that we caught the entire text of the message."

"Can you pinpoint the source?"

"No, sir. It was broadcast in a part of the subspace spectrum no one uses much because of interference from black holes. That's the crackling noise that you heard."

"So it could be coming from anywhere." I watched the last glittering fade of the fourth Falcon and frowned. "Have our sensors picked up unusual ship movements anywhere near the station?"

"Several vessels are in the vicinity, sir, but their flight paths don't seem to be coordinated." Science Officer Christina Schulman sounded as if she was frowning, but then she almost always did when she was trying to interpret long-range sensor data. I had never seen anyone coax more information from sensor arrays and be less satisfied with it. "Some of the ion trails do show an unusual enhancement in the heavier transperiodic isotopes, which means their warp drives are getting pretty old. Other than that, we don't have much information."

"Which means they aren't broadcasting their identification profiles the way most merchant ships do." I swung around to face the station commander, who'd been listening in thoughtful silence beside me. "Commander Barstow, I suggest we stop the transport and place the station on red alert—"

"Based on a single badly translated transmission?" The older man gave me the same tolerant look that had greeted my resupply crew's encounter with Orion swindlers. "Captain Sulu, do you have any idea how many times a week we get hit with this kind of thing out here on the frontier? Garbled messages with just enough words to make the universal translator think it knows the language—and by the time you track it down, you find out it was just a subspace echo that got bounced through a singularity from one side of the quadrant to the other. Or maybe the Klingons along the Neutral Zone amusing themselves by trying to destroy our crew's morale. We can't raise our shields every single time it happens—it would disrupt all our cargo loading operations."

I frowned out at the silver crescent of docking rim I could see through the cargo bay windows. All of those ships, including my own, lay vulnerable to attack unless the station raised its shields to protect them. I might be succumbing to new-captain jitters, but something about the brutal simplicity of those intercepted attack orders told me they weren't idle Klingon chatter. And Captain Kirk always said to trust your instincts.

I shot out a hand and caught the transporter chief's hand away from her controls before she could begin the transport of another Falcon. "I can't force you to shield your own station, Commander Barstow," I said quietly. "But I *can* order this loading operation to be halted so that I can raise the shields on my own ship."

"But if we power down the beam generators now it'll take two hours of recalibration before we can start up again," the transporter chief protested. "We have other ships waiting to be loaded—"

"I'll take full responsibility for the delay." I could see Barstow's exasperation deepen to annoyance. "You can put a reprimand in my file if this turns out to be a false alarm, but for now I'm taking it seriously. I want my ship shielded in case of attack."

"Shut down the transporters," Barstow told his transporter chief reluctantly. She swept a hand across her controls, and I felt the vibration of the immense plasma cables that fed the beam generators fade to a shiver and then vanish. A moment later, the deep-throated growl of the inertial dampeners faded too. Inside the shroud of silence that had fallen over the station's main cargo bay, the chirp of my communicator seemed as loud as the whoop of a distress siren. I thumbed it on, expecting the *Excelsior*.

"Sulu here."

"It's Chekov." His tense whisper probably wouldn't have been audible a moment before. "Captain, our resupply team's not being swindled, they're being held hostage in the quartermaster's office. They must have been forced to call in a false report to explain their delay in returning to the ship."

I lowered my voice to avoid giving his position away in case anyone was listening. "How many Orions are there?"

"None," Chekov said grimly. "I only got a glimpse of the aliens guarding the door, but they don't look like Orions or anything else I've ever seen. And they don't look friendly. I think they're trying to break into the dilithium storage area."

I glanced over at Barstow. "Attack wait explosion," I reminded him and saw his face tighten with dismay. He pressed his own communicator and began calling for security. "Chekov, do what you can to keep those aliens out of there until station security arrives," I told my second-in-command. "They may be trying to sabotage Deep Space Three."

"Understood. Chekov out."

I slapped the communicator to another channel. "Sulu to *Excelsior*."

"Henry here." My crew had obviously taken the intercepted threat as seriously as I had, since they'd summoned the next-in-command back from the shuttle bay to the bridge. "Orders, Captain?"

"Put the ship on red alert. Disengage from the station and back away far enough to raise shields." The interference from a starship's powerful electromagnetic defenses had been known to play havoc with space station circuits, especially if the station hadn't raised its own external shields. "Warn all Starfleet vessels in port that we have a hostage situation in progress, potential sabotage on Deep Space Three, and an attack force of unknown proportions on the way." I glanced at Barstow and found him heading for the turbolift without waiting to consult with me. I didn't hold his departure against him—now that he knew the threat was real, the safety of Deep Space Three had to be his top priority, just as the safety of the *Excelsior*'s crew and her cargo was mine. "Beam me back aboard before you raise shields."

"Too late, sir." The sweeping glare of phasers across the cargo bay windows had already told me that. "We just came under attack."

"Then get those shields up, *now!*" To my relief, I could see docking clamps opening all along the silver rim of Deep Space Three, as one Starfleet vessel after another disengaged and prepared for battle. The *Excelsior* was already several meters from the station and moving fast for all her workhorse bulk. As I watched, a sudden shiver of phosphorescence ran across her starboard side as her rising shields brushed past Deep Space Three's own defensive screens.

Phaser bursts exploded again across the cargo windows, too bright this time to be anything but a direct hit off the screens in front of them. I thought it was a stray shot until it happened again, a few seconds later. I frowned and glanced over at Deep Space Three's transporter chief, but she was so busy recalibrating her instruments that I wasn't sure she even knew an attack was in progress. I tapped her shoulder and got a startled upward look.

"Is there a weapons array near here?"

"Not really. The nearest one is on the lower docking ring."

"What about life-support? Shield generators?"

She shook her head again, looking puzzled. "Cargo transporters are never placed near any critical station systems. The interference from our power circuits would mean constant retuning. Why?"

I squinted up at another burst of light. "Because whoever these attackers are, they seem to be concentrating their fire on us."

"On *us?*" She craned her head upward. "But the screens

over the cargo bay were never designed to withstand heavy fire—"

"I think they know that." I frowned, watching the swoop and flash of surprisingly small and mismatched fighters behind the phaser explosions. This was starting to look more like a pirate raid and less like a military attack. "They're staying tucked between the station wheels, where the weapons arrays can't reach them. And any return fire from the starships out there will just add to the damage they're doing."

The transporter chief looked back down at her panel, winced, then swept her hand across it, taking all her systems back to zero again. "We'd better get out before that hull breaches. At least the Falcons won't mind being exposed to vacuum—"

"No, but they will mind being exposed to phaser fire." I wasn't going to let my very first mission be wrecked by a bunch of alien buccaneers who'd picked Deep Space Three to loot that week. If I couldn't be aboard the *Excelsior,* overseeing this fight, then I could at least be a participant in it. "Get up to Operations," I told the transporter chief, giving her a little push to separate her from her station. "If the station shields fall, tell your security chief to try activating the shields on the other seven Falcons by remote command."

"The other *seven* Falcons?" she repeated, and blinked at me in confusion. "But we only transported four over to the *Excelsior.*"

"I know." I took a step away from the transporter desk and felt the weight of the last five months—the constant decisions, the endless complications, and the unrelenting responsibility—slide unexpectedly off my shoulders. I started to understand why Captain Kirk always insisted on leading all those landing parties himself. "The eighth one will already have its shields raised. From the inside."

Chapter Three

KIRK

IN MY CASE, defending the *Enterprise* from imminent attack wasn't my primary concern. After all, we'd found no evidence of unidentified ships loitering about, and sensors verified that any detectable engine residue belonged only to the damaged vessel in front of us. If you'd asked me at the moment Spock and I arrived in the transporter room, I would have said our biggest challenge would be figuring out our visitors' dietary needs.

I would have been wrong, of course. But I was still young; I had a lot to learn.

So with all the other dire considerations that could have been racing through my head as Engineer Scott activated the transporter, what actually struck me first about them was that they should have been bigger.

Not that I had any expectations—we still hadn't been able to establish voice contact with them, much less visual. The only thing we knew for certain from our sensor readings was that they *weren't* Orions; whether or not they were sympathizers toward that dyspeptic race still remained to be seen. Still, the flashes of transporter cohesion that came just ahead of total solidity suggested terror, speed, and ferocity far beyond anything the Orions had ever achieved.

So when the transporter's whine finally drifted to silence and left behind a half dozen armored creatures not much taller than my shoulder, I felt a little twinge of surprise.

I heard Spock later call them therapods, but at the time the only word that came to my mind was "reptile." Pebble-skinned, a uniform sand gray in color, they had the lidless, jewel-toned eyes of a gecko and the fierce, conical teeth of a crocodile. They were thick limbed, with broad, brutish heads; their crouching, forward-leaning posture would have made them look ready to attack even if they'd been the most gentle, open-minded people in the world, which I had a feeling they were not. The armor was mechanical—no biological elements at all, as far as I could see—but fitted them so tightly that it might have been chitinous plates or thickened skin. When one of them lowered its muzzle to make direct eye contact with me, I swallowed my first surge of alarm and decided I'd interpret the gesture as one of leadership rather than aggression.

Realizing how easily the rod-shaped universal translator could be mistaken for a weapon, I kept my hand scrupulously relaxed at my side as I took a single step toward the transporter pad. "I'm Captain James T. Kirk of—"

They exploded into the room as a single unit, like shrapnel from an old-fashioned bomb. I'd brought an escort of security personnel—I was altruistic, not stupid—and the shriek of phaser fire filled the tiny room as lashing tails and brilliant claws struck out in every direction. I had less than an eye-blink to glimpse two men go down under a powerful double-footed kick from one attacker, then one of the armor-plated monsters slammed me full in the chest and we hit the deck so hard my vision grayed.

It missed gutting me by a few inches—I heard the heavy claws on its feet screech against the decking. Instinctively, I heaved as much strength into my counter blow as I could muster, aiming for the fetid stink of its breath so close to my own face. The translator in my hand impacted with bone and armor, smashing snapping teeth aside but clearly doing nothing to discourage my attacker from another try. Dread clenched at my belly as its big lizard face swung back toward me—

Then the referred jolt of a phaser blast made my hands go numb and knocked the glint of consciousness from the creature's eyes.

I thought I had managed to muscle it aside myself, valiantly ignoring the adrenaline shakes that were making my stomach feel like liquid. But, as it rolled to flop prostrate on the decking, I saw Spock straighten from where he'd bent to haul it off me. I also saw the phaser still in his hand.

"Thank you, Mr. Spock." No sense spoiling the moment by pointing out the legendary Vulcan reputation for nonviolence.

He glanced at the phaser as though unimpressed with how it looked in his hand. "Merely being prudent, Captain."

Because arranging for a new commander officer would prove an annoyance this far away from a Federation starbase? Or because he'd had just enough exposure to the executive officer position to know he didn't want the captaincy? There are some questions better left unasked.

Turning, I made a quick survey of the damage around the transporter room. Spock was one of the few people in front of the console still standing—apparently, our visitors hadn't marked him as a threat when it came to picking targets. Which showed what both of us knew, I guess, since I probably would have discounted a Vulcan, too. But the attackers themselves lay in huddles all over the room, twitching as though in feverish sleep. I was surprised but pleased by how little human blood had been spilled in the brief skirmish. You could say a lot of things about Starfleet security squads, but that they were tough as nails should be top on anybody's list.

"Call sickbay," I told Scott. He and his transporter tech were still safely ensconced behind the control console, wisely staying out of the way. "Get that medical team down here."

"Presumptive, Nykkus sometimes are." The voice was feather-light, and drifted up to us from the dented device still clutched in my right hand. "Incendiary, Nykkus most times are."

The alien still crouched near the back of the transporter

pad blinked at me from beneath the arms he'd crossed over his head. He'd been completely screened from view by the armored creatures now spread out on my floor, who I now realized were probably protecting him. His own armor was lighter, more like a tense skin of protective clothing, and he was slim and more delicately boned. What struck me most, though, was how humanoid his face and eyes appeared when compared to his guards'—like the features of a human compared to those of a gorilla. He stood with a fluid grace that was neither threatening nor submissive and splayed one long-fingered hand against his chest. "Vissith am I." One finger curled out to point down at my side while the little nubbin that was all he had for a tail twitched nervously. "From this elongation, a voice I sense. This alteration, what it eject tells you?"

I glanced down at the translator, then back up at him. "Yes. This is a translation device." Which I very likely addled by bashing it against one of Vissith's guards. It spun out a musical braid of hissing and clicks which I hoped made for better syntax in his language than it did in mine. "Can you understand what I'm saying to you?"

Vissith's head cocked almost over onto his shoulder. His whole body seemed to fidget, fingers moving, knees flexing arrhythmically. "Yes," he said at last. But even the voice given him by the translator sounded uncertain. "Although very bad your decoration of words is."

I couldn't help but smile. "The translation should improve as we talk longer." I was almost hypnotized by his constant movement, and had to make myself blink and look back up at his jewel-tone eyes. "I'm Captain James T. Kirk, of the Federation starship *Enterprise*. We mean you no harm."

He bobbed a short staccato, toes clicking. "Our existence you broken have." Fingers fluttered to dust hissing words over his fallen guards. "My domestic Nykkus killed you have."

"Your Nykkus aren't harmed, only . . ." I glanced at their crumpled forms, trying to decide on the best way to explain "sleeping." Which word should I have used for Vissith's guards—domestic or Nykkus? I chose the one I didn't recognize, hoping it would translate more directly back into the alien's language. "Your Nykkus will wake up again in a few minutes." And, God willing, we'd have everything sorted out with Vissith by then. I wasn't really looking forward to defending myself with a handheld translator again.

The transporter room doors whisked open, and Vissith jumped as though someone had stung him. I responded only a little less strongly—I'd almost forgotten the emergency medical team. I certainly hadn't expected my new chief surgeon to come along with them. Piper'd had a tendency to delegate such duties to his younger medtechs. Snapping an appraising look at the downed aliens and my one injured security officer, McCoy raised both eyebrows at me the way he used to when he was a dorm monitor at Starfleet Academy and I was the cadet he'd caught at an inappropriate party. I waved him to get his team to work without ever really pulling my attention away from Vissith.

"My ship is not the one which attacked you," I tried to explain, turning back to our guest. "But our sensors detect no other vessels in the vicinity—"

"Pirates. Cargos loosened, our pod set adrift."

I resisted an urge to slap the translator against the palm of my hand. Vissith's abrupt interruptions made it hard to follow the flow of our discussion, but the translator's bizarre word choices weren't helping, either. "Any pirates are long gone. We detected your automatic distress beacon and only came to offer assistance."

"Fix our hovel."

The request—the *order*—caught me by surprise. I shook my head slowly, biting back an impulse to point out that someone who'd been minutes away from sucking vacuum was really in no position to be demanding anything. "I'm afraid we can't do that," I explained. Quite reasonably, I thought. "Your ship has sustained serious damage." *And I have no intention of sending a repair crew to poke around a scrap heap so hot that sensors still don't have a definitive fix on the number of life-forms on board.* "But if you're willing, we'll give your crew shelter and medical care, and take you back to your own people."

His rocking and weaving never slowed, but it took him a

long time before he spoke again. "Packages within our belly, these as well you bring."

Spock beat me to that explanation. "Our sensors detect no mass left within your cargo bays, and very little atmosphere beyond where your crew has taken shelter."

I wasn't sure how much of that would make it through a garbled translation, so added, "What your crew has with them is all you have." Then I gave Vissith a moment to absorb the concept, not to mention for the translator to finish skreeling out its own interpretation. "There's nothing left we can steal from you," I said gently. "And if we meant to harm you, we could have done so already. If you'll trust us, and step down from there, we can use our transporter to bring over the rest of your crew and set you up in guest quarters."

For the first time since he'd climbed to his feet, Vissith stood stone still. "Interrogative."

Even the translator had no suggestion as to what he'd meant to say. "I don't understand."

That admission at least seemed to turn into something on its way out the other end of the translator. I listened to what seemed an incongruously long string of hissing, then an equally long silence. "Suspicious your suggestion is." He seemed to be speaking very slowly, carefully. I was more sure than ever that the translator wasn't working any better in his direction than in mine. "Vacuum and vacancy your only improvements will be."

Ah, we got nothing from helping them. Yet from where I stood, we humans actually had a lot to gain—friendship with a new race, expanded knowledge about the galaxy we all lived in, maybe even some information that could help us ferret out any acts of piracy in this sector. Still, I wasn't sure how to explain all that to Vissith, especially through a communications device I wasn't confident could accurately translate our names. "We call it kindness." Could the translator convey the meaning of a smile? "It's a human custom."

Perhaps the slow blinking of alien eyes meant something equally as subtle and untranslatable as a smile. "This gesture to me has no meaning. My people this word do have not."

No meaning in a smile? Or no such word as "kindness." Either way, I should have known right then that something was wrong.

We learned that they were called the Anjiri. There were seventeen of them on board their disintegrating ship, plus another twenty-three of the burly, battle-scarred pit bulls that Vissith referred to as Nykkus. I'd tried to get McCoy to do thorough scans of both, to see if they were related species or no more similar than humans are to Vulcans. Looks can be deceiving. But he was busy inventing appropriate medical treatment for the four Nykkus injured when their ship was first attacked, and his efforts weren't helped by Vissith's continued insistence that he was wasting his time. "Nykkus people are not," he offered, as though that should have been obvious to any casual observer. "Into the dark outside pressure doors toss them you should. This often do we. Injuries unseemly are. To the cold with them."

So when the Nykkus balked at following the Anjiri into the rec hall we'd prepared to house them, I wasn't entirely surprised. How could they be sure there were no airlock doors inside? I let McCoy lead the Nykkus down the corridor to the gymnasium; it wasn't until the last Nykkus rounded the corner out of sight that Vissith and the rest of the Anjiri finally deigned to cross the threshold to the rec hall without them. So much for happy race relations.

"Nykkus people are not," Vissith had said again, seeming to dismiss the whole incident with no more concern than he'd dismissed the Nykkus's injuries earlier. "Nykkus dance fitless ever, flee the face with seeing now."

Which, of course, was the second half of my ever deepening problem. Instead of improving as it sampled more of the Anjiri's language, the translator's syntax and word choice seemed to be getting steadily worse. "It's not working," I complained to Spock. Not unless I planned to believe that the Nykkus "pilled for fees and reasons" or that their Anjiri masters had "baked the halls in the candles of their brains."

"The device is fully operational." Spock didn't even disassemble it—he'd already done that twice on my insistence; this time he simply watched it burble through yet another self-diagnostic, then handed it back to me with no more breach of his Vulcan composure than a testily arched eyebrow. "The Hayden-Elgin model translator has the lowest malfunction rate of any current translation device."

McCoy snorted without looking up from the readings his tricorder compiled. "Fat lot of good that does us." It was the first thing the doctor had said since rejoining us in the rec hall. "We might as well go back to smoke signals and tom-toms."

Spock didn't sigh, but I somehow got the impression he wanted to. He was hitting it off with McCoy about as well as I'd expected. "Doctor, I fail to see the relevance—"

"Bones," I reached past Spock to catch McCoy's elbow, "did you have problems with your translator, too?"

The doctor glanced up, his face an elegant display of disgust. "Who can tell?" he grumbled. "I don't think the Nykkus said two words the whole time I was with them. Not a chatty lot. What they did say made no more sense than a dog barking at the moon."

"Captain . . ." Spock turned quite pointedly to me, his hands gripped patiently behind his back. "Such subjective anecdotes do not constitute a scientific observation—"

I cut him off, already knowing what I planned to do. "I want a communications officer."

He snipped short whatever he'd been about to say, took two mental steps backward, and plowed forward again on a new track. "Translator repairs fall more directly into engineering's purview."

"I don't want repairs." I thrust the translator at Spock until he deigned to bring one hand around and take it. "I want a *new* translator—a living one. I want somebody who'll take into account more than just what comes out of the Anjiri's mouths." When he raised an eyebrow, I qualified, "We've got trained linguists in communications. I say we use them."

And what the captain says, goes.

The young lieutenant who answered my summons fifteen minutes later was in her late-twenties, slim and brown, with the kind of dark mocha eyes that seem to look through you as much as *at* you, and a smile so white it made me blink. I had a feeling she raised attentiveness to a whole new standard. So petite that she could have walked under my outstretched arm, she still managed to exude an ease and confidence that would make me remember her as taller for several months afterward. To this day, I have no memories of ever looking down at her, only of facing her squarely eye-to-eye.

"Lieutenant Uhura." I summoned her with a wave of my hand, then stepped aside to widen our circle when she approached. She joined us with the politeness appropriate to a junior officer, but with no sign of shyness or fear. Her long golden earrings jangled musically as she listened to my quick summation of events with a series of attentive nods. The whole while, her deft hands neatly dismantled the Hayden-Elgin translator so she could examine the pieces, wipe them off, then fit them back together again.

"Well, Mr. Spock is right," she said when I was finished. "There's nothing wrong with the device." She aimed a stunning smile up at Spock, as if either offering him apology or support. "But the inherent problem with all field-style translators is that they're almost entirely dependent on audio and electromagnetic input. There's *some* visual data collection, but the units don't allow for enough storage and processing to really make good use of it." Her eyes danced over the Anjiri, who gathered with their bevy of Federation-supplied security guards around the food service equipment. Her expression reminded me of the way Scotty looked at really tricky technical problems. "Let me talk to them for a few minutes and see what I can do."

Of course, as in all alien dealings, it took more than just a few minutes. Uhura stood in a knot of suspicious Anjiri, tricorder in one hand and translator in the other, for more than an hour—long enough for McCoy to apparently run out of disgruntled comments and head back for sickbay to escape the boredom, long enough for Spock to decide it would be most logical to fill our waiting time by examining two of the overdue crew reports he was finding the most impenetrable, and long enough for me to wish I had insisted on following Uhura when she first strode over to exchange introductions with the Anjiri. I hate waiting. More specifically, I hate doing nothing. Even when there's not a damned thing I can do, I'd still rather be inventing some kind of work for myself than standing around waiting for a junior officer's report.

Still, I'd like to believe that I honestly noticed the moment when Lieutenant Uhura's interactions with the Anjiri moved from linguistic Q&A into actual conversation. Silencing Spock with an upraised hand, I walked away from him without taking my eyes off Uhura and without bothering to notice if he'd even stopped talking.

When neither Uhura nor Vissith interrupted their chatter for my approach, I stopped a few feet away and summoned, "Lieutenant?"

"Captain!" Her eyes shone bright with an unmistakably professional pride. I like an officer who's possessive about her discipline. "I believe we've made some progress."

I could have guessed that from the tangle of wires and patch clips littering the table beside her. The translator, partially gutted again, lay nestled against the bottom of her tricorder, held in place by a wrap of wire and an umbilicus of data cables and conduits. On the tricorder's tiny screen, a little lizard-like simulacrum danced and flowed in rhythm with Uhura's words. I almost recognized some of the movements from Vissith's eternal fidgeting, but they looked awkward and primitive when projected in two lifeless dimensions.

"There's a detailed physical component to the Anjiri language." Uhura stole a look at Vissith, as if knowing—expecting—him to overhear, and eager for his verification. "The position of the body—and various body parts—in space can change the very definition of a word. If anything, the translator's efforts to combine those apparent variations in meaning was only making matters worse."

Rather than meeting Uhura's eager gaze, Vissith's own eyes remained fixed on the dancing lizard on her tricorder screen. "What about now?" I asked. "How do you know what physical movements to attach to whatever word the translator puts out?"

"The tricorder has better visual pickup, and a lot more processing power." She played with one of the wire connections, but I couldn't see that it accomplished anything. "I'm letting it mate the audio portion from the universal trans-

L. A. Graf

lator to its own visual input to create a single English output, then just reverse the process to take the English back into visual and audio Anjiri components." Then a quick smile back at Vissith. "How am I doing?"

His eerie, lidless eyes remained locked on the small screen. "Strange, it is, dealing in conversation with myself in a small black box." The simulacrum did look passingly like him; as near as I could tell, the hissing Anjiri voice it produced was his, as well.

"It's better than struggling with no real communication at all." I studied the little mini-Vissith as it danced out a translation of my words. While Vissith himself said nothing I could hear in response, the translator/tricorder arrangement said, "Yes" in the voice it had given him. I couldn't help but wonder if something in his bobbing and weaving was the equivalent of a human nod. "My apologies for any difficulties we experienced before," I went on. "You and your people are welcome on my ship. Do you understand what's happened? Why you're here?"

"Your podmate much has clarified for us."

I assumed he was refering to Uhura, but nothing in his body language made that clear.

"Returned to our homes, we will be. Honored guests of the captain, until that time we will be."

"Very honored guests," I said. "Our doctor has seen to your Nykkus—"

Vissith brushed off my unfinished sentence so thoroughly that he nearly turned his back on me. "Nykkus people are not. Nykkus live, Nykkus die. Little the concern is to us."

So that much, at least, had translated accurately. I made a mental note to remember this point—how much any race tolerates its siblings tells you a lot about it. And about how it will tolerate you.

"If you'll tell us where you'd like to be delivered, I can have my helmsman set a course."

"Pilots of our own we have." His hands cut short, definitive circles in the air to either side. "Courses of our own we will set. To your bridge you may escort us once we have eaten, have slept."

I blinked at him, caught off guard. "I'm afraid it doesn't

44

work that way. This is my ship." *You lost yours to pirates.* "Tell my crew where you would like to go, and we'll be more than glad to take you there."

"Where we wish to go, our own business is. The path to our own homeworld, the right to know you have not. Our own courses we shall plot, or we shall go not."

Is reason a human concept? It was something I'd have to debate with Spock—later, after we'd managed to off-load our passengers somewhere we could all agree upon. "This is a very advanced vessel. Your crew isn't trained—"

"Anjiri pilots quite cunning are," Vissith insisted with an almost human stubbornness. "Anjiri pilots anything can fly." He turned to Uhura, as though convincing her mattered more than convincing me. "Anything. Our own courses we shall plot or we shall go not."

"Captain . . ." Spock edged about as close as Vulcan comfort would allow. I could almost feel the electric charge building around him, like a capacitor right on the verge of letting go. Because he was a Vulcan, he burst into words, not action. "Captain, I do not advise—"

"All right, Vissith, you can do the course plotting yourselves." I know what you're thinking, but I really don't make it a habit to ignore the advice of my first officers. Usually. The words, the agreement seemed to jump out of me of their own accord. I'd learned a long time ago to trust whatever little corner of my brain tossed out such gems, and I wasn't about to stop listening to it now. "But only if you allow my crew to remain on the bridge in case you need assistance."

Vissith stared hard at the flashing tricorder screen, then flicked his bright eyes up at me. "Watch our piloting they may not. The path to our homeworld, the right to know they have not."

"No one will watch you as you pilot. I only want to make sure my ship can be taken care of if problems should arise." I don't know whether I managed to read something on Vissith's immobile face, or if it was intuition kicking in again. "In case your pirates return," I added smoothly.

This time, Vissith's long silence didn't produce even a flutter from the translator. He had to rattle a whole string of alien sounds before Uhura's device offered up, "Agreed. For you we shall send when our eating finished is." He whisked his hand lightly down Uhura's face, so quickly she didn't have a chance to flinch. "This podmate on the use of your food creation devices instruct us will."

I waited for Uhura to show her acceptance with a curt nod in my direction, then echoed that nod toward Vissith. "Lieutenant Uhura will know how to contact me when you're ready."

I left them all clustered around the food dispenser, their backs turned to me and their hands weaving intricate patterns of talking in the air.

Spock actually managed to keep quiet until we were almost to the turbolift. Then, when he spoke, it was with the cutting precision I'd eventually learn to recognize as the sign of a Vulcan snit. "Captain, Starfleet regulations expressly prohibit granting bridge access to non-Federation personnel."

"Starfleet's regulatory board isn't here." I punched the controls to summon the 'lift. "Besides, I've got no intention of either hauling the Anjiri around indefinitely *or* of handing them over to Starfleet as though we'd collected them as prisoners of war."

He stopped neatly at my side and folded his hands behind his back. "My personal experience is that this practice is unsafe. If we do not know where they intend to take the *Enterprise,* we cannot be properly prepared for whatever we find there."

"Oh, I intend to know where they're taking us, Mr. Spock."

He peered at me with one eyebrow lifted. "I heard you give your promise to Vissith." The coldness in his voice surprised me. "Did you do so intending not to keep it?"

I shrugged. "I promised no one would spy on them while they plotted their course. I never promised to erase the navigation computer's buffer. Or to let them *go* wherever they wanted without my approval." I punched at the call button again, eternally impatient. "We can download the course information from the main computer as soon as they're finished, then I'll decide whether or not we actually follow whatever course they plot. We're not going anywhere without knowing what's ahead of us." The turbolift whooshed open for us, and I graciously waved Spock ahead of me, meeting his skeptical frown with a smile. "A captain never has to lie, Mr. Spock, as long as he's careful about the promises he makes."

Chapter Four

SULU

"AND WHOSE REPTILE might this be?"

Sulu glanced across the bar in surprise. He'd become so engrossed in Captain Kirk's story of his first days serving with Mr. Spock that he hadn't even noticed that the little tailless lizard who'd been sleeping quietly on his hand was gone. Across the bar, a white-bearded old sailor in a gaudy waistcoat and a magnificently oversized hat was holding a fuzzy-looking animal of indeterminate species up off the ground. His pet was scrabbling frantically with all its paws, although since they encountered nothing but air, it wasn't making much headway in its struggle to reach the brownish-gold squiggle crossing the floor.

"Uh—I guess it's mine." Sulu pushed his chair back and went to scoop up the adventurous little lizard. It promptly squirmed out of his grip, but only to leap across to the folded lapel of his uniform. From there it swarmed up the jacket latch to his shoulder where it pulsed the white skin of its throat and made nearly inaudible hissing noises at the leashed bundle of fur below it.

"Sorry about that," Sulu said to the other captain. "I didn't realize it had wandered away."

48

"You ought to've been paying closer attention, lad," the old man said reprovingly. "You don't want to go losing a crewmate in a place like this. No telling what kind of ship the poor thing would end up on."

Sulu lifted an eyebrow, watching an Elasian female captain draped in dilithium jewelry try to fend off a gnomish-looking alien with enormous wrinkled ears. "I see what you mean." He lifted a hand to keep the little lizard in place as he retreated back across the bar to their table. By the time he got there, he found the chairs had been rearranged—the felinoid captain had relocated herself to the lap of the leather-jacketed freighter captain, and her seat had been taken by a human female with a mane of fire-red hair and a dancing smile. For all her youth and merriment, however, the look this new captain threw across the table at the English dandy was sharp as a sword-thrust.

"I heard you mention pirates over here," she said. "And I came to hear the rest of the tale, if you don't mind the extra company."

"Not at all," Kirk assured her gallantly, but the old man with the meerschaum pipe snorted. The swashbuckling Englishman just looked amused.

"Being a pirate yourself, I suppose you have a natural interest in them, Anne," he commented.

"Not all of us choose to be as we are, Peter, which you should know better than most." The redhead reached out to snag his unfinished mug of beer with a rope-calloused hand. "There are those who are forced into the corsair life by sad and evil circumstance."

"And those who take to it like ducklings to water," muttered the white-bearded man through a cloud of pipe smoke.

"And there are those who use it as a shield, to cover even more ambitious and dangerous crimes," Sulu said, before the clash could flare into anything serious. "I suspected that might be the case with the pirates who attacked Deep Space Three, but I couldn't have been more wrong about what those other crimes might be."

The Englishman, his amusement still half-turned on the bold redhead, helped himself to Sulu's drink in turn. "The crime of piracy isn't crime enough where you come from?" he asked.

"More than enough," Sulu told him. Even the memories of that long-ago day still made his stomach churn. "But by the time we found out what else they had in mind, it was more than just a simple crime—it was personal. . . ."

"Sulu to *Excelsior*."

It was the second time I'd made the request, and I was starting to wonder if the FL-70s communicator was functional. I could see the massive shadow of my starship through the occasional breaks in the phaser glare outside Deep Space Three's cargo bay, and she didn't look incapacitated, or even damaged enough to account for my crew's lack of response. "Sulu to *Excelsior*. Come in."

Despite everything, it felt good to be at the helm of a ship again, even if it was just a little Raptor-class reconnaissance vessel with an overpowered warp engine and a bizarre sensor-deflecting design that made it look as if it had crushed its needlenose into a brick wall. It felt even better to hear the airtight thunk of the Falcon's gull-winged door close behind me and listen to the hum of her shields coming online as the phaser explosions outside the cargo bay grew fire-bright through Deep Space Three's fading defensive screens.

I ran a quick systems check while I waited for my crew to respond. I only had a single phaser unit, added almost as an afterthought to the FL-70's reconnaissance systems, but my sensor readouts were almost the equal of a starship's in terms of their sensitivity and swift response. The entire story of the battle outside the space station flickered across my display panel now in symbols and running captions that told me the status of all the participants. I could see the undocked Starfleet vessels shielded and arrayed in protective formation around the defenseless Andorian liner and Earth courier, a thousand meters out from Deep Space Three. The Tellerite merchant vessel was moving to join that sanctuary, but the Orion yacht was still locked onto the lower docking ring.

None of the attackers' fire hit it, though—they were

concentrating their phaser strikes on the centrally located cargo bay with only a few blasts flickering back toward the Starfleet force. The sensor readouts showed only occasional bursts of return fire, whenever one of the pirate ships swooped above the station's circumference on a strafing run. Someone out there must have ordered a limited response to the attack, to keep Deep Space Three from falling victim to our own friendly fire. Not that it was helping much—my Falcon's sensors were also precise enough to show me exactly how little protection remained above my head.

"Sulu to *Excelsior*." This time I used my wrist communicator instead of the ship's larger transmitter, but I still got back the same anomalous silence. Interference from the double set of shields I was trying to transmit through must be jamming my communications signal. I turned my attention to the tentative ship identifications that the Falcon's highly tuned sensors had made based on our attackers' ion trails. One seemed to be a Rochester-class cruiser, a short-range battleship that Starfleet had mothballed twenty years ago. Another looked like a Romulan patrol-ship retrofitted with an Orion warp drive, and the third was a lightly armed Vulcan scientific probe, probably hijacked from whatever mission it had been carrying out. The fourth ship was the most powerfully armed, but seemed cobbled together from so many different recycled ship parts that the Falcon's data banks couldn't begin to guess at its original identity.

The FL-70 shook with the impact of the first phaser blast to break through the station's failing shields. Another blast followed, and another and another, until a sudden crystalline condensation of clouds around my cockpit windows told me the cargo bay had breached to outer space. I brought the impulse engines online with a sweep of my hand. I didn't need them to send the Falcon rising toward the roof of the cargo bay—the decompressing rush of air lifted us along with it toward the shattered hull of Deep Space Three. I used the impulse engines merely to control our upward lurch, intending to keep the Falcon hovering in the phaser-burned rift so no pirates could get through. But as our own upward velocity slowed, the gleaming shadows of seven other airborne ships ghosted past us, drawn toward the stars by the relentless suck of vacuum. I cursed and hit my communicator again.

"Sulu to *Excelsior!*"

"Captain!" There was a surprising tinge of relief in Janice Rand's usually calm voice. "When we lost contact with you and Commander Chekov, we thought—"

"Get me Henry," I said and heard the click of an opened channel, then the familiar background sounds of a bridge on full alert. It wasn't exactly soothing, but the lack of anything that sounded like damage reports did reassure me a little.

"Orders, sir?" said the gruff voice of my chief engineer.

"Tell everyone to stop firing—the FL-70s got torn loose by the decompression blast." Long years of piloting experience let my eyes and hands maneuver my craft through the shattered cargo bay roof while my mind was working out other problems. I tried to scan the Falcon's crowded sensor displays, but the information was scrolling by too fast for me to catch it with a glance. "What are the attackers doing now?"

"They've stopped firing, but they haven't come out from between the docking rims." That was Orsini reporting from the *Excelsior's* weapons panel. "They seem to be just waiting there."

"And I'll bet I know what for." Two of the unmanned FL-70s had gotten snagged by the maze of broken steel and duranium at the top of the cargo bay, but the rest had drifted through and were now spinning aimlessly in the station's microgravity. I sent my own dish-nosed craft surging out beyond them, hoping the unexpected movement would delay the thieves from scooping up their loot. "Break ranks and get the *Excelsior* in position to slap a tractor beam on the loose Falcons. The pirates are after them, not the civilian vessels."

"Aye, sir." I might not have been able to read all the information on the Falcon's sensor display, but I knew the largest symbol on it had to represent my oversized starship. She began moving toward the shattered cargo bay, but I never saw a quiver in the position of the four small red-circled icons that were our attackers. I took another looping orbit around the Falcons, but the pirates had apparently retreated back around the curve of the station—the only place they showed up was on my display screen. I wasn't going to leave the Falcons unguarded for long enough to go and spot them, but I wished I knew why they weren't moving. If I was in command of such a small and ragtag fleet of pirate ships, the sight of something like the *Excelsior* coming after me would have frozen my blood faster than deep space. Unless they had another surprise in store for us—

Ships converge Deep Space Three attack wait explosion capture . . .

"Sulu to Deep Space Three." I was getting more used to the controls of the little reconnaissance ship, and managed to actually read some of my sensor display on my third loop around the drifting FL-70s. Its scan of the station showed severe damage only around the main cargo bay, but my hail was answered as breathlessly as if a total warp core meltdown were imminent.

"Rebovich here—we're in the middle of a firefight with the intruders—Commander Barstow's been wounded and we don't know the status of the hostages. Orders, Captain Sulu?"

"Secure your dilithium supply room and your warp core," I commanded. "Lock down every door and bulkhead in their vicinity and scan them both for possible sabotage."

I heard the instructions tapped into the computer, then another indrawn breath. This time it sounded startled instead of panicky. "Someone with a top-level Starfleet security clearance already gave that order to our computers, sir. About fifteen minutes ago."

Thank you, Chekov. "Then contain the attackers in whatever sector of the station they're in—"

"That's what we did, sir!" Rebovich was starting to sound frantic again. "They massacred the security team that was locked in with them, then they deliberately weakened a section of the main plasma conduit. If we don't let the seals down and send a repair team in soon, we'll lose that whole side of the docking rim!"

"And the hostages will die along with their captors in the resulting plasma explosion," I said grimly. Despite the ragtag appearance of our attackers, their tactics for sabotaging

Deep Space Three were ruthlessly elegant. When their initial attempt to blow up the spare dilithium stocks had been foiled by Chekov's intervention, they'd promptly engineered a wordless blackmail threat that would either get them free or get the station blown up anyway. And that set all my military instincts clamoring. Were these actually Klingons, disguising a border incursion as a pirate raid to avoid diplomatic repercussions? Or was this the first careful probing by a new race of hostile aliens, looking for weaknesses in our defenses? Either way, I was beginning to see why Rebovich sounded so frazzled.

I glanced at my sensor screens again, seeing no movement from the four mismatched ships of the attacking force. The first gleam of the *Excelsior*'s primary hull had just appeared over the curve of the upper docking rim. If they had any sensors of their own, the attackers must know we were only seconds away from securing the floating Falcons in a tractor beam too strong for them to break, yet they still didn't make a move toward the loose flotilla of patrol ships. That surprising inactivity, combined with the tactical brilliance of the landing party on Deep Space Three, let me guess that the ones who'd planned this attack were among the hostage takers rather than the outside forces.

I frowned and glanced back down at my display screens, this time looking for the small symbol that represented the private Orion yacht. It was still firmly attached to the lower docking ring. "Deep Space Three, how far away are the intruders from docking port one-seven-one?"

"About thirty meters, sir. They appeared to be heading in that direction when we locked the bulkheads down on them."

"Then evacuate all personnel from that sector of the ring and open the bulkheads to let the intruders through to their ship," I said. I didn't like giving the saboteurs even a slim chance of escaping with their hostages, but I suspected that nothing less than a clear path back to their ship would entice them to abandon their current position. "As soon as sensors show them moving, slam the bulkheads down behind them and beam in an engineering team to repair the damaged conduit."

"Aye, *sir*." Rebovich sounded so inordinately relieved

that I knew the safety margin on the conduit must be falling fast. The silence that followed her acknowledgment seemed far too long, but that was only the time-dilation caused by my own tension. Even the *Excelsior* seemed to be moving with excruciating slowness, and the diamond glitter of her tractor beam seemed to crawl rather than shoot out to capture the four loose Falcons.

"Intruders are moving, sir," Rebovich said, but she sounded more agitated than ever. "Our sensors still show one life-form near the damaged plasma conduit. Should we beam it in?"

It could be an alien suicide guard, I knew. It could also be my executive officer, although my instincts said that if he had shadowed the hostage takers this far, he would have followed them all the way to their ship, looking for a chance to rescue his fellow crew members. "Can you do a bio-scan?"

"It's a Vulcan, sir. And—and almost dead, according to our sensors."

"Then beam him out," I ordered. "And evacuate the entire lower docking ring while you try to get that plasma conduit stabilized." My sensor displays were showing an alarming instability in the station's normally steady plasma discharge. I swung my Falcon away from its tractor-held siblings, heading for docking port 171. On my display screen, I could see the pirate fleet moving at last, converging to form a tight knot around the still-docked Orion yacht. I felt my stomach clench in dismay, and it wasn't at the military precision of that maneuver. No ship escort needed to fly that close to protect an unarmed vessel. This formation was specifically designed to put the central vessel at risk if any of its escort were fired on. And that meant the hostages had been taken aboard.

"Excelsior to Captain Sulu." I could tell from my chief engineer's voice, harsher than usual with restrained anger, that my bridge crew had come to the same deduction I had. "Request permission to release the tractor beam and pursue the attacking force."

"Permission denied," I said between clamped teeth. "Tow those FL-70s away from the station, at maximum impulse speed. *Now!"* The Orion vessel was disengaging from its docking clamp with such reckless haste that it had nearly slammed one of its clinging escort ships into the station's hull. I sent my own Falcon plunging around to the right, taking advantage of that momentary wedge of opening to aim and fire—

The warning flashed across my sensor displays only a second before the plasma flare punched through the hull of Deep Space Three. I felt the Falcon lifted and hurled helplessly into the backwash of that superheated blast. All I had time to do was throw full power to my shields and hear the howl of the collision warning systems before the little ship sprang violently backward and slammed me into oblivion.

"This," said my chief medical officer crisply, "is the reason why captains should not go running around trying to do *everything* themselves. Haven't I told you before that you should practice delegating a little more of your authority?"

I jerked my head away from the keening hum of the tissue regenerator, not because it hurt but because I knew the cut on my chin barely needed its attention. "All I did was hit my face on the sensor display panel when the collision avoidance rockets engaged—"

"People with glass chins should refrain from piloting ships with uncalibrated inertial dampeners." She might be younger and more detail-oriented than Leonard McCoy, but I had found Judith Klass to be every bit as opinionated as the doctor on the *Enterprise*. Perhaps it was a trait they hammered into them at Starfleet Medical Academy.

"I don't have a glass chin." I rolled off the sickbay bunk with a wince to avoid her skeptical look. I really couldn't complain about the FL-70's automatic collision avoidance system, since it was the reason I was sitting here instead of being splattered across the hull of Deep Space Three. But before we delivered those reconnaissance ships to the Neutral Zone, I was going to make damned sure their inertial dampeners were calibrated. "Call the bridge and tell them I want a senior officers conference in five minutes, main briefing room."

Klass's pale eyes glittered at me from out of her strong-boned face. "I called them as soon as I saw you were almost awake," she said, and caught my chin in her determined fingers again, running the tissue regenerator across the throbbing cut on my chin before I could protest. "They're waiting in the medical briefing room next door."

I couldn't decide what was more annoying—the fact that Klass thought she knew what I was going to want while I was still unconscious, or the fact that she had been right. I settled for saying, "Thank you, Doctor," in as neutral a tone as I could manage before I headed for the door. The amused look I got as she followed me suggested I hadn't entirely managed to disguise my irritation.

It took me a minute, coming into the small and unfamiliar conference room, to place exactly what was wrong. Engineer Tim Henry looked a little grim and Security Chief Nino Orsini was tapping a more urgent rhythm on his data pad than he usually did, but Communications Officer Janice Rand and Science Officer Christina Schulman both seemed as calm and professional as ever. Scott Walroth, my young navigator, kept glancing at my more experienced pilot, Heather Keith, for reassurance, but since this was his first tour of duty on a starship, he had a tendency to do that anyway. It wasn't until I sat down and saw the empty place at my right where by custom my executive officer would have been that I realized it was the reverberations of Chekov's absence that I was feeling in the room.

"Gentlemen," I said. "By my watch, I've been unconscious for over twenty minutes. I assume our attackers are either captured or gone. Which is it?"

"Gone," Orsini said glumly. "Deep Space Three needed the transporters on every Starfleet vessel to evacuate their lower docking ring. By the time we were done, the attack ships had vanished off our sensors and the plasma explosion had erased all traces of their ion trail."

"How many of the Excelsior's crew are missing?"

"Five of the six people on the dilithium resupply team. And Commander Chekov, too, I'm afraid," my young security chief added reluctantly. As a former security chief himself, Chekov had mentored Orsini throughout the shakedown cruise. "We couldn't ping a signal from his wrist communicator, either on the station or among the evacuees."

57

It was exactly the bad news I had expected, but hearing it spoken out loud still sent a stab of dismay through me. You don't lose a friend of twenty years easily. "And none of the pirate ships were caught in the blast?"

"None, sir." That was Schulman's quiet voice. "The brunt of the explosion came straight toward you. If it hadn't been for the Falcon's collision avoidance rockets, you would have slammed right into the station."

I deliberately avoided meeting Doctor Klass's pointed look. "What's the status of the station now?"

Tim Henry cleared his throat. "Between the cargo bay hull breach and the plasma burst, sir, they're operating at about thirty-percent efficiency over there. The other Starfleet vessels in port have sent down some engineers to help get their main power circuits up and running, and a new plasma generator is on the way from Deep Space Two."

"Casualties?"

"None." My chief engineer slanted me a regretful look. "Unless you count the two Falcons we lost when the plasma flare hit the cargo bay—"

I felt the newly healed skin on my chin tug with my half-smile. "A couple of Neutral Zone outposts might cry over those losses, Chief, but I think they're acceptable. How about the station cargo transporters? Any chance of Deep Space Three getting them up and running in the next hour or so?"

Henry couldn't restrain a snort. "About as much chance as they have of sucking all their plasma back in from outer space. Why, Captain?"

I gave him a quizzical look. "Because I'd like to take the rest of those Falcons with us when we leave. It'll slow us by two warp factors to fly with them in formation."

That seemingly simple statement sent a discreet ripple of surprise and confusion through my bridge officers. I watched them think it over for a moment, waiting patiently until one asked the obvious question. There are few pleasures quite as satisfying to a captain as being able to surprise a crew as competent as this one.

It was Nino Orsini who cleared his throat at last and asked, "We're leaving in an hour, sir? Why the hurry?"

"Because we've got pirates to catch," I said. I'd expected that to cause a stunned silence, and it did. I'd also expected the silence to dissolve into a barrage of startled questions, but Tim Henry gave me a single sharp-eyed glance before it could.

"Nano-machined subspace transponder?" he demanded.

I let my smile widen. It was nice to have a chief engineer who kept up with more than just the latest developments in warp drive technology. "Actually, a hundred thousand of them, Chief. The FL-70s are equipped to fire projectile bursts of nano-transponders, enough to blanket an area where you suspect a cloaked vessel to be. They can't penetrate shields, of course, but that Orion yacht didn't have its shields up yet. And I got a nice clear shot at them right before the plasma flare hit me."

Janice Rand was already on her feet and pulling Orsini with her. "Nino, you find the specifications on that transponder frequency, and I'll start scanning for their signal—with your permission, of course, Captain," she added belatedly.

"Granted, with pleasure," I told her. "Walroth, Keith—get up to the bridge and prepare a course as soon as we know the heading. Schulman and Henry, see if you can work out a system we can use to piggyback those five remaining Falcons onto the *Excelsior*. If not, assign them pilots and send out two of our best-armed shuttles to escort them after us. We're not going to slow down for them."

"Aye, sir!" said six voices in unison. A moment later, the medical briefing room was empty except for Doctor Klass and me. She arched one thin eyebrow in amusement.

"Did my lecture about delegating authority sink in, or are you still feeling the aftereffects of the concussion I healed you of fifteen minutes ago?"

I frowned at her. "I had a concussion?"

"Severe, with accompanying brain swelling," she affirmed. "Why else do you think I put off fixing that scratch in your chin for twenty minutes after we beamed you aboard? Do you have a headache now?"

"No."

"Any dizziness or nausea?"

"None." You couldn't really fault Klass for her annoying air of superiority. She was actually an even better doctor than she thought she was.

Her strong-boned face took on the mildly inquisitive look that was her equivalent of a puzzled frown. "So why are you still sitting here?"

"Because I want to know what happened to the sixth member of the dilithium resupply team," I said. "Deep Space Three reported that he was nearly dead when they beamed him out. Is he still there? Did they transfer him back to our sickbay? Or did he die before anything could be done?"

Klass startled me with another amused look. "Indeed not, Captain. Vulcans are capable of sustaining life over a much wider range of physical endurance than humans, as I'm sure you know. And in any case, a great deal of Cadet Tuvok's problems were caused by himself."

"What do you mean?"

In answer, she stood up and gestured me back toward sickbay. "I think I'll let him explain."

The young Vulcan wore the colors of a science officer on his opened uniform and fading bruises on the skin of his neck and chest, despite the time he'd obviously already spent under tissue regenerators. I sat on the stool Klass pointed me to beside him, to spare him the effort he was making to sit up.

"Mr. Tuvok, at ease. I'd like to ask you a few questions." I glanced over at Klass and saw that she had already programmed her medical tricorder to record his answers. "You feel well enough to answer?"

"Of course, sir." The security guard glanced across at Klass. "Did the doctor explain that I was in *us'tar-ja?*"

"The Vulcan healing trance?" I shook my head. "Were you that badly injured?"

"Actually, no." Tuvok rubbed his fingers across the fading bruises on his chest, looking slightly guilty. "I was engaging in what you humans call 'playing possum.' My assumption was that the aliens who captured us would not wish to take a corpse along as a hostage."

"And you gambled they wouldn't phaser you to make sure you were really dead?"

The Vulcan's face never changed expression. "That is correct, Captain. But although our captors were quite needlessly violent, I had observed that they preferred their hands and tails to their sidearms. In fact, some of them seemed almost uncomfortable with the equipment they used, as if it were new to them."

"Hands and tails?" I repeated. "What kind of aliens were they, Cadet?"

"I did not recognize their species, Captain, although I have memorized the appearance and names of the two hundred and fifty known races of this quadrant. But they were clearly of saurian descent—their skins were lightly scaled and they used their tails both as cantilevers and as strong lashing devices." Tuvok paused, looking thoughtful. "They worked as a coordinated unit throughout the sabotage attempt, but I did not get the sense that they were a trained military force."

"A covert terrorist operation? Or a spying mission to prepare for a later invasion?"

Tuvok shook his head. "I cannot be sure, sir. But I am sure of one thing—this was not a chance encounter. The leader of that attack came to Deep Space Three specifically to obtain the FL-70 reconnaissance ships."

I nodded. It confirmed my own guess, although it didn't make me any happier to know we were facing a determined enemy rather than a random pirate raid. "And now that they've failed to get them? Did you get any sense for what they might do next?"

"Yes, sir. That was why I risked entering the healing trance, in the hope of getting the information to you." The Vulcan science cadet sat up despite Klass's glare and his own wince of pain. "Our universal translator did not work well with the language they spoke, and they did not speak much. But toward the end, the leader made it clear through his questions and threats that he wanted the FL-70s so he could take over the Federation outpost at Elaphe Vulpina. He kept asking us if we had any security clearance codes or weapons that would allow him to access it."

I glanced across at Klass's grave face. "And did he get an answer, Cadet?"

"Not from the *Excelsior*'s crew, sir." Even through his Vulcan reserve, I heard the quiet pride in his voice. "But I do not believe the station quartermaster will be able to hold out forever under that kind of torture. The aliens will soon have a Starfleet key to Elaphe Vulpina's defenses."

"Which makes it even more imperative to catch them before they get there. The last thing we want is a firefight that will attract the attention of the Klingon Empire." I pushed him back down on the medical bed. "Relax, Mr. Tuvok. You did the right thing by staying behind."

That got me a surprised lift of his eyebrows. "I never doubted it, sir," said the young Vulcan, and I was reminded again that guilt was not an emotion his race indulged in. "I only regret that the other members of my party did not have the ability to do as I did."

"So do I, Cadet." I stood and winced as my own sore spots complained at the sudden movement. I didn't want to think about how much worse Chekov and the other hostages were probably feeling at this moment, but some morbid part of my brain wouldn't let that thought go once it had kindled there. "So do I."

Chapter Five

KIRK

I KNOW HOW to keep a promise—I didn't spy on the Anjiri. I really didn't. From the central seat of my command chair, I couldn't see much of the helm controls even when a human sat there. The Anjiri, though, had surrounded themselves with their battle-scarred Nykkus so thoroughly that they barely had their own view of the main screen. Even if I'd wanted to peer over their shoulders, I'd have had to practically crawl on top of their heads to do so.

So I made an effort to conceal my impatience by pacing the circumference of the bridge, pretending to micromanage all the other stations while I waited. And waited.

"Captain, please. Can't you make them let us help?"

Sulu shushed Bailey into silence, but I stopped to clap the younger man on the shoulder with as much reassurance as I could muster. "Everybody's got to learn for themselves, Mr. Bailey. Even aliens."

"It's just . . ." His brow furrowed so seriously, you might have thought he was contemplating some great quantum mechanical argument. "Sir—" Another scowled frown from Sulu, and he dropped his voice to a whisper. "They don't have the faintest idea what they're doing! Look at

63

them! I can't believe they even managed to get out of their home star system."

I'd been wondering myself if they actually knew how to get themselves back. Glancing over my shoulder, I watched Uhura carefully explain something to the Anjiri currently in Bailey's seat while he leaned nearly into her lap to watch the translation simulacrum on her tricorder screen. "They probably had a preprogrammed navigation module on their last ship. The kind where you pick a course from a menu, the ship remembers where you started, and all you have to do is reverse your course to get home."

"If that's true, sir," Sulu interjected, "they couldn't possibly have programmed the module themselves."

Bailey gave a defeatist little laugh. "Considering what happened to their last ship, I don't know if we should count on that." I wasn't sure if he meant to blame them for having taken their ship into dangerous space, or for not being good enough pilots to then extricate themselves from an unwanted fight.

My navigator's comment notwithstanding, I didn't think the Anjiri could fairly be blamed for wrecking their own ship. There'd been plenty of battle damage evident, and it wasn't like this whole sector wasn't a prime candidate for an incursion of opportunistic feeders. Still, the Anjiri's total lack of understanding of even the most basic navigation and course-plotting skills was almost surreal.

For three hours—while Sulu and Bailey waited like the true Academy gentlemen they were—the Anjiri had alternated at the helm, a kind of interstellar musical chairs. Occasionally, one of them would hiss viciously at a Nykkus, apparently for stepping in front of the forward screen and blocking their view. I wondered if they could actually tell where in space they were from that display, or whether they'd notice if I had Spock project a view from several weeks ago. For hours they'd touched, sniffed, moved, and activated controls on the helm, making more individual movements for the sake of a fairly straightforward course than Sulu would have made to chart a covert path through the Neutral Zone.

"I think a lot of what they're doing is exploring." I hesitated a moment over how much to reveal. "They've been generating a lot of error messages." At least a dozen for every successful course calculation—and that included making unsupported requests such as access to our library files or attempting to order beverages from the dining hall.

"Let's hope they don't explore too much." Sulu looked apologetic for having brought the subject up. "I don't think that letting strangers know too much about what we're flying is good for business."

But at least we knew exactly how much they were learning. Deciding that wasn't for public consumption just yet, I said only, "Hang in there, gentlemen. You'll have your stations back soon enough," and headed for my own abandoned command chair.

I didn't see the subdued indicator on my command display until I was almost seated, but I glanced up to verify that no one else was looking anyway. While the Anjiri were still hissing and jittering over their arcane course inventions, Uhura stayed intently by their sides, recording every word that passed between them, and Sulu and Bailey continued their extended fret over the nefarious use of their consoles. I thumbed the switch next to my display, and sat back to watch it scroll.

The tiny screen filled with the same convoluted and mostly meaningless data that had been filtered over to me since the Anjiri first began their flight. As promised, we'd been letting them plot their course (such as it was) without interrupting; Uhura had even been on hand to explain anything about the stations they found confusing, and she'd more than once ferried questions back to Bailey and Sulu, then translated their answers for our guests. Meanwhile, the navigation computer stored every keystroke the Anjiri made in a virtual buffer zone until they either accepted it as a final course or input alternative data to overwrite it. I'd assigned Spock the task of creating a shunting program to snapshot the data before it vanished from the buffer, which meant I only examined the data after the Anjiri themselves had declared they were done with it. Whether I looked at the data ten hours after they left the ship or ten minutes after they deleted it struck me as having no real ethical difference, so I had Spock forward the buffer dump to my command console as soon as he'd had a chance to make sense of it.

All of this Spock performed at his science station without sending so much as a glance in my direction. I might have given him credit for some otherwise unexpected theatrical skill, except that he hadn't spoken to me—with the exception of a few well-placed "Yes, Captains" and an equally few "No, Captains"—since our conversation outside the rec hall. I resisted assuming this meant he was irked with me. After all, Vulcan's didn't get irked, they merely withheld comment until they had further data. He was no doubt distracted, thinking about how to phrase his official report on why I had insisted on such an illogical course of action.

So when I first noticed his neat, block-style handwriting on the information drifting by on my screen, I had a perverse moment where I felt like a schoolboy, passing notes during class. Then I saw what he'd written, and my focus galvanized on what was in front of me.

We are within five parsecs of the highlighted station. Orions respond hostilely to approaches of closer than two parsecs. If you choose to allow this course, preemptive radio contact might be in order.

I keyed back to the top of the data, scrolled down through it again twice as fast as before. The station Spock had highlighted in the stats was what the Orions preferred to call a waystation. In reality, it was a place for their pirate skiffs to stop and disgorge ill-gotten gains when being chased by Federation craft, so they could then claim never to have had the goods on board to begin with. The probable cause which might have let us search a fleeing pirate vessel didn't extend to searching an Orion civilian facility. Thus did many Orion pirates escape through legal loopholes and avoid extradition and indictment by our government. It bothered me that the Orions felt it necessary to erect such a station on the border of what had so far been a fairly quiet sector.

I ran across Spock's note again: *Preemptive radio contact might be in order.*

Indeed it might. If I didn't allow the ship to take the heading the Anjiri had chosen, they were sure to notice eventually, and at least figure out that they'd been tricked in some fashion, even if they couldn't precisely figure out why.

At the same time, if I initiated contact with the Orions before their self-imposed two parsec boundary, I was also giving away that I'd been using my own legal loophole to keep track of the Anjiri's doings. I let instinct guide me again, and decided, without giving myself a chance for second thoughts, that we'd never find out precisely what the Anjiri were up to if we didn't find out who they knew. Let the Orions save me from grappling with the dilemma about whether or not to call. I sent Spock the signal to let the course run.

He raised one eyebrow until it nearly disappeared into his hairline, but did as he was told.

"Captain." The advantage of not letting your command crew in on absolutely everything is that they then sound convincingly surprised when they pipe up with such announcements. "We're being hailed on an Orion broadband channel."

I did my best to look surprised in an appropriately commanding fashion. "Put it on screen, Ensign."

An Orion's big, bulldog face solidified out of the stars like a chancre on perfect skin. He wore the dreadlocks of a lower-class citizen, but the wealth of earrings and nose rings dangling from his pushed-in face announced his importance on the station. "I am Akpakken, supreme commander of this station. Identify yourselves and prepare to be destroyed!"

A bold threat, considering most of these floating pawn brokerages didn't have the weaponry to fend off a good case of the chills much less a Federation starship. Still, my mission description didn't include punching holes in over-inflated Orion egos, no matter how great the temptation. "I'm Captain James T. Kirk of the *U.S.S. Enterprise*," I answered with somewhat less bravado. "We're here on a peaceful transport mission. We don't want any trouble."

"Then turn your rodent warren around and flee back to your own space, hairless maggots."

No one ever accused Orions of having the most elevated social skills.

"We have friends of yours on board, Akpakken." I didn't look down at the Anjiri and Nykkus at the front of my bridge. I was waiting for Akpakken to do that first, so I could judge the recognition in his eyes. "Perhaps you'd like to speak with them before you send us packing."

He blew a fierce snort that threatened to fog both our viewscreens. "We are Orions," he announced with phlegmatic pride. "We have no friends."

I offered a little shrug. "Be that as it may, the Anjiri are the ones who brought us here." This time, I angled a quick glance toward Vissith, making sure he was listening via the little figure on Uhura's translation device. All other activity around the helm console had frozen. "They claimed this was their home."

The translation simulacrum in the tricorder danced madly. *I hope it's saying I no longer believe a word you've ever said to us,* I thought at the back of the Anjiri's narrow skull. It's one thing to have someone distrust you so much they won't even let you pilot your own ship, another thing entirely to have them fly you right into the mouth of a compromising situation that could actually lead to fighting.

"We know of no Anjiri," Akpakken insisted. "They lie to you, pink monkey-weasel."

It's a secret vice of mine, but I have always loved listening to what our translators do to Orion speech.

"Now go away!"

Akpakken lifted one meaty fist to slam closed the comm channel, but Vissith leapt in front of the viewscreen before the Orion could complete the movement. "Halt!"

I was surprised first by the speed and agility of Vissith's unexpected movement. I was surprised even more when Akpakken hesitated, squinting down at the lithe saurian with a certain suspicious greed.

I hardly recognized the Anjiri's voice when Vissith first burst into speaking. Not in their language—not in anything that made Uhura's translator activate its display, not in anything the communication channel's translator could turn into understandable English. When Uhura glanced anxiously back toward me, I motioned her to my chair, then leaned forward to whisper, "What are they saying? Why aren't the translators working?"

Uhura shook her head slowly, eyes darting between the two aliens instead of down toward her device. "They keep switching languages, too quickly for the translator to keep up. I think it's some sort of trader argot." She fell silent and listened for a while longer. "I can only recognize a few of the languages myself, but I think Vissith is . . . negotiating with him. He's promising Akpakken something."

I drummed my fingers on the arm of my chair. "As long as it isn't my ship, I don't care what they negotiate for." In truth, I had never liked blind negotiations.

Abruptly, Akpakken declared with traditional Orion directness, "All right—leave them."

Knowing the quality of Orion translators, I couldn't help wondering if what Akpakken thought they'd just discussed bore any resemblance to what Vissith thought they'd been discussing. "We have forty passengers," I began. "Are you prepared—"

He cut me off without even an excusing gesture. "I am prepared. I was mistaken—the Anjiri are our allies. You may approach Pleck Station and leave them." This time his hand completed the termination command. "Akpakken out."

"Food service records indicate an increase of twenty-four point three percent in what is otherwise a consistent average consumption of point seven four liters per twenty-four hours on all other days."

I'd mastered the art of nodding sagely during graduate seminars at the Academy. A necessary component of the practice, of course, was accurately judging when you really had to listen and when you didn't. My elbows propped on a rec hall dining table, hands wrapped around a cup of rapidly cooling coffee, I'd quickly ascertained that the important part of this scenario was the work Scott and his engineering team performed on the hall's exposed machinery. They'd come to make sure the Anjiri hadn't tampered with anything during their stay; I'd come to watch over them while picking through my dinner. Spock had been a last-minute addition after he followed me into the turbolift outside my quarters with a new list of reasons why we had to discuss personnel records before the end of the watch.

Which was why he'd been regaling me with duty schedules and overdue physicals all throughout my roast chicken and potatoes.

I watched the engineers bolt a panel back into place next to an environmental outlet. "Scotty says the only thing he's found missing so far is a programming chip from one of the battle simulation games." I turned to Spock, shaking my head. "All the other useful devices they could have tried to take, and they steal a computer game."

The disparity apparently didn't strike him as fascinating. "Perhaps they did not recognize which among the surrounding equipment was valuable. They might not have known that it was only a simulation game they stole." He tipped his pad meaningfully toward me. "I believe we were discussing Ensign Maudie's caffeine ingestion during his weekend duty tours."

I turned my back to the engineers, facing my first officer full on. "Mr. Spock, I don't care how much coffee Ensign Maudie drinks the morning after he's been out having a good time with his friends."

Spock settled back into his seat, one eyebrow lifting testily as he slowly crossed his arms. "Is there relevant data regarding Ensign Maudie's social activities which I should consider in preparing my report?"

I scrubbed at my eyes to hide my frustration. "Mr. Spock . . ." I really didn't want to snap at him. He was like a child sometimes, honestly trying to do his best even though he didn't fully understand what was expected of him. Dropping my hands to the table, I looked at him as earnestly as I could. "When Starfleet suggests the first officer compile reports on the behavior and performance of a starship's crew, they don't mean surveys on how many hours of sleep the crew is getting or how much caffeine they've ingested."

"However, both are directly relevant to a crew's performance levels. Ingestion of large quantities of caffeine can cause humans to experience light-headedness, trembling, frequent urination—"

"As captain," I cut him off, "my responsibility is to the ship itself, our mission, how we do our job out here. The first officer's responsibility, then, is to the crew—but the details of how they're assigned, who needs disciplinary action, where we need additional staff, not what they choose as their breakfast beverage." My own coffee was too cold now to drink. I set it aside with a sigh. "We're supposed to have a synergistic relationship, Mr. Spock. I decide what needs doing, you help me understand how the crew can best get that done."

The way he stiffened in his seat might almost have been prickly if he'd been human. "I believe I have been timely in providing the captain with assignment rosters and leave requests."

"You have. Your thoroughness and attention to detail is . . . remarkable. Commendable. But . . ." Does it make sense to worry about hurting a Vulcan's feelings? Does a lack of emotional fragility on their part mean I'm no longer obligated to be polite? "This is a primarily human crew, Mr. Spock. That means our feelings will have an impact on the performance of our duties, even when that's not appropriate. Humans will get frightened, or decide they can't work with someone else they don't like, or lose their confidence, or fall in love. I need those feelings to be taken seriously, and tended to, if this crew is going to function at its best." I paused for what felt like a very long time, considering how best to phrase this. "I need a first officer who can understand those details."

He nodded, once, precisely. "Although I am Vulcan, Captain, I have served in the company of humans for many years. Human frailty and prejudice are concepts with which I am well acquainted." The prejudice remark stung. But I didn't try to protest—it would only make things worse, and I didn't really have the right. "In addition, I have had ample opportunity to observe unfettered emotion and its effects on human behavior." A pause, so long I couldn't interpret it in any way but as embarrassment. "My mother was human."

I felt a bizarre impulse to say, "I'm sorry," the way you might if someone just told you a beloved relative had died. It wasn't that I felt there was anything strange or wrong about what he'd said, although it was certainly unexpected, only that he seemed so ashamed for having said it. Like admitting some distant member of your family was a dog. "I hadn't realized."

71

"It is a personal matter," he continued, once it became apparent I wasn't going to say anything more. "It is not a subject for public discussion."

"I understand." And I did, sort of. I understood that he didn't want his half-human status becoming general knowledge among the crew. I didn't entirely understand why.

"Merely because Vulcans have chosen not to let emotional states dictate our behavior does not mean we are incapable of understanding them. Indeed, I am well-versed in human hormonal urges, whether or not I happen to share them." Now he folded his hands on the table and leaned forward as though he were the one lecturing to me. "What you fail to grasp, Captain, is that emotion is not quantifiable. One must rely entirely upon subjective reports from the human in question regarding what that human is feeling, and why. There is no protocol by which to double-blind data collection and verify that such subjective observations are accurate. Nor are the results of emotion reproducible. An event which invokes strong emotion in one human may have no affect on another human of similar construction and experience. A human who responds emotionally to a particular event may be unmoved by a similar event at a later date." He took on that air of effortless pedantry that was apparently coded in the Vulcan genes. "Surak taught us generations ago that emotion is little more than arbitrary responses to arbitrary events. It is not valuable as data, and is therefore ignored."

"But that's where you're wrong, Spock!" I made myself straighten again when he recoiled slightly from my lean across the table. "Whether or not emotions make sense, they are part of the human equation, part of what makes humans behave and function in the ways they do. By refusing to acknowledge human emotions as real when you deal with the crew, you're willfully ignoring a variable, then wondering why your sums don't add up. What matters is that *humans* believe in what they feel. *Humans* will always have that variable in motion, whether or not you choose to allow for it."

I gave him a long time to think about that, watching the path of his thoughts in his dark eyes. After what seemed a small eternity, he said with care, "Your argument is unexpectedly logical." As if he didn't want to get caught saying anything rash. "I must take it under consideration."

I didn't grin at him, but I wanted to. "Mr. Spock, I believe there's hope for you yet."

Just then, the intercom's urgent whistle split the rec hall's quiet. Sulu's voice quickly followed. "Bridge to Captain Kirk."

Exchanging a glance with Spock, I pushed away from the table and jogged to the nearest wall intercom. "Kirk here. Go ahead."

"Captain, we're being approached by four Orion heavy merchant vessels." The official designation of what we all knew were pirating ships. "They've already fired a few—well, I guess they're warning salvos, sir, but they're too far out of range for the shots to even register on our shields."

"Any luck hailing them?" I asked. Spock had moved to my side by now, eavesdropping in the way good first officers always should.

"Not so far, sir, no."

"Patch me through to communications and hit them with a wide-beam transmission. I want to talk to them." I waited for Uhura's go ahead, then declared into the comm, "Commander Akpakken, this is Captain Kirk of the *Enterprise*. You are within the vicinity of my vessel. Cease fire! I repeat, cease fire! If you fire your weapons, and even a single shot comes in contact with my ship, I'll have no choice but to take retaliatory action. Do you understand?"

Addressing Akpakken by name had been something of a calculated guess, but it paid off in spades when his rattling roar came back at me. "Spineless monkey-rodents! To throw your filth into our warrens, then tuck your tailless rear-parts between your monkey legs and flee!"

I raised my eyebrows at Spock, and he merely shook his head. "Commander, perhaps you'd like to tell me what exactly we did to earn your wrath?"

"The pirates!" Akpakken bellowed. "Slimy Anjiri pirates! You fling them into our laps through your deceit, telling us they are victims, without danger. And within hours of your retreat, they have stolen the premiere yacht of our quadrant and escaped with four thousand kilos of precious metals!"

Chapter Six

SULU

There was a unique feel to the *Excelsior* when she was traveling at maximum warp, a repeated subliminal shiver that no amount of fiddling with the inertial dampeners or calibrating the warp drive ever seemed to erase. I didn't mind it myself, although Doctor Klass claimed it drove her crazy and was always requesting Tim Henry to get rid of it. Twenty-five years of piloting experience told me it was only an internal resonance between the hull and the warp engines, but I still often thought of that shiver as my starship's living pulse and a reflection of her crew's eagerness to be out working among the stars. Since we'd left Deep Space Three, that shiver had felt stronger and more persistent than before. I wasn't sentimental enough to anthropomorphize my ship, so I didn't assume that reflected the urgency of our mission to rescue our lost crewmates. All it meant was that we were pushing the envelope of our sustained warp capability.

It had taken us longer than I'd expected to set out after the pirate convoy. Commander Barstow had been injured badly enough in the initial firefight with the aliens that he had to be sent in stasis back to Earth for reconstructive surgery. That meant a quick round of approving new security clearances and promoting people to acting positions of command, a process that had to be carried out by the nearest available starship captain. I had known that by taking command of the *Excelsior* I would become a de facto Starfleet dignitary, but I'd expected that to be a minor responsibility, limited to entertaining ambassadors or making a glittering display of brass at Federation ceremonies. That might be true in the inner systems, but out here on the frontier, a starship captain was the embodiment of Starfleet authority for deep space stations and border outposts like these. Transmissions from headquarters were fine for everyday matters, but when you had a crisis and a crew badly in need of a morale boost, a starship captain was needed to personally fasten those rank pins to the new commander's lapel.

By the time we finally departed Deep Space Three, with our small armada of FL-70s and shuttle escorts trailing behind us, the low-powered signal from the pirate yacht had been entirely overwhelmed by the subspace bubbling of black holes and cosmic strings. The FL-70s' nano-transponders, each no larger than a human blood cell, were designed to be followed from the moment they were launched, not detected long after the quarry had escaped. I ordered a course to be set toward Elaphe Vulpina, then sat gritting my teeth while my communications and science staff searched for the fragile transponder signal along the way. It was a gamble that Starfleet Headquarters had agreed was worth the delay, but if a certain Vulcan junior science officer had misunderstood or misheard the alien pirates' intentions, there was a good chance we might never pick up their trail again. It was a tribute to my hard-working bridge officers that we managed to catch the transponder's call only two hours later, at the feathery edge of its range. My sigh of relief turned to a startled curse when the tracking data were analyzed a moment later—and showed the pirate convoy moving in a completely different direction than we were.

"Plot the transponder's position relative to Deep Space Three and Elaphe Vulpina and put it on the viewscreen," I commanded, as soon as our own course had been altered to match theirs. I watched the outside starscape ripple and dim behind a computer-generated overlay of glowing symbols. "Is this the heading they've been on since they left the station?"

"I don't think so, sir." My science officer frowned down at her panel rather than the viewscreen, although both of them now showed the same view. "If we extrapolate their current velocity and direction backward——" A glowing yellow line shot out from the moving flash of blue that was our quarry to the solid green of Deep Space Three. "You can see that they should have gotten a lot further away from the station than they did. In fact, we should never have been able to pick up their signal at all—it should have gone out of range while we were still sorting out security clearances."

"Maybe they stopped for a while," Orsini suggested. "After all, they don't know we're following them."

"Maybe, but I think it's more likely Cadet Tuvok was right about their original destination." Schulman ran a stylus across her panel and another glowing line, this one red and distinctly dog-legged, snapped into existence on the viewscreen. "If we assume the pirates started out toward Elaphe Vulpina at their current velocity, then turned onto a new heading about an hour into the flight, they would have ended exactly where they are."

I regarded the pattern before us with thoughtful eyes. "Extrapolate their current heading ten parsecs, Ensign Walroth, and tell me what star systems it passes through."

"None, sir." The navigator punched the request into his panel again, more emphatically this time, but even from my command chair I could see that his screen still came up blank. "The pirates are heading straight into one of the empty sectors in this part of the quadrant. There are no inhabited star systems within a month's travel in that direction."

That information made a troubled silence lap across the bridge, while one of my officers after another gave the viewscreen a baffled glance. "Could it be a red herring?" Orsini asked at last. I glanced at him and saw Chekov's wariness looking out of the younger man's eyes. "Maybe the pirates consolidated their forces after the battle and didn't need the Orion yacht anymore."

"Schulman, do long-range sensors detect anything yet at the site of the transponder signal?"

"No, sir. We're still too far away." She glanced over at me intelligently. "But Elaphe Vulpina's sensors should be able to detect the rest of the convoy by now, if it's still headed their way."

I looked back at my communications officer. "Rand, send a message to Elaphe Vulpina on a secure channel. Warn them to scan for ships and prepare for a sabotage attempt or an outright attack if they see anything approaching from that heading." Satisfied that we had given the border outpost all the forewarning we could, I sat back and scrubbed a hand across my face, trying to guess what my enemy's change in plans might mean.

"The sector of space they're headed for now, Walroth—is it part of the Federation or the Klingon Empire?"

"It's mostly Neutral Zone, sir." Ensign Walroth gave his navigation panel a puzzled look, then glanced over at Keith as if her display might show something different. "Captain, it looks as if the pirates have begun to decelerate."

"For another course adjustment?" I demanded.

"No, sir. They seem to be stopping right in the middle of nowhere."

I frowned and rose to my feet, leaning over the young man's shoulders to scan his glowing star charts. He was right—the faint pulse of light that was our transponder source had begun to decrease speed, at a rate that would put it at rest deep within interstellar space. That might have made sense as an evasive maneuver, but the pirates shouldn't have known they were being followed. I swung toward my science officer.

"Are we getting close enough for them to detect us?"

"No, sir," said Schulman promptly. "Our long-range sensors still can't pick up any ships at the source of the transponder signal. I can't imagine that the pirates have better instruments than we do."

"Neither can I." I returned to my chair, still frowning. "What the hell are they up to out there?"

Heather Keith glanced over her shoulder at me, an unusual enough occurrence when we were moving at top warp speed that it caught my attention immediately. "Captain, I spent a lot of time patrolling this part of the Neutral Zone with the *Venture*," she said. "It's not well-known, but there's a traffic pattern the Klingons tend to follow around here, a route through the Neutral Zone that connects the Klingon homeworld with their colonies in the Tregharl cluster."

I lifted my eyebrows. I could see why the Klingons wouldn't make much noise about that, since the Neutral Zone was technically supposed to be entered only on journeys to or from the colonies the Organians had permitted us to establish there. But given the multi-variate curvature of that border zone, there were times when it could put a substantial detour in an otherwise straight journey between one part of the Federation and another. Apparently, it posed the same problem for the Klingon side of the border.

"Transfer the coordinates of that route to the science desk, Lieutenant," I said. "Schulman, how does it correlate with the position of our transponder signal?"

"That's about where they'll be stopping when they complete deceleration," she agreed. "I'm starting to get some reliable telemetry from the long-range sensors as we get closer and I'm fairly sure—"

I waited a moment. It wasn't like my science officer to start a sentence and not finish it, especially when it was something she was "fairly sure" about. Christina Schulman had once admitted to being only "fairly sure" about Plottel's Universal Field Equation and "pretty certain" of Einstein's Theory of General Relativity.

"Lieutenant?" I probed after another minute.

"I think I may have spoken too soon, Captain." She was running one analysis after another on her long-range sensor panel, her troubled look deepening as she did so. "Initial readings suggested there were two ships at the transponder's location, but now I'm picking up four—no, five. And now they're all gone again—"

"Signal interference?" asked Tim Henry from the engineering station in back of the bridge.

"I think you're right, Chief. The number of ships keeps shifting moment by moment." Schulman looked frustrated.

"But I've done three system checks and there's nothing wrong with our side of the link."

Nino Orsini swung around from his weapons panel. "It could be phaser afterglow from a ship battle. At this range, sensors couldn't separate real ships from the reflected images bouncing off their shields with each blast."

"That would make sense of the sensor data," Schulman admitted. "Although it doesn't make sense to *me*. Why would you stop to attack a ship while you were fleeing from Deep Space Three?"

"They're not fleeing if they don't know they're being followed," I reminded her. "And for all we know, that other ship attacked them first. The Klingons can be touchy about finding unauthorized ships in the Neutral Zone." I swung back to Walroth and Keith. "Estimated time of arrival at the battle site, gentlemen?"

"We should be within firing range in another thirty minutes, sir," said my navigator.

"Twenty-five, if we push the deceleration curve." Heather Keith didn't look back at me this time, but she must have heard my quick intake of breath. She added reassuringly, "I know we didn't do it often on the shakedown, sir, but trust me. The *Excelsior* can take it."

"Very well, Lieutenant. Make it twenty-five minutes." I forced myself to take a long, slow breath after I spoke, startled by the surge of adrenaline that had spiked into my blood. What difference did it make, I asked myself, if we met the pirates in twenty-five minutes or the original two hours that I had thought it would take to catch up to them? The sooner the better, as far as the safety of the hostages was concerned.

But that logic didn't quell the churning uneasiness I felt. Neither did a circuit of the *Excelsior*'s bridge, although it did make my officers look more confident to have their various data screens inspected and approved by the captain. The only one who seemed to notice my restlessness was the chief engineer. He gave me a commiserating glance and rubbed at his own stomach.

"Butterflies," he said gruffly. "Always get 'em before a ship's first real engagement."

I nodded and clapped a hand on his broad shoulder as if it

were I and not he who was the veteran of two other prototype ship launches. "We'll do fine," I said, and moved on to the security station. It was there, glancing back across the *Excelsior*'s bridge at the star-streaked viewscreen, that I caught a glimpse of my own empty captain's chair and realized what was really wrong. I'd been through a hundred mock combats and another hundred simulated emergencies with this crew, but in every single one of those situations I'd always had the inner confidence of knowing that my second-in-command could take over if something went wrong. It wasn't the fact that this was the *Excelsior*'s first real crisis that bothered me. It was the fact that Chekov wasn't here to support me through it.

That thought startled me so much that I had to grit my teeth to keep from cursing. Was I really so unready for command, after all the years I'd prepared and longed for it, that the absence of a single one of my thousand competent crew members could disrupt my confidence like this? Granted, he was the only one who'd trained with me under Captain Kirk, who had absorbed that living legend's strategies and maneuvers more thoroughly than I had. And of course, we had the complete mutual trust that came from saving each other's lives more times than we could count. After escaping volcanic eruptions, serving undercover on an Orion pirate ship, and helping each other survive a hundred other critical situations, was it any wonder that I'd come to think of Pavel Chekov as my other self, the man I might have been if I'd been born in cold, grim Russia and not vibrant San Francisco?

I'd asked for him as my executive officer as soon as I'd been given command of the *Excelsior*, knowing he was long overdue for reassignment. Chekov had seemed a little reluctant to accept, perhaps remembering his previous stint as executive officer on the unfortunate science research vessel *Reliant*. But once we'd begun the shakedown cruise, our ability to mesh our talents and working styles had blossomed back into existence as easily as if it had been only yesterday that we'd manned the helm of the original *Enterprise* together. He'd seconded my hardest decisions, volunteered opinions I knew I could trust, and helped me weather all the ups and downs of getting a new crew adjusted to an even newer starship. I had just never realized before how much I'd come to depend on him throughout that process.

"We're nearing Klingon space lanes, Captain." It was the way Scott Walroth had to twist around to glance at me that reminded me I was still frozen beside the security console, staring at the funneling rush of stars that marked our passage without actually seeing them. "We'll be within firing range in twelve minutes."

"Thank you, Ensign." I cast a guilty look down at Orsini, hoping my long silence hadn't unnerved my young security chief. Fortunately, he was still scrambling to update his battle plans for the new ETA, and seemed to think my pause had been for his benefit rather than my own.

"I'm almost done recalibrating, sir," he said. "If you can just wait another minute—"

I did so, leaning over his display panel to scrutinize the battle plans as they coalesced. "Why are you assuming we'll have to fight six opposing ships, Lieutenant? Even counting the Orion yacht—"

"The pirates should only have five," Orsini finished. "But if the vessel they're engaged with is Klingon—"

"They might object to being rescued by Starfleet?"

The security chief shrugged. "Or they might assume we're using the pirates as a cover for an invasion, the same way we suspected them at Deep Space Three. Commander Chekov always says you can't go wrong if you expect the worst."

Despite my tension, I felt a smile tug at the corners of my mouth. I might not have Chekov here to depend on, but I did have a crew that he had shaped and molded as much as I had. "Very prudent, Lieutenant," I said. "Why don't you and Lieutenant Commander Rand work out a message we can send to the Klingons assuring—"

"*Captain!*" Christina Schulman spun around at her station, her urgent gaze sweeping the bridge until she found me. "The transponder signal is moving again."

I strode back to my console at the center of the bridge. "Walroth, can you verify that?"

The navigator hurriedly requested a different set of star charts from his console. "I'm sorry, sir, I was trying to coordinate with Orsini's battle plans—"

"Never mind that now, Ensign. Just tell me if that

transponder heading has changed since the attack on that unknown ship."

"Nine-nineteen mark one. No, sir, it's the same." The young man gave me an almost apologetic look. "The pirates are back up to speed and still heading for nowhere."

"Schulman, do sensors indicate any ships still present at the battle site?"

"No, sir." Her reply came so fast that I knew my science officer had asked herself that question long before I did. "My long-range sensors showed several ships leaving the area together, but I lost resolution before I could get an accurate count."

It was beginning to look as if the caution Chekov had hammered into my security chief had been justified after all. "Could you tell if they were all traveling on the same heading?"

My science officer shook her head. "No. We decelerated below warp five and lost sensor contact before I could determine that."

"Should we resume our previous speed, sir?" My pilot had her hands already poised above the controls, waiting for the order. I was opening my mouth to grant that permission when Janice Rand swung around and interrupted with the confidence of a veteran officer who knows how important her information might be.

"Captain, I'm receiving an automatic distress signal from an emergency life-pod. It appears to be coming from the vicinity of the battle site."

The *Excelsior*'s viewscreen still showed the usual rush of flying stars around us, but a glance at Heather Keith's display screens told me we were decelerating below warp three now. "Did any emergency message or ship identification come in with the distress signal?" I asked Rand.

"None, sir. It's just a simple subspace alarm, the kind most life-pods emit automatically as soon as they're launched." My communications officer glanced over at me, her eyes reflecting the staccato flash of light that marked the incoming alarm on her display panel. "Based on its specific range of frequencies, I'd say the ship it evacuated from was Klingon."

"Just promise me that you won't answer any mysterious distress calls from the other side of the Klingon border . . ."

"What do long-range scanners show at the battle site now, Lieutenant Schulman?"

"They've detected several escape pods at the coordinates of the distress call, sir, but no sign of a wrecked ship. I can't detect any life-signs in that vicinity."

"Would you expect to, at this distance?" Heather Keith asked.

"If there are enough survivors in those pods I would." Schulman threw another aggravated look at her long-range sensors, whose output was never good enough to satisfy her. "But our biodetectors aren't sensitive enough to pick up one or two stray individuals at this distance, especially through the afterglow of that battle."

I frowned, seeing from Lieutenant Keith's piloting screens that I had less than five minutes to decide whether to stop and investigate. "Security, science—rapid analysis of the situation."

"It's a trap," Orsini said at once. "A distress call where no one is actually in distress—any ship can jettison an escape pod and manufacture that."

"Agreed," said Schulman. "But this can only be a trap if someone's waiting there to catch us. According to my sensors, there are no other ships in the vicinity."

"There could be Klingon ships waiting under cloak," said my security chief.

"There could," she agreed. "But Ockham's Razor says that the simplest explanation is most likely to be correct. And those escape pods are drifting in the exact area where our pirate convoy stopped to engage a ship in battle twenty minutes ago."

I glanced at Lieutenant Keith's display again, eyeing the diminishing distance between us and the flashing icon that marked the distress signal. "Ensign, update on the transponder signal?"

"Still maintaining speed and direction on heading nine-nineteen, sir," Walroth said. "Assuming we accelerate back to maximum warp speed now, we'll intercept them in approximately forty-five minutes."

And if we stopped to investigate these escape pods, we would end up a full two hours behind them again. I curved my hands around the arms of my captain's console, feeling uncertainty twist in my stomach. It was so easy to make the right decision in simulated battles, when you were positive there *was* a right decision to be made. But this was the real world, and none of the decisions I could make seemed remotely close to being right. If I stopped to check the distress signal, I might possibly endanger the *Excelsior,* and I would certainly add another hour or so to the time the hostages had to spend in jeopardy. If I didn't stop, I would certainly be breaking Starfleet regulations and possibly condemning battle survivors to death. Depending on what the pirates had decided to do with their hostages after their change in plans, some of those survivors might even be members of my crew.

"Maintain deceleration, Lieutenant Keith," I told my pilot. "Ensign Walroth, plot a course that will put us within maximum transporter range of the source of that distress signal. Schulman, I want a continuous sensor scan of this entire region. If a vessel appears from any heading, put the ship on red alert."

"Aye, Captain," said three voices in unison. The slowing streaks of stars on the *Excelsior*'s viewscreen announced our arrival at the battle site. A moment later, my pilot glanced up from her stabilized display. "We've arrived at the alarm coordinates, Captain."

I frowned up at the unhelpful viewscreen, which showed nothing but deep space and distant stars. "Can we locate and magnify the pod?"

Schulman shook her head, but it was more in bafflement than negation. "Sensors seem to be having a little trouble with it, sir. What we're looking at there is the precise location of the distress signal's generator. It just doesn't seem to coincide with any significant mass in the area."

I glanced back at Rand. The somber look in her blue eyes told me the answer to my question, but for the sake of the ship's records I had to ask it anyway. "Commander Rand, could that alarm continue to generate a distress call if the life-pod itself was destroyed?"

"Most of our distress signal generators are self-contained

and self-powered devices, sir," she replied. "I would assume the Klingons use similar methods."

"So would I." I fought with a brief, treacherous desire to send the *Excelsior* leaping back into immediate pursuit of the pirate ship. But now that we were here, it would be stupid not to take a little time to learn about our enemies. And about their victims. "Lieutenant Schulman, I want you to scan this entire area for wreckage. Chief Henry, beam whatever we can find to a secured cargo bay and see if you can use it to identify the vessel that was attacked. Rand, alert Doctor Klass to be prepared to identify organic remains, if any happen to be found." I glanced at my watch and made a quick calculation in my head. "You have twenty minutes from my mark to reconstruct the crime, gentlemen—the same amount of time the pirates had to commit it. Mark."

The cargo bay was full of bodies. Rows of bodies, large and small, all of them stiff, all of them exhaling the glittery smoke of space-cold flesh put back in contact with air and humidity far too late to do them any good. All of them Klingon.

"I think it must have been a colony ship." My medical officer waited for a response to that statement, but I found myself unable to speak in the presence of so much senseless slaughter. After a moment, Klass cleared her throat and went on. "Chief Henry has only found a few shards of exploded life-pod, but he says the alloy is typical of un-armed Klingon vessels. We found seventy-six adults and eighteen children in the twenty minutes you allowed us to scan and beam them aboard. We might have found more if we'd stayed to sweep the whole area."

"Twenty minutes was all we could spare," I said curtly. Actually, it had been more than we could spare—we had lost the fragile signal of the nano-transponders just before we reengaged our warp drive, and only found it again by following the pirates' last known heading. It was the second time that gamble had paid off, but we were once again two hours behind in the chase. "What killed them? Not phasers."

"No, Captain, or we wouldn't have bodies," Klass said

with patient logic. "Most of the adults and all of the children appear to have been ejected directly from stasis tubes into space. They died from vacuum exposure, and there is no medical evidence to indicate they even regained enough consciousness to take a breath during their last moments."

My throat muscles lost a little of their convulsive stiffness. "And the rest?"

Klass's thin lips tightened. "Judging by the explosive decompression of the capillaries in their lungs, some were thrust into vacuum alive. Others seem to have been killed by blunt force trauma before being ejected from the ship. The tricorder picked up traces of non-Klingon DNA in most of the wounds, indicating the wounds were inflicted by hand. Or by tail," she added dryly.

I nodded, remembering Tuvok's description of the way his captors had fought. "Can that incorporated DNA be matched to any of the known alien races in your medical records?"

"Absolutely none," my chief medical officer admitted. "But the aliens in question are sauroid in morphology, not quite two meters in height, strongly muscled and heavily clawed, and quite possibly passive rather than active endotherms."

I blinked at her. My specialty in biology had been plants, but I'd had the requisite course in zoology and knew the terms she was using. "You think the pirates who did this are literally cold-blooded? Wouldn't that be unheard of in a sentient race?"

"It would be unheard of for them to be *ectotherms,*" Klass corrected me, in the professorial voice all doctors seemed able to assume at will. "But there are several sentient races known to have internal heat generation and warm blood without having the ability to regulate their blood temperature. Studies have shown that this lack of control predisposes them to mood swings, violent outbursts and racial paranoia. Even from the little we know of them so far, I suspect the pirates may be of similar temperament. The presence of ceremonial scarification—"

"Hold it," I said, frowning at her. "How did you infer a social phenomena like scarification from a few genetic samples?"

"I didn't," said my infuriatingly logical doctor. "I inferred it from the abundance of geometrically placed scars on the face, arms, and chest of the body—"

"Body? What body?"

"The single non-Klingon body we recovered in our scan of the battle site." Klass allowed herself a very small smile, one that was more a quizzical upward curve of the lips than any real indication of amusement. "You wouldn't expect Klingons to surrender their ship without inflicting *some* casualties—"

"Show it to me," I interrupted her without ceremony. An austere raised eyebrow reminded me that if DNA analysis and Klass's perfect memory couldn't give our enemies an identity, a quick inspection by a brand-new captain wasn't likely to, either. I didn't bother responding to that look, since I wasn't sure myself what I was going to accomplish. Perhaps I merely needed to see one of my enemies face to face, to have a concrete image of what I was facing in this battle.

"This way." Klass led me through the rows of frozen, fog-shrouded bodies to a form so blocky and solid that it looked as if it had been hewn from ice rather than turned to it. I frowned down at the face, seeing a toothy snout and deep eye-sockets whose unlidded eyes were now ice-punctured and colorless. A strong nasal ridge continued across the forehead with its scarred, lumpy scales, then rose into a cranial crest, vacuum-burned but impressively frilled further down the strong back. The body was covered in scales, ranging in color from mahogany to dark steel-gray. Over them, armor plating like thickened plates of chiton clung to the body, still emitting a warmth I could see in the cold drift of fog off the chilled flesh. That thermal augmenting unit probably kept the passively warm-blooded sauroid inhabitant more active than he could be on his own, but it wasn't doing its owner any good now.

"A single individual of a theropod species, origin unknown, age unknown," Klass reported. "Death resulted from attack with a Klingon *bat'leth*. Ejection into vacuum followed after a period of several minutes."

"Toward the end of the battle, in other words," I said grimly. "He was thrown out into space by his own people."

My chief medical officer lifted an eyebrow at me again, this time inquisitively. "On what evidence do you base that conclusion, Captain?"

"On the evidence of having heard them talk about doing it," I retorted. "Back when I was the helmsman on the *Enterprise* and we rescued a bunch of these guys from what they claimed was a pirate attack."

"Ironic," Klass said calmly, without a flicker of surprise crossing her strong face. "Why was the data on their species never entered into Starfleet medical records?"

I shook my head, still feeling the misty sense of déjà vu that had led to my recognition of this scarred alien. "I'm not sure. It happened a long time ago, and it was never actually an official mission. All I know is that Captain Kirk followed them back to their homeworld and made some kind of deal with the authorities there. And we never heard from them again."

"Until now," she said.

"Yes." I studied the dead face again with its strong projecting muzzle, triangular teeth, and fierce net of ceremonial scars. It seemed as if I should remember the name of such an unusual alien race, yet no word stirred in my memory. If all of Starfleet's computer records were equally blank—

"Put the Klingons' bodies into vacuum storage until we can deliver them to an appropriate location," I told my chief medical officer. "But I want this body kept in stasis until it can be examined."

"By another medical doctor?" Although her tone was polite, there was a spark in Klass's pale eyes that made me realize she had another similarity to Leonard McCoy: a keen sense of professional pride.

"No, Doctor. By the man who's most likely to know why these aliens are here and what they're trying to accomplish." I took a step back from the sauroid's mist-blanketed body, hoping I was doing this for the right reasons and not because I wanted the strong presence of my former captain to support me now that my first officer was gone. "Let's just hope the *Enterprise* isn't on the other side of the galaxy right now."

Chapter Seven

KIRK

"WHO SPREADS VILE LIES about the Gorn?"

Kirk wasn't sure what startled him most—the outraged roar of a familiar alien species, or the equally familiar cadence of its slow words. He twisted around in his chair just in time to come face-to-muzzle with a double row of sharp teeth and a blast of warm, meat-smelling Gorn-breath.

He gripped the edge of the table and leaned back slightly, wincing at the stench. "No one said anything about the Gorn."

The dandy across the table from him ruined the assertion by asking in a voice much louder than necessary, "Captain, isn't this one of the incompetent reptiles about which you've been regaling us?" He returned Kirk's glare with a saber-thin grin that left the starship commander momentarily unsure which fellow captain he would end up hitting.

"No!"

The Gorn lurched upright with a steamy hiss. Whatever thick, stinking fluid had been in the bucket in its hand splattered its feet and the floor around it. "What stringy human dares call the Gorn incompetent?"

89

Kirk noticed with some annoyance that not all the fingers that rose up to point at him came from his table.

"We weren't talking about the Gorn," he began, in what was meant to be his most soothing and reasonable voice.

He interrupted himself to duck out from under the Gorn's sluggish roundhouse swing.

I remember this, he thought as his chair overturned and he hit the floor rolling. Slow, deliberate, but persistent and strong as hell. Kirk watched the Gorn's second swing impact with the table, sending glasses, patrons, and wood flying off in all directions. It occurred to him that a drunk Gorn was probably the scariest thing he'd seen in the last few years.

"My lizard!" Sulu jumped to his feet, away from the alcohol-soaked mess. A few meters ahead of him, a squiggling flash of gold-and-brown whisked under the boards of the staircase and out of sight.

If the Gorn noticed either the fleeing lizard or the other Starfleet captain, it gave no indication. Swaying mightily, it turned in a laborious circle to snap pearly teeth at Kirk. "Hold still, leaping mammal! I will be merciful!"

"I've heard that before." Kirk bounced into a squat, ready to dive in any direction. No matter how slow moving, this was still the creature who, while sober, had once heaved a rock the size of a shuttlecraft at him. Kirk had no intention of taking this Gorn captain lightly. "Captain, let's discuss this like civilized creatures—"

The Gorn's languorous swipe would have passed over him by a good half-meter if not for the dangling bucket. Ducking, Kirk scrabbled sideways to avoid being drenched.

"You've had too much to drink—"

No bucket this time, just a talon-filled swipe wide enough to let Kirk jump to his feet and out of range.

"And I think you've misunderstood—"

The sauroid's roar rattled like a snake's angry tail. "You claim now that I don't even understand your speaking?"

"You've gotta admit," the human freighter captain leaned his elbows back against the long bar, looking almost as puckish as the dandy, "the translation devices seem to be working a lot better this time around—the stuff he says almost makes sense!"

Of course there were no translation devices—there never were here, and never needed to be. Which is why Kirk felt perfectly justified in raising his voice loudly enough for everyone present to hear. "This is a Gorn, not an Anjiri *or* a Nykkus!" He swept a chair between himself and the staggering Gorn, more for the appearance of distance than because he thought it would protect him. "They look completely different, and don't function even remotely the same. This is *not* the race we had dealings with!"

"Lies!" the Gorn raged, stretching up to its full, towering height. "The Gorn have had dealings with the humans for decades—one long history of conflict!"

It crushed the chair with one foot. Kirk took refuge behind another table as its patrons fled.

"So," the dandy asked mildly, "exactly how many different reptile people have you managed to irritate in your career, Captain?"

Obviously one more than was good for him. Dodging swiftly to his right, Kirk let the Gorn get halfway into a slow-motion spin to confront him, then dashed just as quickly leftward to place himself behind the alien's broad back. He might have felt guilty about kicking anyone else between the shoulder blades, but he'd done enough hand-to-hand grappling with this mighty species to know that any kick he delivered was likely to feel more like a friendly thump on the back. Much as he expected, the Gorn barely stumbled under the blow. It wouldn't have fallen at all if it hadn't tripped over Sulu.

The whole bar seemed to shake as the Gorn hit the floor. Sulu threw himself valiantly toward the struggling lizard he'd finally relocated, barely managing to avoid being crushed by the toppling behemoth. Even so, the little tailless reptile seemed to squirt from the middle of the imbroglio like a watermelon seed, beelining for the cracks in the stone fireplace. Kirk performed what felt like a particularly blundering tap dance around the fleeing gecko and his former helmsman, and ended up pouncing on the Gorn's chest more to cover his own stumbling than because he'd actually intended to pin the alien.

As long as he was there, though, he planted his knees on

the Gorn's shoulders and caught the end of its muzzle in both hands to protect his face from being bitten off. "Now, listen to me." Its hot breath whistled past his fingers, stinking eloquently of something pale and fermented. "Yes, we've been talking about a reptilian race that we clashed with a number of years ago. No, that race was *not* the Gorn, although the Gorn have been our worthy opponents in the past." That seemed to mollify the Gorn captain a little. He gave a little burp and stopped trying to shake off Kirk's hands. "The Gorn have always been honorable," Kirk continued. "The race we're talking about was very different."

The Gorn captain's voice hissed against Kirk's palms, but his grip on its muzzle blocked whatever words it made against the back of its own teeth.

Lifting his hands away, Kirk asked civilly, "What was that?"

"What became of these other people who were not Gorn?"

A request was always better than a blow. Rocking back on his heels, Kirk took his weight off the Gorn's chest and rose neatly to his feet. "That's what I've been trying to tell you." He offered the Gorn a hand, but was still a bit surprised when the big creature reached up to take it. "Why don't you join us over here—" Although he had to lean back into his pull to heave the other captain upright, they both managed to make it without falling down. Sulu still stood, looking disconsolately around for his gecko, but the others had already regrouped at the bar and resupplied themselves with fresh beverages. "I'll buy you a drink," Kirk offered the Gorn, "and you can let me explain what happened. . . ."

"Captain Kirk, I'm detecting another heading shift in the *Nevekke*'s ion trail."

Before I could order our own course change to compensate, Lieutenant Sulu quickly scanned his own helm readings, then leaned over to examine Bailey's navigations console. "No . . ." Even in correcting the younger man, his voice was calm and nonjudgmental. "The yacht moves back to its original course twelve kilometers later." He glanced over his shoulder at me. "I think they're flailing. They either don't know how to use the *Nevekke*'s controls, and are changing course without meaning to, or this is their idea of evasive maneuvers."

I had a feeling I knew which it was, but didn't want to take anything for granted. "Keep on them."

Sulu nodded curtly, swiveling back to his controls with only a brief pause to murmur some words of encouragement to Bailey. I fidgeted in my command chair, too mad at myself now to even pace the bridge.

I hadn't taken the Anjiri lightly—hadn't been impressed with their technological savvy, perhaps, but also hadn't assumed they were harmless because of that. Their original ship had been such a mishmash of different technologies that I'd simply taken for granted that they were a poor race, the kind that couldn't afford the high-quality technology that made spaceflight safe. That they were living off other races' leavings. In a sense, I was right. In this case, though, the "leavings" weren't whatever obsolete technology their trading partners were willing to part with, but whatever the Anjiri themselves could find lying around. Or whatever they could steal. Technological scavengers, opportunistic feeders off of more advanced races who probably should have known better.

"You are indulging in an exercise of fruitless emotional narcissism, are you not?" When I angled a dark look at Spock, he added, "I meant no disrespect. You are human, I understand. It is your lot."

Before he was promoted to first officer, he stayed at his science console instead of hovering at my right shoulder. "I'm reassessing how I handled the Anjiri," I sighed. It was strangely gratifying to have him standing there, as though his presence gave me the right to vent. "I was so damned eager to get them off the ship, I didn't even care where we off-loaded them."

He seemed to consider that for a moment. "As I recall, you exerted no undue pressure on Commander Akpakken to accept the Anjiri."

"I should have warned him," I grumbled.

"Illogical." Spock folded his hands behind his back, warming up for full lecture mode. "Contrary to human conviction, data obtained after the fact cannot be applied retroactively. We had no reason to believe Akpakken would be incapable of taking the necessary precautions to protect his station from the Anjiri."

In fact, the Anjiri didn't even attempt a sophisticated hijacking once they got on board the station—they took the Orion yacht in a straightforward smash and grab, without bothering to string the Orions along, much less come up with a believable excuse to get access to their hangar bay. After blasting their way off the station—the Orions were threatening to bill the Federation for repairs to their hangar bay doors—they then made no attempt to mask their drive signature or damp their ion emissions. Not exactly the actions of your top-flight pirate crew.

"At least Akpakken had the sense to map their course for the first few parsecs." I sighed again, but this time without the conviction of a true sulk. "Saved us a lot of time."

"And presents us with interesting data on Orion sensor and navigational techniques," Spock added. "Given the Orions' skill in predicting the location of Federation patrol ships, Akpakken's information should prove quite useful in avoiding future pirating activity in this sector."

I managed a wry smile. "I'm glad we could at least provide you with interesting study material, Mr. Spock." He didn't seem to get the joke.

The chirrup from the helm's long-range sensors caught my attention, and I knew what it meant even before Sulu announced, "Picking up a small craft dead ahead."

"Put it on screen. Full magnification." I hadn't expected a lengthy chase—there hasn't been a yacht built with any hope of outrunning a starship. I watched the *Nevekke* ripple into view against a hazy ribbon of gas and debris and cocked a look toward Spock. "Asteroid belt?"

He was already back at his station, bent over his sensor display. "Planetary remnants, including residual ring structures." He gave the viewscreen a pensive frown. "The outermost of fifteen planets around a class K star."

At the helm, Sulu was suddenly a whirlwind of activity. "They're accelerating!"

On the screen, the Orion yacht's small warp engines brightened, squeezing a rippling puff of exhaust leakage out of the belly of the ship. They were pushing the little ship way too hard, and I had a feeling why.

"Close with them!" I shouted, half-vaulting from my chair. "I want a tractor beam on them before they make that field. All hands, yellow alert!" That last was peremptory—if we ended up dodging and weaving through that debris field in a ship the size of the *Enterprise,* I wanted the crew ready for anything.

I felt the *Enterprise* gather herself for the leap forward, like a racehorse plunging in the gate, but I knew with sick certainty that we'd never catch *Nevekke* before she made the debris field. Still, I almost snapped at Bailey to take a stab at them with our tractor beam, even though they were woefully out of range. Instead, I cursed at *Nevekke*'s vapor trail when she didn't so much as fire her retrojets before diving into that sea of gas and distraction.

"Mr. Sulu," I ordered grudgingly, "cut speed. One half impulse." We weren't *Nevekke.* We wouldn't win this battle with speed, any more than they'd made any headway with cunning.

Spock jerked his head up from his console. "Captain . . . ?"

"We promised the Orions we'd bring back their yacht, Mr. Spock." I fumed as discreetly as possible, clenching my fist against my thigh. "We can't do that unless we follow them in."

Ahead of me, I saw Bailey start, and even Sulu's voice carried a certain note of skeptical acceptance when he acknowledged, "Aye, aye, sir. One-half impulse."

Instead of leaping into action, the warp engines pulsing at my ship's heart growled down to a frustrated rumble. The asteroid belt no longer rushed up on us like the edge of a cliff, and we lost visual with the yacht a lot faster than I would have liked. All that was left was the ripple of her warp exhaust where she'd ducked into a cloud of tumbling rock.

"Look at their speed!" Bailey shook his head at that

visual remnant of the Anjiri's escape. "They're going to ionize themselves on a planetoid."

We should be so lucky. "Let's try not to follow their example," I cautioned. "Be conservative, Mr. Sulu, but keep that ship in range."

Sulu gave only a terse nod in acknowledgment—he was already fixated on his controls as the forward screens began to glow with vaporizing dust and microimpacts. Our treacherous waltz had begun.

Proximity alarms exploded into life all around me.

"Kill those sirens." I waved irritably at Giotto at the security console. He hurried to comply, and I hunkered down in my chair to glare at the blurring starscape before me.

You have to understand astronomical distances—there wasn't a one of those rocks closer than several kilometers away. If the Enterprise had been a human on foot, traversing this debris field would have been like navigating around a set of football goal posts without slamming into one. But the Enterprise wasn't a human—she was a huge, massive, warp-powered vessel that has more inertia than some small moons and enough of her own gravitational field to perturb the orbit of every piece of space debris she passed. "Several kilometers" in a Constitution-class starship starts to seem a lot more like tiptoeing across a trampoline covered with hand grenades.

Screen magnification adjusted itself downward, then downward again as we crept deeper and deeper into the morass. I couldn't see a damned thing to justify our caution. Most of the planetoids and asteroids we brushed past weren't even close enough to get a meaningful visual, and once magnification reached zero the stars beyond the nose of the ship looked hardly different than what I usually saw there, just a little more cloudy and yellow.

Spock's deep voice interrupted my glowering. "Captain . . ."

I spared him a glance, then realized that whatever he'd picked up on his sensors had seized his full attention. I doubted he'd have noticed me looking at him if I bounced a hand phaser off his head. I thought about Sulu, equally engrossed in the business of keeping us out of any unfriendly gravity wells, and stood to join Spock at his station so that whatever he had to say wouldn't distract my helmsman. "What is it?"

He still didn't look up from his readouts, but his response was more alert than I'd expected. "I'm detecting signs of primitive industrialization on one of the planetoids currently within sensor range."

I don't know why I glanced at the viewscreen. I didn't really expect to see anything—there wasn't even a discernable star this far out, and no other full-sized planets in sight. "Intelligent life? Here?"

Spock lifted his shoulder in a minimalist Vulcan shrug. "Not indigenous, certainly. The planetoid in question does not appear to support even a noxious atmosphere, or show any indication of tectonic activity. Logic suggests that these are colonists, perhaps shipwreck survivors."

"The Anjiri?"

"Possibly." But his voice gave no indication how likely he thought that possibility to be. "Readings reveal the same eclectic collection of technologies and metals."

"A good place to hide, if you've got ships agile enough to access it." Which an Orion yacht wasn't, really. "What about reinforcements? Any sign of other ships in the vicinity?"

He bent back to his sensors for a moment. "I assume you are only interested in ships which are capable of lifting off to engage us in combat?"

What the hell kind of question was that? "Do you detect some other kind?"

"The inhabited planetoid is . . ." He hesitated, just enough to make the hair on the back of my neck start to rise, "encrusted with a great variety of vessels. I read no engine activity, yet their life-support systems appear to be powered and fully operational." He turned a cool look toward me without straightening from his station. "The Anjiri appear to be using them as living quarters."

And what could make for nicer living quarters than a well-appointed Orion yacht?

"We can't let them land that yacht." Taking the steps to

my command chair in a single stride, I swung into the seat as I demanded, "Mr. Sulu, where are we relative to the *Nevekke?*"

The helmsmen stole a series of short but directed glances at his readings. "Ninety-three kilometers," he shook his head apologetically, "and pulling away. I'm sorry, sir. We're losing too much velocity on the turns."

Damn. "Don't blame yourself for the laws of physics, Mr. Sulu." I slapped open a channel on my chair console. "Bridge to Engineering."

"Engine room. Scott here."

"I've got a civilian yacht at a hundred klicks dead ahead that I need to stop. Can you route extra power to the tractor beam so it'll hold across that distance?"

Scott sounded wary of my request, as always. "Aye, I can route half your shield output through the tractor beam array. I can't promise your civilian ship'll hold up to the stress, though."

"Let me worry about that. You get me that power." I closed our connection before he could protest further. "Mr. Sulu, where's our quarry?"

"A hundred twelve klicks, still pulling away."

"Mr. Bailey, activate tractor beam. Let's see if we can slow our friends down a little."

I heard Spock stir slightly to my right. "Captain," he interrupted, "if we should attach our tractor beam to an asteroid rather than the *Nevekke*—"

We'd be a living example of that old joke: What's the last thing to go through a starship commander's mind when his ship hits a moon? Answer: His warp drive.

"Mr. Bailey will endeavor to be careful."

The jolt of deceleration hit the ship so powerfully, I came out of my command chair and went down on one knee. "*Careful,* Mr. Bailey!" I reminded the navigator.

He shook his head frantically, hands flying across his panel. "That wasn't me!" he protested with youthful indignation. "I mean, that wasn't us! The engine room hasn't even given me the go-ahead yet."

So when the second tremor rocked the ship, I swung an urgent glare at Spock. It was wasted—he'd already buried his attention in his station, and didn't need me to prompt him for a report. "Captain, we've been caught by someone else's tractor beam."

I leaned hard over the railing between us. "*What?*" In the background, somewhere decks away, I could hear the ship's core systems straining as the *Enterprise* tried to plow forward despite the drag.

"Two tractor beams," Spock continued, as calmly as though we were discussing dyes in a petri dish, "at a one hundred twenty degree angle from each other."

I twisted to shout at Sulu, "Helm, full stop!"

Sulu went to work without replying. Nothing betrayed our drop in speed, but the third jolt which rocked the ship didn't jar us so violently, thanks to our reduced momentum.

Spock's announcement was only what I expected. "Captain, we're suspended in a triangulated tractor beam. The beam generators appear to be situated on three separate planetoids around the main industrialized homeworld."

Maybe the Anjiri weren't so ignorant of how to use their stolen technology after all.

"Any of them within phaser range?" I asked. I prowled back to the command chair, but couldn't make myself sit down.

"Negative. The power of each individual beam is unprecedented, allowing them to be situated a great distance from our position." Spock actually looked impressed. "I will speculate that this is how the Anjiri make use of the reaction piles from their various captured ships."

What a nice little lesson in recycling. I chewed my lip, absently bouncing a fist off the edge of my chair back as I pondered our options. "Uhura, open hailing frequencies. Broad band."

"Sir, I—" She hesitated, and I turned to face her. "We're being hailed," she told me, looking a little startled. "The channel's low frequency and the coding very primitive, but . . ." Her eyes glazed with listening for a moment longer. When they cleared again, she said, "It sounds like they're speaking Anjiri."

Of course they were. I rounded my seat, glaring at the still obstructed view. "Put them on screen."

The already dusty and fragmented stars fragmented further, shattering into a pale, unremitting buzz. I waited for a face to appear, but instead heard only the growling hiss of a voice that might have been Vissith's, yet was somehow clearly not Vissith's. The tortured translator-syntax was unmistakably Anjiri.

"Your ship to our revered coordinates shall proceed. Into our company yourselves you shall present. All of this within one specified unit of time you shall accomplish, or torn into prenatal bits you shall be."

Chapter Eight

SULU

Captain's Log, U.S.S. Excelsior, Stardate 8730.1

   We are in pursuit of the alien pirates who attacked
Deep Space Three and took six members of our crew
hostage, then slaughtered ninety-four innocent Klingon
colonists. Their heading and velocity have put them
deep within an uninhabited portion of the Neutral
Zone and their ultimate destination remains unclear. So
far, we have received no answer to our requests for
either a conference with Captain Kirk or the records of
his previous encounter with these aliens. What we have
received are strict orders from Starfleet not to cross the
Klingon side of the border. We are therefore proceed-
ing at maximum warp to intercept the pirates.

I RELEASED the recording button on my console arm with a
quiet, guilty sigh. In these days of visual computer records,
a captain's log was a personal journal, intended to docu-
ment its maker's mental and emotional state in case his or
her command decisions were later brought into question. I
could remember Captain Kirk back on the bridge of the
Enterprise, pouring out his frustrations and venting his

fears into his log entries. So far, all I felt able to record in front of my crew were brief and banal statements of fact: Where we were, what we planned to do, what our orders were. I suspected that later examination of this journal would merely conclude that its captain lacked the inner confidence he needed to carry out his duties.

"Captain Sulu, long-range sensors are picking up some telemetry on the transponder source," said Lieutenant Schulman. The aggravation in her voice added the unspoken words, *"at last."* "It looks like six ships, traveling together in tight formation. We're not close enough to separate out their ion trails and identify them yet, but from the size of the sensor reflections, I'd say one is much larger than the others."

"The Klingon colony transport," I guessed and saw my science officer nod agreement. "Time to intercept, Ensign Walroth?"

"Nine-point-three minutes, sir." The words might have a Vulcan precision, but the suppressed excitement in the young man's voice betrayed an all-too-human sense of anticipation.

"And our current distance from the border?"

"Fifty million kilometers and closing," said my pilot without looking away from her display. "We're going to be kissing Klingon space by the time we catch up to them, sir. We can't let them run any further."

I swung around and caught my security chief in the process of doing the same thing, so that our glances caught and held. "Battle strategy, sir?" Orsini demanded.

"Overshoot before engagement," I said. "If we come at them from the direction of the Klingon border, their best hope of evasive action is to break back toward our side."

"Assuming they're not running for that border as a sanctuary," Henry put in from his engineering station.

Heather Keith snorted. "After killing almost a hundred Klingons, I doubt they'll find a warm welcome in the Empire, Chief."

"Unless they captured that colony ship to use as a Trojan horse," I said. "We'll concentrate our fire on it first and see if that draws the other ships in to protect it."

"If it doesn't?"

I paused, trying to decide how best to balance the safety of our missing crew with our urgent need not to let their captors cross the Klingon border. In the part of their missive coded for my eyes only, Starfleet Command had made it very clear that any incursion into the Empire's space right now was likely to set off a round of attacks and reprisals that would at the very least rouse the Organians' wrath. At the very worst, it might catapult us into full-scale interplanetary war with the Klingons before those superior beings even had time to intervene. Balanced against that, the six lives that had drawn us here were clearly of lesser importance—and yet every fiber of my body rebelled against subjecting them to the kind of crushing attack the *Excelsior* was capable of.

Janice Rand interrupted before my internal conflict could betray me into a jumble of contradictory battle orders, or even worse, no battle orders at all. "Captain, we're getting another message from Starfleet, security code alpha."

That meant all of my bridge officers had the clearances needed to hear it. "Put it on the main viewscreen, Commander."

The glittering rush of stars going past us at maximum warp speeds vanished, replaced by the calm face and piercing dark eyes of Rear Admiral Hajime Shoji. "Captain Sulu," he said with the politeness he was legendary for, even at the times of greatest crisis. "I apologize for the delay in responding to your earlier request for information, but it was necessary to consult with Captain Kirk before we made a decision." The slightly ironic emphasis the rear admiral put on the word "consult" suggested that it was a tactful euphemism for "cross-examine." Given that no official medical records seemed to have been filed from the *Enterprise*'s previous encounter with these aliens, I could see why Starfleet Command might have been a little vexed.

"Were you able to discover the identity of the aliens?" I asked, since the rear admiral seemed to be waiting for some response.

"Indeed," he replied, as imperturbably as a Vulcan ambassador. "And I'm pleased to be able to tell you that upon hearing of your encounter with them, Captain Kirk volunteered to assist you in any way he can. He has just finished a mission in an adjacent sector and should be arriving within two standard hours."

That news, which would probably have made me bristle with offended pride a day ago and sigh in relief two hours ago, now felt like nothing more than extraneous information. "We're five minutes away from contact with the alien convoy, Admiral." I tried to sound as imperturbable as he did, but I wasn't sure I succeeded. "Is there *any* information you can give us that might be of some help?"

Shoji inclined his head in a gesture as ambiguous as it was gracious. "Starfleet Command is forwarding you all the information we can—"

"Captain!" It was a tribute to Rand's poise and confidence that she felt no more compunction about interrupting a rear admiral than a fellow bridge officer. "We're being hailed on a Klingon emergency channel—but the message says it's from our resupply team!"

"Match and verify voice patterns," I ordered my communications officer. "Orsini, raise shields and prepare for attack in case this is a trap. Schulman, locate the source of that transmission and cross-check it with the flight path of the alien convoy. Admiral, if you'll excuse me—"

The appreciative glint in those dark eyes told me the order in which I'd issued my commands hadn't been lost on my sector commander. "By all means, Captain Sulu. Shoji out."

I swung around without waiting to see the uninformative stars that replaced him on the viewscreen. "Schulman, let me know as soon as you've received and scanned the information Starfleet sends us. Where are the alien ships now?"

"Two are continuing on their original heading toward the Neutral Zone, Captain," she reported. "Three others have split off on a heading which is roughly parallel to the Klingon border, and the largest one—the former Klingon colony transport—seems to have come to a complete stop, then turned around to go back to where it came from."

I glanced at Rand. "Status of the emergency hail?"

"Voice patterns are matched and verified, sir. It's Ensign

McClain from Ship Services Division. He says the rest of the resupply team is there with him."

"Put him on the main screen," I commanded and swung around to face it. This time, the transition from star-streaks to a human face was much less smooth, fragmented around the edges in a way that meant the transmitter was calibrated for a different type of rastering system and had been transformed to fit our screen. Inside that fractal halo, a young and swollen face squinted back at me through a splatter of deepening bruises.

"Ensign McClain, what is your status?"

"Alive and abandoned, Captain." McClain's voice held the kind of toneless exhaustion I'd heard before in survivors of torture, the same tone Chekov's voice had held when the Klingons had used an agonizer on him so many years ago. "The damned snakes who took us killed the station quartermaster trying to get a Starfleet security override code he didn't even know. When they started in on us, Commander Chekov managed to cut some kind of deal with them. They kept him and threw all the rest of us out in a Klingon lifepod."

I wasn't sure whether the tightness I felt in my throat was pride that my first officer had been able to save his crew, or dismay about his own fate. "What kind of deal did Chekov cut?"

"I don't know, sir. The universal translators could barely make sense of the snakes when they talked. All I know is that as soon as he cut it, the aliens changed course away from Elaphe Vulpina and stopped slapping us around. They didn't get around to actually throwing us out until later, after they'd attacked that Klingon ship and had the lifepods to spare."

Something about that sequence of events didn't feel right to me, but now wasn't the time to dissect it in detail. "All right, Ensign. We've got the coordinates of your signal fixed and will be within transporter distance in just a few minutes." I could see the flashing beacon of his emergency signal on Heather Keith's piloting boards, and years of piloting experience told me exactly what its position meant in terms of travel time. "Does anyone in your party need to be beamed directly to sickbay?"

"It looks like Neely has a pretty bad concussion, sir, and Vanderpool thinks her wrist might be broken. The rest of us are just banged up."

"Good. Notify us if anything in your situation changes, Ensign. *Excelsior* out."

Before I had even touched the button that closed the channel, his battered face vanished from the screen, replaced by a dim vision of stars and a glowing overlay of ship movements. "Captain, our long-range sensors show that the convoy ships have all come to a stop just outside normal sensor range," my science officer said urgently. "They seem to be massing for some kind of surprise attack."

"Red alert," I ordered, then scanned that sensor-constructed array, wishing I had the kind of running captions the FL-70s used to identify each vessel. The large image now somewhere behind us was certainly the Klingon colony transport, lightly armed but a significant threat if she made any kind of suicide run. Off to the side, where their parallel course had taken them, the three smaller images probably represented the smallest ships of the pirate convoy: the former Orion yacht, the captured Vulcan science probe, and the retrofitted Romulan patrolship. Of the three, only the patrolship was much of an offensive threat. Still out in front of us, close to the Klingon border, the final two images must be the Rochester-class cruiser and the unknown alien battleship. With their heavier armor and powerful phaser banks, they were the most threatening part of the little fleet.

"Walroth," I said without turning away from the screen. "How long will it take those ships to reach the coordinates of our resupply team's life-pod?"

He punched the request into his board and visibly stiffened at the answer. "Under one minute for most of them, sir. The Klingon transport would take longer."

"And our current ETA for the life-pod?"

Lieutenant Keith answered before he could. "One minute and forty-three seconds, sir. Even at maximum deceleration, we're not going to beat them to it."

"Then take us to the outside edge of transporter range. I don't want that pod getting caught in the cross fire if a battle starts." I vaulted out of my chair and crossed to the weapons desk. "Orsini, those ships are probably going to wait for us to drop our shields and start beaming our crewmen aboard before they attack. As soon as we stop, I want you to cut power to our shields—"

"*Cut* power, sir?" he repeated, looking puzzled.

"Yes, Lieutenant. We want to look unshielded and defenseless just long enough to lure them toward *us*. When they're all within firing range, raise shields and counterattack."

My security officer slanted me an inquiring glance. "Won't that still put the life-pod on the edge of a battle, sir?"

"Yes." I was beginning to regret having left our two strongest shuttlecraft to escort the remaining FL-70s to Elaphe Vulpina. One could easily have defended the life-pod from attack while the other tractored it out of danger. Instead, I was forced to rely on split-second timing and luck, that most fickle of allies in outer space.

"Sulu to main transporter room," I said into my console's communicator panel, and waited for the response of Transporter Chief Renyck. "Lock on to the five life-forms in that Klingon life-pod and prepare to beam them out on my command. If the pod gets hit by a stray phaser shot, we're going to lower shields and beam the crew aboard. If we've disabled the strongest attack ships by then, we can probably endure a few minutes of unshielded phaser fire—"

"Nearing life-pod coordinates, Captain," Walroth interrupted. Hearing Commander Rand cut off a rear admiral seemed to have given him a little more confidence in his own ability to issue reports. "We've established a stationary position at a distance of approximately twenty-five thousand kilometers."

"Shields down," I told my security chief, and heard the almost subliminal whisper of the power generators fade. "Schulman, can we get an image of that life-pod now?"

"I'll put it on-screen," she said, and a magnified image of a tiny Klingon life-pod floated through the glowing diagram of alien ambush still covering the screen. The flimsy hull of plastic and raw duranium barely reflected the deep space star-glow, and not a sign of light leaked from its single porthole. It didn't look like it could survive too much more exposure to vacuum, much less a glancing phaser blast. Doubts about my strategy started to creep into the confidence with which I'd begun this encounter.

At the communications station, Rand cleared her throat. "Sir, I'm getting another message from Ensign McClain. He says they can see the *Excelsior* from their porthole, and want to know why we're not beaming them aboard."

I scowled, knowing there was no way I could send a secure message back on that Klingon frequency. "Tell him we're dropping shields and will be beaming them over soon. With any luck, overhearing that exchange will kick our friends out there into motion."

But five long minutes crawled by and the glowing symbols on the viewscreen made no attempt to converge on my unprotected ship. More doubts began to cloud my conviction that I knew what the pirates were up to. Could they be waiting out there for some other reason? Perhaps this close to the edge of the Neutral Zone, they were hoping the lifepod's distress call would draw in some Klingon border guards and precipitate a military confrontation they could then take advantage of. But that strategy implied Pavel Chekov had made the destruction of the *Excelsior* part of his deal with the "snakes," and I knew that was the last thing my executive officer would ever do.

"Captain, we've received the information packet from Starfleet on the *Enterprise*'s previous encounter with these aliens," my science officer said, in what was obviously an attempt to fill the silence. "I've scanned over it, and there doesn't seem to be very much there. It mentions the same kind of translation problems we've noticed in their speech, and it refers to them as interstellar pirates, but there's not even a consensus about what they're called. Sometimes they're referred to as the Anjiri and other times as the Nykkus."

I scrubbed a hand across my cheeks and chin, amazed I didn't feel beads of sweat popping out as the impasse lengthened. "That's because there were actually two species working together in the group we rescued back then, Lieutenant," I said absently. "I remember thinking at the time that they looked like congener species—"

Neither of whom had evinced very much respect for the life of the other. I felt my frown deepen as I recalled the cavalier way both those sauroid species seemed unable to value others' lives. Now that I had time to think, I also remembered what had bothered me about Ensign McClain's story. It wasn't the fact that Chekov had cut a deal to save his crewmen from torture—that part rang utterly true. But why had the Anjiri and Nykkus, whose regard for each other's lives was minimal to say the least, needed to wait until they had a *spare* life-pod available for the hostages to be freed in? Surely the Vulcan science probe had life-pods large enough to carry five humans, and if they didn't the Orion yacht certainly would have. Just as surely, neither the Anjiri nor the Nykkus would have worried about saving all those life-pods for each other. So why did they wait for several hours after Chekov convinced them to turn away from Elaphe Vulpina before they released the hostages in a Klingon pod several sizes larger than it needed to be?

I didn't like any of the reasons I could think of.

"Lieutenant Orsini, I want a thorough security scan of that life-pod," I said crisply. "Life-forms, systems integrity, possible explosive devices—"

"You think the *life-pod* is the Trojan horse?" demanded Tim Henry.

"I think there's some good reason we're being watched and not attacked," I said somberly. "And if there aren't any Klingons on the way, I suspect they've planted a surprise for us along with the crew. They seem to be awfully fond of trying to sabotage their victims before they come in for the kill. If they're really smart, they didn't even let the hostages realize anything was wrong."

"We're out of range of my weapons sensors, sir," Orsini said. "If we could get a few thousand kilometers closer—"

I eyed the hovering threat that ringed us on the viewscreen, and shook my head. "That might be exactly the move they're waiting for, Lieutenant. Schulman, what can you get on the long-range instruments?"

"Life-forms all read human, sir, and there are only five of them," my science officer said promptly. "But I am picking up an unusual power drain from the pod's impulse engines. Their fuel cells seem to be functioning normally, but all the power is getting siphoned off before it reaches the cabin."

"That's why it looks so dark?"

"Yes, sir."

"Captain!" At the helm, Heather Keith stared up at the viewscreen. "One of those ships out there is moving!"

I sat up straighter, noticing the slight divergence of one of the three smaller glows from the others. "Projected course," I said sharply, and heard the tap of orders input to both Schulman and Walroth's stations. Instants later, twin white lines appeared on the viewscreen, lancing out from that moving ship directly toward the drifting Klingon life-pod.

"Pirate ship will enter firing range in twenty seconds," said my security chief. "Orders, Captain?"

I paused, feeling nearly overwhelmed by mounting doubts and indecision. "Hold your fire," I said, just before the twenty-second deadline passed. "Prepare to raise shields and counterattack if she changes course to come at us. If she doesn't, scan for weapons activity or subspace transmissions. I want to know if they're planning to attack the life-pod or rendezvous—"

"Captain." The tangible calm of Rand's voice made me realize how much tension was vibrating in all the others, including my own. "I'm picking up a transmission from the approaching ship to the rest of the convoy, on the same subspace frequency they used before they attacked Deep Space Three. But this time our universal translator can barely make sense of it—" She broke off and keyed a tab on her communications console. The familiar deep growl that emerged made the hair on my forearms rise in apprehension.

"Wait explode escort wait explode escort . . ."

"It must be another sabotage attempt," I said, but the confirmation of my suspicions about the Klingon life-pod didn't make me feel any better about losing the innocent crewmen who were stranded there. "Do we have scan results on the approaching ship yet?"

"Fifteen life-forms aboard, of a type unrecognizable to the sensors," Schulman said. "I assume they're either Nykkus or Anjiri. Power flows from impulse engines—"

"Phaser banks are charging, sir," Orsini broke in on her unceremoniously. "They'll be within firing range of the life-pod in thirty seconds."

I tapped the button that made my communication console reestablish its most recent connection. "Transporter room, get those hostages out of there!"

"Aye, Captain," said my transporter chief's competent voice. "Transporter beam is locked and engaged. We have partial recovery—"

Rand swung around from the communications station, and for the first time that I could remember since our voyage began, her voice actually sounded strained. "Captain, I'm receiving a transmission from the Klingon life-pod. It sounds like Ensign McClain—"

I clamped my jaw shut on the urge to say something time-consuming and useless like *What?* or *That's impossible!* "Main screen," I said between my teeth. I didn't wait to hear what Ensign McClain had to say—one glance at his bruised and frantic face, and I smacked a hand back on my communicator controls.

"Transporter room, abort transport!"

"Captain Sulu!" McClain's voice was no longer toneless, but the note of terror I heard in it wasn't much better. "You beamed over five snakes instead of us! They were in stasis tubes programmed to snag the transporter beam—"

I pressed the reconnect button again, this time even harder than before, as if that could somehow get me through to my endangered transporter chief. "Renyck, abort transport! Can you hear me?"

"It's too late," Schulman said. "The ship's logs show that transport was completed ten seconds ago."

That made Renyck's lack of response ominous rather than frustrating. I swung around toward Orsini. "Get security—"

"Captain, the pirate ship is firing at the life-pod!" He had his hands poised over his weapons array, his face lifted to watch the brilliant flare of phasers across the viewscreen. "Orders?"

I gritted my teeth again, this time on an impulse to curse this entire chain of insanely impossible events. "Hold your fire until we have those hostages out! Helm, take us on an intercept course between the pirate ship and the pod. Try to draw their attack back toward us." The glowing sensor-pattern of ambush disappeared into a stomach-churning swoop of stars and a quiver of phaser beams as Keith launched us into the middle of that strafing run. I could feel the ship shake as one blast caught us amidship, and a few seconds later a damage alarm began to sound at the engineering desk. "Rand, contact the auxiliary transporter room and get those hostages beamed out of there, *fast*. We'll be unshielded and open to attack until we get them."

They may have responded to my orders with shouted "aye-ayes" or they may have carried them out in silence for all I knew. With the external crisis taken care of, my attention immediately snapped back to the crisis on my own ship. "Security alert, all decks. We have hostile intruders on deck five, repeat—"

"Not deck five, sir," Schulman said grimly. "There was another transport forty-five seconds after the first, but this one was intraship." Transport at such close range was always dangerous, but given the *Excelsior*'s brand-new and carefully calibrated transporter pads, I knew we couldn't depend on finding our intruders splattered across a bulkhead. "Four life-forms were transported that time. One of them must have stayed behind to make sure the transporter chief didn't send them back to where they came from—"

"Where *did* they go?" I demanded. On the viewscreen, radiance scythed and lanced its way across the nearby sky, laying down a lattice of destruction for our helm to dodge through. But the *Excelsior*'s workhorse bulk wasn't exactly built for evasiveness. I saw Lieutenant Keith wince as the ship shuddered with impact again, more strongly this time.

Schulman glanced over her shoulder, a surprising clench of anxiety on her normally composed face. "According to my records, sir, the second transport was to the ship's main shuttle bay."

"Where the FL-70s are." I knew I was the one who said that, although I barely recognized that grating voice as my own. I could hear the ominous silence that followed and wondered if my officers felt as betrayed as I did by the fact that all the shakedown cruises in the world could not prepare us to meet this crisis. "Orsini, beam down to the shuttle bay and secure those Falcons. If the pirates capture even one of them, they'll be able to gut the whole ship." He vanished a step away from his security console as Schulman punched the emergency order into the computer. Without a word, Scott Walroth left navigations and took his place at the weapons panel. "Henry, can you throw a stronger version of the phaser dampening field across that shuttle bay?"

"No, sir. It's too broad to span without internal amplifiers."

"Then beam some in there," I said sharply. "If the Falcons can't fire their phasers, it'll take a suicide run to damage us from the inside." A phaser blast glanced off our bridge carapace, making the ablative armor scream in a protest I hadn't heard since the last explosive decompression I'd survived. I remembered that we still weren't shielded. "Walroth, target phasers on that ship! Rand, did we manage to get the hostages out of the life-pod yet?"

"Yes, sir."

"Then I want full power returned to shields—"

"No, sir!" Henry's words were as gruff as ever, but the unusually deep pitch of his voice caught my entire attention. "Our shields were designed to ward off phaser fire from *outside.* If any of those FL-70s fire at them from the inside while they're in place, they'll set up a runaway internal resonance through the entire node-generating network. It'll blow the ship apart within minutes."

I grimaced, feeling the shudder of another glancing phaser blast. This one slanted past one of our warp nacelles, then caught the drifting Klingon life-pod in a brilliant embrace. The little pod promptly blew itself to bits in an explosive decompression whose shrapnel slammed against the *Excelsior*'s unguarded hull. I winced and hit my communicator panel.

"Orsini!" I was probably yelling louder than I needed to, but by then I didn't care. "Are those Falcons secured yet?"

"Sir . . ." His strained voice barely emerged from the noise of what sounded like a hundred cascading waterfalls. I didn't need to hear any more of my security chief's response than that. I recognized the sound of several impulse engines throbbing in a confined space, and felt my gut twist in painful dismay.

"Captain Sulu." Walroth turned from the weapons desk,

his smooth face suddenly looking older than its years. He knew what that sound meant, just as did the rest of the bridge crew. We weren't going to be able to put up our shields to defend ourselves, and we weren't going to be able to stop the Falcons from blasting their way through the *Excelsior*'s undersized shuttle bay doors. "The other members of the pirate fleet are all converging on us now. Orders?"

I took a deep breath, bitter with the smell of smoke from overloaded circuits and the knowledge of my own failure. "Return fire, Ensign. Take out as many of them as you can." In the time I had left before my brand-new ship was reduced to a ruined hulk, the least I could do was make these unknown aliens pay a steep price for what they had done. "Keith and Henry, prepare for imminent hull breaches in sectors six, seven, and eight. Schulman, track each of those Falcons. The minute they're out of the cargo bay, I want our shields back in place." That was assuming the shields still worked by then, and that the pirates weren't smart enough to remain inside and blast the *Excelsior* into oblivion.

I turned toward Rand last, barely able to make my throat muscles spit out the last set of commands I had to issue. "Order all nonessential crew to begin evacuation procedures. Alert essential crew that total ship destruction is possible within the next few minutes. And send Starfleet—" I had to pause to swallow something that tasted like bile. "Send Starfleet an emergency distress call along with a complete copy of our ship's log."

I paused, wishing I were done there, but the most unpleasant task still remained. Bad enough that I had made a wreck of my very first mission and turned my ship into a blackened and possibly lifeless hulk. Even worse, though, was the fact that I had to send the news of that disaster back to the one man who probably could have avoided it, if he'd been the captain here. But I had no choice—for the safety of my crew and for the Federation, I had to let go of my last shreds of personal pride. "And Rand, I want you to send the same message directly to Captain Kirk on the *Enterprise*."

After that, I sat back in my captain's chair, scowling out at the glowing viewscreen and preparing to direct the last few evasive maneuvers and phaser blasts we could get in before the hammering I could already feel in the *Excelsior*'s gut spread out to destroy all her essential systems. For the sake of my crew, I had to pray that the *Enterprise* was close enough by now to come to our rescue. For myself, however, James Tiberius Kirk was the last man in the galaxy I wanted to see.

Chapter Nine

KIRK

"*COSA PENSA!*" Lieutenant Commander Giotto crowded between the pilot and copilot's seats, staring out the shuttle's front window like a kid staring into an adult establishment he'd never be allowed to enter. "This place looks as bad as the hull of my grandpap's fishing boat."

I eased back on the throttle for what felt like the hundredth time since leaving the *Enterprise*, irrationally afraid of bumping into something. "Your grandfather should have cleaned his ship more often."

Giotto's snort was as crass as it was eloquent. "Yeah—so should the Anjiri."

I couldn't argue with him there. If the asteroid ahead of us had been an ocean liner, the barnacling on her hull would have kept her from leaving port at all. Except these barnacles were the size of shuttles, the size of houses, the size of ships. Passenger transports had been sunk into the rock's upper layers right alongside ore carriers; private skiffs were welded nose-to-nose with garbage scows. The original dimensions of the planetoid were impossible to determine. Individual life-pods distorted its silhouette like warts on a frog, and what could only be disconnected cargo trunks formed an uneven seam around its middle like a poorly stitched-up scar. I found myself counting the number of individual ship designs represented in this coagulated flotsam, but quit when I reached the mid-twenties.

"Are any of those Federation ships?" Uhura asked.

I'd brought her along for the same reason I'd left Sulu back on board the *Enterprise*—I wanted the best I had in the places where I could use them most. Given the universal translator's problems with the Anjiri language, I was hoping Uhura and her improved equipment would let us avoid any fatal misunderstandings once we were in front of whoever had levied this summons. Meanwhile, if this little trip to the Anjiri principal's office didn't go well, I wanted a pilot at the helm who could thread the *Enterprise* between these rocks and back to open space at record speeds. Sulu was my best bet for that, which left only me to pilot the shuttle.

I split my attention between the shuttle's controls and the couple of likely Federation candidates in the junkyard now filling our view. "I don't think so," I answered Uhura at last. Then, because it seemed more honest than any flat statement about the Anjiri's architecture, "At least, I don't see any Federation ships among what's there."

"We're not exactly deep in Federation space here." Giotto all but braced his elbows on the control console to maintain his view out the window between us. His dark eyes scanned along behind mine. "With all the troubles we've been having with your translators, Lieutenant, I'm almost sure these Anjiri have never run across us before."

I was more than just almost sure—I would have bet my command on it. Their twisted mistranslations and inappropriately self-important behavior would have fueled too many good stories for a captain to keep quiet about them, and their own lack of knowledge about our equipment and ways was too thorough to be feigned. As if that weren't enough, these asteroid-bound Anjiri had repeatedly insisted we come to them in a ship—no mention of beaming. No mention, even, of *not* beaming. No indication at all that they even realized such a thing was possible. I was hoping we could keep it that way, at least for a little while. Even though their tractor beam generators were out of our phaser range, the coordinates they'd given us for this rendezvous were well within the range of our transporter. As long as the Anjiri didn't know that, it increased my chances of snatching my people out of there when *I* decided we were ready to leave, and not just when the Anjiri decided they were ready to let us go.

As if alerted by my musings about them, the female Anjiri who'd radioed us before—or at least the same translated voice—announced grimly, "Near to our landing specifications you are. Speed reduce you shall, docking undergo."

I looked up, past Giotto's shoulder, and focused on a set of rusty bay doors just as the docking lights circling it blinked into life one at a time. "And there she blows . . ."

The sleeve that housed the doors was half-sunken in the asteroid's surface, not even attached to a recognizable ship anymore. I could glimpse metal plating along the outer edges, but couldn't tell if it continued on to become part of some buried transport or had been cut free of the bigger structure for mounting here. All I knew for sure was that the doors began their slow sideways rumble much later than I would have liked. I down-throttled again, waiting for the gap between the doors to widen enough to admit us.

It felt like an optical illusion—movement so gradual as to seem like no movement at all, then a sudden increase in the distance, then no movement again for an achingly long time. I think I noticed the chains about the same time my heart started racing with the realization that we were moving too fast and the doors were moving far too slow.

"Oh . . ." Giotto's exclamation sounded more like a soft moan, "Oh, I don't like this, sir."

I couldn't see exactly how the chains were being taken up inside the doors' mechanism, but the stop-start nature of the movement hinted at living creatures, not machines, struggling to haul the huge bay open. The gigantic bolts on the exterior of the doors might have been welded in place, or even simply screwed forcibly into the metal, although both options assumed the incongruity of a Nykkus inside an environmental suit. I couldn't believe the Anjiri had risked themselves for such a task. The chains on either side passed through what might have been natural holes in the rock, terminating somewhere out of sight in what could only have been a hundred Nykkus engaged in the galaxy's largest tug-o'-war. "Not comfortable with technology" didn't even begin to describe this.

"Captain, this is bad," Giotto insisted, in case I hadn't heard him the first time.

"Observation noted, Mr. Giotto." Again easing back on the throttle, again feeling strangely as though nothing I did at the controls was having enough effect on the shuttle's velocity. "Now you and your team go strap in. That's an order."

He proved the worth of his training by ducking back beyond my range of sight with nothing more than a crisp, "Aye, sir." Then I heard him in the passenger compartment, ordering his security squad into their seats with no trace of resentment in his voice. He was a good officer, never misjudging when to speak his own mind and when to just obey.

I wish I could claim my own judgment was as good. About all I can say in my defense is that I'd had the same minimalist pilot training as every other Starfleet commander—just enough to think I can pilot my own shuttles into danger, but not enough to reliably get them out of it again.

Uhura stirred uneasily in the copilot's seat beside me. "Captain . . ."

She had *not* had pilot training, which was why I'd inactivated the console in front of her. This, however, didn't mean she couldn't tell a bad approach when it was happening right in front of her.

"Captain . . . !"

"Lieutenant—" I gritted my teeth and killed the shuttle's engines completely. "Please, don't sideseat drive . . ."

It was already too late, of course. I'd brought us in too close to bleed off any more momentum before impact, and the view through the doors had grown just wide enough to reveal that the entire bay was much shallower than I'd expected. Not a bay at all, as it turned out, just a pair of stolen doors mounted over an uneven hole. If I made it through the narrow gap they called an entrance, I didn't see how I was going to keep us from crumpling *Galileo*'s nose against the back wall.

Inspiration is nine-tenths desperation. I didn't so much

plan to flip us ninety degrees starboard as I suddenly found us that way while trying to squeeze past the slow doors. Our drive nacelles scraped metal so long and hard that the whole ship rumbled. My own stomach crawling up my throat, I heard Uhura gasp, and saw her hands shoot down to grab the edges of her seat. I hoped Giotto had succeeded in getting his people strapped down in back. Snapping us upright as swiftly as I dared, I let the rough bottom of the bay drag on us until I could almost feel the friction heat eating its way through our hull. When the nose bumped the rear wall, though, our momentum was down to only a few meters per second. It sounded more like a love tap than the shaking we'd just been through.

I did a quick check of the boards to make sure no breach alarms were flashing, then tried to disguise my own pounding heart by showing Uhura a charming smile. "Any landing you can walk away from . . ."

The shaky expression on her face was probably meant to be a smile, too, although she looked neither amused nor reassured.

"I don't think we need to mention the details of this to Mr. Spock," I continued, prompting her with a small nod. I waited for her halting echo of the gesture, then reached across in front of her to open our channel to the ship. "*Galileo* to *Enterprise*. We're in."

"*Enterprise,* Spock here." As though somebody else might have answered and I wouldn't have known who it was. "Landing noted, Captain. I shall place Mr. Scott on standby for shuttle chassis repairs when you return." I knew he couldn't see the color that flushed into my cheeks, but it annoyed me that Uhura would. "Might I suggest a lower velocity approach on our own shuttle bay?"

The lieutenant bent over her pile of translation gear, a stifled giggle bringing the warmth back into her face.

"Thank you, Mr. Spock. I'll keep that in mind." Then, in the hopes of avoiding further embarrassment, I directed him toward business. "Do you have a lock on our transponders?"

Spock proved willing as always to follow my lead. "Affirmative. Sensors indicate no evidence the Anjiri are capable of generating an energy shield which might interfere with either reception or transportation."

"Good." But I tried not to worry about how deep we could go beneath this planetoid's heavy metal cladding before it amounted to the same thing. "One word of warning from any one of us, and you pull us all out."

"We shall be standing by."

"I'm counting on it. Kirk out."

I couldn't hear those big slow doors bang shut on the vacuum, but the whole stone bay shuddered with their impact. Unbelting, I joined Giotto and his team in the rear, peering out the shuttle's side windows while the security squad checked their weapons and pulled themselves together. Nobody waited for us in the bay, and the pinging and moaning of slowly building outside pressure made me wonder how long it would take before anyone could safely stand in that cramped chamber. We weren't entirely alone, though; the walls all around us were filled with cloudy windows. And every one of those windows was crowded with row upon row of staring Nykkus.

I waited for one of the inside doors to slide open, and even then made no move to open our own hatch until I glimpsed a few rounded Anjiri heads protruding above the emerging Nykkus. If they'd sent a group of Nykkus all alone, I wouldn't have trusted the atmosphere was something any of us could survive—after all, Anjiri threw Nykkus out airlocks when they became inconvenient. Who knew what they did with meddling starship captains? I was trusting they wouldn't sacrifice members of their own elite class for the sake of a crude trap.

Poising my hand above the door controls, I waved for Giotto and the security team's attention. "Stay here, and keep the hatch closed. I don't want to find out we've been welded into the scenery when I get back."

Giotto nodded brusquely. "Anybody tries that, they go through us." He took one polite step backward to leave Uhura a place at my side. "We'll be here, sir," he promised. "Just don't keep us waiting."

I didn't intend to.

The air in the bay felt thin, and it carried just enough chill to sting my nose and make my breath feather steam in front of my face. The Anjiri and Nykkus, I noticed, either didn't breathe or didn't steam when they did so. I'd assumed when we first met them that their quick metabolisms meant they couldn't be true ectotherms. Now I wondered, and wondered as well how they kept moving when the temperature was so low. Perhaps their armor had built in thermal-circuits to keep them warm.

Three of the Anjiri stepped forward as a unit. They didn't even need to elbow the Nykkus aside—the guards simply parted for them as though knowing all along what was expected. "My image, you will follow." The voice offered by Uhura's translator was male, and I couldn't tell which of the three Anjiri had spoken. "The Egg Bringers to you will speak."

They all turned away just as abruptly, striding back for the door.

Glancing aside at Uhura, I found her frowning over her translator, playing with the readings and giving no sign she realized our hosts were walking away. I caught her elbow and hurried her along beside me. I didn't want to find out what would happen if we ended up left in the bay all alone.

Once we'd been ushered into the only slightly warmer hallway, I leaned down to ask her quietly, "Egg Bringers?"

Still frowning, she tapped through several screens of data. I don't know how she kept from stumbling along the rough-hewn floor. "The concept's confusing—the translator is offering other possible meanings. 'Mentor/teacher,' 'wise one,' 'life bearer,' 'mate.'" She glanced up from her readouts, looking almost embarrassed to suggest, "Sir, I think they mean females."

The dark, winding interior of this cold rock's tunnels didn't look significantly different than the surface. Stone-carved walls gave way to scarred stretches of steel, various hatches and doors and even partial ship's hallways jerry-rigged one into the next like a huge three-dimensional crazy quilt. I felt surrounded, smothered, weighed down by this metal-and-mineral termite mound. I didn't want to be part of this—I didn't want my ship to end up as part of this. With a start, I realized that my biggest fear all along was that the Anjiri had only brought me here as a diversion, that their real goal was the *Enterprise*. How to explain to Starfleet that your first command was dismantled and turned into part of some floating alien apartment complex? How to reconcile that horrible prospect within yourself?

I shook the idea off. It wasn't going to happen. Even before I left the ship, Spock had already figured out how to overload at least two of the Anjiri tractor beam generators using our own defensive screens and a fatal feedback cascade. I didn't like thinking about Anjiri and Nykkus civilians caught in the explosions that kind of tactic would cause, but I liked thinking about the *Enterprise* in pieces and my crew exposed to vacuum even less. Spock had his orders. If I couldn't work things out with the Anjiri, he was to make sure the ship and crew got free, no matter what the cost.

I don't like to lose.

Uhura drifted ahead of me, unconsciously placing herself as close as possible to the sibilant voices of the Anjiri who led us. She reminded me a little of a Vulcan just then, so intent on her tricorder and its cascade of linguistic codes that it didn't seem to occur to her that Anjiri might not appreciate tailgating any more than starship captains appreciated piloting advice. I realized our escort was slowing as the tunnel widened into an anomalously bright and smooth-sided room, and I had just reached out to pull Uhura back to my side when the trio of Anjiri spun on her, snapping at the air.

"What weapon?" they rattled, flashing their claws at the device. They'd dissolved into a single stalking cacophony, but still only one voice spiraled out from Uhura's small speaker. "What weapon this is?"

My communications officer looked up, her face registering startled hurt at their suggestion. "Why, it's not a weapon." She turned the tricorder carefully, so as not to tear loose any of its eccentric connections. "It's a translation device. See the figure?" As it metamorphosed into an Anjiri simulacrum, her words seemed friendly and warm. "It turns my words into language you can understand, and turns your words into my language."

Alarm spiked through me as the Anjiri rushed to cluster around her. But the Nykkus fell back, almost as though unwilling to listen in on their masters' translated thoughts, and I imagined I recognized the childlike tilt of utter fascination in the Anjiri's hairless heads. When Uhura shuffled around to stand shoulder-to-shoulder with two of them, lifting the translator so they could see, I couldn't help but smile.

I think that's when I realized what a treasure I had standing before me. In an outfit like Starfleet, competence is easy to come by; brilliance is only slightly harder. More valuable than either, though, is the ability to transcend species and transfix creatures you have never even met before. In a communications officer, that skill becomes priceless. It's what elevates a comm officer's job beyond mere talking and makes him or her a vital member of the crew. I knew she belonged on a starship's bridge, and felt an instant of shame that I hadn't seen fit to place her there sooner.

Then a hoarse, breathy rumble swept over us with almost physical force. I jerked around, expecting the frigid rush of escaping air through a breached hull, or, at the very least, a weakened seal on one of the many stolen airlocks we'd passed for the last hundred meters. Instead, I was met with a wave of confused movement as the Nykkus on all sides dropped as though pole-axed, and the Anjiri around Uhura shrieked before flinging themselves prostrate to the floor. When I saw what had swept into the alcove behind me, I had an irrational moment when I considered the wisdom of joining them.

What could only have been the threatened females ducked through the doorway one right after the other, bursting upright as though furious with the restrictive hallways they escaped. They were startlingly similar to the Anjiri males, and because of that, somehow more frightening. Bigger and sleeker, their heads sculpted into the suggestion of an elegant crest and their eyes swirling with colors I can't even begin to describe, there was a heat to them, a presence or a smell. I was suddenly acutely aware of how much taller than me they all stood, how much more quickly their rangy muscles could move. With no defining sexual characteristic but their size, they seemed strangely more male than the males; any possibility of external variation in their structure was hidden by the close-fitting armor wrapped around their gracile frames. It was some sort of environmental suit, I decided. Something that kept them warmer, primed, eternally faster than I had any hope of being. My instincts wanted to give way before them, offer them apologies for things I'd never done. So instead, I got angry. The fact that their impact on me was clearly something as natural to them as breathing didn't make me feel any better about it. It just made me rail against my own apparent frailties, and promise to prove that I was better than that.

"Such clucking cease you will." A strange chill laced the females' translated words. They swept in so close against each other that they might have been one big creature. Behind them, inching along the floor like the train of a living gown, Vissith and his Anjiri crew couldn't have looked more obsequious if they'd had hair to pull and clothes to rend. What had to have been the group of Nykkus we'd originally rescued with them slithered silently along in their wake. I realized with an unexpected jolt of discomfort just how indistinguishable the individual Nykkus were, and wondered if that was why the Anjiri viewed them as such interchangeable cogs.

"Robbers of our vessel these things be?" The largest of the females hissed the question back toward Vissith, her bright eyes glittering for all that she never truly deigned to look at him. The rest of them glared unblinkingly at me. They all bobbed and danced as though carrying on some inner conversation. I got the impression all of their gestures impacted the one speaker's meaning, but decided this wouldn't be the best time to initiate that conversation with Uhura. "Stealers of the ship which to your weakling fangs we granted?"

I'm a loyal mammal—if I'd had hackles, I'd have raised them. "We didn't 'take' anything," I objected. I tried hard to keep my voice civil, but guessed from the sharp glance Uhura cast my way that I wasn't entirely successful. The consummate professional, though, she kept her translation device aimed at the cluster of females, even though only half of them watched what it had to say. "We found your people stranded on a ship so badly damaged that I was under the impression we *rescued* them." I scowled down at Vissith, taking what satisfaction I could in the way he nearly wormed himself through the stone flooring. "We *offered*—very generously, I believed—to return them home."

The females rounded on Vissith like a pack of lions. One of them planted a taloned foot in the middle of his back, and I thought for a moment they would shred him. "And to *here* you bring them did?" The voice from Uhura's translator sounded so calm, so untroubled. I found myself wishing the Anjiri had tails, so I would have some way to gauge the subtlety of their moods beyond just what I imagined I could read in their expressionless faces. I didn't like having to wait until they struck at something. "To these dens and nurseries lead them you did?"

"No!" His translated voice equally dispassionate, Vissith's body language, at least, was clear even to me. Splayed hands crept up to cover his head, and he turned one eye toward the floor as though he could barely stand to watch the females circling. "Fooled them did we! Clever we were, so as to prideful make you—to a place of fine ships take us did we make them. A ship new, clean did we abscond!"

The threatening foot shifted, and a bright rake of purple-gray blood blossomed on the male's exposed back. "Tiny what you have brought home is."

"Inside you must yet see," Vissith insisted. If he felt any pain, he didn't display enough in either his speaking or his movement to change the timbre of the translation. "Inside this ship very fine is."

"Yet these creatures a huge ship behind you do trail." They all looked at me then, and I made myself meet their combined gaze with equal fierceness. "Careless."

Vissith squirmed beneath the shelter of his own hands. "Many fine things from that ship did we salvage." He made no coordinated movement that I could recognize, but some communication obviously passed through the males groveling behind him. It ran aground among the silent Nykkus. A knot of them slithered forward without ever really standing, and produced double handfuls of all-too-familiar trinkets. It was like magic—I don't know where on their bodies they could have been hiding it all. Perhaps inside the seams of their body armor. Perhaps inside alien orifices I didn't want to know any more about. Either way, it was an astonishing volume of trinkets, things Scott hadn't even reported yet as missing. Knobs and buttons, probably from the transporter room, computer chips, decorative trim, and a few pieces of McCoy's medical equipment. There were even two communicators and a phaser jumbled into the mix. I didn't know whether to be horrified or amused.

I didn't make a move to interfere when the females spread themselves to each pick up their own piece of the loot. "They took useless things," I announced, trying to keep an eye on everything as they began to pass them around. "Games and trinkets. And the ship they brought here was stolen. It belongs to someone else."

Three of them shrugged, then squatted to examine the phaser. "To us belongs it now."

"None of this belongs to you." I wanted to know where in hell the Nykkus had picked up that weapon. Its presence in the pile bothered me more than everything else combined. "You can't simply take things."

The biggest of the females tipped her head toward me. "Interrogative."

I dared a glance at Uhura. She looked at me, then back down at her translation equipment. "I think she means, 'Why not?'"

I felt like someone had elbowed me in the stomach. How do you explain human morality to an alien?

"Where we come from," I said, rather slowly, "we have respect for the other peoples we live with. We feel that stealing things from others is disrespectful."

It took a long moment for the translator to make something of that. At least half the females lost interest in the jittering simulacrum before the audible sounds of my speech had finished translating. "Needed things are," the larger female informed me as she turned a communicator over in her hand and watched the golden lid drop open. "Needed is needed. Our eggs quickly mature do, we more room soon require. What other should do we? Our children to crowd and die we must allow?"

I didn't have an answer that.

"Can't you make your own living spaces?" Uhura finally spoke up. She looked impossibly tiny and fragile, wedged in among those powerfully muscled bodies. "You have plenty of room here. You could tunnel—"

When two of the females slashed their hands through the air near her, I was terrified they meant to strike at her. But Uhura calmly held her ground, so I gritted my teeth and refrained from leaping to her rescue. "Tunnel? No. When ships there are all about for our use lying? Tunneling for rodents is."

That was the second time I'd been called a rodent in a single day. "These ships aren't just lying about," I tried to explain. "They belong to someone—maybe someone a lot bigger and more powerful than yourselves." I reached out to scoop the communicator out of her hands. She hissed at me, but didn't resist. "When you go around taking things that don't belong to you, you run the risk that the actual owners are going to come take their ships and equipment back."

The dorsal ridge only hinted at on the Anjiri males lifted into a stubby crest of anger on the females. "A threat from yourselves this is?"

Even as she asked it, the stinging tingle of an ultra-close transporter beam chased itself all through my hands. I could almost smell the ionization of the air molecules as the communicator in my grip shimmered and evaporated into nothing.

No one said anything for an elongated moment. Then I heard myself announce, as if I'd known all along what I'd intended to say, "Yes, that's a threat."

The second communicator sparkled away in the wake of the first, with the phaser not far behind. The females rattled with alarm, dropping whatever else they held and leaping together in a protective circle

"Trickery! Foolery!" Their leader tore through the Nykkus closest to her like a whirlwind through paper. I knew the guards were dead even before their bodies spun to the floor, but I hadn't a hope of interfering with that terrifying speed. I thought for sure Vissith and his companion males were next, but instead the females only crouched menacingly atop them, howling. "Items of false death, these be! Items to

destroy themselves made these be!" One of them I couldn't
see clearly struck a male who was already on the ground.
"Cold-born! Foolish!"

"No! No!" I'd never heard the Anjiri make such shrill
noises before. Vissith writhed and twitched in submission
as he pleaded with them. "Their pod this trickery reaps!" he
squealed. "Things to dissolve and remake elsewhere they
have! Stole my pod from our ship in this way they did! Seen
it we have. Felt it also we have."

Sparkles rang into thin air from random places on the
floor, but I couldn't tell what had dematerialized.

"He's telling you the truth." I recaptured the females'
attention, at least half in the hopes of preventing any further
bloodshed. "We can take back every item you stole from us
by making it vanish here and reappear on board our vessel.
We could take anything else we wanted the same way."

They'd pulled into an elongated formation, the largest
female still boldly facing me while her sisters arrayed
themselves by descending size behind her. "Disrupt our
breathing bubbles would you?" Only one of them was
speaking now. "Vanquish air and heat from our hatchlings
would you?"

"I *could.*" I paused for effect, letting the transporter's
whine underscore my silence. "But I won't." That announcement seemed to upset them even more than the
prospect of my potentially beaming away sections of their
hull. The rearmost females lowered themselves halfway to
the floor, mouths agape. Ah, culture shock. "My people are
peaceful. We have no intention of harming you or your
hatchlings. All we ask in return is that you give us the same
courtesy. Don't abscond with our starships. Don't steal our
devices."

The females fell very still. "Conjunction of query."

This time I didn't have to look toward Uhura for the
translation. " 'Or'?" my communications officer suggested.
"As in, 'Or else you'll do what?' "

I didn't want to make threats. Peaceful people didn't
make threats to their less sophisticated neighbors, especially
threats they honestly had no intention of keeping. Once
you've promised something dire, you'd better be prepared

to deliver the first time they decide to test your resolve, otherwise it's as good as making no threats at all. And that didn't get us anywhere.

"You should be more concerned about what races less peaceful than mine could do," I said at last. "There are many powerful peoples out there who wouldn't hesitate to destroy your colonies and expose your hatchlings to vacuum." I was thinking about the Klingons when I said it, but even the Orions had been known to unleash some nasty vendettas on trading partners gone astray. "You could never defend yourselves against them, and even my people wouldn't be able to help you."

"Always dangers have there been." She threw a snarl toward the males, but they couldn't have cowered more deeply if their lives depended on it. Which they probably did. "Cold-born males by these dangers culled should be. Fool-born males to steal and never fight commanded have been. Things of use to their homes and pods they must bring. Far from pleasantness of society until hours of breeding to keep them we prefer."

"Instead of stealing," Uhura said gently, "have you considered establishing trade friendships with other peoples?"

A short snap of sound, which the translator converted to the familiar, "This word no meaning for us has."

I found myself wondering if the word they lacked was "trade" or "friendship." It didn't really matter. "I can't tell you how to conduct yourselves with other races, I can only give you my advice. And my advice—my *strong* suggestion—is that you direct your scavenging expeditions away from my people's region of space." That would at least steer them clear of most of the galaxy's major powers, and send them instead to contend with the master merchanters who tended to array themselves behind the Orions the way flies gathered on rotting meat. If anyone could usher them into the world of interstellar capitalism, it would be that cabal. And if they couldn't survive that . . . Well, then they wouldn't survive the Romulans or Klingons or Rigelians, either, and Darwin was right after all.

I like to believe it was serious thinking the females did

when they drew back into a tight knot and fluttered and shushed at each other. At least what their leader proclaimed at the end of their strange conference was a point both well considered and true. "Useless scavenging be if goods return home do not."

I nodded. "My point exactly."

"Cold-brained males elsewhere to scavenge shall be sent." They flashed a unified look of some fierce emotion straight at me. "From our dancing, lidded eyes of yours away shall you turn. To ourselves leave us you shall."

"You have my word." And I had the last of my equipment. I kept half-an-eye on what could only have been the chip from the simulator game as it shimmered in to nonexistence from where it had ended up beneath a female's talons. Males and females both were already skittering away from that last transportation site when I flipped open my own communicator and startled them with the chirp. "Kirk to *Enterprise*. Mr. Spock, lock on to me and Lieutenant Uhura and beam us directly to the *Galileo* on my mark." And to hell with the Orion pleasure yacht. We'd made unexpected progress in our negotiations with the Anjiri; I wasn't about to compromise that by dickering over a ship we could just as easily claim had been destroyed in the pursuit.

"Transporter locked on," Spock answered briskly. "Captain, your coordinates prompt me to ask if you noticed that I successfully located—"

"I know what you did, Mr. Spock." Which didn't mean the Anjiri needed a full explanation right at this moment. "Now energize, please."

The song of imminent dissolution was louder now, strong enough to make the polished walls sing. A few of the bolder females kept their intent eyes on us as the transporter began to catch hold and fade us into transparency. Most of them, though, averted their eyes, or took positions on the floor next to their kowtowing males. I had a brief glimpse of what it must feel like to be a young god.

"Bright and fierce your heat is." The large female even came a step closer, and I felt a strange, undeserved pride in her bravery. "Eggs of many great fire may bear you."

131

At the time, I thought it just some untranslatable Anjiri good luck wish that had no English meaning. As it turned out, I was both right and very wrong.

"They thought I was *what?*"

"It is the only logical explanation, Captain." I tried to remember that Spock couldn't possibly be enjoying himself as he sprang this on me. The emotions were certainly just too complex for a Vulcan—enjoyment itself, vindictiveness over my perhaps not so open-minded treatment of him these last few weeks, and of course the undeniable necessity of empathy with my own very human sense of pride. But as he folded his hands atop the briefing room table and turned that studiously considering frown in my direction, the only thing I could think was that he'd determined ahead of time what reaction his observation would elicit, and he was now tickled green to see things playing out as planned. "Judging from your and Lieutenant Uhura's observations, females hold the dominant positions in Anjiri society. You allude to a strong biological basis for this situation, similar to that among primate species on Earth. However, even on Earth, female-dominated aggressive hierarchies are not unheard of. In the Terran species *Crocuta crocuta,* for example—"

McCoy's delighted chuckle cut off whatever long explanation was sure to have followed. "They thought you were a girl, Jim."

What in hell did everyone find so funny about this?

Spock seemed to be thinking something similar, although I still found it hard to believe he hadn't expected as much. He turned an imperiously arched eyebrow on McCoy, for all that he ostensibly addressed only me. "In acknowledging your position of power, it was the only conclusion they could draw. Indeed, Captain, you should be flattered."

I tried not to look too sour as I played with the cream at the bottom of my coffee cup. "I'll remember to thank them if we ever cross paths again."

"Do you think that's likely?" Scott asked. He seemed a little surprised when we all turned to look at him. "That they'll break their word, I mean. It's sure to get them into all manner of trouble."

"I don't think they'll bother us." Uhura had conducted

herself throughout the briefing with the same quiet dignity she'd displayed when surrounded by volatile Anjiri breeders. She was proving an excellent addition to my command crew. "Their main concern was for the safety of their children and their homes. No matter how their intraspecies behavior might seem to us, they weren't outwardly hostile—they weren't doing any of this because they wanted to pick a fight, and they never once put us in any real danger, even though they could have."

"Either that," McCoy pointed out, "or they're just smart enough not to pick a fight they can't win."

"Whichever the case," I said, "we've got to give them a chance to keep their word. It's hard to find your sea legs in a great big galaxy—it's not our place to tell them which way to go." I swept together my own notes as a signal that this debriefing was over. "Let's keep our reports minimal on this encounter. I'll recommend to Starfleet that we send an occasional scout to check this border for the first year or so. After that—" I shrugged. "They're on their own."

McCoy downed the last of his coffee as he stood. "Aren't we all?"

In a very big sense, yes. And sometimes that was the point.

Other times, the point was to learn how to step beyond our independence and forge a bond with the species that Fate had arrayed all around us. I tried to catch Spock's gaze as he stepped past me on his way to the door. "Mr. Spock, a moment please."

He paused, ubiquitous data pad in hand, but didn't retake his seat.

I waited for the door to close behind McCoy and the others before saying, "Good work retrieving those items." I tried on a smile more for my benefit than his. "It might have proved embarrassing to explain how they all disappeared on my watch."

He acknowledged that with a minuscule tilt of his head. "As property of the ship, they fell into the realm of the first officer's responsibilities, did they not?"

I smiled, forced once again to give him credit for a sense of humor that I suspected he'd had in him all along. "Yes, Mr. Spock, they did." Settling back in my seat, I punched up an order for a large pot of coffee and two cups. I didn't think Spock would use his, but it seemed the proper gesture, given the hours we'd be putting in together over the next five years. "Take a seat, Mr. Spock. First officers don't have to stand during their weekly meetings with their commanding officers. Now—isn't there the matter of some eight hundred crew evaluations we need to get through before tomorrow?"

Chapter Ten

SULU

"A *MOST* SATISFYING TALE." The red-haired pirate captain thumped her mug of Martian ale on the bar to emphasize her approval of Captain Kirk's story. They had repaired to the long polished counter while a twitchy young boy and the unruffled bartender replaced the smashed remains of their previous table. The arrangement would have suited Sulu fine, except that his skittish little lizard had disappeared at some point during the fracas. He'd have worried that the massive Gorn had stepped on it, but the entire fight had happened in such drunken slow-motion that even a gecko could have kept out of its way. "Oh, what I wouldn't give to be one of these fierce lizard-women, who can tether their men with just a flash of their claws!"

"I wish you were one, too," Sulu said, eyeing the potted Andorian palm whose delicate fronds draped one end of the bar. He saw a gauzy spider perched on one inner leaf, but no sign of the gold-and-brown reptile that had ridden into the bar in his sleeve. "Then maybe you could get my little lizard-friend to come out from wherever he's hiding."

That brought the Gorn's heavily scaled muzzle up from his bucket of Gondwana Pale Ale. "I am not hiding," he said with ominous slowness. "Any skittering mammal who says otherwise insults my honor!"

"No, no!" The last thing Sulu wanted was to start another barroom brawl with their new drinking companion. It wouldn't be as easy to replace the mahogany bar as it was to replace the table, and for all its sturdiness, he wasn't confident it could stand up any better under a direct impact from the Gorn. He leaned forward, trying to phrase his response in the same slow syllables the big sauroid used. "I said 'little' lizard-friend, Captain. No one could *ever* think that referred to you."

The murmur of agreement that rippled down the bar seemed to soothe the alien captain's vanity. "In that case, I no longer say you skitter," he said magnanimously. "Even though you do."

"Thank you," Sulu said wryly. The Gorn grunted and dipped his muzzle back into his drink, throat muscles bulging and compressing like a snake's with each swallow. Across the broad expanse of glittering greenish scales that was his massive neck, Sulu saw a tiny patch of gold-dusted brown stir and then settle back happily among the warm folds of skin. He thought about reaching out to pluck the little gecko from his new perch, but decided that had too high a probability of being interpreted as another attack on the Gorn. Instead, he finished the last of his own ale and glanced at the time display built into his wrist communicator. It seemed as if far too much had occurred in the brief span of time the chronometer said had passed since they'd entered the Captain's Table. Sulu consulted with his own internal clock and reluctantly decided against a second drink.

"If you'll excuse me, gentlemen . . ."

Kirk lifted an eyebrow at him. "What's your hurry? I thought you had two hours before your new executive officer was due in port."

"That's true, but—" Sulu wasn't sure quite how to phrase his suspicions that inside these comfortable walls, time wasn't running quite at the pace it should. It seemed ungracious to accuse Captain Kirk of bringing him to a place where you couldn't trust the clocks. "I still need to get some dinner."

"Eat here." The large sauroid head lifted from its bowl to bare an immense jawful of teeth. Sulu hoped that was a smile. "Finish story."

"Yes." The felinoid captain squirmed out of the freighter captain's lap and over the polished top of the bar, coming back with a menu and a large bowl of Elyrian spice-almonds, which she pushed toward him. "You cannot leave us in suspense."

"Indeed." The elderly captain still chewed all his words around the stem of his meerschaum pipe. "The Captain's tale may be well-finished, but yours was left at a most sorrowful pass. What became of your gallant new ship and her crew?"

"And why did those wayward Anjiri and Nykkus males commit those atrocities on *Excelsior* more than twenty years after Captain Kirk had negotiated his truce with them?" The English captain might look like a debonair Elizabethan dandy, but he had the keen instincts of a seahawk. "Did the females of their species send them out to attack and pillage for some new purpose of their own? Or were they cannons loosed upon the deck by some twist of fate?"

"Precisely what we wondered at the time," Kirk agreed. "But that part of the story is Captain Sulu's to tell."

Sulu paused, strongly tempted to stay and enjoy the strong feeling of camaraderie he'd found among this strange assortment of captains. While he debated, the quiet bartender came back to his station and made his choice for him by pouring out another Martian Red Ice Ale. Caught between its mellow honeyed scent and the spicy aroma of the almonds, Sulu sighed and opened the menu.

"Pot-stickers and the satay chicken," he told the bartender, then passed the menu on to Kirk. "You're sure we'll have enough time to eat?"

"Steak sandwich, extra fried onions. Don't worry, Captain. We'll be done before the sun sinks over the yardarm."

That promise brought nods of agreement from the red-headed pirate, the elderly captain, and the Englishman, but made both the Gorn and the felinoid look puzzled. "What iss thiss planet called Yardarm?" the felinoid asked the freighter captain. "And why must we be done before local sunset there?"

He scrubbed a hand through his salt-and-pepper beard to hide a smile. "Uhh, I think that's just another way to say 'happy hour.' So, Captain, what happened after the pirates boarded your ship?"

"They didn't board it," Sulu admitted. "I wish they had, we might have had a chance against them then. But all they did was blast the Falcons free and rake our warp nacelles and impulse engines with enough phaser fire to keep us from following them. Then they vanished, leaving us unarmed and defenseless—right on the edge of Klingon space."

"Bridge to Captain Sulu."

I reached out and caught hold of the nearest bulkhead, to keep myself from drifting into some critical piece of equipment while I tapped my wrist communicator on. The entire secondary hull had lost gravity in the pirate attack, and the large room that housed our gravity generators had become a floating minefield of debris, spare parts and old coffee cups. After working in this chaos for two hours, my chief engineer's temper had become understandably short. Even the captain who'd stopped in momentarily to check his progress wasn't immune to being snapped at if he bumped into the wrong thing at the wrong time.

"Sulu here."

"Sir, we're being hailed by the *Enterprise*. Captain Kirk would like to speak to you personally."

I winced, but my dismay was muted now by exhaustion and a resurrected sense of pride. Despite all the damage that the Anjiri and Nykkus pirates had inflicted on my ship— the shuttle bay breached to space where the Falcons had blasted their way out, the warp nacelles blackened by phaser fire, the shields still offline, and the computer networks out in over half the ship—not a single member of the *Excelsior*'s huge crew had been lost. Our months of training might not have prepared us to avoid the pirate's attack, but they had paid off in smooth emergency evacuations and flawless disaster response both during and after it. On deck after deck, my resilient crew had begun repairing equipment and reconnecting circuits within minutes of our opponents' departure. It might not have renewed my faith in my own decisions, but it reassured me that one way or another, the *Excelsior* would survive my tenure as her captain.

"Put the call through to me here, Marquez." From the dazzled tone in which the other captain's name had been spoken, I'd known the voice emanating from my wrist communicator wasn't Janice Rand's. Like my other command officers, Rand was roving through the ship, troubleshooting, coordinating and approving the crew's repair efforts. Only Tim Henry had been excused from that morale-boosting duty—his engineering intuition was needed to put the severed control circuits of the secondary hull's gravity generator back together.

"Sulu." The crisp voice from my communicator brought back wistful memories of the days when all I had to do was carry out orders to the best of my ability, without worrying about whether or not they were the right ones. "We're fifteen minutes away. Is there any chance the Anjiri are using you as bait in another trap?"

My first instinct was to protest that my ship's long-range sensors were down and I had no idea what the pirates might or might not be up to. But the *Enterprise* had long-range sensors every bit as good as ours. If they were within minutes of a rendezvous, Captain Kirk wasn't asking me for raw data—he was asking for a fellow captain's analysis.

"Possibly," I said after a pause. "The Falcon reconnaissance ships they stole from us are designed to deflect long-range sensors and might not appear on your screens. However, they're only very lightly armed and shouldn't be able to damage the *Enterprise* as long as its shields stay up."

"Then we'll launch our big cargo shuttle and run both it and the *Enterprise* into the area fully shielded," the captain said with his usual decisiveness. "The *Jocelyn Bell* should be large enough to bring over all the repair equipment as well as the extra team of engineers you requested."

I cleared my throat. "Sir, you won't be able to use our main shuttle bay—it was breached to vacuum in the attack. And I'm afraid the *Jocelyn Bell* won't fit into our auxiliary bay."

"How do you know that, Mr.—I mean, Captain Sulu?"

"Because I flew her prototype back at White Sands, a few

years ago." There were people who said I'd spent too many years as a Starfleet pilot before I'd applied to a command post, but I'd never regretted the experience. "You'd have to dock her at the emergency airlock on the primary hull, which would still leave you exposed to a pirate attack."

"We could fly into your main shuttle bay, then drop our shields and let you beam us in from there," Kirk suggested. "Your transporters are still working, aren't they?"

I glanced over at Tim Henry, surrounded by the glowing ends of so many severed optical cables that he would have looked like a haloed saint if it hadn't been for the irritated frown on his face. "Are the main transporters back on line, Chief?"

"Yes, but Klass says the dais is off-limits until she's done collecting DNA samples," he said absently. "They'll have to use the auxiliary transporters in the secondary hull."

"DNA samples?" my former captain repeated, sounding as if the overheard words were disturbing. "What for? You're not worried that Chekov was one of the infiltrators who beamed aboard to steal the Falcons, are you, Sulu?"

"No." My mouth had framed that answer before my mind could even decide if the question was a valid one. I forced myself to spend a moment thinking about it, and decided that it was impossible. If Chekov had been one of the infiltrators who'd stolen the reconnaissance ships, he'd have turned his phasers on the others before he'd let them destroy the *Excelsior*. "My chief medical officer has been studying the dead Nykkus we've got and she's noticed some discrepancies with the report Starfleet sent us. Can you bring Doctor McCoy and Mr. Spock over so we can examine the bodies and compare notes?"

"We'll be there in ten minutes," was all the captain said in reply. "Kirk out."

I really didn't remember much about our initial encounter with the Nykkus and Anjiri. It had been my very first mission as chief helmsman for the *Enterprise*, and so mostly what I remembered was my intense concentration on every technical detail of the voyage. The only distinct visual memory I had of the aliens we'd rescued and then chased after was of the several hours they'd spent canoodling with the ship's navigational systems, while navigator David Bailey and I watched from the back of the bridge and fretted. I remembered the Anjiri officers looking as slender and elegant as the house geckos who used to live among my boyhood plant collection back in San Francisco. Their Nykkus security guards and subordinates had seemed much more burly and brutish, with a stronger predatory tilt to their sauroid torsos and a twitchy animal nervousness in their eyes and tails. I vaguely remembered that they spoke, although not often, so they were sentient but you could hardly call them sophisticated. Certainly not the kinds of minds who could have planned and carried out the shrewd infiltration of the *Excelsior*.

I hadn't thought much about finding a Nykkus body in the wreck of the Klingon colony ship—I assumed he'd just died in the course of guarding some Anjiri superior. But when the suicide guard we'd found floating in the airless space of the breached shuttle bay had turned out to be Nykkus, too, I started to wonder exactly who our attackers were. A visit to sickbay to interview the former hostages had yielded a description of the pirates that seemed to fit the Nykkus far more closely than the Anjiri. And Doctor Klass's examination of the two dead Nykkus bodies had, as I had reported to Captain Kirk, raised some additional questions.

Questions that now lay on the autopsy table between us, shrouded by a gentle shimmer of stasis.

"Notice the hypermorphosis of the cranial crest," Klass said, without looking up from the screen of her medical tricorder. She didn't need to glance at the body she was discussing, since she'd spent the last hour dissecting and analyzing every part of it, but I couldn't look away. This limp gray body, with its lacing of thick ritual scars and the dark vacuum bruises under the swollen and lightly scaled skin of its throat and face, seemed to stare back at me as aggressively in death as in life.

"So he's got a big bump on the top of his head." That was Leonard McCoy, of course. His years sat lightly on him— the eyebrows he lifted at my chief medical officer were still brown and the sardonic note in his voice was as tart as ever. "Without any real knowledge of physical variation within the Nykkus as a species, we can hardly conclude—"

"Doctor." That Vulcan voice was just as measured as Klass's but significantly deeper in pitch. Spock said nothing more, nor did he stir out of the watchful pose I remembered from years of serving together—hands behind his back, chin tucked into his chest, one eyebrow slightly elevated. Still, McCoy scowled and settled back into silence with grudging respect. It was as if, after all their years of sparring with each other, these two best of enemies had distilled their arguments down to single words loaded with meaning only they understood.

Klass cleared her throat and continued. "Note also the significant increase in bone thickness, tooth differentiation, and secondary sexual characteristics such as the dorsal frill. These physical features suggest elevated levels of hormones linked with sexual differentiation and sexual dimorphism. This hypothesis was confirmed by the discovery of significant concentrations of cortico-steroids in the blood—"

"Measured after being freeze-dried in outer space?" McCoy demanded, as if he couldn't keep himself quiet any longer. "I hardly think you could make a valid case for comparison there."

Klass glanced up from her tricorder, exchanging steely looks with her fellow physician. "I cannot make *any* case for comparison, Doctor, since blood samples were never taken from the Nykkus specimens encountered by the *Enterprise* twenty years ago. All I would postulate is that these hormone levels seem unusually high for an adult, even in a fast-growing, passively endothermic sauroid species like the Nykkus."

For all his years of decorated service, McCoy didn't seem to take that amiss. I had noticed before that there was very little attention paid to rank in Starfleet Medical Academy, or among ship's doctors. "Hmpphh," he said. "Have you looked at chromosomal abnormalities?"

"Indeed," said Klass. "The DNA I collected from the two specimens and from the transporter pad all showed similar, and thus presumably normal, chromosomal patterns. I did note a great deal of complex coding in the regions which appear to control sexual development. If similar samples had been taken on our previous encounter with the Nykkus, we'd know whether that was an inherent feature of their genetic heritage—"

"Or a recent mutation, or even a result of genetic engineering," McCoy said testily. "But until you've tried to get blood samples from a batch of grouchy reptiles who can barely communicate through a universal translator, young woman, I suggest you refrain from pointing any fingers!"

Klass lifted an eyebrow at him with steely hauteur. I intervened before she could make matters even worse. "I don't think Doctor Klass meant to criticize you, Doctor McCoy. She's just trying to say that we don't have enough data to know exactly what's causing this physical change in Nykkus."

"It's not just a physical change," said the trim, hazel-eyed man at the end of the autopsy table. Captain Kirk had been eyeing the dead alien even more intently than I had, but his words showed that he hadn't missed any of that medical exchange. "The Nykkus we met twenty years ago could never have planned the kind of attack that sabotaged Deep Space Three and disabled the *Excelsior*. Hell, I'm not even sure the *Anjiri* we met back then could have carried off something like that. At least," he amended thoughtfully, "not the males. Are we sure these *are* males?"

It might have seemed a strange question to ask in front of a naked corpse, but like many sauroid species, the Nykkus did not have or need external reproductive organs. Their passively warmed bodies probably put less stress on genetic haploid cells than our hot mammalian blood did, allowing their reproductive systems to be kept in safe internal storage until needed. Spock lifted an eyebrow in thoughtful consideration of the question, but Klass was moving her chin in a precise and tiny motion of negation.

"Chromosome analysis of all the DNA I collected turned up the single shortened variant that we universally assign to the male of the species, Captain. Unless the females dispatched the males here while they remained on board the ship, I believe we are dealing with a single-sex expedition, just as you were twenty years ago."

"Then something's changed their whole mentality and

level of intelligence." Kirk paced from this autopsy table to the next one. This Nykkus body was far more damaged around the eyes and muzzle, since he'd still been alive when he'd encountered the absolute chill and emptiness of space. "Although not their willingness to sacrifice themselves, it seems. Your transporter chief said this guard beamed himself into empty space after he forced her to transfer the Nykkus who stole the Falcons?"

"That's what she told me," I said. "But I had one of the other transporter technicians check the coordinates he had her beam him to. If the shuttle bay had breached to vacuum five minutes later, he'd have been right next to one of the Falcons and able to climb aboard."

"So he just mistimed his getaway." Kirk frowned down at the rictus of asphyxiation that distorted this alien's vacuum-bruised face into a more savage expression than life could have given it. "I see why you thought we should compare notes, Captain. These may be Nykkus, but they're not the kind of Nykkus I encountered twenty years ago." He leaned closer to the damaged face with its lidless eyes frozen milk-white. "Spock, do you remember the Nykkus we transported having these elaborate scars?"

"No, Captain," his science officer said. "The scars I recall seeing on those Nykkus looked like random relicts of battle, nothing more."

It was my turn to lift an eyebrow across at McCoy, who rolled in his eyes in wry response. Only a Vulcan scientist as brilliant and retentive as Spock could recall minor physical details of beings he had seen for only a few hours, twenty years before. "What do you think these scars represent?" I asked him.

"Tribal identification," McCoy said before Spock could answer. "Rite of passage ceremonies. Military hazing."

"All of which," said Klass clinically, "are dysfunctions associated with excess levels of masculine hormones during and after adolescence."

Kirk made a face. "You don't have to talk about it like it's a disease—"

"But indeed, Captain, it can be," Spock replied. "In many species, unusually high levels of normal reproductive hormones can result in unacceptable levels of antisocial behavior among both males and females."

McCoy snorted. "Don't beat around the bush, Spock. Are you saying that we're dealing with nothing more than a case of testosterone poisoning here?"

Klass gave McCoy another cold look, but the Vulcan science officer didn't even lift an eyebrow. After so many years, I supposed he was resigned to McCoy's insistence on rephrasing all his insights in more casual and less precise language. "That might indeed be one part of the change that has occurred in the Nykkus," Spock agreed. "Although I do not believe it satisfactorily accounts for their increased intelligence and remarkable military strategy."

"But the excess levels of reproductive hormones are not in themselves the cause of this problem," Klass said. "They are merely a symptom of whatever disease or mutation or genetic engineering the Nykkus have been subjected to."

McCoy opened his mouth as if he planned to continue that cause-and-effect debate, but I cleared my throat and intervened. "This—er—hormone poisoning might explain how the Nykkus were able to do what they did these past two days, but it doesn't explain *what* they're trying to accomplish by it."

Captain Kirk threw me a frankly approving look, and I found to my surprise that it felt as good now as it did back when I was a young helmsman making suggestions on battle strategy. "You're right, Sulu. Whatever their medical problems are, we can't solve them if we can't find them, and to find them we have to figure out what they're trying to do."

"That's obvious," said McCoy. "The reports I read said they attacked Deep Space Three to steal those new Falcon reconnaissance ships, right? And when that didn't work, they lured in the *Excelsior* with the hostages they held and went after the Falcons again."

"Yes, but now that they have the Falcons, we don't know what they plan to do with them," I said.

Kirk steepled his fingers, looking down at the fallen face of our enemy. "We're on the edge of Klingon space," he said. "And the Nykkus just brutally attacked a Klingon civilian ship, something that's bound to lead to reprisals once it's discovered. If these were Orions, I'd say they were trying to stir up a war between the Federation and the Empire for their own purposes."

Klass gave him an inquiring look. "Does the fact that these are not Orions preclude them from having the same motive?"

"I suspected the pirates might be Klingons in disguise when they first attacked Deep Space Three," I admitted. "If we hadn't stopped to answer that Klingon distress call, we might never have realized the Nykkus were the ones attacking us."

"And the Klingons would sure as hell assume we were the ones who attacked *them,*" McCoy agreed. "Starfleet Command's already chewing their nails to the quick about *that* situation."

"But from what we know of the Anjiri, they seem determined to stay as isolated as possible from galactic politics," Captain Kirk reminded us. "They're subsistence spacefarers with only a small asteroid for a homeworld, unable to manufacture their own ships or homes or weapons. A little raiding to augment their aging technology was all the dominant females were willing to sanction their males to do. They knew any attacks more ambitious than that would have brought down the wrath of a superior race upon their heads."

"Do you think these hypermasculine Nykkus would subscribe to that same caution, Captain?" Spock inquired.

"Perhaps not—but I don't think they're just out to raise a little manly hell, Spock. Or to steal whatever kind of technology they come across, the way their Anjiri cousins were twenty years ago. If that were the case, they'd pick easier targets than Starfleet and the Klingon Empire." Kirk was pacing around the stasis table now, his stride as restless and energetic as ever. "No, they've got some more specific plan in mind and the FL-70s are crucial to accomplishing it. What advantage can those four little ships give them?"

It might have been a rhetorical question, but I answered it anyway. "They're lightly armed, but they have the best sensor-evading technology in Starfleet right now. It's not as good as a Klingon cloaking device, since you can still see them once they're in visual range, but until then they can fly virtually undetected through space. And they're almost impossible to target with weapons sensors."

McCoy shook his head, looking puzzled. "But if the Nykkus need stealth for whatever they're planning to do, doesn't that imply an attack against a superior enemy after all?"

Captain Kirk and I exchanged thoughtful glances. "Quite possibly," he said. "Or a terrorist attack against their own species. If they've already been outcast for their—er—anti-social and hypermasculine tendencies—"

"But that wouldn't explain why they captured that Klingon colony ship," I pointed. "Unless it's going to be used as a decoy . . ."

The silence that followed my remark was a profound one, with both Klass and Spock slitting their eyes in the most thoughtful look they could manage and even Kirk looking arrested and enlightened. Only McCoy was left to stare around at the rest of us in puzzled expectation. "Well?" he asked after a moment. "What does that mean?"

"It *could* mean the Nykkus do plan to attack their own homeworld, and will use the Klingon ship to lull the suspicions of their siblings," Spock said. "Or—"

"It could mean that the Nykkus plan to attack a Klingon outpost," Klass finished.

I had already tabbed on my wrist communicator. "Sulu to Keith," I told the computer. After a brief pause, I heard a background wail of duranium welders, so loud that I could barely hear the sound of my pilot's voice shouting for them to be silenced. Someone had heard her, though—the wail dropped to an idle whine.

"Keith here, Captain. What do you need?"

"Information," I said. "When you used to patrol this area with the *Venture*, where were the closest Klingon border outposts?"

She paused, but like any good pilot she didn't need to think about it long. "There're no nearby border patrol stations, Captain, but there is some kind of research station out at Kreth. It's in a system we call Alpha Gaudianus, an uninhabited red sun with only a few gas planets."

"Thank you, Lieutenant." I thumbed the communicator off and turned back toward Kirk. "Does that sound like a potential target for the Nykkus to attack?"

He nodded, looking grim. "But we can't discount that they may also be heading back to their homeworld, armed with weapons that are far superior to anything the Anjiri ever dreamed of."

"So what do we do?" demanded Doctor McCoy. "Flip a coin to see which way we go?"

The lines engraved between Kirk's eyes deepened. "If there's even the slightest chance the Nykkus are heading for Kreth, we have to stop them. We can't afford to take even the risk that their attack might incite the Klingons to war."

I'd expected McCoy to be the one who objected to that cautious strategy, but to my surprise it was Spock who did so. "The borders of the Federation may be endangered by a Klingon incursion, Captain, but the future of our united races is not cast in doubt. However, if these Nykkus outcasts are allowed to raze their homeworld with weapons that we gave them—"

"Sulu didn't *give* them those Falcons," the captain said in exasperation. "And we don't know that they want to use them for anything more nefarious than a palace coup."

"Their treatment of Deep Space Three and the colony would argue otherwise," Klass pointed out. "I agree with Mr. Spock. The Nykkus and Anjiri's homeworld at least deserves to be warned about this threat."

"That's easier to say than do," Kirk said regretfully. "Even if we send a subspace signal to the coordinates of their homeworld, we have no idea what frequencies they use or if they even use subspace communicators at all."

"So we actually know the coordinates of their homeworld?" I asked in surprise.

A corner of Captain Kirk's mouth jerked up wryly. *"We* know it, even if Starfleet officially doesn't. The record of our voyage to the Anjiri homeworld was erased from the official ship's log with Starfleet's permission, but it's still preserved in my captain's logs. Why?"

An idea was starting to glimmer in my head, one I found both seductive and frightening. It would give me a chance to solve the current dilemma, but at the same time it would take me away from my ship. Was that separation what I really wanted? Was I running away from my problems, or was I trying to surmount them? I was unsure enough of my own motives to rephrase my original proposal.

"If the Anjiri females are dominant, and can only be overcome by stealth, a warning may be all they need. You could send Mr. Spock and the *Jocelyn Bell* to the coordinates of the Anjiri homeworld, Captain, while you take the *Enterprise* out to Kreth."

"A good idea, except for one thing, Captain Sulu." Kirk gave me a speculative look. "Why should I lose a first officer when there's a perfectly good Starfleet captain sitting around twiddling his thumbs while his ship gets put back together?"

I frowned. "But with the *Excelsior* this close to Klingon space—"

"The *Enterprise* can easily tow her to a safer distance before we leave for Kreth," Spock said. "And upon your return from the Anjiri homeworld, Captain Sulu, you can use the *Excelsior*'s own tractor beam to attach her to the *Jocelyn Bell*, and finish towing your ship to safety that way."

I took a deep breath. "How far away are the Anjiri from here?"

Kirk grinned at me, as if he knew that asking that question was as good as saying yes. Which perhaps it was. "Several hours, at top warp speeds. Spock will program the coordinates into the *Jocelyn Bell*'s navigational computer before we leave. And I'll let you pick your shuttle crew from your own ship, Captain Sulu. Once we enter Klingon space, I'm going to need every crewman I've got to keep the *Enterprise* in one piece."

"I'd like to take one of your officers, sir, if you don't mind," I said. "If I remember correctly, Commander Uhura was the only one who really seemed to understand what came out of our universal translators when the Anjiri talked to us. If we post Janice Rand temporarily to the *Enterprise* to take her place—"

"That's acceptable." Kirk cast a grim glance at the dead Nykkus lying on the autopsy tables. "Somehow, I suspect that even if I manage to catch up to the Nykkus between here and Kreth, they're not going to do much talking to us. Any other questions, gentlemen?"

"Yeah." That was McCoy, predictably enough. "Am I the only one who's noticed that we've got two of everyone in this meeting except first officers? What are we going to do to rescue poor Chekov?"

I exchanged glances again with Kirk, reading the grim reality in his face that I already felt in my heart. "We'll do what we can, Bones," the captain said. "But that may not be much."

"And Chekov would understand that," I said quietly. After twenty years of friendship, I knew in my bones what my first officer would have said if he'd been there. "He'd be the first to tell you that his life isn't worth saving if it means putting the Klingons at war with the Federation."

"No," Kirk said somberly. "No more than any of ours would be."

Chapter Eleven

KIRK

SHE WAS A BIG, awkward, front-heavy girl, with a fragile rear end and inertial dampeners that were shot all to hell. As willing as her captain might be, I knew if we just slapped a tractor beam on her and started to pull, we'd stress her structural frame badly enough to compromise seals and welds all across her secondary hull. Looking at the damage wrought on her shuttle bays after the FL-70s' exit, I was frankly afraid we'd snap her in half. So I sent over my chief engineer and the best team of tube-crawlers he had, and we waited nearly three hours for the combined *Enterprise-Excelsior* tech force to wake up the red-lined impulse engines enough to break the huge ship's inertia.

The *Enterprise* took over as soon as the *Excelsior* was drifting free. Even so, we accelerated her along as smooth a vector as we could manage, and I kept wishing Hikaru Sulu was the one piloting the *Enterprise* as we did it. They say it's hard sometimes for young officers to "grow up" out from under their charismatic commanders. I'm here to tell you that it's also hard to be the commander who lets them go, especially when you know that kind of talent doesn't come along every day. Even without Sulu at the helm, we managed to safely tow *Excelsior* a good ten parsecs into Federation space; it took another ten to ease her to a full stop and send word back to Starfleet that she'd be sitting here for a while.

The *Excelsior*'s crew breathed a collective sigh of relief when we finally released her. I wasn't celebrating just yet. McCoy once told me I'd be a captain until the day I died—if not longer—because something inside of me just wouldn't let it go. I suspect that something is the niggling certainties, the agitating instincts that tell you where to go and what to do, even when you have no clear idea what you're reacting to. Good commanders learn to trust those silent impulses; I'd given myself over to them years ago. Apprehension with no direct target had started burning in my belly about halfway through our oh-so-careful tow, and by now it had almost eaten me through. There was something about this mission already not going as planned, something still an unreachable distance away, something I wouldn't know about until it was too late. I didn't say anything to Sulu. He had his own problems, his own ship to worry about, his own peace to make with whatever urges and instincts his captaincy woke in him. It was bad enough that my instincts already insisted we wouldn't be bringing his first officer back; I didn't need to complicate his mission with worries about the safety of my ship and crew as well.

Still, we left Sulu and his shuttle crew still gearing up for their trip to the Anjiri homeworld. "No time to waste," I'd insisted. In reality, if I'd had to hover around doing nothing even one moment longer, I was going to explode. At least on the way to Kreth, I could be doing nothing at maximum warp.

When Spock's call found me in my quarters late that night, more than ten hours after we'd left the *Excelsior* picking up her pieces on the friendly side of the Neutral Zone, I had raised doing nothing to a fine art. I'd undressed at bedtime, and had centered my head on the pillow the way you're supposed to when trying to guarantee you get enough sleep to be a fit commander for your loyal crew. Then I'd stared at the ceiling and thought about the Anjiri we'd met twenty years ago, worried about Chekov, and faced head-on every horrible thing I could think of that might result from the Nykkus reaching Kreth ahead of us.

The chirrup of the bridge channel, then, didn't exactly wake me. Stretching one arm toward my bedside comm, I hit the switch with the side of my hand without actually bothering to roll over. "Kirk here."

"Captain—" Spock's deep voice sounded as awake and unbothered as always. "We have come within sensor range of the first FL-70."

I bolted upright, scowling down at the dark comm panel as though Spock himself were sitting there. "The first?" The lights in my cabin bloomed to half-brightness when I stood, and I had to shade my eyes with my fingers to keep from being blinded as I made my way toward the viewscreen on my desk. "What about the others?"

Spock's face appeared on the small screen, looking as neat and alert as when I'd left him on the bridge three hours ago. "Unknown. We only became aware of this craft's presence because sensors detected leakage from damage to its engines and weapons array. Its shields are not active and life support appears to be nonfunctional."

"Do we have a visual?"

An inset view from the ship's main screen took over the bottom half of my display. The little Falcon floated in a cloud of luminous particles; I could see the faint, corkscrew trail of its drift over the last hundred kilometers or so. Phaser burns streaked its flanks, and a good portion of its blunt, shovel-nose was simply missing. I tried to tell if there were lights on in the cockpit, but couldn't see past an opaque glaze of fog on the windows. "Looks like she's been in a fight."

"A ninety-nine point nine nine percent probability," Spock agreed. His own image was turned in profile, apparently examining the ship as it appeared on the bridge's main screen. "Damage to the aft quarter is consistent with that sustained by ships retreating from a more heavily armed opponent."

I scrubbed at my eyes, getting used to the light, and considered the options. "Maybe the Klingons found them." The FL-70s might have been minimally armed, but they were still more powerful than a lot of small ships. And I found it hard to believe that any battle this deep into the Neutral Zone hadn't attracted a whole swarm of Klingon cruisers eager to share in the glory.

Spock was quiet for a time, turning to consult his sensors until all I could see was the back of his dark head. I stood to dig a clean pair of trousers and a tunic out of my closet, so was halfway across the cabin pulling the tunic over my head when he finally said, "Klingon attack is unlikely. Weapons residue suggests phaser cannons of Federation design."

So much for easy answers. "Well, who else out here—" I pulled the tunic's collar down past my eyes, and so saw the Falcon and its mist-whitened windows as though for the first time. Fog. Condensation.

Breathing.

"Spock, somebody's alive in there." He'd reported that the life-support systems were inoperable, not that the ship itself was in vacuum.

My first officer's answer was so studied, so carefully precise, that I knew he'd made this same deduction minutes ahead of me. He must have been hoping to present all the truly relevant information before inconvenient human emotions came into play. "May I remind the captain that the *Excelsior* was enticed to drop her screens, and thus nearly destroyed, using much the same ploy."

I thrust my arms through the sleeves of my tunic and hastily shook out my pants. "It's human, isn't it?" I knew the answer without having to demand it of him. "Spock, it's Chekov."

"It is not possible to obtain a positive identification using only ship's sensors."

"Who else could it be?" I insisted. I'd left my boots by the door, so swept my jacket off a chair back and started buckling up. "The Federation phaser fire—it's from the other Falcons. Chekov got his hands on one somehow and used it to escape." And got this far before the systems finally failed. "He must know what the Nykkus are planning."

"Provided the human life-form inside is Commander Chekov and not some other human hostage of whom we are unaware." He met my gaze across the channel with frank coolness. "And provided the Nykkus have maintained

Commander Chekov in a fashion which leaves him still capable of communicating."

In other words, not dead, but maybe even worse than dead. The thought made my stomach turn sour. "Point taken." I paused in latching my last shoulder clasp to drag one hand across my face. "All right," I said, sliding back into my desk chair. "The last time, the Nykkus used *Excelsior*'s own transporter beam to bring soldiers aboard straight from stasis. Any chance they're counting on the same tactic here?"

I pulled up a general schematic of the FL-70s while Spock spent what felt like hour-long moments verifying his own sensor scans. "I detect no anomalous power usage," he reported at last.

"And the Falcon itself is barely big enough for two people, much less a cargo of stasis pods." I looked up from my private research. "What about outside attack once our screens are down? Is there any way we can be sure those other Falcons aren't hanging around?"

"Assuming they are all still fully functional?" Spock gave the micrometer headshake that I sometimes suspected less-experienced observers couldn't see. "No. Not until they come within visual range. However, the window of opportunity afforded by a single transporter operation would not be sufficient to put us in any appreciable danger from such small craft."

Unless, of course, the Nykkus had managed to add a few more ships to their arsenal. Like a nice cloaked Bird of Prey.

I caught sight of the small ship's clouded main window again, and my heart clenched like a frustrated fist. It's easy to maintain your professional objectivity as long as you don't remember that the officer who's suffocating inside his damaged shuttle while you debate is someone you know.

"Send a double security squad to the main transporter room." I sounded marvelously decisive, as though I was already sure this was exactly the right thing to do. "And keep an eye on our internal sensors—if anyone beams in *anywhere* except that main dais, I want to know about it." But I keyed off the screen before turning to retrieve my boots, unwilling to watch the little deathtrap's tumble any longer. "Do I have time to get to the transporter room?"

I couldn't see him turn toward his sensors, but I recognized the slight delay. "Carbon dioxide within the Falcon will not reach fatal concentrations for approximately fifteen minutes."

Oh, good—we'd be saving a man's life with barely ten minutes to spare.

"Have McCoy meet me at the transporter." I palmed off the lights, then turned my back on the darkness. "I'll call you when we're ready."

There are times when I feel like the transporter is really just some malicious genie. We let it out of its bottle, point it at something we can't really see, and it snakes out like a giant hand to bring back whatever we've wished for, uncaring of the consequences or details. That genielike literalness had brought a nest of vipers aboard the *Excelsior* and nearly caused her destruction. I didn't begrudge my security team's caution, then, when the transporter dais began its wailing song and a dozen phaser rifles leapt to a dozen shoulders. Whoever first said, "Better safe than sorry" must have been a Starfleet security chief. Or, if not, they must all have it tattooed on their hearts during their training.

But when the first cloud of randomized matter coalesced near the floor of the transporter pad, the bundle it formed looked fearfully still and small. By the time colors had solidified and the last molecule of doubt was erased, I knew there was no Nykkus ambush waiting to blow my ship apart. Just a Starfleet officer curled into a motionless huddle, the sour stench of sweat and stale air hanging over him in the bubble of atmosphere we'd brought along for the ride.

I let McCoy move in first, before the incoming carrier wave had fully faded, and took the extra second to wave the security team at ease. The moment of post-transport stasis broke before I turned back; I heard Chekov take a hoarse lungful of oxygenated air, and caught a glimpse of purple-gray Nykkus blood sprayed so liberally across his front and arms that I didn't want to imagine what had happened to put it there. Then McCoy knelt in front of Chekov, blocking my view, and I heard the doctor's gentle voice murmur, "Easy does it—you're safe now."

I don't think Chekov hit him. McCoy reared back when his patient exploded into movement, nearly overbalancing himself down the transporter steps, but I caught him by the shoulder of his jacket before he could fall. He looked startled, not injured, and he still had the good sense to fling an arm out to stop me when I would have vaulted the rest of the way onto the dais. Chekov, in the meantime, had ended up with his back to the alcove wall, crouched on one knee with both hands thrust out in front of him. He shook so hard, I expected him to shatter. What must have been an energy weapon burn traced a thin line up one cheek, and it looked like his nose had been broken. Still, I found myself strangely reassured that he wasn't anywhere near as battered as the survivors we'd left back on the *Excelsior*. I think I noticed all of this, including the stark panic in his eyes, a good second or two before I noticed the gun. "Chekov . . ."

It was an impossibly old Romulan pulse cannon, almost as long as his arm. I'm not sure he even realized he had it. It was corroded and damaged, like everything the Nykkus owned, and just as spattered with gore as its holder. I had a sudden, clear insight into how he'd managed to wrench himself free from his captors, but it was smashed aside by the clamor of booted feet thundering up the dais stairs behind me.

I twisted a stern glare over my shoulder. "Freeze!"

The rumble of their halt was almost more frightening than their advance. The whole security squad was so close I could have roundhoused them, a staggered arc around the floor and steps of the transporter. Their commander, tight on my right shoulder, didn't even twitch when I informed her evenly, "Lieutenant Benni, take your team and fall back."

Benni's eyes remained fixed and passionless, like a hunting dog unwilling to be called off her mark. "Sir—"

I saved her the dilemma by reaching out calmly and closing my hand over the front of her phaser. "We're dealing with a fellow Starfleet officer," I told her, pushing her arm gently but firmly to her side. "No one's is going to be shooting anyone. Now fall back."

If she'd hesitated an instant longer, I might have tipped over into anger. But she was new, a veteran only of one so far woefully pedestrian tour. She didn't understand yet how I did things, and she didn't understand the fragile tightrope command sometimes walked between controlling a crew and losing your temper with them—much like being a parent. I gave her an extra instant, and Benni saved herself from a reprimand by stepping her squad back so carefully they might have been moving through a minefield. Phasers dropped dutifully to their sides, but I noticed not one team member put them away.

When I turned my attention back toward Chekov, he met my gaze with a feverish intensity I wasn't sure how to interpret. "You're on the *Enterprise.*" I came a step further up onto the dais. "We picked up the engine discharge from the Falcon you hijacked, and we pulled you aboard."

He nodded, as though my announcement only confirmed what he already suspected. "What about the *Excelsior?*"

I made the mistake of trying to placate him. "The *Excelsior*'s fine—"

"She's *not* fine!" He let the old Romulan cannon drop, but didn't let go of the grip. "I saw what they did to her!" One hand strayed to clutch at a patch of wetness high on his right thigh, and I realized that the black of his trousers had hidden a fairly substantial flow of blood. It pooled now into a dark stain beneath his knee. "I saw what I helped them do to her," he insisted, less forcefully than before. "She's *not* fine . . ."

I wished McCoy had been able to sedate him, and wondered how long we had before he passed out on his own. "All right, she's not fine." I mounted the last step and came forward to squat right in front of him. "But she's not destroyed."

He didn't believe me. I could tell by the bone-deep sorrow that flashed into his eyes, and by the way he brought one shaking hand up to cover his eyes, and by the way he asked, very, very quietly, "Where's Sulu?"

Even knowing I was telling the truth, I felt a liar's rabbit-punch of guilt. "He's not here." So often, it's how things are perceived that really matters.

He nodded again, resigned this time, and sank wearily back against the wall. The ancient gun finally clattered from his grasp, and he drew his knees as a brace for his elbows as he buried his face in his hands. Edging closer, I leaned in to slip a finger through the cannon's trigger guard and slide it back across the transporter pad.

"You should have left me out there." He said it so softly, I almost didn't hear him over the clatter of security guards dashing forward to take custody of the gun. He didn't even sound bitter.

I stared at him, acutely aware of McCoy rushing up from behind me but not wanting to leave the remark just lying there. "You know I couldn't do that."

"But you should have." He brought his hands away from his face with a sigh, lacing them atop his updrawn knees. It was such a strangely casual gesture, it worried me more than everything else that had gone before. "You should have just left me to die."

"Captain, I have the *Jocelyn Bell* online."

I glanced aside at Chekov, trying to gauge his reaction to Rand's announcement. Waiting quietly, his hands folded on the table, he proved as impenetrable as he'd been since I spirited him out of sickbay. His silence made the empty briefing room feel huge.

Punching the button to answer Rand, I leaned over the pickup to order, "Put them through, Commander." Then I moved to a seat just far enough to one side that I could watch both Chekov and the small comm screen without having to give away my thoughts to either.

I'd had this idea while pretending not to loiter in sickbay, supervising from afar while Scotty towed the Falcon's remnants into our own shuttle bay and trying hard not to interfere while McCoy did whatever a doctor could with Chekov's physical injuries. For maybe an instant, I'd even entertained the thought of speaking privately with Sulu before I let this call go through. Had everything on the *Excelsior* gone well over the last few months? Had Chekov given Sulu any reason to suspect he had unfinished business from his last starship assignment? One look at our silent guest now, though, and I knew I'd done the right thing by letting this contact go through cold. My former navigator was many things, but inattentive was never one of them. He'd have sensed immediately that there'd been words between Sulu and me, and the last thing I needed was to give him more reason to suspect me of trying to fool him.

Distance stole some of the detail from Sulu's face, but none of the animation. I was suddenly fiercely glad I hadn't polluted this—no one could have feigned the pure relief that flooded the captain's face when he first caught sight of his pale and weary first officer. "Pavel! Oh, God, I'm glad they found you. Are you all right?"

"Yes." A lie, but not mine to expose. Sulu could see enough of the truth without my interference. Chekov had been patched up but not fixed. With broken bones mended and the wound in his leg mostly healed, the bruises under his eyes still stood out so starkly that he looked like he hadn't slept in a year. "What about the *Excelsior?*" he asked his captain. "What about the crew?"

"Henry's going to be a while getting everything glued back together, but we didn't suffer any casualties. Even the resupply team made it home all right." Sulu met his first officer's eyes with touching sincerity. "You did good by getting them out of there," he said, stressing each word as though pressing it into his friend's palm. "I'm just glad you got yourself out in one piece, too."

Chekov cast such a faint glance in my direction, it barely registered as a look at all. "Blame that on Captain Kirk."

"Is the captain with you?"

I responded more to Chekov's shift away from the comm than to Sulu's question. But once Sulu's exec had averted his eyes, I pulled the screen slightly aside to put myself in the captain's view. "Yes, Captain."

"I take it we're now sure the Nykkus are headed for the Kreth research station and not for home. Do you want us to turn around?"

I'd already thought about that and decided on my answer. "No. If we're going to have to fight the Nykkus, I want all the information we can get. Check in at their homeworld and see what you can find out."

He gave me a brisk nod of understanding. "Aye-aye, sir." Then, his expression relaxing again as he turned to his XO, "Commander Chekov, take care of yourself."

What hopes I had for Chekov's recovery lay entirely in

the warmth that passed briefly through his eyes when he answered, "You, too, Captain."

We sat in silence for what seemed a long time after Sulu closed the channel. I let the screen go black, then settled back in my chair to let Chekov sort through whatever must have been churning behind his studiously controlled expression. "Are you satisfied now that I'm not lying to you?"

He nodded mutely. That was all.

I remembered only once before when he'd been so uncharacteristically stoic. We sat near a row of windows during a grim San Francisco winter, waiting our turns at a Starfleet Command inquest I'd strenuously insisted should never take place. But it was what Starfleet did when starships were destroyed—they questioned the survivors and everyone involved in rescuing them until even the most gruesome details became rote and polished smooth from too much handling. I'd watched Chekov then, as gray and quiet as the weather outside, and wanted to make sure, incongruously, that everything was all right. But I hadn't said anything. I'd respected his silence, and the silence of the more than two hundred *Reliant* crewmen whose deaths had brought us to that place. And now we were here, and I couldn't believe the silence had done any of us any good.

"Does Sulu know?" It wasn't what I thought I'd say.

But it broke the ice-jam. He shook his head, still not raising his eyes toward mine. "I didn't even know." He pushed himself to his feet, and limped away from me down the long length of table. It would take a lot more than twenty minutes with a tissue regenerator to put that leg to rights, but that was more than could be said for the Nykkus whose body we'd scraped out of the Falcon once we got it on board. It had gotten in only the one good blow before losing to the Romulan pulse cannon. "I got so good at . . . not thinking about any of it. And it isn't as if I ever run into old crewmates . . ."

Of course not—everyone he had served with on the *Reliant* was dead. But I couldn't have said that out loud. I didn't need to. I could tell by the way he paused to lean heavily against a chair back that not a moment went by when he wasn't painfully aware of that reality.

"I thought if I kept busy with another assignment, another crew, it wouldn't be a problem," he went on, very deliberately. I could almost see him picking through his turmoil to choose the proper words. "I thought it wouldn't be the same."

Yet apparently it had been. "What did you promise the Nykkus to free the resupply team?"

"The aliens—the Nykkus?" He glanced at me to verify the word, then looked away again once I nodded. "The Nykkus weren't well-armed when they left Deep Space Three. They wanted the Falcons to use as Trojan horses against Elaphe Vulpina—they somehow believed that the research facility there was working on technology to replicate matter using the transporter."

Information no doubt pried from the crew of the Vulcan science ship Sulu had reported among the pirate force. Information which also hadn't trickled down below the rank of admiral, as far as I knew. Chekov couldn't possibly know how prescient the Nykkus were in choosing their target. "Something had gone wrong on their homeworld; there weren't very many of them. They intended to replicate themselves into an army." He turned to face me, one hand still braced on the chair, the other clenched at his side. "I couldn't let them torture my crew." It was the most passion I'd heard in his voice since leaving the transporter room. "I couldn't just stand by and watch another research facility be destroyed. It's supposed to be my job to protect them from that." Pain, raw and earnest, made his eyes almost glow. "I convinced them that Federation replication equipment had governors to prevent its use with living organisms. But that Klingon transporter duplicators didn't have the same restraints."

The logical leap caught me temporarily off guard. "But you knew the Klingons weren't doing replicator research," I guessed. I realized only after I said it how much of the reality I gave away.

If my slip meant anything to him, he didn't show it. A ghost of his old smile threatened. "No one's doing it," he pointed out. "It only mattered that they believed someone was. The Nykkus had a handful of out-of-date warships and an old pleasure yacht. I traded them the coordinates to

Kreth in exchange for the resupply team's release. I know how Klingons arm their stations. By the time the *Excelsior* was close enough to be in any danger, the Klingons would already have destroyed the Nykkus fleet."

And you along with them. But maybe that had been part of the plan. Maybe that had seemed easier than facing the loss of another starship and another crew. I kept my mouth shut and let him finish.

"I didn't mean to help them bait an ambush. If I had known what they were planning—"

Another damned platitude escaped me before I could stop it. "No one's blaming you."

And the steel doors slammed down in his eyes, so bitter and dark that I despaired of ever breaching them again. "Of course not," he spat, so choked with self-loathing it made me wince. "The first time—with the *Reliant*—all I did was turn my ship over to a madman and do *nothing* while he massacred my captain and crew. And Starfleet declared it nobody's fault, so everyone forgave me. Well, this time I gave the enemy everything they need to start a war between us and the Klingons." He slammed his empty chair against the table and turned his back on me for the final time. "I don't need anyone else to blame me anymore. I know whose fault this is."

Chapter Twelve

SULU

FOR A LONG TIME after Chekov's signal cut off, I sat quiet at the helm of the *Jocelyn Bell*, trying to decide what it was that had bothered me about that call from my first officer. Was it the briefness of the contact, or was it the far-too-normal sound of his voice in those few sentences we had exchanged? I remembered the bruises and broken bones, the troubled looks and numbed voices of the hostages we had beamed out from the Klingon escape pod. My frown deepened. Chekov's face had worn the same bruises, but not the same traumatized expression. Had his age and past experience allowed him to survive being tortured by the Nykkus? Or did that carefully correct demeanor of his hide an experience so much worse that it couldn't be expressed at all?

"Something about that didn't sound right." Uhura glanced over at me from the communications station of the cargo shuttle. Her coffee-colored eyes were as warm and thoughtful as ever, but the years had subtly chiseled her good looks, adding distinction to their beauty. "Was Chekov giving you some kind of coded message?"

"Not that I could tell." I kept one eye on my helm control

164

while I talked, although our course hadn't varied since we'd left the *Excelsior* a few hours ago. Piloting the *Jocelyn Bell* myself wasn't just an attempt to keep my mind and hands occupied during this long, tense trip. It freed up another of the cargo shuttle's limited seats for a xenobiology specialist to accompany my science officer, my borrowed communications chief, and my handful of security guards. The fact that it also kept my mind and hands occupied was a fringe benefit. "Why?"

"Because Janice Rand is filling in for me back on the *Enterprise,*" Uhura said. "If Chekov wanted to make sure the *Excelsior* and her crew had survived, all he had to do was ask her."

"I'm not sure why he needed to ask anyone." Lieutenant Sandi Henry was never shy about sharing her concerns and opinions, which was one of the reasons I'd brought her along as our xenobiology specialist. The other reason was that it gave her something else to worry about besides the amount of overwork her chief engineer husband was currently subjecting himself to. "Surely Captain Kirk told him the *Excelsior* was all right. Why wouldn't Commander Chekov believe him?"

"Maybe for security reasons," Nino Orsini said loyally from where he sat in the back of the shuttle with his squad of eight security guards. "Commanding officers can't always tell the truth in front of everybody. Not if there are important Starfleet secrets at stake."

Uhura shook her head, making the beaten gold sunbursts and silver moons that dangled from her ears chime. "That can be true sometimes, Lieutenant—but I'm not sure what secrets the Anjiri and Nykkus could have that would matter to Starfleet or to the Federation. You never saw their homeworld, did you?"

"No," I said, knowing the question was directed at me instead of my security chief. I wasn't the only one on board the shuttle who had served on the *Enterprise,* but I was certainly the only one old enough to remember that particular mission. "I was back on the ship, preparing to make a quick getaway in case the Anjiri stormed out at us. Why?"

"Because if you had, you wouldn't have been worried about them storming out at us." Amusement danced in her voice the same way the shuttle instrument lights danced over her jewelry. "They had the most ragtag technology I've ever seen, even worse than on Omega Four. I can remember thinking it was a miracle the Anjiri were there at all, considering they lived in unshielded shipwrecks on a hollow planetoid. They must have inherited their first spaceships from an earlier civilization, or maybe were given them by the Orions in payment for some term of service. By the time we ran across them, everything they had was secondhand, stolen or rescued from scrap."

"Including their weapons?" asked Orsini.

Uhura shook her head and her earrings chimed again. "I really didn't see those. I was too busy trying to translate the Anjiri's language by watching their body language."

"I don't remember them having much in the way of handheld weapons," I told my security chief. "But they had a real kicker of a tractor beam. They used it to drag in small ships and space debris from parsecs away."

"Like Charybdis in her cave, pulling in all those Greek and Roman ships," Schulman said whimsically.

Orsini gave her an uncertain look. "Uh—right. That's probably how they got that little Vulcan science vessel. Don't the Vulcans have a scientific prospecting treaty with the Orions in this sector, Cadet?"

"Indeed," said a deep, collected voice from the row behind him. I glanced back at Tuvok and thought that for all his youth and inexperience, he looked much calmer than I would have felt about returning to the stronghold of my torturers. There were advantages to the rigid training in emotional control that his culture practiced. "I reviewed our tapes of the space battle as you suggested, Lieutenant, and deciphered the Vulcan ship's identification number from them. The Vulcan Science Academy reported it missing only two weeks previous to our encounter with it as a pirate vessel."

"And its last reported location, Cadet?" I asked, frowning.

"The Orion system Greshik Tyrr, sir. Approximately two parsecs from the coordinates Captain Kirk gave us for the Anjiri-Nykkus home system."

I glanced at the helm display and saw that we had ten

parsecs remaining in our voyage. "Can you calibrate our long-range sensors to scan for the fringes of that tractor beam, Lieutenant Schulman? It might be good to let the Anjiri bring us in as unpowered flotsam rather than drop out of warp at their doorstep."

"I'll try, sir." Far from being frustrated with her task of scraping data out of the cargo shuttle's less sensitive sensors, my chief science officer seemed positively energized by the challenge. I was beginning to suspect that her ongoing battle with the *Excelsior*'s long-range sensors had less to do with the quality of our equipment and more to do with Christina Schulman's delight in getting a system to perform above and beyond its specifications. "I should be able to give you at least a parsec of warning."

"Good enough." I checked our heading once again to make sure it hadn't wavered, then swung back toward Uhura and Henry. "All right, tell me everything you know about the Anjiri and the Nykkus."

Uhura inclined her head at the xenobiologist first. "I looked over Doctor Klass's autopsy and the DNA reports on the two dead Nykkus, as well as the limited information from the previous contact mission," Lieutenant Henry said promptly. "I agree with the doctor's conclusion that some sexual hypertrophy exists in the specimens we recovered, but nothing in their DNA patterns looked genetically engineered to me. And given the extreme improbability of random genetic mutations producing beneficial results, I would also hesitate to attribute the change to any kind of teratogenesis."

"What *would* you attribute it to?" asked Schulman, glancing over curiously from her sensor panel. "Environmental toxicity?"

"That would be possible if the Anjiri and Nykkus lived in a natural environment," the other scientist agreed. "Pollutants that mimic natural reproductive hormones have been known to cause serious disruptions in sexual development, particularly among herptile species. However, I would be very surprised if a ship or manufactured planetoid, with all the filtration systems that are needed to recycle the air and water, could create the same kind of chemical poisoning."

"Even in an old, cobbled-together environment like the Anjiri's?" I asked.

Henry nodded. "The extent of filter breakdown you'd need to cause hormonal poisoning would cause other effects, like heavy metal toxicity and pernicious anemia. The Nykkus we found didn't have any of those problems."

"So what's the bottom line, Lieutenant?"

"The bottom line," said Sandi Henry, "is that we simply cannot make generalizations about the range of genetic variability in an alien species from a few minimal encounters. For heavens sake, look at the Klingons—judging on appearance alone, you can't even tell some of them are the same species."

Uhura gave her a quizzical look. "So what you're saying is that these 'new' Nykkus who attacked the *Excelsior* may be genetic variants that have existed all along in the home population?"

"Or whose genetic code existed all along in the gene pool, at least," Henry agreed. "Perhaps as a recessive trait, like the gene for dark color that only showed up occasionally in white English moths until the Industrial Revolution. Traits like that are essentially in storage, waiting for conditions to change—"

"And favor them," Schulman finished, nodding. "At which point the recessive gene becomes selected and begins to be expressed more frequently."

"Exactly."

The shuttle was silent for a moment. I suspected that most people aboard were wondering, as I was, how the conditions at the Anjiri homeworld could have changed to favor the devious, savage intelligence we'd experienced from their sibling species of Nykkus. Had the same change occurred to the Anjiri as well? If so, perhaps a state of war now existed between the former allies, and any incoming ship would be regarded as a threat.

"Three parsecs to the Anjiri homeworld." My pilot's instinct had told me that even before I glanced at the helm display to confirm it. "No sign of a tractor beam yet, Schulman?"

"No, sir. No sign of any sensor sweeps, either. Either the

Anjiri are tractoring in any random debris they hit, or they're just not out fishing today."

"Keep looking," I ordered. "They may pulse their sweeps to avoid detection." I glanced across at Uhura. "No hails from that direction either?"

She glanced across her boards and shook her head. "Not from any direction, Captain."

"All right, then, Commander. It's your turn to tell us what you know about the Anjiri and the Nykkus."

"About the Nykkus, not much," she admitted. "The Anjiri did most of the talking back when we encountered them. Although the Nykkus clearly understood the Anjiri's commands and could think for themselves, they weren't very verbal."

"Neither were the Anjiri, were they?"

She shook her head, suns and moons jangling at her ears. "Most of their language was nuanced through their body postures. They only had a few basic sounds—hisses, snarls, intakes of breath—so they made each combination mean different things according to how they stood and moved as they said it."

"And the Nykkus didn't make any of those sounds?"

"They made all of them, but their posture was always so defensive and submissive that with the additional body language added to it, the universal translator just kept repeating 'sorry, sorry, sorry' for everything they said." Uhura picked up the communications tricorder she had brought with her and toggled its display on. "I did a preliminary linguistic analysis of the original signal the *Excelsior* picked up and translated just before the attack on Deep Space Three. It codes out as essentially the same language as the Anjiri and Nykkus spoke twenty years ago, but with an emphasis on deeper growling vocalizations rather than higher-pitched hisses. A different accent, perhaps, or maybe a new kind of military slang. Either way, I have to agree with Lieutenant Henry. We could just be seeing a segment of Nykkus society that we were never exposed to before."

I nodded, glancing back at my helm display. "One and a half parsecs from Anjiri homeworld. Still no sign of a tractor beam or any sensor sweeps, Schulman?"

"No, sir." She gave me a worried look. "Actually, Captain, I'm not picking up much sign of activity from the homeworld at all. I should be getting some ionic emissions from their power plants by now, or some signal leakage from their communications circuits."

"Perhaps they've relocated their floating planetoid to another solar system," Orsini suggested. "It sounds like the whole thing could have been towed with a few good ships."

"Perhaps." I watched the distance between us and the Anjiri homeworld dwindle, eaten away by the *Jocelyn Bell*'s powerful warp engines. At half a parsec, I could finally make out the sullen twinkle of the Anjiri's home star by its unmoving position in the center of the helm display. At twelve billion kilometers, we streaked through the unseen halo of space-dark ice that was the system's cometary belt and the twinkle kindled to a dim charcoal glow. At two billion, the ember brightened to a flare, and at half a billion it became a furious boil of bloody fire at the center of a crowded gas-giant system. I swept a hand across the warp controls and brought the *Jocelyn Bell* sweeping out into normal space, at a deceleration rate fast enough to make the safety warnings on our inertial dampeners strobe as redly as the Anjiri sun. Uhura winced and braced herself against her communications panel as the shuttle continued its weapons-evading slam to the position I had selected for our stop, just outside the heavy metal gates of the Anjiri's manufactured worldlet.

"Sulu," said my old *Enterprise* crewmate between her teeth. "This is exactly how fast Captain Kirk brought us in the last time I was here. Please tell me I was right in thinking for twenty years that we wouldn't have crashed into the Anjiri's docking bay if you had been our shuttle pilot."

"We're not going to crash into the Anjiri docking bay." I watched the exponential downward curve that was keeping our inertial dampeners stretched to their limit. Nonpilots never realized just how much tolerance was built into Starfleet's systems, but I had spent a few lost years of my life determining the width of that safety margin to a hair. We would end that deceleration a safe kilometer away from the Anjiri's fortress, arriving too relativistically fast to aim at and stopping too close to fire at. "Don't worry, the sensors are picking up the planetoid and it's still in the same position—"

"Yes." Uhura's somber voice told me that wasn't necessarily a good thing. I spared a look up from my controls as the dampeners stopped flashing their warnings, and saw the dark shadow of the Anjiri's little planet, wearing its haphazardly welded encrustation of spacewrecks and flotsam. That looked familiar enough, but as soon as my eyes adjusted to the dim reflection of red star-shine, I saw what Uhura had already seen. The great metal gates of the Anjiri docking bay were blasted through as savagely as the *Excelsior*'s own shuttle bay. And not a trace of light leaked from within.

"Schulman," I snapped while the *Jocelyn Bell* swooped to a graceful but completely unnecessary stop inside the asteroid's safe firing range. "Sensor readings on life-support and life-signs inside there."

"Negative, sir, at least for the sectors I can read from here." My science officer frowned at her sensors, for once looking justifiably frustrated. "The problem is, these systems just don't have the power to sweep through more than a few hundred meters of that metal cladding. There could be lots more areas intact deeper inside, or on the other side, and we'd never know."

"Well, we're damn well going to find out." I saw Uhura's lifted arch of eyebrow and realized how grim I must have sounded. But I hadn't come all this way, leaving behind a wounded starship and a damaged first officer, just to turn and leave at the first hint of an obstacle. Even if not a single Anjiri or Nykkus remained alive in there, we needed to know what had happened to them to understand the rampage on which their survivors had embarked. "Schulman, keep scanning. I'm going to loop around this rock and give you a chance to scan as much of the first hundred meters as we can."

"And then what, Captain?" Lieutenant Henry's clear blue eyes couldn't mask her doubt the way her well-trained voice could. "We don't have a transporter aboard, and even if we use the environmental suits, we may be breaching all the rest of their atmosphere just by going in."

"I know that." I sent the *Jocelyn Bell* into a slow spiral

around the augmented Anjiri planetoid, watching its welded carapace slide past. Most of the flotsam I saw was unrecognizable, but here and there a space-blackened nacelle or carelessly welded weapons turret caught my pilot's eye. The blackest, most buried ones were ships I'd only seen in books or museums, while the ones that still gave off an occasional glint of steel gray or duranium silver beneath our scanning lights were spaceships that had flown in my boyhood. None of them had what I was looking for.

"What are your sensors reading, Lieutenant?"

"Atmosphere, I think, sir. But it seems to be pretty deep inside—no, wait, it's starting to hold a lot closer to the surface." We'd passed a barren projection of the planetoid's original iron-nickel core a moment ago, and seemed to be orbiting now around a different sector of this manufactured world. The welded wrecks were fresher here, and carefully arranged to allow views of the sullen red sun through scattered portholes.

"This side looks better than the other one." Despite her curious gaze and comment, Uhura's hands never stopped moving across her communications panel. She was scanning all possible frequencies, not just the normal subspace channels, in search of a distress call. I doubted the secretive Anjiri and Nykkus would ever resort to begging the outside galaxy for help, but I didn't try to dissuade her. Even a slim chance was better than not looking at all. "I wonder why."

"Maybe it's how the other half lives," Sandi Henry suggested. "The Anjiri half. From the reports filed after the *Enterprise* encountered them, there seemed to be a wide social gap between the two species."

"Despite their obvious relationship," Uhura agreed.

"Captain, I'm reading life-signs inside," Schulman said abruptly. "Bearing five-fifteen mark nine."

"Affirmative." I sent the cargo shuttle slanting over to the new heading without taking my eyes off the barnacled mass of welded ships passing beneath our lights. The pack rat Anjiri had apparently used anything they'd found to expand their limited space habitat. I recognized an early Vulcan unmanned probe, an antique Orion colony supply ship, an M-class Starfleet courier—

"Captain?" Schulman gave me a puzzled glance as the

Jocelyn Bell swerved from its heading into a back-looping spiral. "The life-signs are still seven hundred meters away."

"Is there atmosphere in the section right below us, Lieutenant?" I asked, bringing the shuttle to a slow idle over the familiar Starfleet insignia. On one side, I could see a crudely welded patch over the dusky star of a photon torpedo hit. Since the Nykkus had never used torpedoes against us, I presumed that meant this was a wreck from some early space battle with the Romulans or Orions, found and salvaged by the sauroid space-gleaners.

"Yes, sir, there is." Schulman's startled look had melted into comprehension. "Oxygen levels and pressures are a little low, but well within human tolerance."

"No worse than paying a visit to the cloud-cities on Ardana." I made a tighter looping spiral around the wreck. The port side of the courier ship was preserved intact, welded into the planetoid's metal husk in a way that seemed to deliberately leave her emergency docking port clear and accessible. I wondered if the Anjiri had used it as an airlock themselves. "Orsini, have someone pack along a few oxygen bottles from the emergency lockers in case anyone gets sick."

"Yes, *sir,*" my security chief said enthusiastically. Uhura glanced over her shoulder at the away team he was already forming from his squad, then back at me. Her lifted eyebrow would have done Spock proud.

"You're actually planning to *dock* here?"

"Why not?" I had the *Jocelyn Bell*'s own emergency docking port already centered over the courier's airlock, her guide-lasers locked onto target and her impulse engines adjusted for a slow descent. Without an order being given, Schulman began downloading data from her sensor station to a tricorder and Henry fastened her xenobiology equipment belt around her waist. "Starfleet emergency docking ports have been made to the same specifications for the past ninety years, Commander, for situations just like this."

"I don't think this was *exactly* what Starfleet had in mind." But Uhura scooped up her own communications tricorder as soon as she heard the solid thud of the magnetic docking plates latching onto each other. I cut the *Jocelyn Bell*'s impulse engines and engaged the cargo shuttle's autothrusters to keep her from pulling away as the Anjiri homeworld rotated beneath her. Fortunately, this little planetoid had an unusually strong gravitational pull that would help keep us mated. It must have been a chunk of pure iron-nickel core blasted free when its primordial planet was destroyed in a cosmic collision. And the outer layers of duranium and metal cladding slathered onto it by the Anjiri had only added to its density.

"We've got the old docking port plugged into ship power and online, Captain," called Nino Orsini's voice from the back of the cargo shuttle. I couldn't see him behind the advance group of guards, but suspected he'd be the first one through that airlock when I gave the order to enter it. "We're ready to go when you are."

"Proceed at your discretion, Lieutenant." I spun my pilot's chair around and moved to join Uhura, Schulman, and Henry in the center of Orsini's carefully arrayed security guards. For all its age, the M-class courier's emergency port made no more noise irising open than our own shuttle's had. The only sign that we had opened a gateway to the Anjiri homeworld was the gust of air sucked out of the ship and a drop in air pressure so sudden it made my ears pop. As a former test pilot, I was used to ignoring that, although I saw Henry and Uhura both wince and rub at their ears.

"I don't remember the air being this thin before." Uhura watched the first party of security guards climb down into the open airlock and disappear. "Or this cold."

The temperature change that followed our exchange of atmospheres with the planetoid was striking, especially in an artificial habitat created by a sauroid species. "Maybe the life support systems are failing and causing environmental problems after all," I said. "Schulman, did the life signs you picked up show any indication of medical distress?"

"Not that I could see, sir. There was one that seemed much weaker than the others, but it could have just been coming from deeper in the planetoid. The metal alloy this world is made of is highly recalcitrant to sensor scans." Schulman grimaced at the tricorder she'd brought with her.

"The bioscan on this thing probably won't work for more than a hundred meters in any direction."

All of the advance guard had now vanished through the airlock, leaving a tense silence behind them. I pushed past our own escort and risked a glance down through the short tunnel made by the magnetically mated portals. All I saw was darkness, lit by an occasional distant gleam from a security guard's hand lamp. A strong smell, tart as corroded metal but at the same time more musky, rose up to prickle at my nose. I frowned and toggled on my wrist communicator. "Sulu to Orsini."

"Orsini here." My security chief sounded a little breathless from the change in oxygen levels, but otherwise untroubled. "The advance team has secured the courier hull and adjacent tunnel passages, sir. It should be safe for the rest of you to enter. It's a drop of about twelve feet, but the gravity change will soften it."

"Tell your men not to explore more than a hundred meters away from the airlock until we're all through," I ordered, then tapped off my wrist communicator and swung myself down into the airlock first. I felt the Anjiri homeworld's lighter gravity make my stomach lurch when I dropped below the courier's hull, but I still hit the metal floor below with enough of a thud to make my teeth clack together. I stepped back, shaking my head at Orsini's idea of a soft landing. When the next guard to drop through the airlock also grunted with pain on arrival, I told him to help the rest of the party down, then went in search of my security chief.

There didn't seem to be much else left of the M-class courier beyond its docking port and upside-down bottom deck. A jerry-rigged Romulan bulkhead had been used to close the area off, in case of accidental portal opening I supposed. The glow of a handheld light inside its opened door panel shed enough light to let me recognize Orsini's aquiline features.

"Any sign of recent Anjiri or Nykkus activity in this sector, Lieutenant?"

Orsini shook his head, looking puzzled. "Not really, sir. Certainly no evidence of a recent attack or any kind of space battle. All we found was a lot of toys scattered around down one of the tunnel passages."

"Toys?" My voice must have been loud enough to catch Uhura's attention even as she dropped through the airlock—I recognized the soft jangle of earrings that accompanied the sound of approaching footsteps. "What makes you think that's what they were, Lieutenant?"

He held out what looked like a limp bundle of fiber cable. On closer inspection, I could see that it was knotted at each end to form a series of oil-darkened handholds. One of the knots still wore the embedded glitter of an ash-dark scale. "If that's not for playing tug-of-war, sir, I don't know what it is," Orsini said apologetically. "We found a lot of other ropes like this strung along a high tunnel wall and across a section of roof. There seemed to be a lot of claw marks in the metal around them."

"A jungle gym?" Uhura asked.

"That's what it looked like to me, sir."

"Or maybe a military training ground," I reminded them. "That military strategy the Nykkus have been using on us didn't come from nowhere." I glanced back to see the rest of the landing team gathered on the courier's lower deck. "Schulman, what direction were those life-signs from here?"

"Seven-nineteen mark nine, sir." She came to join us, scanning her tricorder around the spokes of metal-walled tunnels radiating out from this docking port. "That tunnel seems to lead in the right direction, sir."

I nodded at Orsini, and he called his guards together with a single snapped command, then led us down the passageway the science officer had selected. Its welded walls must have been torn from several generations of wrecked spacecraft—engraved Orion filagree gave way to the simple gleam of Vulcan steel, then to the rusting crunch of ancient Klingon armor. After a while, the crazy-quilt passage gave way to the dull purple-black of the planetoid's own native metal. It seemed to suck the light from our massed handlamps into itself, leaving me with an uneasy sense of being surrounded by echoing space instead of solid walls.

"Anything showing on the bioscan, Schulman?"

"No, sir. My calculations show we're still approximately

four hundred meters from where I first picked up the life-signs."

I frowned. The strange smell that had reminded me of corroded metal and a carnivore's breath was growing stronger the deeper we penetrated into this passage. "Orsini, pull back your advance guard," I said after a moment. Maybe I was being overcautious, but a captain doesn't have to explain his orders. My security chief not only didn't question them, he pulled his rear guards in as well to make a solid protective diamond around us. He'd apparently mistaken my unease for the kind of battle intuition I'd always envied in Captain Kirk.

"What is it, Captain?" Uhura asked.

"I'm not sure, but I think—"

"Life-signs," Lieutenant Schulman interrupted, her voice crackling with frustration. "Only forty meters away and moving toward us fast, *damn* this tricorder—"

"Phasers set on stun," I snapped and heard the adjustments click around me. "Heavy stun," I added after a moment when I felt the passage shake with the approaching thunder of footsteps and roaring voices.

"Twenty-five meters," said Schulman.

The din rose to a clamor. At a sign from Orsini, the front line of security guards dropped to one knee to give the rear line a clear line of fire. I crouched behind them, seeing Uhura and Henry join me, while Schulman still stared down at her tricorder. Before I could snap out an order, the xenobiologist tugged Schulman down with us, out of the line of fire. "Fifteen meters," the science officer said without even seeming to notice. "Ten . . . five . . ."

A massive glitter of purple-black hurtled around the curve of the passage ahead of us, and for a moment it looked as if we were being attacked by the metal planetoid itself. Then the solid onrush broke for an instant into the chaotic surge and eddy of a charge arrested in mid-stride, and the thundering roar dropped into startled silence. Ten meters away, the knot of attacking Nykkus had crashed to a stop and now stood staring at us like a stymied pack of natural predators, interlacing restlessly through each other without taking another step toward us.

"Hold your fire," I said softly. "Wait and see what they decide to do."

They were undeniably Nykkus rather than Anjiri, this hunting pack in front of us. They had the same savagely muscular shoulders, the same strong sauroid skulls, the same gleaming teeth. But the flaring rills on their skull-crests brushed the top of the two-meter tunnels they stood hunched in, and their jeweled reptile eyes blazed in the darkness like fire-opals lit from behind. They lacked the ritual scarring on their scales that had distorted the two Nykkus bodies we had found. In its place they wore a glittering network of copper and silver droplets that they'd either pierced through their overlapping scales or somehow soldered to them, in intricate patterns that followed the curves of their environmental armor and their own strong muscles. The brightness of that metallic bodywork was reflected and intensified by the rich luster of the scales beneath.

The Nykkus and Anjiri we'd met twenty years ago aboard the *Enterprise* had been sand-gray and dust-brown, Captain Kirk had said. The Nykkus who'd attacked Deep Space Three and the *Excelsior* had been significantly deeper and richer in color, their scales grading from polished mahogany to wet steel. But the Nykkus before us made the previous ones look like pale imitations of themselves. Their scales had the intense shine of dark gemstones—the charcoal gleam of smoke quartz, the dried-blood glitter of garnet, the gray-black glint of polished hematite. The colors seemed to shift and melt as they gradually stilled into silence, cooling from their original overcast of angry purple-black to a more watchful midnight-blue. I suspected it was a side-effect of their scales settling back into place as they cooled and lost the purple-gray flush of blood vessels in the exposed skin below.

Their restless shifting had settled at last into a wedge formation that almost echoed ours, the tallest and darkest Nykkus at its point and the others arrayed behind in order of descending size. A deep rumbling snarl broke the silence, but before any of our nervous security guards could take it for a threat, Uhura's specially adapted translator had already transformed it into a rush of words. I was so startled that I rose from my crouch and stared across at our attackers. The universal translator was always sensitive to gender, and armed with Uhura's Anjiri-Nykkus database, it had turned that snarled demand into a strong but undeniably *female* voice.

Twenty years ago, James T. Kirk had found the females of the Anjiri species to be more powerful, assertive, and intelligent than the males. Now we were facing their Nykkus equivalents—even stronger, even more aggressive, and perhaps even more intelligent than the military strategists who'd blown up Deep Space Three and left the *Excelsior* in ruins.

God help us all.

Chapter Thirteen

KIRK

KLINGON RESEARCH. The ultimate oxymoron.

Racist of me, I know, but I've always found the concept of Klingon scientists a little hard to wrap my brain around. What did Klingon science look like? Steel-jawed geologists extracting information from rocks using agonizers and *d'k tahg*? Armor-clad physicists smashing atoms with *bat'leths*? After all my years in the service, the only thing I knew for sure was that the Klingons defended their research outposts as ruthlessly as their military bases.

Kreth was apparently no exception. From parsecs away, we could see the flash and glow of weapons discharge like lightning against a black storm sky.

"So much for avoiding a war," Benni muttered from her weapons console.

She had a lot to learn if she thought I gave up that easily.

"Sensors detect massive damage to most station sections." Spock, already well familiar with my tenacity, had bent to his sensors the moment the Alpha Gaudianus system, which was Kreth's home, came within range. "Quantum interference in the region is anomalously high, but I believe there are only three ships engaged in the attack."

I heard Chekov stir to the left of my command chair. "The Falcons." McCoy had released him from sickbay with no caveats more than an hour ago, but he still looked tired and a little lost with no position to go to, no job to do. He must have seen the movement when I glanced at him, because he turned to face me before continuing, "The Nykkus will use the FL-70s' stealth capabilities to get in close and pick the station apart without risking their weaker ships. They've got their soldiers—the ones they plan to duplicate—packed into the other ships like livestock. They won't put them in danger."

"Not yet at least." Once they were on the station and faced with hand-to-hand combat against the Klingons, I had a feeling they'd have to be a little more free with their resources. "Spock, any sign of damage to those Falcons?"

He hadn't yet lifted his face from the sensors. "Negative."

Which meant the damned things could keep nickel-and-diming the station for days. Clenching one fist in frustration, I told myself it wasn't reasonable to resent Starfleet for building a reconnaissance craft that was everything they claimed it would be. "Mr. Benni," I called to my weapons officer, "shields up. Helm, warp three."

"Captain—" Spock took a single step away from his station, a sure sign that I'd startled him with the order. I will admit to occasionally feeling a sting of pride that I can still startle my Vulcan first officer after so many years.

"Those Falcons are Federation property, Mr. Spock. They're also the only thing in sensor range, which means Kreth's record of this attack is going to look one hell of a lot like a Federation invasion."

He gave that reasoning the considering nod it deserved. "Bringing a Constitution-class starship into the fray will not go far toward convincing them otherwise."

"It will if we can clear out those Falcons," I insisted. "And if we make sure there are Klingon eyewitnesses left to tell the tale."

The Nykkus themselves certainly weren't going to stick around to greet the Klingon cavalry. From everything

Chekov had said, they were unsophisticated but not stupid. Smarter, even, than their Anjiri counterparts from two decades before, who for all their flailing managed to do quite well with other races' stolen technology. It wouldn't take the Nykkus long to figure out that there were no prototype replicators on Kreth. Once they realized they'd been duped, they'd abandon the station, leaving only the misleading battle records to explain what had happened. And, unless I missed my bet, they'd be back at Elaphe Vulpina about the time the first salvo was being fired in the Federation/Klingon war.

When the first rough judder rattled my teeth, I put it down to the quantum wreckage ringing any battle whose main projectiles were photons and gamma rays. Then the ship rocked as though we'd skipped her belly across an open moon, and I gripped the arms of my command chair in alarm. "Spock . . . ?"

He ran down the list with stoic precision. "Debris from at least two Birds of Prey . . ." The traditional guard dogs of Klingon posts. "Also remnants of a Veth-class Klingon colony transport . . ." The Nykkus's Trojan horse. "A vast amount of subspace fracture as well."

"Subspace fracture?" That hadn't been what I'd bargained for when I first called for this heroic swoop to the Klingons' rescue. I swivelled my chair to frown at Spock. "From what? Some sort of natural phenomenon?" At the time, I was thinking a nearby singularity, or perhaps the fading wavefront from a long-ago supernova.

My science officer merely lifted both eyebrows in a thoughtful Vulcan shrug. "Insufficient data at this time. However, it is not consistent—"

It was no subspace fracture that slammed us broadside. The whole ship seemed to buck like a startled horse, and I shouted, "Shields *up*, Lieutenant!" toward the weapons panel even as I dragged myself back into the command chair. Chekov, on his knees now, wisely took hold of the bridge railing but made no move to stand.

"Shields are up, sir!" Benni's hands were already flying across her controls, her face contorted in what I knew was anger at that situation, not me. "Whatever hit us—"

It came to her call, kicking us so hard I could almost feel the strutwork break.

"God . . . !" she breathed. Her face had the stunned look of someone facing a power greater than she'd ever conceived. "That's off the scale."

I motioned sharply at Chekov. "If you're staying, Commander, take a seat." Because I had a feeling things were only going to get worse, and it was no time to ride out a battle on your knees.

He gave me a brusque nod, then scrambled under the railing toward the empty auxiliary engineering station. I don't know if he picked that seat because it was the first his eyes happened upon, or because it was immediately behind the weapons console. Whatever the reason, he was poised between the two when the third impact slammed us, and barely made it past the weapons alcove before being all but thrown into his chair.

A breach alarm for somewhere in the lower decks shrilled so loudly I couldn't hear which department sent out the call for a medical team. "Spock, where the hell is that coming from?"

He stared now at the light show on the viewscreen, as though that could tell him something more than his sensors. "As the Falcons are outfitted with only a single phaser array, I must infer that we are being fired upon by the station."

What does Klingon science look like? Weapons research.

I mouthed a fistful of profanities as I swung toward Janice Rand. "Commander, get that station on the comm!"

"Trying, sir." She already had one hand to her earpiece, that familiar glazed look in her eyes as she played across the bandwidths. "There's no response."

Of course not—if I were a Klingon, the word "surrender" wouldn't even exist in my dictionary. And in the height of battle, what else could an enemy commander possibly want to discuss?

"Then punch through to them," I snarled. "Tell them what we're here for and get that gun turned away from us!" I turned to find Benni's eyes already fixed on me, awaiting her orders. "Lieutenant, let's prove our good intentions. Lock on to those Falcons."

She was working before I'd even finished the command. I heard the telltale beep of the weapons system searching for its target, but never the staccato chirrup signaling an imminent phaser strike. "I can't get a fix," she finally complained after what felt like a dangerous eternity. "The readings have them all over the place."

"Then go to visual," I told her. "Get a manual lock."

This time, the target-lock sang out triumphantly. A blue-white burst of phaser fire stitched the vacuum behind a Falcon, between two Falcons, seeming to pass through the body of both without even generating a defensive flicker in their screens. Even inertial dampeners couldn't completely negate the stomach-wrenching shift in vector as the *Enterprise* slewed toward port and shouldered downward. A bouquet of gas-shrouded fires bloomed along the damaged curve of Kreth's silhouette as our own phasers tore aside its outer plating.

"Dammit . . . !"

The helmsman, Plavi, shook his head in apology but didn't glance away from his boards. "I'm keeping her as steady as I can without getting us hulled."

No one was blaming him. The rending pulse of whatever the Klingons were firing distorted the space in front of us like a column of heavy water. It sheared aside as if changing its predatory mind, and I realized we'd dropped into another laborious half-roll only when my ribs collided roughly with the arm of my chair. If the Klingons didn't kill us, we were going to tear our own ship apart trying to avoid it. The only thing the Klingons weren't hitting with their damned cannon was the Falcons.

"Spock—" God, I hated to do this. But if the Klingons destroyed the *Enterprise,* the Falcons would keep at Kreth until she fell, and there'd be no way to keep that from looking like a Federation attack when the Empire came to pick up the pieces. "Can you get me a fix on the station's weapons array?"

Spock, wisely, didn't bother to point out that firing on the station ourselves wasn't exactly stacking the deck in our favor. "Two four seven mark three eight three one mark one seven five."

What's that old saying about making an omelet by breaking some eggs? "Weapons, lock on phasers, half power—"

"Wait!"

Chekov's shout brought my heart up into my throat. But I bit off the command I would rather not have been giving and swung my chair around to find him already out of his seat, sliding into the back of the weapon's alcove. "Targeting's off by forty degrees." He pointed at the readings as though I could see what was displayed there. "The Falcons—it must be part of their detection avoidance mechanism—"

"We're on visual—" Benni argued sharply.

Chekov scowled at her with senior security officer's disdain for the uppity young. "Then they're throwing chromatic echoes," he said, reaching over her shoulder for the targeting controls, "or projecting false visuals off their shields, but they aren't where we're seeing them!"

Benni glanced an irate question in my direction. I felt only a moment of guilt about betraying a current officer in favor of the instincts of a previous one. "Give it your best shot, Mr. Chekov." Because if it didn't work, we'd be opening fire on the Klingons. I would grasp at any straw that might avoid that.

Even standing, he seemed oddly relaxed at the controls. As if by touching the station where he'd spent so much of his youth, he temporarily rediscovered the unquestioned self-assurance that came with that territory. A spiral of phaser fire circled the closest Falcon like a bracelet of fire. I started to bite down on an oath when no single shot hit home, then the Falcon kicked back suddenly on a ball of exploding gas, and went tumbling.

My heart felt like it would explode with relief. "Keep on them!"

Unlike the Falcons, we made an all-too-easy target. Another great fist of force smashed us almost head-on, and I saw Chekov's next shot swirl so wild not even a forty degree deviation in tracking would help put it close to its target. "Dammit, can't they see—?"

I don't remember how that angry shout would have

finished. When I caught sight of the wounded Falcon bearing down on the Klingon weapons array, all I could think was that they were idiots if they thought they stood a chance by putting themselves in such close quarters. Then I remembered the Nykkus we'd seen on board the *Excelsior*, who had trustingly beamed himself into vacuum because that was his part in someone else's greater plan.

And I realized what this crippled Falcon had been ordered to do.

"Mr. Chekov, stop that ship!"

He didn't take the time to acknowledge, only opened fire. He couldn't possibly have been faster—I don't even think he'd been waiting for the order. I saw what I thought was the flash of shields repelling a phaser blast across the Falcon's aft, but its nose carved into the station at too close to the same instant for me to be sure. Or maybe the Klingons unleashed their big weapon in one last defiant attempt to take the little ship down. All I know is that the energy pulse that swelled out from the ruptured station when the Falcon ignited was tremendous. The wave of supercharged subspace slammed the *Enterprise* full in the face, throwing her almost ninety degrees straight upward. It sounded like the whole world exploded, then reality tore itself out from under me, and everything went black.

Whatever stimulant Starfleet arms their medics with tends to tear through your nervous system like a phaser bolt, yanking you into wakefulness just before it exits out the top of your head.

At least, that's how it always felt to me. For all I know, it had more to do with being knocked unconscious than with how Starfleet chose to wake me up. I must have been lifted into a sitting position. All I remember is rolling onto my hands and knees with my skull throbbing like a pulsar. Blood stung my eyes, and something skin-warm and slick moved just under my hairline. I didn't need to touch my hand to my scalp to know it was more blood.

Smoke blurred the air on the bridge into a gray pall. Lighting had dimmed to emergency levels, and the ghostly chatter of distant voices over the intercoms filled the background with requests for medical help, damage teams, and rescue. Helm and navigation were mostly dark, with a lower section of the helm console blown completely open. My helmsman, Plavi, was nowhere to be seen, and Navigator Chambers did her best to attend both positions, although I didn't know what good she could possibly be doing. Just keeping herself busy, maybe. A badly burned corpse, half-obscured by the singed duty jacket draped across its face, lay neatly arranged on the deck between the weapons and auxiliary engineering stations. When Chekov slid, sans jacket, out of the maintenance hatch beneath the weapons console, I realized the corpse was Benni.

I caught the arm of my chair to crawl upright and check the starboard half of the bridge. My attendant medtech made the mistake of trying to pull me back down to the deck. "Go take care of someone else," I told him. When he didn't let me go, I shrugged him off with captainly force and turned to look for Spock.

My first officer—my friend—worked at his own station as calmly as if we weren't up to our asses in dead machinery and dead crew. I've never been sure if the too-hot stench of burned circuitry and burned flesh simply didn't faze a Vulcan's discipline, or if some peculiarity of biology rendered them unable to smell it. Either way, I envied him.

Dragging myself to the front of my command chair, I summoned the closest thing to a command crew I had left. "Spock, Chekov . . ."

I could tell as soon as they started toward me that both officers had escaped any serious damage. Spock had a tear across one shoulder of his jacket, but the tinge of emerald that marked Vulcan blood was so faint that I doubted he'd bled much even before the medics reached us. Chekov, meanwhile, rounded the railing with most of his attention focused on the blackened circuit boards in his hands. He shuffled through them like a gambler displeased with a poker hand, and didn't seem to notice the fresh bruise running up the length of his cheekbone.

For just an instant, I wondered if I should send him below. Wasn't this the mistake I'd made last time? Letting him stay as though the only way to deal with losing your starship was to keep working as though nothing unusual had happened? I'll admit, I didn't know what else I could do. Especially now, with casualties so high, I couldn't afford to turn down any experienced officer's help. The fact that the message sent by banishing him from the bridge would have been intolerable was only incidental.

I eased myself into my seat as they joined me. "Report." God, what had I done to my shoulder? My whole arm ached like mad.

Spock folded his arms behind his back in that gesture that always made him look like a student about to deliver an oral presentation. But his voice now was low and serious. "We have sustained seven fatalities shipwide, including Lieutenant Benni. Ensign Plavi and thirty others are listed by sickbay as having serious injuries, and there are hundreds others still being treated at their stations."

Better than I had feared, but worse than any captain ever hopes for. I used my sleeve to wipe blood away from my eyes while I let him go on.

"Hull breaches in sectors four and five of the secondary hull," Spock continued. "Life-support systems are down all over the ship, and gravity is unavailable below deck twelve. Warp engines are off-line, impulse engines are marginal. Commander Rand is confident she can reinstate communications within the hour, but we are at seven percent shield strength and without long-range sensors."

I realized then that part of the background comm noise had been Rand reestablishing vital ship channels. "So we can't defend ourselves." I turned toward Chekov. "Can we fight?"

He looked up from his damaged boards for the first time, shaking his head. "Most of the torpedoes in storage survived undamaged, but launch bays one and two both took crippling hits. Automated targeting systems are off-line. Phasers are functional at one-quarter power, but only for microbursts." A little gesture with the boards, as though showing me something there. "We can't put up a sustained barrage."

Settling gingerly into my command chair, I aimed a silent curse at the shattered station still drifting near the bottom of the viewscreen. It took me a moment to realize that the screen's snowy resolution wasn't damage to its systems, but just the physical debris and waste plasma from our combat. "So they got in one last good shot." I couldn't even see the Klingon weapons array from here. "Dammit."

"I do not believe our damage was caused by the Klingons." Spock frowned up at the station as well, his head cocked ever so slightly. "At least, not directly. Based on my analysis before we lost power, I infer the Klingons here on Kreth were experimenting with focused multiphasic resonance waves." He seemed to feel that peering at me intently would help me better understand the more lofty concepts of his profession. "This would explain how their weapon was able to inflict such great damage even through our shields, as well as why destruction of the weapon would create such a powerful subspace pulse."

Chekov, on the other hand, believed in placing lofty concepts in perspective. "Like trying to disable a hydrogen bomb by blowing it up."

So it was the destruction of the weapon that crippled us, not the weapon itself. I felt weirdly sorry for the Klingons. However much that exploding resonance wave rocked us, it must have been immeasurably worse for them. "I suppose it's too much to ask that the Nykkus ships were caught in the pulse."

"Except for the Falcons," Chekov said, "they were all out of range. They came in after the resonance wave had passed, and the *Rochester* battleship towed the Falcons in to dock."

"And left us alone . . ." That detail ate at me. I tried to find the Nykkus ships through the sullen subspace glare— the Vulcan science probe, the Orion yacht, the overgunned mutt that had torn up Deep Space Three. But they were all out of sight beyond the edge of the viewscreen. If it weren't so damned unimportant, I might have asked Chambers to realign the pickups to provide a more satisfying view. "The way they used that damaged Falcon to take out the Klingon array . . ." I caught myself thinking out loud, and made an effort to carefully arrange what I was trying to say. "They'd counted on the Falcons being impossible to hit," I explained, including both men in my brainstorming.

"Counted on them to clear out the Klingon weaponry before moving in their more valuable personnel carriers. But once we proved we could shoot them, they couldn't take their time anymore. So they sacrificed one damaged ship to clear the way for the rest of their fleet." Which proved they were not only clever, but ruthless as well. Always a chilling realization. Made worse by the fact that they obviously had someone calling the shots who thought fast enough to take advantage of downturns during combat.

"They cannot have known the result of their actions would also disable the *Enterprise,*" Spock pointed out.

"No," I agreed. "But they could recognize that it had happened." I had to wipe my eyes clear again, and my head responded by banging my pulse against my ears. "So why not attack us? Why just leave us sitting here?" It occurred to me for the first time that I could conceivably pass out from loss of blood. The thought made me angry at my own human weakness.

Before I could take advantage of our silence to summon the medtech back over, Chekov said with sudden conviction, "We're the red herring." And a whole host of certainties poured through me.

Klingons were not known for broadcasting distress calls, but that didn't mean no one would come to find out what had happened here. If nothing else, patrol ships somewhere between here and the Federation border would pick up on the pulse sent out by the dying resonance gun, and one of them somewhere would know what that had to mean. They'd come expecting a tragic laboratory accident, perhaps, but they'd find the *Enterprise.* Would the two seconds they spent blasting us to atomic dust give the Nykkus time to sneak out under the confusion of the local space distortions? Who knew? We certainly wouldn't be around to find out.

"This is where we could really use those Klingon eyewitnesses," I sighed.

Spock turned to head back toward his sensors. "We have seven."

I spun so sharply in my chair that my head felt like it would explode. "What?"

"Short-range sensors are functioning at reduced range." He brought up a display on the viewscreen as though to prove his claim. "We have located a small concentration of Klingon life signals in one of the intact areas of the station."

Of which there were not many. I looked at Kreth's blackened hulk and the aurora of quantum fury suspended around it. "Let me guess—we can't beam them out because of the local subspace damage."

Spock lifted a thoughtful eyebrow. "I suspect that would present additional considerations during transporter operations," he admitted. "However, our primary obstacle is the station's own defensive screens."

"Shields?" This time I actually came up out of my seat and leaned across the railing between us. "Spock, you're kidding—that thing still has operational *shields?"* I was unexpectedly envious of the fruits of Klingon research.

"I can only infer the Klingons employed some form of multiple node shield generator network, in which part of that network remained operational even after the resonance wave."

That part must have been shielded like all hell. I forced my thoughts back to the problem at hand. "All right, so we can't pull them out. Maybe we can lead them out." I turned, still holding on to the rail, and asked Chekov, "Can you get past whatever general security measures they'd have in their labs and corridors?"

He looked only a little surprised by the question. Chekov hadn't worked full-time in security for more than eight years, but he had always been meticulous about detail and, as near as I could tell, remembered every damned thing Starfleet had ever put into his head. He'd all but majored in Klingon weaponry at the Security Academy, which made him the closest thing to an expert I had on board.

"With the right equipment," he said at last, very slowly, "yes, sir, I think I can."

From a Starfleet officer, that promise had always been good enough for miracles. I gave Spock a nod toward his console. "Tell Mr. Scott to start working on those 'additional considerations during transporter operations.' I need a one hundred percent reliable transporter for local conditions in under an hour." Then one last look at the battered research station before motioning Chekov toward the lift. "We've got Klingons to rescue."

The inside of a stripped-down FL-70 is cramped, hot, and a little too close to vacuum for my tastes. We'd torn out the weaponer's seat—along with the weapons, the engines, both wings, and just about anything else with more than ten grams of mass—to make room for a portable airlock and both environmental suits, not to mention reduce the Falcon itself to as close to a pressurized tin can as possible in under forty minutes. As it was, Chekov and I ended up wearing the torso shells and carrying our helmets, but it still made for a damned uncomfortable way to drift into the dragon's lair.

Of course, the plan was to arrive without being noticed by the dragon. Thus the removal of anything that might possibly be detected as an energy source, and our faith in the Falcon's naturally sensor-deflecting design. In the shuttle bay, long minutes before two dozen flight technicians joined forces to heave our unpowered vault into space, I suffered a moment of doubt about whether it might actually be safer to risk the half-repaired transporter and beam over. McCoy would probably say I had some unexpressed need to flaunt my own perceived immortality. But, then, he said that every time duty placed me in physical jeopardy, and it hadn't yet altered how often the situation arose. Doctors don't really know everything. Still, it was the physical limitations of the Kreth station that finally decided what form our little rescue mission would take, bulky environmental suits and all.

Spock had used one of the detached wings to spread a surprisingly concise version of the station's schematics in front of me while Chekov helped the engineers finish welding gas canisters to the Falcon's ruined nose.

"Docking facilities here, here, and here were destroyed in the combat." Spock pointed to the most convenient airlock sites, all on our side of the station. "This sector of the facility housed the resonance wave cannon—"

"So is no longer there," I finished for him. I sat down on the edge of the wing, not liking where this was going.

"The Nykkus have control of the only landing bay," he went on, "as well as all of the external docking airlocks."

I studied the clean lines of the printout, trying to reconstruct it in three dimensions with all the little alterations Spock's report implied. The end result was a very sorry picture. "That doesn't leave us a lot of places to access the station." At that point, I'd still been hoping to mate with an airlock and get on board the easy way.

Spock turned the schematic to show me the details of the section blown open by the resonance cannon's destruction. "You should be able to wedge the Falcon between decks here." He indicated a wide open gap that used to be someone's sleeping quarters. "Portions of these decks are necessarily breached to vacuum, which will guarantee you meet no Nykkus resistance while securing the Falcon."

"We'll have to go aboard in environmental suits . . ."

I glanced back at Chekov, who'd approached so quietly during our discussion, I hadn't even realized he stood on the other side of the wing until then. Behind him, what maintenance personnel Scotty would spare us busily collected their gear before heading off to tend to the ship at large. Chekov stared at the station map with his lips pressed tight, reading something in its layout that I wasn't able to see.

"Is there a problem, Commander?" I asked when he didn't say anything further.

His eyes flicked up to mine, his train of thought apparently disrupted by my question. "No . . ." Then, more firmly, as though whatever he'd been thinking was trivial and he was now convinced of the answer. "No, sir. I'm just concerned about doing the delicate bypass work in full suit."

He wasn't the only one.

"Trust me, we'll get into atmosphere as soon as we find some." I rapped my knuckles against the station proper. "Where are the Klingons in all this?"

Spock circled an area surprisingly deep in the structure, the lines of its decks and bulkheads highlighted in bright green. "They have not moved since we first detected them." He didn't have to say that this could mean anything—from the Klingons all being massively injured, to them being in stasis, to the readings being just plain wrong. I chose to believe it simply meant they were prudent, and had chosen not to roam about. I couldn't afford to have any of the other options be true. "The Nykkus are here." A much bigger area, in red, radiated outward from the airlocks the Nykkus had claimed. I noted the main operations center right in the middle of it all. "To avoid interference from the station's shields, you will need to bring the Klingons at least this far outside the shields' operative range. I would recommend the highlighted path as the most efficient route of travel."

Not to mention the one that kept us nicely away from where the Nykkus had established their foothold.

I gave us two hours to accomplish our objective. "If you detect Klingon cruisers approaching," I ordered Spock as I climbed inside the gutted ship, "or the Nykkus start pulling their ships away from the station, get the *Enterprise* out of here." In either situation, Chekov and I would have failed. The only question remaining would be whether or not the *Enterprise* could get back across the border in time to warn the Federation about the impending war.

Chapter Fourteen

SULU

"NOT-NYKKUS YOU ARE."

The dark-scaled female heading up the wedge formation blocking our tunnel passageway may have repeated her words, or my dazed brain might just have finally realized what she'd said before. The emphasis put on the connected words "not-Nykkus" made me wonder if it was a derogatory term for all beings who were not their own magnificently scaled selves.

I glanced over at Uhura, and she rose from her crouch, stepping forward with a calmness few communications officers could have summoned under the circumstances. She stood between two of the kneeling security guards, careful to go no further than that, then lifted her tricorder and held it out so the Nykkus females could see its translating display. A dozen fire-opal eyes swung from me to her, hot as predators watching prey, but still not a member of that female hunting pack stirred out of their careful wedge. They were waiting, with what might have even been termed politeness, for a spoken response.

"I am a human, and an officer of Starfleet." I spoke slowly, to give Uhura's jittering figures a chance to be seen on the tricorder display. "I cannot speak your language well, but the drawings you see on this machine might help you understand me better."

"Nykkus speech in machine this stored is," said the lead female, her powerful torso tilting forward then swaying side-to-side to nuance each of her rumbled words. "Nykkus you before met have. Where?"

I tried not to let her see how much she startled me with that swift deduction. Instead I glanced at Uhura, wordlessly giving her permission to answer that question.

"Nykkus and Anjiri we have met in this place, many years ago," said the communications officer. "Anjiri speech we have studied and kept in our machines since then."

That response, watched with all its visual nuances by a dozen intent eyes, seemed to send a jostling tide of surprise and disappointment through the pack. "Anjiri speech Nykkus speech now is." The bobbing head and lashed tail of a slightly smaller female in the second row of the wedge showed that she was the one speaking now. "Anjiri withers and gone soon is."

"Nykkus only soon remain," echoed another female. The translator ran their words together, but I suspected that was because their deep rumbling voices overlapped almost as closely as their own scales. The physical movements of their powerful torsos, lashing tails and rising heads was what really distinguished one speaker from the next in this species, and even that seemed to ripple across this coordinated hunting pack like a wave across a kelp forest. "Nykkus walk—"

"Nykkus wait," said a third.

"Nykkus return," finished the leader. It sounded like a war chant, or perhaps a sort of prayer. "Your docking hear we, Nykkus are you think we. Attack we not, if we otherwise knew."

This time the look I exchanged with Uhura was one of pure astonishment. The last thing I'd expected, when this pack of fiery-eyed predators had lunged around the corner, was an explanation and an apology for their thundering approach. I tried to remind myself that these creatures might be even more devious than their spacefaring brothers, but something about their steady gazes and interwoven voices didn't seem to allow that possibility.

"We have come to find out why *some* Nykkus have attacked our ships and space stations in the past few days," I said, putting as much emphasis as I could on the word "some" to avoid giving offense. My vehemence expressed itself by making one of the stick Nykkus figures on Uhura's display screen leap high into the air, something that seemed to amuse the females watching it. At least, I assumed that the hisses, slitted eyes and in unison swaying represented amusement.

"Rebellion *some* Nykkus made have," the lead female replied at last, her opalescent eyes still narrowed to brilliant slits. Her voice seemed to echo the emphasis I'd put on the word "some," although perhaps with a more mocking tone. "Atrocities *some* Nykkus committed have. On homeworld ours, on Egg Bringers. Meeting would wish we, dominance would do we, blood would spill we from *some* Nykkus."

I frowned, trying to follow the sense of her words. "Were they slaves of the Anjiri, these Nykkus who rebelled?" A slave uprising would explain the decimated homeworld, especially if some environmental or genetic change had altered the willingness of the Nykkus to remain subordinate to their Anjiri cousins.

"Nykkus slaves *never* were!" The leader flattened her powerful torso so that her frilled crest-rill had room to rise and express her indignation. Behind her, her sisters snarled and hissed their own rills erect in swift support. "Cold-born Nykkus leaders required, Anjiri cold-born no better would be. Cold Anjiri may have us made, but Nykkus slaves never were." Her eyes narrowed again, as if a new thought had occurred to her. "Lies *always* told are, tricks *always* played are, by Nykkus too warm born yet not hot enough. This truth you have obtained not yet?"

I opened my mouth, then closed it again and thought over her statement. I might not understand all of its subtleties, but I couldn't differ with the gist of it.

"This truth we have begun obtaining," I agreed. "These Nykkus who play tricks and tell lies—did they play a trick and leave you here when they abandoned this place?"

That question brought a chorus of deep hoots from the

entire group. I waited impatiently for the translator to give me the meaning of those sounds, and only understood them to be laughter when Uhura turned to give me a wry smile of her own. She had her fingers flexed on the controls of the translator so that her words remained in English.

"I'm glad you're amusing them, Captain. But remember that for all their politeness, these Nykkus females could be even more unpredictable and quick-tempered than the Anjiri females Captain Kirk and I met twenty years ago."

"I haven't forgotten." I listened to the roar of hooted laughter continue. "What did I say that was so funny?"

"I'm not entirely sure," Uhura admitted. "But when they were referring to the Nykkus who were 'warm-born yet not hot enough,' something in the way the translator handled that made me wonder if it wasn't another way of saying 'male.'"

"Male?"

Uhura began to answer me, but the soft echoes of the last Nykkus hoots were already dying. She turned back and released the translator's input control, holding the display screen up again just in time to catch the female leader's definitive snarl.

"Of Nykkus ignorant you must be, to think warm-born could us disdain or defy!" She paused, tilting her head to regard me with her swirling, fire-bright eyes. "If tormented by warm-born you now are, with the wisest speak you must. Come!"

It wasn't until the Nykkus had led us several hundred meters along the twisting length of one passageway and down the descending spiral of another that I noticed they weren't carrying lights. The glow of our handheld lamps didn't seem to bother them, but clearly they didn't need them to see, even in the thick darkness cast by the purple-black metal into which these tunnels had been carved. The realization made me clutch my lamp in sweaty fingers, abruptly aware of how much of a disadvantage we could be put at even if all the Nykkus did was take our illumination and leave us. I glanced over my shoulder at Schulman.

"You've recorded the route we've taken since we left the ship, Lieutenant?"

"Of course, sir." Her response was absentminded rather than indignant, even though I was questioning her on one of the most basic rules of landing party safety. Clearly, her mind was elsewhere. "Lieutenant Orsini is keeping track, too."

"Yes, sir." My security chief spoke softly, although with Uhura's augmented translator again turned off, none of our Nykkus escorts should have been able to understand him anyway. Still, after all that we had endured from this surprising alien race, I couldn't entirely blame Orsini for his caution. "I've linked my tricorder's recording loop to my communicator, so the rear guard we left aboard the *Jocelyn Bell* will know exactly how to get to us if they need to."

"Good." Most security guards would have simply assumed the signal from our communicators could provide enough information to track us down in an emergency, but in a three-dimensional maze like this planetoid, precious time was lost finding the correct route to the final location. Reporting the entire path was the kind of extra precaution Chekov would have taken, if he'd been securing this mission. Just as questioning the science officer about her distraction was the kind of extra initiative Captain Kirk would display if he'd been leading it. I slowed down a step so I could fall into stride beside her.

"What are these strange readings you're getting from your tricorder, Lieutenant?"

Her frowning gaze lifted from her display for a startled moment. "How did you know, sir?"

"By the expression on your face," I said wryly. "What's the matter?"

The corners of her mouth kicked downward. "I don't know if it's interference from all this metal ground-matrix or the way I tried to reprogram the bioscan after it did such a bad job picking up those approaching Nykkus. I thought I had fine-tuned it, and it did start picking up more life-signs ahead of us a while ago, but none of the readings look right. One seems to be the weak one I caught before, and it's still weak, which suggests an organic rather than instrumental cause—"

"In other words, a person who's sick or injured?"

"Yes, sir. It's the other ones that really bother me, though.

I'm getting at least a dozen life-signs that just don't make sense to me at all. There's a definite pulse and associated brain activity with each of them, but absolutely no respiration or thermal signature."

"Eggs," said Uhura from several steps ahead of us.

Schulman looked thoughtful. "I suppose that could explain the readings—"

She broke off as we passed through a metal-carved arch and unexpectedly found ourselves in a huge, echoing space. After a moment, I recognized it as the inverted belly of a cargo ship, welded onto the planetoid and lit with the anomalous flicker of firelight instead of the usual ship's fluorogens. The red-gold dance of flames was bright enough to drown out our hand-lamps and warm enough to banish the metallic chill of the tunnels we had traveled through. It was also wide enough to encompass a ring of what looked like large fire-charred stones in its halo of warmth.

"Eggs," Uhura repeated, as we joined her in gazing at the blackened lumps. Each was almost a meter long, smoothly rounded on one end but sharply pointed on the other, and each sat in a hollow scooped out of the native metal of the planet. Other hollows pocked the metal floor around us in concentric circles around that fire, and further out in the darkness, I thought I could see the charred pits where other fires had once burned. "This must be their nesting grounds—the place where they incubate their young."

"Lieutenant?" I asked Schulman, who'd discreetly managed to point her tricorder at the nearest lump. Our Nykkus escorts had paused with us, making respectful gestures with tails and lowered frills toward their incubating cousins. "Are these your mysterious life-signs?"

"Aye, sir. All except for the single weak one." My science officer stooped to press her hand against the purple-black metal of the floor and looked surprised. "Whatever this alloy is, it's holding a lot of the fire's warmth. In fact, it's hot enough all the way out here that I wonder—" She scanned her tricorder across the ring of eggs again, and her surprised look darkened into a frown. "Henry, can this be right? It says the ambient temperature inside those eggs is sixty degrees centigrade."

"*What?*" The xenobiologist came over to frown at the

tricorder readings. "That's not incompatible with life—but it's highly unusual. Most of the sauroid species I've encountered incubate their eggs between thirty and forty degrees."

I glanced around the ring of eggs again, seeing their fire-blackened shells in a new light. If they'd been kept so close to the fire's heat that even the crystal matrix of the eggshells had been charred—a ghost of boyhood memory rose to tickle at my consciousness. I'd never been allowed to keep all the reptiles and insects I would have liked to propagate my exotic plant collection, but that hadn't stopped me from reading everything I could about them, in the hopes that my parents would someday relent. They hadn't, and a few years later I'd transferred my enthusiasm to flying lessons instead of reptile husbandry, but I still remembered some vague rules about incubation. I glanced out at the shadowy marks of all those other empty egg-hollows, arrayed in concentric arcs farther away from the leap of flames, and my suspicions deepened.

"Henry, what effect would an overheated incubation generally have on a sauroid species?" I asked softly.

The xenobiologist threw me a glinting but unsurprised look, as if I'd caught the trend of her own thoughts. "It depends, Captain. The eggs of some species have very little temperature dependence, other than the basic threshold required for survival. Others sauroids can link sex, size, and even life-span to the temperature at which the egg was gestated." She paused, glancing back at our escort of female Nykkus. Their tails had begun to rasp impatiently across the floor and their fierce eyes refracted the firelight into blood-opal glimmers. "In temperature-dependent species, excess heat could cause malformed limbs, fused spinal disks, and infertility in extreme cases. In less severe cases, you might get more rapid development both in and out of the egg, aberrant color patterns, and inappropriate—or exaggerated—sexual behaviors."

The lead Nykkus female roared out a warning, then leaped into a powerful surge of motion again. Orsini hurriedly motioned for us to follow her, then spread his security guards around us in a protective cordon. I suspected the large, echoing space had made him fear an attack from behind or from the flank, and given the way these gem-dark Nykkus blended in with the native shadows of their homeworld, I wasn't sure I blamed him.

The resounding crash and thunder of Nykkus footsteps led us across what seemed like half a kilometer of nesting ground, until the glow of the fire looked as dim and sullen behind us as the red cinder of the Anjiri sun did in front, glittering through some salvaged porthole. The sides of the inverted cargo ship swept in like metal wings, and the space between its deck and the raw metal floor dwindled until the Nykkus had to slow to a walk and go single file, flattening their rills against their skulls for protection. I was the first to follow them, with Orsini treading right at my heels. As the space narrowed even further, the smell of corroded metal that permeated the Anjiri homeworld finally faded, but only because it was overlain with such a strong smell of musk and fetor that I could no longer smell anything else.

The dull red eye of the Anjiri sun seemed to wink at us, and the dark female Nykkus slowed to a stop, dropping to her knees with all her sisters in a single, coordinated motion. I followed suit, but it wasn't until a moment later that I realized the sun's temporary darkness had been caused by the jerky lift of a dark hand from a cluttered dais, heaped with thermal blankets and pillows. The pile looked so utterly still and crumpled in the dim sunlight, I hadn't realized there was a body buried in it. And the sound that followed that painful gesture was barely recognizable as a voice—hoarse coughing like distant gusts of wind, interspersed with long whistling noises that must be painful breaths.

"Comes . . . is . . ."

The universal translator had again given us a female voice for this speaker, but it had parsed the words out with long pauses between them, as if there were missing pieces it couldn't translate. I glanced over my shoulder at Uhura, who had lifted her augmented translator up over Orsini's shoulder. The slanting red sunlight threw exotic shadows across her sculpted face, but lit her coffee-dark eyes with sympathy.

"What's going on, Commander?"

"I'm not sure, sir, but I think she's too sick to do anything but whisper. The translator will need a little time to recalibrate for her."

Unfortunately, I wasn't sure we were going to be given that time. The female Nykkus leader had twisted around to stare at us with sun-flamed eyes and an aggressively outthrust jaw.

"Egg Bringer answer you must." Her snarl sounded like a whipcrack after the ghost-whisper of the sick female's voice. "Respect, obedience you show!"

"I wish I could," I said, hoping both she and the senior female could see the translating dance of stick figures on Uhura's screen that nuanced my words. "But our speaking machine can't hear all of the Egg Bringer's words."

"Perhaps if you could repeat what she says for a while, our machine could understand her better," Uhura suggested politely.

The tall female Nykkus tipped her head, as though listening to something we couldn't hear, then lashed her tail in swift acknowledgment, pushed herself to her feet, and launched herself toward us. I struck Orsini's hand away from his phaser, hoping to God I had guessed right about this. The massive hematite-dark body came to a halt only centimeters away, so close I could smell her own reptile musk and feel the exuded heat of her thermal armor.

"Close to Egg Bringer this machine take," she ordered. "Her own speaking to your ears must go."

I reached back to take the translation device away from Uhura, but she had already slipped past me on the Nykkus's other side and was approaching the bundle of blankets with her usual calm fearlessness. I went to push after her and bumped into a scaled, breathing wall of Nykkus instead. I scowled up at the female leader.

"Allow me through to answer the Egg Bringer!"

"Reason?" she demanded. "Not hottest of your egg pod you are."

I scowled, but before I could try to argue about something I wasn't even sure I understood, an audible hiss from the invalid interrupted. The lead Nykkus female's head snapped around and then, with a hot exhaled breath that sounded remarkably like a human sigh, she stepped back and let me through.

I joined Uhura at the edge of the blankets, crouching down as she had so the female lying there wouldn't have to lift her head too far to look at us. It was clear, now that I could actually see her painfully thin, shriveled body slumped across the stack of pillows, that this Egg Bringer wasn't just sick—she was old and probably dying. The hand she lifted to point at Uhura was twisted by some kind of degenerative bone disease into what looked like a single massive claw, while a dowager's hump of softened bone lowered her sauroid head deep onto her sunken chest. Even her lower jaw looked deformed by her illness, slid sidelong and drooping. Only in the gemstone glow of her eyes did she seem to resemble her Nykkus companions, but her far slimmer build and complete lack of tail told me the resemblance ended there. This was not an older Nykkus—it was one of the more aristocratic Anjiri species, the first we had seen in all our current dealings with these formerly allied races.

"Memory of you have we." Now that we were closer, the augmented translator seemed to be working a little better, although without the ability to nuance her words through movement, I suspected the Anjiri invalid had difficulty articulating even in her own language. "Trinkets by wanderers stolen, to air turned by you were. Promises kept."

I opened my mouth to ask what she meant, but Uhura's gentle tug on my sleeve stopped me. "She thinks you're Captain Kirk," the communications officer said softly, her fingers flexed on the translator's control panel so no figures danced her words through to the old Anjiri. "Tell her we know she kept her promise, and that we kept ours, too."

"Promises were kept on both sides," I said, as soon as Uhura released the controls again. "We left your area of space alone, and you did ours. Until now."

Her bright eyes followed the stick figure's interpretative dance across Uhura's display screen with enough understanding that a breathless snarl bubbled out of her deformed jaw when the final words were spoken. "Until now, Nykkus with Anjiri worked, promises together kept we." The bitterness of the words sizzled even through the imperfect translation. "Until fire touched. Nykkus warriors perfect were, Anjiri blood on their hands not, no eggs they

destroy. Cry the day when fire Nykkus eggs did touch!
Promises broken all, Anjiri warm-born by they killed all.
From then ever, eggs all fire-touched, eggs all Nykkus were.
Gone, gone, this world's future all. With warm-born Nyk-
kus gone, returning never."

The ancient Anjiri's coughing of words stopped, seemingly exhausted by that final spate of fury. I spared a glance
back at our Nykkus escort, but they didn't seem to be
offended by the old Anjiri's rant against their own species. I
remembered their apology when they first met us: "Nykkus
are you think we. Attack we not, if we otherwise knew."

"What happened to cause such a tragedy between the
Nyykus and Anjiri?" I asked, although I was starting to get a
glimmer of the answer. The crumpled figure on the dais
jerked a hand up again, this time pointing the fused claw
past us at the largest of the Nykkus.

"Of birthing tell," she ordered, in her hoarse snarl. The
dominant Nykkus ducked her powerful head in respectful
submission, then turned her opalescent eyes toward us and
the translating device.

"Hatched in fire, hot-born Nykkus, first in millennia are
we," she said simply. There was no pride in her voice, just a
simple realization of anomaly. "Nykkus eggs always warriors hatch, Egg Bearers and young guard they. Cold-born
obedient warriors hatch, no eggs lay, no eggs destroy.
Nykkus eggs far from fire kept, pale their shells remain.
Anjiri eggs closer and darker are, heat in brains and loins
burn they."

I frowned, beginning to see the pattern. With temperature
the deciding factor in intelligence among these sibling
species, it was clearly to the Anjiri's advantage to keep their
stronger and fiercer cousins as cold as possible while they
incubated, so that the Nykkus hatched out slow-witted and
docile. But if fertility was also predetermined by the effects
of temperature on the egg, as the young female Nykkus
seemed to imply, why hadn't her species died out centuries
ago?

I didn't have time to ask—the dark female had drawn
another exasperated human-sounding breath and was continuing her story. "Mistaken, one pod of eggs long ago was.
Anjiri eggs thought to be, close to fire set were they. Put to

be Egg Bringers well would be, hot-born danger make not we. Warm-born Nykkus instead hatched, heart-hot but brain-shadowed always are they. Skulls crushed at once, well would be, but cold-born caretakers this truth obtain do not. Warm-born live, warm-born fast grow, warm-born rebellion against Anjiri make."

"They made smarter Nykkus males by mistake," Uhura said, lifting her fingers from the translator during the next, longer pause. "And then paid the price for all those years of repression."

"Yes," I said.

The dominant Nykkus female threw us a fiery opal gaze, as if she'd guessed what we were saying without the need of a translation. I reminded myself that if the females of her species were as superior in intelligence to their males as the Anjiri females had been to theirs, I was quite probably dealing with a being much smarter than I was.

"Lies *always* told are, tricks *always* played are, by Nykkus too warm-born yet not hot enough," she repeated fiercely. "This truth in times past all obtained, to make no warm-born Nykkus agreed *all*. Lost to time, this knowledge was— in blood and murdered pods regained was it. No Anjiri warm-born alive left they, all Anjiri eggs destroyed did they! Nykkus eggs only to be hatched were, an army of glorious renown to make."

I frowned. "But how could they—"

"Captain." I recognized the urgent voice from my wrist translator, so nearly noiseless that even Uhura's translator didn't detect it as that of my xenobiologist. "I've done preliminary DNA scans on the Nykkus and Anjiri, and you need to know the results. These aren't sibling species, sir, these are co-sexes of the same species. The females can lay fertile eggs for both variants, probably because they have two different kinds of ovaries."

I glanced over at Uhura, startled, and saw her pitying look swing back to the last female Anjiri. "The warm-born Nykkus forced the Egg Bringers to bear too many eggs, so they could raise more of themselves, didn't they?" she asked.

The Anjiri female didn't answer, but her Nykkus sister— or daughter—tilted her torso far forward and opened her jaw to bare her scimitar teeth, a position that made the translator's voice roar with anger. "Egg Bringers birth-killed, bone-rotted with swift bringing did they, stupid warm-born. No more Anjiri Egg Bringers made they, stupid warm-born. Nykkus Egg Bringers to make and use thought they, *stupid* warm-born!" Her teeth glinted, reddish-purple sunlight dripping across them like blood. "One pod only in the fire burned and hatched. Even wet from eggs, *dominance* did we, blood from warm-born Nykkus spilled.

"Crush our skulls ordered they, but cold-born caretakers knowledge obtained and wiser were. Taken far were we, taken far to ancient burrows. By cold-born alone raised were we, come the time to return and dominance do." Her gape became what looked distinctly like a grimace. "But the warm-born Nykkus in theft of ships spent, too late to do dominance came we. One bone-rotted Egg Bringer alive left they. Into space all warm-born young took they, only one pod in fire put to burn left they, more Nykkuss Egg Bringers. Here wait we, here with sisters yet unborn, to dance dominance when the wanderers return do."

"But *will* they return?" I asked grimly. The question wasn't meant for the Nykkus or Anjiri around me, but Uhura's translator made it snarl and dance across the display screen nonetheless. The crumpled Anjiri female lifted her deformed snout from the thermal blankets and fixed me with a steady glare. Her coughing voice was fainter still, as if her last reserves of strength were fading, but the translator gave its human equivalent a steely note.

"Warm-born Nykkus your ships among the star battled have?"

"Yes," I admitted.

"Warm-born tricks and lies and cunning traps witnessed have you?" she persisted.

"Yes." This time the admission nearly got snapped between my teeth on its way out.

"The warm-born to this refuge return do, here to stay they forever, would have done you?"

"If possible, yes."

The sway of her head, so precariously slung on the calcium-exhausted bones of her spine, might have been either a nod or a shake or some other more alien gesture, but the triumphant gleam in her eyes was unmistakable. "This dilemma of warm-born, foreseen long have I. Broken promises vengeance upon their breakers bring, as long ago foretold you. But if complete vengeance is, disaster upon our race brings also. No more eggs can make I, warm or cold, Nykkus or Anjiri. Without warm-born to quicken them, no eggs these hot-born daughters make. Gone, all this world's future, gone with warm-born Nykkus." Her eyes flared with a last spike of determination, and her fused claw lifted to point directly at me. "Unless the hot-born to dominance among the stars bring you."

My immediate reaction was to step back in surprise, to frown at her, to ask her what she meant. But something hard and inexorable rose up inside and stopped me before I could do any of those things. It wasn't newfound strength or newly acquired wisdom. It was the relic of my defeat at the hands of the Nykkus, something I could thank them for all the rest of my life—a deep conviction that the easy, unthinking, natural response to a situation could sometimes be utterly the wrong one.

This time, that conviction held me silent and impassive as I thought over what the ancient Anjiri was suggesting. "Are you sure," I asked her at last, "that these young hot-born of yours can dominate the older Nykkus?"

Her misshapen face gaped with the ferocity of her hoarse snarl. "When wet with egg-blood, dominance did they on Nykkus many hatchings older," snapped the translator. "Close enough to warm-born see and touch, these daughters bring must you. No further battles, tricks, or lies upon your stars must Nykkus do. Home to quicken eggs and serve will come they, and glad at their bidding be."

I glanced at Uhura, not so much for consensus as to check the depth of concern in her eyes. It might be risky to take intelligent female Nykkus out into the galaxy, but their behavior had been honorable even before they'd known who we were, and their Anjiri sisters had certainly kept their end of the previous bargain they'd made with Starfleet. I thought we could count on these gem-dark female warriors to do likewise, provided we could get them close enough to get their rogue males back under control. We had to at least give them the chance to save their race—we had no other alternative. Members of the Federation are taught from childhood to avoid the needless loss of any species, and to abhor the extinction of any sentient alien race.

"We will take your daughters to the stars, to do dominance on the warm-born there." I didn't look back at my officers for consensus or support before I made that promise. It was a command decision, made because there wasn't any other choice. "But by now, your warm-born will have made enemies of other powerful starfaring empires besides our own, and we may not come in time to save them from vengeance wreaked by others."

"Swiftly go, and what can be saved, save you." The crippled Anjiri made a final gesture of benediction toward the powerful female Nykkus, then closed her fire-bright eyes and slumped torpidly down into her blankets. "For one more turning of sun alive will stay I, hope of future generations homeward brought to see. If not, then in fires of my birth will burn at last these weary bones, and to hell the souls of Nykkus with them take."

Chapter Fifteen

KIRK

THE SECURE PANEL blocking the mouth of the maintenance tunnel leapt aside so unexpectedly, I steeled myself for an out-gush of poison gas, or the concussion of a plasma grenade. Instead, we were met with only a gentle exhalation of cool air changing places with warm, and Chekov leaned inside to squint up into yet another long column of darkness. "Don't Klingons believe in emergency lights?"

A question which had grown near and dear to my heart during the last half hour. We'd stumbled across atmosphere barely a hundred meters into the station, but a positive pressure hadn't come with the other amenities I'd hoped for. Our helmet lights provided enough illumination to install the portable airlock and fill its narrow confines with gas. They could not, however, show us any way to coax open the bulkhead door which led into the pressurized station. That required an extra ten minutes of suit time while we ate most of our airlocked oxygen by cutting through the massive door with a phaser torch.

"I don't like not being able to secure this door again," Chekov had complained when we finally crawled through to the pitch black hallway on the other side. "If anything happens to our lock, we're going to evacuate the rest of the station."

With us inside. Not an unreasonable fear. Also, I suspected, not the reason he peeled out of his environmental suit soaked with sweat.

"What's your suit temperature?" I'd asked, tossing my own helmet into the web sling I'd bolted to the corridor wall. I'd managed to just reach the lower end of uncomfortable during our short trek, nowhere near hot enough to plaster my hair to my forehead much less drench my jacket.

Chekov glanced almost peremptorily at the reading on the inside collar of his breastplate, then stuffed it into the storage sling alongside mine. "Twenty degrees Centigrade."

What my mother used to call "room temperature." Perfectly normal. Unlike almost everything else about this mission.

By the time we'd reached this maintenance passage, a good kilometer further along, I'd started to wonder about the nature of equipment failures. Here we were, picking apart a space station's defenses one security door at a time, then sealing them behind us so that a casual glance would look like nothing at all had happened. Deceiving through appearances. Lying by the expediency of what others believed of what they'd see. And I thought about how easily humans could accomplish the same trick, by locking all their doors behind them, by allowing the appearance of functionality to substitute for the real thing whenever no one took the time for more than a casual glance.

The cool dry air of the station had dried Chekov's hair, but there was nothing to be done about his heavy uniform. I stood a little behind him as he verified there were no other security measures on the maintenance tunnel's hatch, and I wanted to ask him if he'd been in an environmental suit since losing the *Reliant*. If he'd known when he agreed to come with me that the first ten minutes of our trip would be the longest of his life. If he'd considered what might have happened if we'd been forced to stay in suits for thirty minutes—or an hour.

Instead, I rolled up the map in my hands and said, "Sixteen Klingon security points in less than thirty minutes. I'm impressed."

He tossed a look back at me that seemed both surprised and slightly pleased. "It only looks impressive because no one's home." He scooted away from the opening and pushed the cover plate completely aside before stuffing his tools back into their case. "Unlocking a few security doors is one thing. Doing it without anyone noticing is something else."

I went first up the open-runged ladder, my hand lamp wedged into my grip alongside the ladder's holds. The climb was the worst. Twelve steps up, the only thing I could see below me was the flicker of Chekov's light as he brought up the rear; ahead, my lamp cut a pitifully small swath out of the darkness. We could have dangled four hundred miles above the abyss and it wouldn't have been more black. We had phasers we couldn't reach, communicators that did us no good whatsoever now that we were deep inside the Klingons' shield, and a satchel filled with security-technician paraphernalia that was only worth its weight against pass boxes and sector doors. If someone closed in behind us or swooped down from above, about the only good either of us could do would be to warn the other. Not exactly my idea of an equitable division of risk.

I felt better once we reached a side passage. It was decadently wide by human standards, built to accommodate Klingon shoulders. I couldn't have hit my head on the ceiling without standing almost upright. All fours still made for the best mode of transport; I clenched the wrist cord on the lamp in my teeth and let it dangle as I pushed the map ahead of me one arm's-length at a time. The cone of light swung and jiggled, but it managed to catch enough details off the conduit-crowded walls and ribbed flooring to give me some vague idea where we were. Impressionistic map interpretation. Pausing, I settled back on my heels to stretch my spine, and to give my eyes a break from the headache-inducing wobble of light against dark. "We need to start looking for an exit hatch," I called back to Chekov. "If the Klingons haven't moved, we should be practically on top of them by now."

The floor in front of me shattered with enough force to pitch the map into the air and slap the light out of my teeth. A flurry of self-indictments raced across my mind—I should have sent Chekov first to search out booby traps; I should have led with a tricorder, not a phaser, to verify each centimeter of the structure's integrity; I should have known that Klingons would never let themselves be rescued without a fight.

The *bat'leth* twisted savagely into the metal, ripping it like paper. The floor beneath me tore downward in a single ragged sheet, and I had time for only one abortive grab at an overhead conduit before pitching down into blinding brightness.

Instinct made me roll the instant my shoulders slammed into a hard surface. In theory, this would be the deck, and being in motion would render me harder to hit while I tried to explain what I was doing here. In reality, the table now forced to catch my weight, in addition to a Klingon's armored mass, collapsed with a splintered crash. My attempt at evasion gained me only a metal-clad boot in the chest, and I ended up sprawled face-up beneath a *bat'leth* with someone's heel grinding into my throat.

A harsh female's voice commanded, *"Mev!"* just as my own eyes flashed to a movement in the hole above me and I saw Chekov lean through with his phaser armed.

"Hold your fire!"

Klingon and human both obeyed with laudable speed. The Klingon froze in midswing, his *bat'leth* swept back over one shoulder in what I'm sure would have ended up as a clean decapitation. Chekov more prudently shrank back from the opening, leaving only the washed-out glow from the lantern he'd discarded in the passageway behind him.

"What unexpected guests." This time I recognized the flat burr of an intercom in the still distinctly female voice. "Vardok, release him."

I've never understood how Klingons manage to balance their enthusiasm for battle with unquestioning obedience to sometimes less than blood-happy commanders. Vardok, though, proved himself a warrior with mettle. Taking two long strides away from me, he let his *bat'leth* fall across his front, the way a ballplayer might stand while awaiting his turn at bat. I noticed he was missing most of the flesh along one side of his face, and three of the fingers on one hand had been torn away. I'd never seen anyone, excluding Vulcans, sustain such hideous injuries in stoic silence. I didn't know whether to be respectful of the Klingon's inner strength, or just very, very afraid.

I opted for keeping one eye on him while doing what I'd come for. Heart pounding, I rolled carefully to my knees and took stock of the surroundings before trying to stand. At first glance, it looked like a sickbay. Then I realized there were no beds, no diagnostic tables, not even the shelf after shelf of hyposprays that I'd grown used to seeing in McCoy's domain. The six other Klingons detected by Spock's sensors all clustered behind a long stretch of transparent aluminum. They wore jumpsuits of a trim, pocket-filled design, with silver and hematite piping that I suspected denoted rank, or position, or perhaps what areas of the station they were allowed to access. I wondered if they were part of some closed environment experiment, or if they'd fled here seeking safety when the Nykkus attack began.

Then I remembered that even Klingon scientists probably never fled.

"Captain—" The speaker turned out to be a female young enough to be Vardok's daughter. Her angular face showed only the disdainful pride I'd learned to identify as the Klingon default expression, but near her hip she clutched a small data pad so tightly that she'd cracked the screen. Perhaps Klingon scientists weren't quite as fierce as their military counterparts after all. "Please," she said, sounding strangely like she meant to be both fierce and courteous, "do us the honor of bringing your soldier down to join us."

I stepped clear of the hole Vardok had torn in the ceiling, keeping my hands carefully away from my sides. "Chekov, come on down. This is what we came here for."

He slid through the hole without answering, catching the edge in both hands and lowering himself toward the ground. All in all, a neater landing than my own. As he moved to stand beside me, the female behind the transparent wall remarked to the other five crowded in with her, "What more proof do you need that Federation ships do not necessarily mean Federation attackers?" But she said it just a bit too loudly, as though meaning it for my ears as much as theirs.

"Even Starfleet is not foolish enough to send only two human warriors to deal with us."

I took her assertion as a promising sign. "We're not here to fight. I'm Captain James T. Kirk—"

It was Vardok, his voice slurred and bloody, who rumbled, "We know who you are."

I've never been sure how to react to having my reputation proceed me. I turned partway toward Vardok, including him in the discussion. "Your attackers are pirates who hijacked Federation ships. We came to try to stop the attack, but our ship was caught in the subspace pulse when your resonance cannon was destroyed."

A little murmur of what might have been recognition passed through the Klingons behind the barrier. Vardok had returned to stoicism, not even meeting my gaze when I looked at him.

"So your ship is crippled," the female said. Implying they understood at least a little of what their cannon could do, and perhaps even what it had done to their own station. "Surely you did not come here to apologize for being defeated in combat."

"I came to appeal to your honor." I felt Vardok's eyes on the back of my head, and reminded myself to tread carefully. The Klingons behind the partition might seem to be calling the shots, but Vardok was still the one out here with the sword. "Even if the Nykkus haven't found you yet, they will soon. You'll be killed, the Nykkus will leave, and your government will arrive to find a research outpost that was apparently destroyed by the Federation." I gave them a moment to follow that thought a few months, or years, into the future. "There is no honor in declaring war against the wrong enemy."

The female nodded slowly. "You have a keen understanding of Klingon honor, James T. Kirk." She seemed to notice the data pad in her hand for the first time, and slipped it out of sight into one jumpsuit pocket. "So you would have us stand witness for what truly happened here. How did you plan to use your crippled ship to ensure that?"

"We have a transporter. Right now, you're underneath one of the station's remaining defensive screens. If you would follow us—"

She pounded one fist against the transparent aluminum wall, so hard I would have expected the material to crack. But it didn't even rattle. It just made a deep, dull thumping, like stones against a starship's hull. I understood what she was telling me even before she said it. "We can follow you nowhere. The automatic security systems sealed these rooms when the attack began. It cannot be opened from inside, or from where you stand." She spread her arms in the almost universal gesture of helplessness. It looked particularly ill-fitting on a Klingon.

That stirring in my gut that had kept me awake nights since leaving the *Excelsior* kicked in with renewed vigor. I didn't like the precedent set by having the fundamental elements of a plan go awry. "If we can't move you out from under the shield, then we have to bring the shield down." I extended a helpless gesture of my own. "Where's the generator?"

Hesitating only momentarily, she motioned me to approach the divider. Inside, probably the last working computer terminal on the station cast a pale glow across her face as she sat to wake up its system. It must have be shielded inside this isolated clean room, along with at least some small computer dedicated to keeping it alive. The other Klingons clustered in a ring barely big enough to let me see what she was doing.

"The generator is here." The kind of layout starships often keep on hand for new personnel popped up on her screen, and she pointed with authority at the general operations center. Smack in the middle of Nykkus country. She split the screen to display an innocuous square housing, its front marked by nothing except the Klingon "Do Not Enter" that Chekov and I had gotten so skilled at ignoring lately. "You need to use a maintenance command code to open the housing." She glanced over her shoulder at an older male Klingon in a dull gray robe. He spoke to her briefly, and she typed the run of figures onto the screen. "Lork says this code will serve that purpose. The generator itself is inside."

I studied the numbers, but the code was really the least of my worries. "There are Nykkus all over that part of the station. We can't very well just walk in and turn it off."

She swivelled away from her computer to look at me, then beyond me. "This warrior with you—he understands how our weapons work?"

I didn't have to glance back at Chekov to know where she was looking. "Yes. He knows them well."

"Then we will show you the place on Kreth where research was done on directional explosive devices." I knew the kind she meant—the kind you planted ahead of your own troops that projected its force so specifically, you could be sure it would only wipe out things in one direction. "You should be able to find everything you need to build a very useful bomb," she assured me with great sincerity. "Blast your Nykkus out into space. You will have us alive to speak on your behalf to our people, and we will have our revenge for the dead." A truly Klingon smile bared her teeth, and I wasn't sure I liked how they gleamed. "An elegant solution to both our problems, don't you think?"

The fact that any explosion which destroyed the operations center would probably also suck most of the air out of the rest of the station didn't seem to concern them. Why should it? They were in an airtight room, and had nothing better to do with their time. They could be beamed out once the explosion was over. Vardok, meanwhile, would be honored to join his fallen comrades at the gates of Sto'vo'kor. At least, so they assured me. Vardok himself had surprisingly little to say on the matter.

Unlike Vardok, we had suits, which made me feel only marginally better about it. I hailed the *Enterprise*. "Pick up any Klingon life-signs not grouped tight with the others," I told Spock. "Beam him in first." But it was a messy, interference cluttered communication, and I wasn't entirely sure he understood what I'd asked him to do.

"Still no word from Sulu," I announced once I'd closed the channel and turned back toward the inside of the lab. It didn't seem prudent to mention that, with as spotty as our own communication with the *Enterprise* was, it probably wasn't reasonable to expect to hear from the other captain until he was right on our doorstep. "Are we ready to go?"

Chekov sat in front of the workbench with his hands folded on top of it, his chin resting on his hands, and his dark eyes boring into the exotic contraption he'd just put together one piece at a time. "I'm thinking it through." It was a bit unnerving to watch—I could almost see him reexamining the parts in his mind, stepping through each of their functions until the final point where detonation destroyed them all. About the time I was thinking of urging him to hurry, he sat back with a sign and reached for the small, studded cylinder that he'd already told me was the detonator/timing device for the bomb. I remembered finding it eerie to be saving such an innocuous yet deadly piece for last. "It's not as focused as I would like," Chekov admitted as he quickly examined the detonator under his light, "but it should work."

So we stood a little farther behind it, or we would do what armies sometimes did and completely retreat from anywhere near the device before setting it to explode. If it could do even half the damage Chekov predicted for the little device, it would work more than just well enough.

I stayed in the laboratory doorway as he primed the last piece for insertion. It was dark in here, just like everywhere else. I'd let Chekov take both lanterns so as not to ruin my night vision as I crouched outside to guard the hall. Now he sat in the midst of their combined glow with half the contents of his equipment kit spread out on the workbench, a confusion of Klingon tools, devices, and parts discarded nearby. In that moment, while he put the finishing touches on the one item that meant the success or failure of everything we'd come here to do, he seemed so comfortably settled and sure of his work, so far removed from the guilt-wracked officer I'd beamed aboard a few hours ago, that I had to ask, "What's the difference?"

He tossed me a silent question out of the corner of his eyes, but didn't stop working.

"Between this and command," I added. I stepped inside the doorway, as though for privacy, even though there wasn't anyone within this whole section of the station who might possibly hear. "At this moment, you're responsible for the ship, those Klingons, for both our lives . . ."

He gave a little nod of understanding, finally catching up to my thought processes. "No, sir," he said, clicking the detonator firmly into place, *"you're* responsible. I'm just one of the tools you use to get the job done." A single white light blinked alive on top of the device. "I wasn't very good at taking care of my own tools."

I watched the care with which he collected his kit together, checking each piece for damage, wiping each one clean on the sleeve of his jacket. I found it hard to believe he'd been any less conscientious with his people. "You had some pretty heavy extenuating circumstances."

"That doesn't bring them back." He slipped the last piece into its slot in the satchel, and closed the case. "I thought at first that I should somehow make up for being the only one left . . . by not running away from my duty, by taking the new assignment and being better . . ." But then he shook his head, as if even he realized how little sense thoughts like that made when you had to speak them aloud. "Now . . ." He slid the bomb into one hand and stood. "I'm ashamed at how good I am at this." He looked not at the bomb, or at his tools, but just at me, presenting himself with all these pieces as his evidence. "At being someone else's tool, and not the craftsman."

I wished—not for the first time since bringing him aboard—that we had the leisure to do more than just stumble across these things in the midst of crisis. Instead, all I could say was, "You have nothing to be ashamed of. You'd make a fine addition to any crew."

An unexpected flush dashed up his cheeks. "We should get going." He reached back for the lanterns, tossing mine toward me with a neat underhand. "It's a long walk back to our suits."

Not as long as the walk out from them. The already opened security doors helped, I'm sure, but it was adrenaline that pushed me at a near-trot the whole way. Just before we rounded the last corner leading to the storage sling where we'd left our suits, I mentally cautioned myself not to get too comfortable with this apparently abandoned station. We'd traveled the same routes too many times now, grown too used to the idea that the routes Spock had marked for us were somehow magically more safe than others. Once we were suited up again and making our clumsy way through the corridors closest to the Nykkus base of operations, we couldn't afford to be so cavalier.

In that regard, then, the Nykkus clustered around our ruined suits were not a complete surprise. Nor was their speed in dashing in to surround us, nor was their fierceness in tackling Chekov and slamming me against the wall. In retrospect, the only thing that I could never have expected, even after reading the *Excelsior* crew's reports, was how hideously a Nykkus tail could hurt when it smashed into you at full, whistling speed.

I crashed back into consciousness while half-choking on pain.

"Captain . . . easy . . ."

It was like zero-G, with no concept of up and down, only brighter and smelling pungently of reptile musk and Klingon blood. I couldn't see clearly, couldn't seem to remember how to breathe. I tried to push myself away from whatever crowded against my cheek and shoulder, but just the thought of shifting my elbow ripped such pain through my chest that I shouted profanities and curled in on myself.

"Sit up!" Hands gripped the front of my jacket, heaving me upright through pain's sticky surface tension. As soon as I was vertical—even before I realized it was a wall that patiently took my weight—the crushing heaviness lifted off my rib cage. I took a careful, pain-clouded breath as Chekov instructed me, "Captain, take this."

It's amazing what being able to breathe does for one's perspective. Taking the wadded-up jacket he thrust into my arms, I hugged it against myself like a lifesaving float. More stress removed from my protesting rib cage, and a return to vision as my blood pressure came down. Much more practical first aid than anything I'd ever been forced to study. They must teach them this stuff at the Security Academy.

We'd made it to central operations a bit more straightforwardly than I might have preferred. A big, open room with dark metal walls and only the ghost of emergency lighting ringing the ceiling and every empty panel. Stations cluttered the space in what seemed a thoroughly nonergonomic manner, but perhaps it was just an expression of Klingon aesthetics. There were no chairs.

Nykkus milled in groups of two, three, seven, walking

over what was left of dead Klingons with as little reaction as when they walked over their own filth. Moving, upright, their dark, metallic scales flashing, they were more intimidating than they'd seemed on a cold morgue slab. Infinitely more intimidating than a mere two decades ago. Four of them entertained themselves by chuffing and barking into our confiscated translators, but they were too far away for us to hear what they were saying. Probably the Nykkus equivalent of "the quick brown fox." Two others sat together in a corner, one studiously carving fresh whorls into the other's cheeks. The largest group of them, though, busied themselves with our phasers, targeting objects all throughout the room. They'd apparently discovered the heat generation settings. Every time they fired on something and sent it bursting into flame, they went into a frenzy of excitement, racing in and out among each other, leaping into the air. They reminded me of a bunch of nine-year-old boys shattering glass bottles with an air rifle.

It was the angular lump of gray metal on the far side of the room, agonizingly distant from my hurting self, that made my stomach twist in frustration. "The shield generator."

"I know." Chekov, on his knees in front of me, twisted a grim look over his shoulder. "I don't think they've even tried to get it open."

Of course not. The housing could have been a seat, or one of a dozen other strange structural irregularities that jutted out from walls and floors around the place. It occurred to me that I had no idea what all those other boxes might contain. I found myself wishing we had the time to examine them all.

But we had time for very little, really. Regaining my sense of command, I focused on Chekov for the first time since he'd pulled me upright. "Are you all right?" The sleeve of his blue tunic was wet with blood from the elbow down, as though one of the Nykkus had gripped him a bit enthusiastically, but his eyes looked remarkably bright and clear from pain.

"Better than you." He stretched his arm out—to flex his hand and prove nothing was broken, I thought. But then he closed his fingers firmly around my wrist and squeezed. I felt the smooth regularity of metal pressed against my skin, and realized with a start what it was: my wrist communicator. I glanced down and saw Chekov's own communicator on his wrist, its little status display informing me that it was turned on and a channel to the ship already open. Apparently, the Nykkus were better at recognizing weapons.

"The Nykkus found our environmental suits and destroyed them," Chekov explained. His eyes never left mine, but I knew the words were for the sake of whoever else might be listening. "You have at least a few broken ribs, and probably a concussion—you've been unconscious for nearly twenty minutes. We have fourteen minutes left of the window you afforded Mr. Spock for this mission."

And we were either close to completing that mission or farther from it than ever before. "Whether or not Mr. Spock sticks around past that will have to be up to him." We might as well supply him with some useful information in the meantime. "We're obviously in the main operations center. Why are we still alive? What are they waiting for?"

"The Raask has to visit each of their cargo ships in order to check with the crews." He added with a certain amount of satisfaction, "I don't think their communications equipment is working very well."

I frowned, still on his first bit of information. "What's the Raask?"

A commotion at the other end of the room sucked the attention of all the other Nykkus like a fireball sucks oxygen. They dropped their toys, jumped away from their wrestling and dancing, and clattered for the source of their fascination with high, grating squeals and breathy hisses. In front of me, Chekov shuffled quickly back as though anxious to make room between the two of us. The glare he threw toward the approaching band was pure hatred.

"The Raask," he said grimly, "is them."

They stood out from the rest of the Nykkus the way a mastiff stands out from a herd of deer. Seven of them, their bodies a mass of ritual scarring, their dorsal crests erect, their muzzles crowded with at least one extra row of teeth. They were obviously older than the less scarred, less finished males around them, their dominance dripping off them like hot wax. All of them carried Klingon disruptors, and three had what looked like raw Klingon skull plates fastened to their body armor. Their tails were plated with scales so sharp, I knew they must augment their natural shape with filing. If I'd been hit with one of those tails, there'd have been little left between my collarbones and pelvis for Chekov to worry about taking home. Every detail of their hot, closely knit unit was so intensely beautiful, so terrifying that I momentarily despaired of ever standing up to them.

They spread into a flying wedge as they drew close to us. Chekov stood, drawing their attention, and they swept into a prowling circle around him, tails rattling against the floor in a private rhythm that seemed to pass back and forth between them.

"Hurtful things from this creche fine are. Objects beauteous . . ." They each wore a Starfleet translator—stolen, no doubt, from the *Excelsior*'s resupply team. Their voices— one voice—slithered out of all the units at once, granting them a strange sibilance that wasn't at all inappropriate.

One of them, taller and more heavily boned than the others, halted its prowling to roll our newly made bomb out of the pouch it wore around its waist. "The Raask this thing as one with the others knows. Design and housing, prettily the same are." It leaned close to breathe the question into Chekov's face. "What this creates?"

Chekov tipped his chin a bit defiantly upward, and told them, "It's a bomb."

The Raask blurred into movement. I rocked up onto my knees in alarm, choking back an uprush of pain and praying I didn't see one of those sharpened tails lash out in a spray of blood and human entrails. "Scaleless!" The large, dark Nykkus—the leader?—pummeled its siblings aside and bent low over where Chekov had ended up sprawled on the floor. "Toothless-born! Think mammals not their faces the Raask can know? Think this mammal tricks and lies no payment to the Raask bear must?"

I tried to see past the swarm of their bodies, but even after struggling upright, I had to content myself with watching for signs of blood on Nykkus teeth and tails.

"Know this mammal well the Raask do. Lies and slinking dance this mammal do." It sank into a squat, the bomb cradled like a baby on its taloned hand. "Star-bright vast expansion not," it declared, almost sweetly. "This mammal always lie do. The Raask this so knows does. Thing hurtful the Raask believe this does do. Object beauteous to mammal for all lying pay. See?"

It rolled the bomb from hand to hand, metal-polished talons clicking against its duranium surface. When one arching thumb claw pried at the detonator tab, I couldn't keep my mouth shut any longer. "Stop!"

Half the Raask whirled on me, crouching in suspicion. Their leader simply ceased all movement, its gemlike eyes staring into space with what I could only take to be annoyance at my interruption. "What mammal dancing so this is?" it asked at last.

I heard Chekov's voice call frantically from within their cluster, "Captain, don't—!"

He had caught their attention again with horrifying efficiency. I lurched a few unsteady steps forward, still hugging the balled-up jacket against me and hoping it would prove enough support to save us both. "I mean it!" Shouting made my head spin in sick circles. "If you kill him, I won't tell you a damned thing, and you'll all die."

One of the Raask slammed its tail against the floor, making the younger Nykkus around their edges skitter back and sink low. "Dancing so this mammal also touted." The words came from all of them, any of them. "This mammal lies make did."

"But I'm not lying." I shuffled a few steps close, still trying to get a good look at Chekov where they kept him pinned to the floor. "And neither is he. He's trying to trick you. He's counting on you not believing him so that you'll experiment with that device and blow yourselves up."

A ripple of coordinated movement passed among them. "Mammal's death also this dance make would."

Yes, but I don't think he cares about that right now. "Why do you think I'm stopping you? I don't want to die." I staggered to a stop next to one of the dead control consoles, only to discover that nothing feels like useful support when your ribs are too battered to let you lean. "You think I'm lying? This mammal—" I jabbed a finger toward Chekov, who was in the middle of their bundle. "You believe he hates you? You believe he would do anything to destroy you, even destroy himself?"

For the first time, very little movement wove through their pod. I wondered if they were thinking, or if there were gestures in their language so subtle the human eye couldn't even see what they were.

"If you think I'm lying," I said, "then hand that device to him and see what he does with it."

Tails rattling, teeth clacking in obvious threat, the Raask drew apart like a door irising. Chekov stood slowly, relieving at least a little of my breathlessness, and looked at me with incomprehension clouding his expression. He wasn't hurt, though. For all their speed and ferocity, they apparently knew how to temper their outbursts so as to preserve a victim for torture. What interesting evidence of civilization.

The lead Raask balanced the bomb on the palm of its broad hand, and thrust the device toward Chekov. My officer stared at the bizarre gift while I thought as fiercely as I could, *Do what you said you're good at—be the tool! Let me be the captain, and just do what I expect of you without questioning it.*

As though my thoughts arced across the distance and into his brain, Chekov gave a decisive little nod, took the bomb from the Raask, and pulled out the switch. Squawking a brief Klingon warning, the bomb began its countdown.

If they'd learned nothing else in capturing Kreth station, the Nykkus had learned the difference between a handgun and a weapon of mass destruction. They fell on Chekov like football players all going for the same ball. One of them came up with the gleaming metal device in both hands, and dashed toward me while commanding shrilly, "Undo! Undo!"

I jerked my chin toward where the other members of the Raask might very well have killed Chekov already. "Let him go." They might not be able to read the Klingon numbers marching across the face of the bomb in their hands, but I could. I knew exactly how much time we had.

I made them place Chekov next to me and back two large steps away before finally taking the heavy device. I pushed the timer back inside the body, and the countdown stopped. The Raask insisted on examining the quiescent, but not defused, bomb.

"Why this mammal's entrails safeguard you do?" one of them asked, tossing the bomb to one of its companions now that it was no longer interesting. "Why its bones protect you do?"

I looked at Chekov, who still bore the slightly stunned expression of a man who'd avoided unwanted death by far too close a margin. I took that as a good sign. "Because he still has uses. I'm not done with him yet." I stood as straight as possible, hoping that made me appear honest. "I can show you how to find the replicator equipment you came here for."

"No objects of duplication smelled have we!" But there was a certain hopeful lust in the lead Raask's eyes when it dashed foward. It never shifted its eager attention from me, but still slashed a hate-filled glare at Chekov. "Lies this mammal do!"

"He's not the one telling you this—I am." Clinging to my wad of jacket like a lifeline, I pushed away from the station I'd been using for support. Chekov caught my arm, and I leaned on him as heavily as I dared as I limped toward the generator housing. "This station belongs to our enemies. You can build a hundred armies in their space and I wouldn't care. You'll just keep them busy." It was smaller than the upright consoles, just the right size to sit on when you didn't think you could stand a moment longer. "They know how dangerous their replication technology could be in the wrong hands. So they've hidden it under a masking field. That's why your sensors don't work well around this station, why you're having trouble communicating with your ships." I thumped one foot against the innocuous housing. "The controls are in here."

I motioned Chekov to slide aside the access door, but the Raask was faster. Snatching him away from me, their leader flattened its hand across the commander's middle in a gesture whose threat was more than merely obvious. "Like this mammal you falsehoods do, like this mammal also you die do."

I attempted a thin smile. "I was already clear on that."

Thank God for Starfleet training and the sense to pay attention to everything. I hesitated only long enough to recall the Klingon figures Lork had donated to our cause, then keyed open the housing with an authority I didn't entirely believe myself. The inside surprised me with an intricate network of displays and colored lights. I'd almost forgotten how working Klingon equipment looked. I found the master circuit near the rightmost edge of the generator's system board; prying it out was harder. Sweat stung my eyes, and I felt more than just a little dizzy by the time I succeeded in wedging a finger under the flange and popping it upward. Almost immediately, the lights on the face of the generator died. I imagined I could feel the mighty shielding fall.

Straightening, I clenched the master circuit in my fist as tightly as I could. And I smiled. All triumphant traitors should face their captors with a smile.

The lead Raask dashed forward to thrust its big muzzle into the open housing. It's throat rippled with a purr of delight. "Field of masking gone now is. What now we do?"

"Now we see if Mr. Spock decided to stick around."

Even these new and improved Nykkus were faster physically than mentally. By the time the transporter's whine grew into a wail around us, it was already too late for them to stop us. Too late to do more than swipe harmless talons through our fading silhouettes, too late to seek another sheltered part of the station.

Too late, even, to snatch back the shield master circuit that I still held safely clenched in my hand.

Chapter Sixteen

SULU

"STILL NO CONTACT with the *Enterprise*?"

I'd made the request enough times in the last few minutes that Uhura didn't even bother to glance up from the controls of her communications console on the *Jocelyn Bell* when she answered. "No, Captain. I've even tried tight-beaming a signal directly to her presumed location at Kreth, but there's no reply."

I swung my frown to the console on the left and my chief science officer. "The *Enterprise* still hasn't appeared on our long-range sensors? We're within ten minutes of arrival."

Christina Schulman shook her head. "The integrity of subspace itself seems to be badly damaged around that Klingon research station, Captain. It's almost as if some kind of phase demodulation of space has occurred there. I don't think you're going to get sensor or communications contact until we're within visual range."

"Warm-born there known still to be?"

I glanced over my shoulder at the two-meters-plus of Nykkus leaning forward to peer at the *Jocelyn Bell*'s small viewscreen. I could remember thinking on the journey out to the Anjiri homeworld that this wide-bellied cargo shuttle was almost too big for comfort. The once roomy command console in front of the two long rows of passenger seats now seemed small when the rear cargo area held a restless coil of Nykkus, conversationally snarling and snapping and jostling each other with powerful shoulders as they vied for places behind the viewscreen. My nervous security chief hadn't taken his eyes off them since we'd boarded, but there'd been no attempt to break the agreement we'd made back in the sullen red light of their own sun. Unlike their male counterparts, the hot-born female Nykkus seemed to understand the wisdom of not making enemies when you didn't need to.

"We won't know that until we get there," I told her. The Nykkus made the snapping sound with her jaws that seemed to be their equivalent of a nod without even glancing at the jittering stick figure on the augmented universal translator. The Nykkus were growing more and more comfortable with just the sound of our translated voices as this trip progressed, at a rate I might have found disturbing if I didn't have more important things to worry about. Like whether Captain Kirk and the *Enterprise* had fallen victim to the warm-born Nykkus the way the *Excelsior* had, or if the Klingons had simply annihilated all of them together in a fit of imperious wrath at the infringement of their territory.

"This vessel cannot faster go?" The female's fire-opal gaze slanted past my shoulder at the *Jocelyn Bell*'s display of warp output and velocity. It was such a reasonable thing for someone to do while asking that question that it took me a minute to realize this particular young sauroid had never been trained in space-flight procedures.

"No," I said flatly.

She snapped her scimitar teeth together again, equably enough, and gave up her place to another of her sisters. This one used her time to simply stare at the viewscreen for several long moments. Then, just as I began the *Jocelyn Bell*'s smooth deceleration curve, she stabbed a single onyx-colored claw at the display's polysilicon surface. "This star our destination is," she said, not making it a question.

"Yes," I said, wondering how she'd calculated that. We decelerated out of warp and promptly entered a region of normal space lit with a pale, ghostly glow, as if a shred of nebula or planet-forming plasma had streaked through and left it subtly energized. I ran a quick systems check of all my piloting controls, but saw no interference on the boards. "Schulman?"

"I think we're seeing the effects of that subspace dephasing I picked up earlier on sensors, sir." My science officer was hunched over her sensors now, running one analysis after another. "I don't think it's natural, sir. Some kind of subspace explosion or cosmic string eruption—"

"Or space-battle?" I asked grimly, seeing the darkened silhouette of a Klingon station slide into view without any indication of lights or power glowing within. There was still no sign of the *Enterprise,* but at this range the station could be blocking her from us.

"Possibly, sir. But if so, the weapons used don't match the output of anything in Starfleet's data banks."

"This world builds, who?" asked the Nykkus, peering at the station on the viewscreen so intently that her powerful head hung nearly level with my own. "You?"

"No. It belongs to our enemies, a race of warriors called Klingons." I began to cut back the *Jocelyn Bell*'s impulse engines as we drew closer to Kreth. From behind me, I could hear Lieutenant Orsini whistle in soft astonishment at the black stabs of phaser burns and lesions of hull breaches that marred the station's sides. "Why?"

"Built too simple it is," said the charcoal-colored female, crinkling her muzzle in distaste. "Windows too few, floors too few. And to space, too many holes is."

Before I could explain that hull breaches hadn't been included in the original Klingon blueprint, the architectural critic was shouldered aside by the largest and most dominant of the pod. I was starting to be able to tell the Nykkus apart by the different undertones of garnet, sapphire, and amethyst that gleamed like a raku pottery glaze across their dark scales. The leader of the group was almost completely black, with only a splash of twilight color at her throat. I wondered if that meant her egg had received the most charring and heat.

"Weapons of distant murder at this place have they." She pointed to the phaser scars showing on the viewscreen, confirming my suspicions that she was not only the biggest but also the brightest of her pod. "If warm-born now this place control, dominance afar must we first do, with our own distant weapons use. Weapons powerful enough we have?"

I gave her a startled look. These hot-born sauroids with their gleaming hematite scales and opalescent eyes had seemed utterly adapted for their simple life back in the tunnels of the Anjiri homeworld. I'd wondered how they would react to the cultural shock of Starfleet technology, but I'd never suspected they would absorb and encompass it in a few short hours. They'd given such close scrutiny to every move we made since boarding the *Jocelyn Bell* that by now I had the uneasy feeling they could have flown the ship themselves if they wanted to. That swift Nykkus adaptability helped me understand how their rogue male counterparts had cut such a swathe of destruction through two overwhelmingly superior space-powers. It also made me wonder what would have happened if this complex sauroid species had decided long ago to control their disruptive Nykkus males by incubating warrior eggs too hot rather than too cold.

Uhura swung around before I could answer the hot-born female's question. "Captain, I'm getting a reply from the *Enterprise!*"

"Sulu." That was Kirk's grim face, unmistakable even through the drizzle of interference on the viewscreen. "Security protocol delta."

I nodded as the communications officer made the necessary encryption modifications to her console. "Protocol engaged, Captain," I said and saw his own confirming nod. "What is your situation?"

"We've got the leaders of the Nykkus pirates in our brig, but we're not going anywhere with them soon," Kirk said. He looked tired. We'd all had a very, very long day. "The Klingon station sent a distress call out when the Nykkus first attacked it. About an hour ago, our old friend Captain Koloth showed up with a couple of Klingon warships."

"Is he holding the Federation responsible for the attack on the research station?"

"No, thanks to a few surviving Klingon eyewitnesses." Kirk threw a wry glance over his shoulder, and I finally realized that the familiar figure manning the *Enterprise*'s security station was my own executive officer. Chekov's dark gaze lifted to meet Kirk's—and mine—for a rueful moment, then dropped to his panel again. "But Koloth is demanding that we give the Nykkus ringleaders over to him for the execution of Klingon justice."

"Which usually boils down to plain old execution," added Doctor McCoy sardonically, from his usual place beside Kirk's command chair.

I glanced back at the knot of hot-born Nykkus in the cargo shuttle, guessing from the way their scales had lifted and flushed with purple blood that they'd had no problem following this conversation. A strong tang of musk now pervaded the shuttle's atmosphere. "Is Koloth threatening to attack if you don't surrender the Nykkus to him?"

"No, but if we don't he's threatened to take his revenge against the shipload of younger Nykkus he captured when he took control of the station." Kirk's face turned grim again. "That's why I need to know what you found out at the Anjiri homeworld, Captain. Are these Nykkus pirates criminals in their own society? Can we turn them over to the Klingons with a clear conscience?"

The image of a crippled and dying Anjiri female rose in my mind and I opened my mouth to say "yes." But my new inner reluctance to accept easy solutions at their face value stirred again, forcing me to stop and turn toward the silent Nykkus at my back. She opened her mouth wide, in the snarling gape that seemed to be an expression of both anger and resolution among her species.

"Criminals are they, criminal to us before all others!" she declared. "But to us must these criminals return, or else forever our race dies. Warm-born males by mistake were made, and their tricks and lies on Anjiri first they played. Now only hot-born females we remain. Warm-born Nykkus need we, both race of Nykkus and Anjiri to re-create." Even their translated syntax was getting better.

Kirk's eyebrows shot upward. "Sulu? Is that true?"

"Yes, Captain. The Anjiri and Nykkus are members of the same species, their sexes and personalities decided by the temperature at which their eggs are incubated. Thanks to those megalomaniac pirates out there, the Nykkus males on their ships and these few females are the only ones left. We need to save as many as we can, to give their race a chance to survive."

The dominant female had listened to my succinct report in silence, but her fire-opal eyes glowed with determination by the time I was done. "Survive must we and dominance must do we," she told the viewscreen. "But even if not so, first victims of the warm-born are we. Belongs justice first to us, before to any other."

Captain Kirk stared at her from the viewscreen so intently that I wondered if he already saw the potential danger—and opportunity—in these intelligent sauroids as clearly as I did. "You want to punish the pirate ringleaders yourselves?"

"Punish, avenge, and dominance do!" The bubbling snarls that echoed her own roar showed the sentiment was shared by her sisters. "This right on our world have we. This right among the stars have we also?"

"Considering Klingon concepts of justice, you just might," Kirk said thoughtfully. "Commander Rand, hail Captain Koloth and patch a three-way contact through to the *Jocelyn Bell*."

While we waited for the channel to open, our shuttle finally rounded the shattered corner of the Klingon research station, and the equally burned and blasted silhouette of the *U.S.S. Enterprise* floated into view with two sleek Klingon warships hanging ominously above her. I took a deep breath, feeling suddenly and quite illogically better about my entire engagement with the Nykkus. If they could do this to Captain Kirk, there was no shame in their having done it first to me.

A dark face with slashed eyebrows above glittering black eyes appeared on half the shuttle's viewscreen. From the way Kirk's frown jagged deeper into his forehead, I could tell that Koloth's scornful look was aimed at him. "Please don't tell me you're going to dither at me some more about justice, Captain," he said. "Just transport those reptile criminals over to my custody, and I might be able to forget that you're currently invading Klingon territory."

Kirk's scowl deepened. "The criminals you're referring to have been claimed by a third party in this dispute, Captain

Koloth. It seems the Nykkus themselves have a claim to settle against these pirates."

"And how many fleets of starships do the Nykkus have, that I have to worry about their claims?" Koloth asked coldly.

"None," Kirk said between his teeth. "So far. But they are an emerging and warlike race who own a highly strategic piece of Orion real estate, close to the Klingon border."

I saw the considering look that entered Koloth's dark eyes at that information, despite the fact that he must have known Kirk had deliberately thrown it out to make him pause. I added my own quiet persuasion. "Captain Koloth, isn't there a Klingon proverb that says, 'Choose your enemies more wisely than your friends. Your friends do not come back to kill you later.'"

"Indeed, there is." The Klingon captain turned his gaze slightly in the viewscreen and his slanted eyebrows went up. I suspected the fierce wall of Nykkus arrayed shoulder to shoulder behind my back, teeth bared and frills defiantly erect, also had a salutary impression on him. "Well, what crimes do these Nykkus have to complain of, and what justice do they intend to exact for them?"

Kirk opened his mouth to reply, but a roaring Nykkus voice drowned out whatever he meant to say. "Murder of our species, would commit they!" spat the dominant Nykkus female. "Of justice final givers are we, dominance dance upon their bones until remains defiant none!"

"That sounds interesting," Koloth admitted. "Would you mind an audience?"

Kirk scowled into the viewscreen at him. "You don't have the right to interfere—"

The Klingon's mouth curled into a cruel smile. "Oh, indeed, I do, Captain. My two *undamaged* warships give me that right." This time, it was the mocking emphasis in his voice that made Kirk's face darken. "Your Nykkus friends will dance their dominance right here, on my ship and in front of me, so that I can see that it satisfies the demands of Klingon honor. Otherwise, I will simply blow them and you to bits."

"Where dominance is done care not we," declared the

lead female, before I could interfere. "Fire's daughters are we, the Vorsk, first to hatch in centuries. Dominance on the most-scarred, the Raask, will do we, matters not the place or time."

"That sounds like agreement to me." Koloth was still smiling. "In precisely three minutes, Captain Kirk, I will drop my shields and beam over the—er—reptile ladies. You can beam over the gentlemen you're holding at the same time, along with any witnesses you care to bring. A truce of encounter will hold until justice is delivered to my satisfaction. After that, you can—as you humans say—go on your merry way. Provided that the merry way you go takes you straight out of Klingon territory. Agreed?"

"Agreed," the captain said grudgingly. "Kirk out."

Koloth's cynical face vanished from the viewscreen, leaving only my former captain to look at me with foreboding in his eyes. "Sulu, how many of these female Nykkus were you able to rescue?"

"A full pod of twelve, here have we," said the Nykkus leader before I could answer. "Why ask you?"

Kirk snorted. "Because we have at least seven of the Nykkus ringleaders in custody, the ones marked with all the scars, plus another twenty younger ones who supported their attack. And they all seem to be just as big and strong as you are."

"Strength in more than tail and teeth have we," said the dark female, her teeth parting then meeting again with a startling rasp instead of the usual click. "Sufficient to this meeting be we."

"I hope so," Kirk said grimly. "Because if you're not, Koloth will be doing dominance on all of us."

We materialized in yet another cargo hold, this time one dank and chill to suit Klingon cargo, but well-lit and cordoned off by a watchful line of Klingons armed with *bat'leths* and stern looks. I arrived with Kirk, Spock, and Chekov as the designated Starfleet witnesses in this distinctly odd court of justice. The Nykkus females had already been transported over by the Klingons, punctual to the minute on their promise. We arrived only a moment later, but Koloth was already scowling. The expression pulled his pencil-slim beard into a sour curve across his face.

"Gentlemen," he said reproachfully. At first I thought he was addressing us, but a moment later his voice surged into a peal of annoyance. *"Gentlemen.* Where are the reptile gentlemen these ladies are so eager to punish? You gave your word of honor to bring them over, Captain Kirk."

"And I'll keep it," Kirk said. His voice had taken on the tone of no-nonsense curtness that irritable Klingons so often brought out in him. "In stages." He saw Koloth's face darken and added, "Even a trial doesn't put everyone in the dock at the same time."

"They do on Qo'nos."

Kirk ignored that petulant protest, turning instead to the impatient line of female Nykkus. They were unarmed and unarmored, except for the links of thermal plating that kept their temperature up. Their gold and silver scale-piercings glittered in the light. "Which of the criminals do you wish to confront first?"

"Dominance on the Raask, the first-to-hatch, would do we," said the largest. In the actinic Klingon lights, her opalescent eyes had turned an eerie, opaque white, and a tense flush of purple shone through her lifted black scales. "Now, while strong we are."

Kirk lifted his wrist communicator and toggled it on. "Scotty, beam over the main set of prisoners," he ordered.

There was almost no pause—Montgomery Scott must have been waiting for that order with the Raask already targeted and caught in the transporter's clutches. Forms with familiar sauroid tails began to coalesce in the middle of the open area framed by Klingon guards, forms as broad-shouldered as the female Nykkus who waited for them, but neither as tall nor as dark. Nor as quick.

I wasn't sure what I had expected from this clash of warring sexes. A negotiation, or even an exchange of threats and counter-threats seemed unlikely, given the participants' nonverbal natures. Perhaps I thought the mobile Nykkus bodies would establish heirarchy through gestures and posturing, or that some invisible interplay of pheromones and female musk would bring the rogue males under control.

I couldn't have been more wrong.

The female Nykkus slammed into motion as soon as the glitter of the transporter had faded, as if the smell and sound of their snarling male counterparts had ignited something explosive inside them. Almost thirty meters separated them from the Raask, but they covered the distance in enormous, leaping steps, hurtling into the knot of males while the Raask was still swinging around to see where the thunder of footsteps was coming from.

The scarred Nykkus met that charge with fierce aggression, powerful tails lashing and jaws snapping fiercely for a hold on gem-dark skin, but in even in the chaotic roil of battle, it was clear who the superior warriors really were. With swift and silent precision, the female Nykkus split into pairs and harried five of the scarred males into separate areas of the cargo bay so they couldn't back themselves defensively together. The two largest females took on the remaining males as a pair, leaping in and striking, then flashing away again before marginally slower male reflexes could catch them.

Purple-gray blood ran across the clean metal deck, and roars of anger turned slowly to snarls and groans of pain. And still the male Nykkus battled, stubbornly refusing to yield to their dominant sisters. There was a single instant, more felt than actually seen, when it seemed to me as if all the females of that jeweled fighting group somehow paused in the midst of battle to confer with one another. Before I could even be sure if it had happened, a chorus of final unbelieving shrieks ripped out of the males. A moment later, they all lay dead, their throats bitten across so fast and lethally that no human eye had even seen the killing blow.

Their panting, amethyst-flushed killers stepped back from that carnage, grimacing a little at their various bites and bruises. The largest turned toward us, her opaque white eyes brilliant as a sodium flare against her hematite skin.

"The next domination ready to do are we."

I glanced over at my fellow witnesses to Nykkus justice. Koloth looked as surprised and delighted as if he'd found a secret treasure, while Chekov's pale face wore the half-stunned, half-pained look of a torture victim unexpectedly released but not yet healed. Spock's face remained impassive, of course, but Captain Kirk scowled at the ruthless sauroid killers in what looked like deep anger and dismay.

"Is this how you will preserve your race? By killing all those who are not yourself?" he demanded fiercely.

The lead Nykkus female shook herself, head to tail, in a powerful gesture that still managed to seem surprised at its own power. "To murder planned not we," she said, but she sounded resigned rather than repentant about that. She watched the Klingon guards drag the dead bodies from the combat ground. "If dominance had accepted the Raask, alive would they now be. But to live wished not they anymore."

"I think I agree with her, Captain," I said quietly. "I don't think those particular Nykkus could ever have agreed to stay quietly at home after what they'd done."

"And I don't think we could have trusted them to stay there." Chekov finished my thought in the way we'd fallen into doing during the *Excelsior*'s shakedown cruise. I glanced at his still-pale face and hoped that whatever demons seemed to have been plaguing him had begun to settle now.

"It should also be remembered, Captain, that these Nykkus pirates had the blood of ninety-eight Klingon colonists on their hands. They were not innocent victims." His first officer's words finally eased the troubled look from Kirk's grim face. Despite his own Vulcan imperturbability, Spock had known better than the rest of us what was causing his commander's anger.

"Death honors them with its swiftness." Koloth gave us a look of glittering amusement that didn't quite match his solemn Klingon proverb. "Now please don't be a spoilsport," he added, sounding more like his usual self. "That was a superb clash of warriors. Bring over the others and let us see more!"

Kirk frowned, but lifted his wrist communicator nonetheless. "Scotty, send over the second party."

This time, there were more sparkling transporter beams than usual—Scotty must have had both the main and auxiliary transporters locked in to work together. I watched twenty slighter and less scarred Nykkus forms materialize in the middle of the cargo hold. From the outset, these males seemed less aggressive, perhaps because they were younger, or perhaps because they smelled the blood of their slain leaders under their feet with their first indrawn breaths. The change didn't seem to affect the females—they lunged at this overwhelming group of twenty with the same explosive ferocity as they'd used on their seven older siblings. There was a moment filled with snapping jaws, lashing tails, painful snarls, and more than a few startled yelps as the Nykkus seemed to realize just who was attacking them. For another moment, a few small pockets of resistance roiled within the mass, as one male Nykkus or another tried to break and run. But by the time I'd finished taking my third tense breath, the snarls subsided into a chorus of plaintive hissing, and the young Nykkus males had lowered themselves in crouching submission to the bloodstained victors.

"Now that wasn't anywhere near as much fun," complained Koloth. "In fact, it reminded me entirely too much of a bad Klingon marriage."

Kirk snorted. "You can spare yourself any further sight of it by releasing the rest of the Nykkus into our custody."

The Klingon captain frowned, but with seven blood-soaked bodies heaped along his deck, he couldn't very well claim that his demands for justice hadn't been served. "Release the rest of the little lizards from that Orion yacht we captured, and bring them up here, Tulrik," he ordered one of his lieutenants, sulkily. "And don't forget, Kirk—I expect you to be gone within the hour."

"We will be," the captain said, although after Koloth had turned away, he added under his breath, "Although we may have to row to manage it. Spock, get back to the ship and tell Scotty to prepare for departure. Chekov, I want a security team ready to meet the Nykkus when we beam them back aboard, and quarters arranged for them on a secured deck of the ship." He glanced out at the mass of subdued young sauroid males, looking wry. "Not that I think they'll be causing much trouble, but it never hurts to be safe. We'll beam over with them as soon as the younger ones are here."

"Aye, sir," the two men said in unison. I waited until the transporter beam they'd called for had swept the last gleaming motes of them away before I let my concern and indignation show.

"You're demoting Chekov back to security chief?" The way he'd given my executive officer those orders told me that, even if Chekov himself hadn't felt able to. "Why? Because he helped the Nykkus when they held him hostage?"

"Of course not." Kirk put a hand out to catch my shoulder, looking for once almost as old as I knew he was. "Sulu, you know what happened when Chekov was first officer on the *Reliant*. That's a lot for anybody to stand up under, and he might have found his way through it if you'd managed to get a year or two of routine missions on the *Excelsior* before this happened . . . but you didn't. And this Nykkus disaster has got him doubting everything except the one thing he knows he can still do. Take orders, and carry them out."

My frown deepened. "But, Captain, he's first officer material—"

"I know that, and you know that," Kirk agreed. "But right now, Chekov doesn't know that. Give him a few more years, and maybe he'll remember it again. Until then, let him take his old position on the *Enterprise*. He'll be the better for it."

No doubt he would, but would I? For a minute, clinging uncertainty and self-doubt still insisted that I needed Chekov on the *Excelsior,* that having him there with me would be the easiest way to handle my own new and stressful position. But that inner voice that now mistrusted every easy, obvious answer rose up and informed me that was exactly the reason Chekov shouldn't be there. Maybe, in a few years when I knew for sure that I *didn't* need him, it would be time for us to serve together again.

"Whenever he wants it," I said at last, "there'll be an executive office on the *Excelsior* waiting for him."

"I'll let him know that." Kirk gave me an approving thump on the back, then turned to survey the Nykkus again. A flood of half-grown, snarling males had just been herded into the room. They headed instinctively for the little groups of females and sub-adult males that had coalesced out of the general submission, clustering around them in obedient formations that soon looked as tightly bonded and efficient as trained military teams. The transition wasn't lost on Koloth—I could see him looking across at the Nykkus with speculation gleaming in his dark, shrewd eyes. Apparently, Captain Kirk saw it, too.

"After all this, I hope we didn't just give the Klingons a new ally in this sector," he commented dryly.

I looked across at the dark army of Nykkus and shook my head with determination. "Not if we play our cards right. We'll just have given them a new reason to respect the Federation's allies."

"Spoken like a true captain." Kirk reached out and wrung my hand in his own sturdy grip. I smiled and returned the handshake just as strongly. "Congratulations, Captain Sulu. It's nice to have you in the club. Oh and by the way," he paused with his wrist communicator not yet toggled on, "there's a nice little place on Utopia Planitia that I should probably show you someday. Remind me, next time we both happen to be in port."

"I will," I promised.

Chapter Seventeen

THE CAPTAIN'S TABLE

"AND DID YOU?"

Sulu glanced up from his empty mug of Martian Red Ice Ale, wondering who'd asked that question. The English sea-captain was draining his own mug, and the old man with the meerschaum pipe was busy trying to get it to light for about the fiftieth time that night. The felinoid and the human freighter had slipped away, arm in arm, to some more private part of the bar during the last part of the storytelling session, and the Gorn was lying facedown in his beer bucket. The voice had been too low to be the red-haired pirate's, which meant that it either belonged to the barman or to Captain Kirk himself. Both of them were smiling at him, so he gave up trying to track down the source of the question and simply answered it.

"No," he admitted. "It's been so many years, I'd forgotten all about that promise until I told the rest of the story. Captain Kirk was the one who remembered it, and came to find me." He returned his mentor's smile. "You're right, sir. It was a good way to pass the time."

"I thought you'd like it," Kirk said, pushing his own glass away and buttoning up the flap of his uniform jacket. He slid off his bar stool, then gave the Gorn captain's massive green shoulder a comradely thump. "I hope you enjoyed the story, Captain."

The Gorn lifted an enormous ale-stained snout from his bucket. "What story?" he rumbled. "I forgot to listen." Then he fell back onto the bar and began to snore again.

"Well, now that you know about the place, Captain Sulu, you can come back and find it on your own anytime," the barman said, twisting a rag through a long, triangular glass. "We're open whenever you're passing through."

"I'll remember that." Sulu reached in his pocket for a handful of coins to throw onto the bar, but the red-haired pirate reached out and caught his hand before he could drop them. She had perched herself cross-legged on the bar across from him for the last part of his story, so she wouldn't miss a single exciting detail of the triumph of female Nykkus over their rogue males.

"You can't leave now," she protested. "You haven't finished your story!"

Sulu threw Kirk a rueful look. "That's true, I haven't, but that's because the epilogue hasn't actually happened yet. If you can wait until after I pick up my new first officer tonight—"

"No, I meant about the lizard-women! Did the evil Klingons add them to their archipelago? Or were they invited to join your federation of good nations?"

"That's a whole other story," Kirk informed her. "You'll just have to wait until the next time we drop in to hear it."

"Or ask some other captains to tell you." Sulu couldn't be sure, since the Captain's Table bar was so crowded and wide, but he thought he'd seen a pod of familiar faces enter the room from the other side, dressed in the same Starfleet red Kirk and he wore. The glitter of their dark scales reminded him of his short-tailed stowaway, but he glanced around in vain. The slump of the sleeping Gorn's neck showed no brown and gold gecko anywhere in sight. "Has anyone seen the little lizard I came in with tonight?"

The barman shook his head, looking concerned. "I hope the little furry animal didn't eat him."

"No." The white-maned sea-captain pointed with the

stem of his pipe. "I saw him squiggle off toward those dark-skinned girls, over there."

Kirk evidently had a better view of the group than Sulu did. He lifted his eyebrows in amusement. "Your gecko knows superior officers when he sees them, Mr. Sulu. You'll have to get another pet tonight."

"Actually, sir, I think I've had enough exposure to reptiles for a while." Sulu stepped away from the bar, then paused to give their companions a respectful nod. "It was a pleasure meeting all of you. Fair skies."

"And fairer stars," said the Englishman seriously. "Travel safe among them."

Sulu smiled and followed Kirk out into the midnight-blue Martian night. The two small moons weren't up yet, and the desert-clean atmosphere made the stars burn like diamonds sprinkled on dark velvet. He glanced up, wondering just how many of them he'd visited so far in his life, and just how many more he'd get to see before he died.

"It was good to work with you on the *Excelsior*'s first mission, sir," he said, as they matched strides down the avenue that led back through the spaceport. "I don't remember if I ever thanked you for everything you did back then."

Kirk shook his head, smiling. "Maybe not, but it doesn't matter. You'll pay back the favor to some other young captain who rises out of your ranks someday. That's the way Starfleet works." His smile widened. "And in any case, I got a superb security officer out of the whole mess. If I weren't retiring soon, I'd try to keep him a while longer."

Sulu laughed, knowing from the way Kirk had let his voice drift ahead of them that the words weren't meant for him, but for the dark-haired man waiting at the spaceport's gate. "And he'd probably let you, Captain, but I wouldn't. I've got a hundred free flight simulator games coming to me, after the bet we made about whether you really were going to retire after the Khitomer treaty signing. And with the *Excelsior*'s schedule of deep-space missions for the next five years, the only way I'm ever going to get my payoff is if he comes along as my first officer."

"Very funny," said Chekov. "You're late."

Sulu glanced at his watch, suddenly worried that all that time in the Captain's Table had really been the hours that it seemed. The time displayed there assured him otherwise. "By ten minutes, Pavel! Don't tell me you never found a nice little Russian bar on shore leave and forgot exactly what time you were due back at the ship, because I remember—"

"That was different, there were two diplomats and an alien tax collector involved—"

A hand fell on both their shoulders, warm and friendly. "It's good to see you two working out so well," said Captain Kirk. "Enjoy your mission on the *Excelsior,* Mr. Chekov. And Captain Sulu—let me know how everything goes next time we happen to be in the Captain's Table together."

He left them with a final clap on the shoulders, his strides fading away into the night. Chekov looked curious.

"The Captain's Table?" the Russian asked. "I've never heard of that bar here on Mars. Is it new?"

"New to me, but I think a lot of people have already found it." Sulu paused, remembering what Kirk had said about passing the favor on to a captain who would someday rise out of his ranks. He smiled at his new second-in-command. "Maybe I'll get the chance to take you there someday. I don't suppose you want to bet on whether—"

"No," said Chekov firmly. Sulu laughed, and swung around to walk beside him, heading back toward the spaceport, toward the *Excelsior,* and toward the stars.

Captain Jean-Luc Picard looked around at the thickening fog and decided he would never reach his destination.

In the pea soup that surrounded him, every building looked like every other. Floating street illuminators were few and far between. And as Madigooran cities were known to have their deadlier sides, he wasn't at all comfortable not knowing where he was going.

Turning to his friend and colleague, Captain Neil Gleason of the *Zhukov,* Picard shrugged. "Maybe we ought to turn back," he suggested. "Return to the conference center."

"Nonsense," said Gleason, his face covered with a thin sheen of moisture, his blue eyes resolute beneath his shock of thick red hair. "We can't turn back. We're almost there."

Picard cleared his throat. "Forgive me for sounding dubious, Neil, but you said the very same thing ten minutes ago, and—unless I'm mistaken—ten minutes before that."

Gleason stopped and clapped his colleague on the shoulder. "Come on, Jean-Luc. I've never attended a more useless excuse for a conference in my life. Trade routes, transitional governments, border disputes . . . it's enough to make me wish I'd become an engineer."

Picard had to agree.

A year earlier, the Federation had signed its treaty with the Cardassian Union, with each side ceding certain planets to the other. After that, matters along the border had gotten complicated rather quickly.

For one thing, the Maquis had entered the mix, using guerrilla tactics to make it known they weren't going to accept Cardassian rule—treaty or no treaty. Like it or not, that compelled Starfleet Command to formulate a whole new line of policy.

Hence, the strategic conference on Madigoor IV, which Picard and Gleason had been asked to attend. But in its first day, the conference had dealt little with practical matters—such as where and how the Maquis might strike next—and more with a host of attendant political considerations.

"We owe ourselves a little relaxation," Gleason insisted with a smile. "A little diversion, if you will. And there's no place in the galaxy as diverting as the Captain's Table."

"Yes," Picard responded. "You told me. A pub to end all pubs."

"An understatement, I assure you."

The captain ignored the remark. "At which point, if you'll recall, I said my pub-crawling days were well behind me."

"That's right," Gleason agreed. "And I told you *this* pub would make you change your mind."

Truth be told, Picard had had another reason for trying to decline his friend's offer. He'd had a lot on his mind lately—an *awful* lot—and he still needed to sort it out.

However, there had been no arguing with the man. So

Picard had accompanied him—a decision he was rapidly beginning to regret.

Looking around again, all he could make out were vague shapes. Fortunately, none of them were moving, so there was no immediate danger. But the fog was getting denser by the moment.

"I'm sure you're right," he told his companion reasonably. "I'm sure this Captain's Table is a perfectly wonderful establishment. But if we can't find the place—"

"Oh, we'll find it all right," Gleason assured him. He frowned and peered into the fog. "It's this way," he decided, though he sounded even less sure of himself than when they'd left the conference facility. "Yes, this way for certain, Jean-Luc."

And he started off again. With a sigh, Picard followed.

But after another ten minutes, they still hadn't gotten where they were going. A little exasperated by that point, the captain took Gleason by the sleeve of his civilian garb.

"Listen," he said, "this is absurd, Neil. At this rate, we'll be wandering these streets all night."

Gleason scratched his head and did some more looking around. "I just don't get it," he replied at last. "Last time, it seemed so close to the conference center. And now . . ."

"That was a year ago," Picard reminded him. "Maybe it's closed down in the interim. Or moved."

Gleason didn't say anything, but his look admitted the possibility his friend was right.

"At any rate," said Picard, "this is looking more and more like a wild-goose chase. And as someone who actually chased a wild goose in his youth, I can personally attest to the fruitlessness of such an endeavor."

Clearly, Gleason wasn't as sure of himself as before, but he still didn't seem willing to admit defeat. "Look," he sighed, "maybe if we just go on a little further . . ."

Having reached the end of his patience, Picard held his hand up. *"You* go on if you like. I'm going to call it a day."

Of course, he was so lost at that point, finding the conference center would be no mean feat. But at least he knew the place still existed. That was, unless the Madigoorans had hidden it as well as they'd hidden Gleason's pub—which seemed fairly unlikely.

Gleason squinted into the fog. "It's here somewhere," he insisted. "I could've sworn it was . . ." Suddenly, his face lit up. "Right there!" he announced triumphantly. And he pointed.

Picard followed the man's gesture. Through the concealing, befuddling fog, he could make out a whimsical sign handpainted in bright colors. In flowing Madigooran characters, it read: G'kl'gol Ivno'ewi.

Gleason translated. "The Captain's Table." He held his arms out like a performer seeking applause. "You see? I told you I'd find it."

"So you did," Picard conceded.

Funny, he thought, how that sign had seemed to loom up out of nowhere. Looking at it now, he didn't know how he could have missed it.

"Come on," Gleason told him, tugging at his arm.

They crossed what appeared to be a square and reached the door beneath the sign. It was big, made of dark wood and rounded on top, with a brass handle in the shape of a mythical, horned beast. All in all, a curious entrance—even for Madigoor, which had its share of antique architecture.

Without a moment's hesitation, Gleason took hold of the handle and pulled the door open, allowing a flood of noise to issue forth from inside. Then he turned to his colleague with a grin on his face.

"After you, Jean-Luc."

Picard took Gleason up on his offer. Tugging down on the front of his uniform shirt, he went inside.

His friend followed and allowed the door to close behind them. "Well?" Gleason asked over the sounds of music and clattering glasses and conversation. "What do you think of it?"

Picard shook his head. After hearing his colleague's description of the place, it was hardly the sort of ambiance he had expected. The place wasn't a pub at all, was it?

Rather, it was reminiscent of a French country inn, from the elegant but faded wallpaper to the violin melody coming from somewhere to the ancient hearth blazing in the far wall. There was even an old French nation flag hanging from the smoky, dark rafters.

Also a stair, off to the side and just past the bar, that led upstairs to another floor. No doubt, the captain mused, there were rooms to let up there, for those who had drunk a bit more than their fill.

Tables stood everywhere, a veritable sea of them, each illuminated by an oil lamp in the center and liberally stocked with half-empty wine bottles. And there was hardly a vacant seat to be had, except in the farthest reaches of the place. Nearly every table was surrounded with guests, some sitting and some standing.

Picard couldn't help but remark—if only to himself—on the assortment of species in evidence there. He had run into almost every kind of being in space at some point in his career, and he was hard-pressed to think of one absent from the proceedings. In fact, there were a fair number of patrons whose like he'd never even heard of.

As he continued to examine the place, something caught his eye. A display case, actually, with—unless his eyes were failing him—something remarkable inside it.

Something *quite* remarkable.

"Jean-Luc?" said Gleason.

"Just a moment," the captain replied.

He wound his way through the closely packed crowd, drawn by his curiosity. Moments later, as he stopped in front of the display case, his initial conclusion was confirmed.

There was a bottle inside the case. And inside the bottle was a model of a Promellian battle cruiser—much like the one he had built as a boy, which stood now in his ready room on the *Enterprise.*

Picard had never seen another such model in all his travels. It was hard enough to believe another child somewhere in the universe had been so fond of Promellian ship design. But the chances of that child being inclined to build something in a bottle . . .

He shook his head. It boggled the mind.

Yet here it was, an exact replica of his boyhood trophy. The captain turned to comment on the coincidence. "Look at this, Neil. I—"

But Gleason was gone.

Picard looked about, imagining his fellow captain had merely strayed in another direction, toward the bar, perhaps. But the longer he looked, the more certain he was that Gleason was nowhere to be found.

Now, that's strange, Picard thought. Gleason was so eager to show me this place. Why would he bring me in and then abandon me?

The captain didn't wish to jump to any unfounded conclusions. However, it occurred to him he knew almost nothing about this establishment. The hair prickled on the back of his neck.

If Gleason *had* somehow fallen victim to foul play . . . perhaps someone he'd met here on a previous occasion and offended . . .

Picard was starting to grow uneasy when he felt a hand on his arm. Turning to its owner, he found himself gazing into the shadows of a large hood—in which he could make out a vaguely lizardlike face.

The being said nothing. He looked at the captain without any discernible expression. But as Picard gazed into the yellow slits of the being's eyes, a strange feeling of calm came over him. A sense that there was nothing at all to worry about.

It wasn't hypnosis or anything of that nature. The captain was still thinking as clearly as ever—clearly enough, certainly, to question the effect of the hooded one's presence on him.

But then, Picard told himself, he'd probably been overreacting anyway. A massive conspiracy aside, the place was too crowded for Gleason to have been shanghaied without witnesses. And not every bar was a playground for kidnappers and cutthroats, despite his experiences to the contrary.

No sooner had he come to that conclusion than the hooded one patted his arm and walked away. And all without a word of explanation.

The captain watched the being go. He had half a mind to catch up with him, to ask him why he had done what he'd done—whatever that was. But he had a feeling he wouldn't have gotten an explanation anyway.

As for Gleason . . . he'd simply give the man a chance to turn up, which he would no doubt do in the fullness of time. And in the meantime, Picard would take a closer look at the bottled ship.

As he did this, Picard found himself marveling at the model—at both the care that had gone into its construction and the choices that had been made. For instance, the method used to put the metal hull joints together.

They weren't glued, as one might have expected. They were fused, just the way *he* had done it. In fact, if he hadn't known better, he would have suspected the thing had been taken from his ready room and placed here only a few hours ago.

An unlikely event, the captain conceded. A ridiculously unlikely event. Still, the resemblance was—

Suddenly, he saw something out of the corner of his eye. Something shiny. And it was flying in his direction.

Whirling, he snatched at it—and found himself holding a foil by its leather-wrapped pommel. For a moment, he stared at it, for it was clearly an antique—six hundred years old if it was a day. Then he looked up to see how it had come hurtling his way.

There was a man standing not twenty paces away, carving the air between them with a twin to the foil. He was human, about Picard's height, with a roguish mustache and the fine, worn clothes of a swashbuckler. No doubt, one of those who fancied period styles.

The man smiled. *"En garde, mon ami."*

The captain held a hand up for peace. "Excuse me," he said with the utmost diplomacy, "but I think you've mistaken me for someone else. I didn't come here to duel with you."

"Ah," said the man with the mustache, "but I believe you have."

"Jean!" came a deep, commanding voice.

Picard whirled. Unless he was mistaken, the summons had come from the direction of the bar. Sure enough, the bartender seemed to be looking in the captain's direction.

He was a tall, heavyset human-looking fellow with long, silver hair and a starched white apron. His gaze looked sharp enough to cut glass. Not unlike his tone of voice, it carried something of a warning.

"Are you speaking to me?" Picard asked, wondering how it was the man knew his name.

"I'll have no bloodshed here," the bartender insisted. "Not like the last time, Jean."

The *last* time? the captain wondered. There hadn't been any last time. Not for him, at least.

"You needn't worry," the swashbuckler said. He inclined his head to the bartender even as he pointed his blade at Picard. "There will be no dire injuries tonight. Only a few welts in the name of fun."

Abruptly, Picard realized the swashbuckler was called Jean as well. And with narrowed eyes and rippling jaw muscles, the man was advancing on him, his point extended.

The assembled patrons pushed a couple of tables aside and scurried out of the way. They seemed eager for a little entertainment, and the swashbuckler seemed only too happy to give it to them.

Under most circumstances, the captain would have declined. After all, he stood a chance of getting hurt, and in a strange milieu at that—and he still didn't know what had become of his friend Gleason.

However, the challenge, delivered so recklessly, had stirred in him an emotion he thought he'd suppressed long ago—the bravado of a young cadet. Besides, the swordsman had said he intended no serious violence. And if it were welts he was eager for, as he had announced . . . Picard smiled. He would do his humble best to oblige the man.

"Well?" asked the other Jean, stopping a couple of strides from the captain. "Will you fight me?" He tilted his head slyly. "In the name of good fellowship, if for no other reason?"

Picard chuckled. "In the name of good fellowship . . . why not? The game is one touch. Agreed?"

His adversary grinned broadly. "Let us make it first blood."

The captain frowned. He was somewhat less comfortable with that approach, but he agreed to it.

"First blood, then," he said.

They raised their swords and advanced on each other. Before Picard knew it, he was engaged in a storm of clashing blades.

The captain's opponent was clearly an expert with the

foil, flicking it about with deadly accuracy. But Picard was no novice either. He had studied in some of the most famous fencing dens on Earth, under some of the most exacting masters. Before long, he proved himself equal to any assault his adversary cared to mount.

Then, after about thirty seconds or so, the fellow's attacks began to speed up. It became clear to the captain that his opponent had been testing him to that point, gauging his skills. And now, having educated himself on that count, mustached Jean was beginning to fence in earnest.

Still, Picard kept up with every cut and thrust. He foiled every attempt to bind his blade. And all the while, he looked for an opening, an opportunity to beat his opponent with minimal risk to himself.

But then, was that not what fencing was all about? Anyone could become a swordsman on the physical plane. But the mindgame, the contest of wills and wits, that was another matter entirely.

Picard barely noticed the cheering of the crowd. He was too intent on keeping up with the play, too focused on seeking a weakness he could capitalize on before his opponent discovered one in him.

Their blades whipped back and forth as if they had a life of their own. It was lunge and parry, counter and retreat, over and over again. Each exchange was a thing of beauty—even to Picard himself, though he had little time to appreciate it.

And then he spotted his opening. The other Jean, a little fatigued perhaps, had lowered his blade a couple of inches. Picard pretended to launch an assault on the fellow's shoulder.

Seeing it, the other Jean reacted, bringing his weapon up to fend Picard off. But the captain's true target wasn't Jean's shoulder at all. In mid-lunge, he dropped his blade and came in under his opponent's armpit.

Not hard enough to hurt him, of course, but hard enough to pierce his white, ruffled shirt and break the skin beneath it. After all, the game *was* first blood.

"Alas!" Picard bellowed suddenly, commiserating with his adversary as fencing tradition demanded.

The other Jean took a step back and raised his sword arm.

Clearly, the fabric of his shirt had been pierced. And there was a blood-red mark just to the side of the hole.

Eyeing Picard with a mixture of disappointment and admiration, the fellow hesitated for a moment. Then he brought his blade up to his forehead and swept it down smartly in a fencer's salute.

"You've won," the other Jean conceded.

"So it appears," Picard replied, returning the salute with one of his own. "But it was well fought."

His opponent nodded. "I thought so, too."

A hearty cheer went up from all assembled, shaking the very walls of the place. And before it died, someone had thrust a glass of wine into the captain's hand. From the background, he could hear the stirring strains of ancient France's national anthem.

As the patrons of the Captain's Table clinked their glasses and put their own words to the music, Picard wondered at their careless enthusiasm. What kind of place *was* this? he asked himself.

He had a thought. A very disillusioning thought, at that.

Could this be his old nemesis Q at work again, showing off his vaunted omnipotence for some purpose the captain couldn't begin to fathom? He searched for Q in the crowd, but couldn't find him.

Suddenly, the captain felt an arm close around him like a vice. He looked up into dancing eyes and a dense, white beard and for a moment—just a fraction of a second—imagined he was face to face with Santa Claus. When the stranger laughed, filling the room with his mirth, it didn't do anything to dispel the illusion.

"Why, you're more solid than you look," the big fellow guffawed. He thrust a meaty paw at Picard. "Name's Robinson, lad. Just Robinson. It's a pleasure to make your acquaintance."

The captain took the man's hand and found his own enveloped. "Jean-Luc Picard. The pleasure is mine."

"There's a lad," Robinson rumbled. He pulled the captain in the direction of a table in the corner. "Come and say hello to my friends. They want to meet the man who bested the best sword-fighter in the place."

The best? Picard considered the inn in a new light. Did that mean there were *others?*

A moment later, he was deposited in a chair. Looking around, he found himself in the company of Robinson and his friends. The big man introduced them one by one.

The tall, slender being with the green skin and the white tuft atop his head was Flenarrh. The muscular Klingon female was named Hompaq. Bo'tex was the overweight, oily looking Caxtonian nursing his oversized mug of ale—and exuding an unfortunately typical Caxtonian odor. And Dravvin was the heavy-lidded Rythrian with the loose flaps of skin for ears.

"And this is Jean-Luc Picard," Robinson announced. "Master swordsman and captain extraordinaire."

Taken aback, Picard turned to the man. "How did you know I was a captain?" he asked.

Robinson laughed and slapped Picard on the back, knocking him forward a step. "Didn't anyone bother to tell you, lad? We're *all* captains here, of one vessel or another."

Picard looked around the table. "I didn't know that," he said. And of course, he hadn't.

"That was some duel," Bo'tex remarked, changing the subject a bit. "Best I've seen in this place in quite a few years."

"Admirable," agreed Flenarrh, placing his hands together as if praying. It gave him an insectlike look.

"Here," said Hompaq, pouring a glass of dark liquid into an empty glass. "There is only one drink fit for a warrior."

Picard recalled his tactical officer's dietary preferences. He couldn't help wincing as the glass was placed before him.

"Prune juice?" he ventured.

Hompaq's eyes narrowed. "Of course not. It's bloodwine—and you'll find no better on Qo'nos herself!"

"Not everyone *likes* bloodwine," Dravvin noted, his voice as dry and inflectionless as the other Rythrians of Picard's acquaintance.

"He will like it," the Klingon insisted. She thrust her chin in Picard's direction. "Drink!"

He drank—though perhaps not as much or as quickly as Hompaq would have preferred. To be sure, bloodwine was a powerful beverage. The captain didn't want to be caught at a disadvantage here—especially when his comrade was still missing.

"Excuse me," he said, "but has anyone seen a fellow named Gleason? He's human, a bit taller and broader than I am, with bright red hair turning gray at the temples."

His companions looked at one another. Their expressions didn't give Picard much hope.

"I don't think so," Bo'tex replied, speaking for all of them.

"Worry not," Robinson assured Picard with the utmost confidence. "People have a way of appearing and disappearing in this place. Your friend'll surface before long." He sat back in his chair, as if preparing himself for a good meal. "What's important now is the storytelling contest."

Picard looked at him. "Contest?"

Robinson nodded. "Indeed. We have one every night, y'see." He eyed the others with unmitigated glee. "This evening, we're out to see who can tell the most captivating tale of romance and adventure."

"Yes," Bo'tex confirmed. "We were just about to begin when you and Lafitte started flashing steel."

Picard looked at him. "Lafitte?" he echoed. And now that he thought about it, the bartender had called the man . . .

"So?" Hompaq rumbled, interrupting Picard's thoughts. She leaned across the table toward Bo'tex, accentuating an already ample Klingon cleavage. "You have a story for us, fat one?"

The Caxtonian's complexion darkened. "I'm afraid I'm not much of a storyteller," he demurred. "The . . . er, exigencies of command haven't left me much time to perfect that art."

"Rubbish and nonsense," Robinson boomed, dismissing the idea with a wave of his hand. "You always use that excuse. But captains make the best storytellers of anyone, and Caxtonian captains are no exception."

"If that's so," Bo'tex countered in a defensive voice, "why don't you get the ball rolling for us, Robinson? Or is it possible you haven't *had* any romantic experiences?"

Robinson shot the Caxtonian a look of reproach. "As it happens, Captain Bo'tex, I've had not *one* but *three* great loves in my life. All of them transcendant beauties, and educated women to boot." He cast his eyes down and sighed. "One died young, bless her soul. The second died in middle age, just as I was about to propose marriage to her."

"And the third?" the Rythrian inquired.

Robinson's features took on a decidedly harder line. "She died not at all," he said.

But he didn't go on to say how that could be, or what affect it had on him. And since no one else pressed the man for an explanation, Picard thought it best to keep silent as well.

Robinson turned his gaze on Bo'tex again, obviously not done with him. "And what of you, sir? Is it possible any female could stand the unwholesome smell of you?"

Bo'tex smiled a greasy smile. "I'm not smelly at all—at least, not to other Caxtonians. In fact," he went on, waxing poetic, "my full-bodied scent is actually a pheromone bouquet unequaled on my homeworld. I've often got to fight females off with a stick."

Dravvin closed his eyes. "Somehow, I'm having difficulty conjuring that image in my mind."

"You're not the only one," said Flenarrh.

Hompaq spoke up. "I once had a lover," she growled.

"Oh?" said the Rythrian. "What happened to him?"

The Klingon grinned fondly, showing her fanglike incisors. "I had to gut him, the mangy targ. But he'll always live in my heart."

Dravvin rolled his eyes. "Delightful."

Hompaq eyed the Rythrian with undisguised ferocity. "You mock me?" she rasped, challenging him.

Dravvin was unflustered. "Me?" he said dryly. "Mock you?"

It wasn't exactly an answer. However, it served the purpose of keeping the Klingon in her chair while she pondered it.

Suddenly, a half-empty mug of ale slammed down on the table, causing it to shudder. Picard turned to see its owner—a short, stocky alien with mottled, gray skin and tiny, red eyes. The fellow leaned in among them, between Bo'tex and Robinson.

"Kuukervol," Flenarrh sighed.

"That's right," said the newcomer, who seemed more than a little drunk—though not so much so he hadn't caught the gist of their conversation. "Kuukervol, indeed. And I've got a story that'll make the heartiest of you quiver and the weakest of you weep for mercy—a tale of blood and thunder and love so powerful you can only dream about it."

The assembled captains exchanged glances. Picard noted a certain amount of skepticism in their expressions.

"He was on his way to Rimbona IV—" Hompaq growled.

"Minding his own business," Bo'tex continued, "when he ran into a Traynor disturbance. Level one, perhaps a little more."

"Enough to rattle my sensor relays!" Kuukervol protested.

"And necessitate repairs," Dravvin amplified.

"There he was," said Hompaq. "Blind on his port side, vulnerable to enemy attack and the vagaries of space—"

"Except he *had* no enemies," Bo'tex noted, "and he'd already stumbled on the only real vagary in the sector. Nonetheless—"

"I hurried desperately to make repairs," Kuukervol pointed out, "when who should show up but—"

"A Phrenalian passenger transport," Dravvin added. "And lo and behold, it was headed for Rimbona IV just as he was."

"Of course," Hompaq said, "it wasn't going to stop for him."

"It was full!" Kuukervol declared. "Full to bursting!"

"So it was," Dravvin conceded. "Which is why it could rescue neither our friend nor his crew. However, its commander promised he would alert the Rimbonan authorities to Captain Kuukervol's plight."

"Which he did," said Robinson.

"And they would have arrived just in the nick of time," Bo'tex gibed eagerly, "had they seen any reason to effect a timely rescue—or indeed, effect a rescue at all."

"Unfortunately," Dravvin went on, "there was no discernible danger to ship or crew."

"No *discernible* danger," Kuukervol emphasized. "But the *un*discernible lurked all around us!"

"Under which circumstances," said Flenarrh, "Captain

Kuukervol and his courageous crew had no choice but to take matters in their own hands—and repair their sensor relays on their own."

"At which point," Hompaq chuckled, "they went on to Rimbona—"

"Warier than ever," Kuukervol said.

"And," Dravvin finished, "arrived without further incident."

The newcomer's mouth shaped words to which he gave no voice, as if he hadn't spoken his fill yet. Then he gave up and, wallowing in frustration, took his half-full mug and wandered away.

The Rythrian looked pleased. "I think we've taken the wind out of his sails. And good riddance."

Robinson made a clucking sound with his tongue and turned to Picard. "The poor, benighted sot tells the same story every night. Except for a few middling changes, of course, so it'll fit with the evening's theme."

Flenarrh smiled benignly. "If we've heard him tell it once, we've heard it a hundred times."

"Come to think of it," said Bo'tex, "we never did get to hear the juicy part. I wonder . . . would it have been the Phrenalian commander who served as Kuukervol's love interest? Or perhaps he would have singled out some member of his command staff?"

"The possibilities boggle the mind," Dravvin observed ironically.

"Minds being boggled," said a voice from over Picard's shoulder. "Sounds like my kind of place."

Picard turned and saw another fellow coming over to join them—one dressed in a navy-blue pullover with a white symbol on the upper right quadrant. He had dark hair with hints of gray and a goatee to match. Also, something of an antic sparkle in his greenish-brown eyes.

"Ah," said Robinson. "The captain of the *Kalliope.*"

The newcomer smiled. "Good to see you again, Captain Robinson. What's it been? A year or more?"

"Time has little meaning in a place like the Captain's Table," Robinson replied. "How's your wife? And the little ones?"

"Not so little anymore," said the captain of the *Kalliope.*

"The big one's trimming the sails now and his brother's taking the tiller." He glanced at Picard. "I wondered if you would drop in here someday."

Picard looked at him. The fellow seemed awfully familiar, somehow. Picard tried to place him, but couldn't.

"Have we met before?" he asked the captain of the *Kalliope*.

The man shrugged. "In a manner of speaking. Let's just say your fame has preceded you." He raised a mug of dark beer until it glinted in the light. "To Jean-Luc Picard, Starfleet's finest."

The others raised their glasses. "To Jean-Luc Picard."

Picard found himself blushing. "I'm flattered."

"Don't be," said the captain of the *Kalliope*. "These guys will drink to anything. I learned that a long time ago."

The others laughed. "How true," Hompaq growled. "Though I am not, strictly speaking, a guy."

Bo'tex snuck a sly look at her bodice. "It appears you're right," the Caxtonian told her.

Her eyes narrowing, Hompaq clapped Bo'tex on the back, sending him flying forward across the table. "How clever of you to notice," she said.

As Bo'tex tried to regain his dignity, the captain of the *Kalliope* sat and winked at Picard. "Some group, eh?"

The fellow reminded Picard of someone. It only took him a moment to realize who it was. Riker was a little taller and more sturdily built, but otherwise the two had a lot in common.

Picard nodded. "Some group."

"Now, then . . . where were we?" Robinson asked.

"A tale of romance and adventure," Flenarrh reminded him. "And we still haven't got a volunteer."

"Don't look at me," said the captain of the *Kalliope*. "You know I can't tell a tale to save my life."

Flenarrh looked around the table—until he came to Picard, and his eyes narrowed. "What about you, Captain? You look like a fellow just steeped in romance and adventure."

Robinson considered Picard. "Is that true, Captain? Have you a tale or two with which to regale us?"

Picard frowned as he weighed his reponse. "In fact," he said, "I do. But it's one I would rather keep to myself."

His companions weren't at all happy with that. Dravvin harrumphed and Hompaq grumbled, both clear signs of displeasure.

Robinson leaned closer to Picard. "Come, now," he said. "We're all friends here. All *captains,* as it were. If you can't share your tale with us, who the devil can you share it with?"

Picard looked around the table. Normally, he was a man who kept his feelings to himself. Nonetheless, he felt remarkably at ease in this place, among these people. He drummed his fingers.

"All right," he said at last. "Perhaps I'll tell it after all."

Robinson smiled. "Now, there's a lad."

"A warrior," said Hompaq.

Indeed, thought Picard. And he began weaving his yarn.

To be continued in
The Captain's Table
Book Two
Dujonian's Hoard

James T. Kirk

by
Michael Jan Friedman

His Early Life

James Tiberius Kirk was born in 2233 in the region called
Iowa, on planet Earth. He and his older brother, George
Samuel Kirk, grew up on their father's farm, where they
learned hard work and an appreciation for the facts of life
and death.

In 2246, at the tender age of thirteen, James Kirk was one
of the surviving eyewitnesses to the massacre of some 4,000
colonists on Tarsus IV by Kodos the Executioner. Later on,
as a Starfleet captain, Kirk would identify and apprehend
Kodos, thereby bringing a sense of closure to the surviving
members of the colony.

Kirk was admitted to Starfleet Academy in 2250. One of
his most influential instructors was a man named John Gill,
who would later violate the Federation's Prime Directive by
inadvertently creating a tyrannical regime on the planet
Ekos.

Early on at the Academy, Kirk was tormented by an
upperclassman named Finnegan, who frequently chose
Kirk as a target for his practical jokes. Kirk found a measure
of satisfaction years later, in 2267, when he had a chance to

wallop a replica of Finnegan created on an "amusement park" planet in the Omicron Delta region.

One of Kirk's heroes at the Academy was the legendary Captain Garth of Izar, whose exploits were required reading. Years later, Kirk helped save his hero when Garth became criminally insane and was being treated at the Elba II penal colony. Another of Kirk's personal heroes was Abraham Lincoln, sixteenth president of the United States of America on Earth.

As an exemplary student, Kirk was asked to serve as an instructor at the Academy. One of his students was Gary Mitchell, a fellow human who would become Kirk's best friend. Years later, on the planet Dimorus, Mitchell would risk his life by taking a poisonous dart meant for his friend Jim. Mitchell also arranged for Kirk to date an unidentified "little blonde lab technician," whom Kirk almost married.

Another of Kirk's friends from his Academy days was Benjamin Finney, who named his daughter, Jamie, after Kirk. A rift developed between Finney and Kirk in 2250 when the two were serving together on the U.S.S. Republic. Kirk recorded a mistake that Finney had made in the duty log, and Finney blamed Kirk for his subsequent failure to earn command of a starship.

Shortly thereafter, Kirk and the Republic visited the planet Axanar on a peace mission. The operation was a major achievement for Captain Garth, who spearheaded the mission, while Starfleet awarded Kirk the Palm Leaf of Axanar for his smaller role in the effort.

Kirk continued to serve aboard the Republic until his graduation from the Academy in 2254. Before leaving, he distinguished himself as the only cadet ever to have beaten the "no-win" Kobayashi Maru computer-simulation problem. Kirk accomplished this by secretly reprogramming the simulation computer to make it possible for him to win, earning a commendation for original thinking in the process.

After graduation, Kirk's first posting was as a lieutenant on the U.S.S. Farragut, under the command of Captain Garrovick. While serving aboard the Farragut in 2257, Lieutenant Kirk encountered a dikironium cloud creature at planet Tycho IV. The creature ended up killing some 200 members of the *Farragut's* crew, including Captain Garrovick.

At the time, Kirk felt guilty for the deaths, believing that he could have averted tragedy if he had fired on the creature more quickly. However, he learned years later that nothing could have prevented the deaths of his captain and his comrades.

Sometime in his youth, Kirk was exposed to and almost died from Vegan choriomengitis, a rare and deadly disease which remained dormant in his bloodstream. In 2268, the disease was used by the people of the planet Gideon to infect volunteers willing to die to solve their planet's overpopulation crisis.

In 2263, Kirk was promoted to the rank of captain. A year later, he assumed command of the *U.S.S. Enterprise,* taking over for Captain Pike, and embarked on a five-year mission from 2264 through 2269 that made him a legend in the annals of space exploration.

It was during this five-year mission that Kirk's friendships with Commander Spock and Chief Medical Officer Leonard McCoy developed. These were friendships that would last the three men the rest of their lives.

The Legendary Five-Year Mission

In 2265, Kirk and the *Enterprise* discovered a strange energy barrier. Exposure to the energies in the barrier initiated a transformation in Kirk's friend and colleague, Lt. Gary Mitchell, changing him into a being with tremendous psychokinetic powers. An attempt to quarantine Mitchell at the Delta Vega mining facility was unsuccessful and Kirk was tragically forced to kill his friend to save the *Enterprise.*

Kirk demonstrated his ability to "tap dance"—in other words, to create innovatative solutions to urgent problems—when he encountered a giant spacecraft which identified itself as the *Fesarius.* When the commander of the *Fesarius* threatened to destroy the *Enterprise* if it didn't move off, Kirk told his alien counterpart that Starfleet vessels are equipped with a "corbomite" system which would destroy any attacker. The *Fesarius* refrained from initiating hostilities and Kirk eventually established friendly relations with its lone occupant.

Kirk lost his older brother, George Samuel Kirk (whom only James called Sam), and sister-in-law, Aurelan Kirk, on the planet Deneva when it was invaded by neural parasites in 2267. Kirk's nephew, Peter, survived the invasion. Sam Kirk also had two other sons who were not on Deneva at the time of the tragedy.

James Kirk became the first starship captain ever to stand trial when he was accused of causing the death of Benjamin Finney. However, Kirk's court-martial, held at Starbase 11, exposed a plot by the embittered Finney and proved the captain innocent of any wrongdoing.

Early in his five-year mission, Kirk recorded a tape of last orders to be played by officers Spock and McCoy upon his death. Some time later, while trapped in a spatial interphase near Tholian space, Kirk vanished with the *U.S.S. Defiant* and was declared dead. Spock and McCoy honored their captain's last wishes by working together against the Tholian threat, despite their differences—at least until they realized he wasn't dead after all.

In 2267, Captain Kirk and a handful of his officers were thrust into a mirror universe after trying to beam down to a planet during an ion storm. They found it to be a savage place, governed by a brutally oppressive regime. In this frame of reference, Starfleet officers climbed the ranks through assassination and mutiny.

One of Kirk's earliest nemeses was Harry F. Mudd, a slippery interplanetary swindler. In the captain's first meeting with Mudd, the con man was trying to sell off his "cargo" of three women—the beneficiaries of a Venus drug that kept them young and beautiful.

In another encounter, Kirk's ship was taken over and brought to a planet full of androids—among whom Mudd resided. Mudd had made plans to rule the androids as they expanded throughout the galaxy, but the androids—recognizing Mudd as a flawed example of humanity—decided to strand him with the crew of the *Enterprise* when they left the planet. With Mudd's help, Kirk took back his ship. But when the *Enterprise* departed, Mudd was left behind.

Of course, not all of Kirk's adversaries were completely

human. In 2266, Kirk took aboard young Charles Evans, the lone survivor of a spaceship on the planet Thasus 14 years earlier. When Charlie demonstrated remarkable telekinetic powers, causing crewmen to disappear and taking over the *Enterprise,* Kirk was presented with the difficult problem of dealing with this enfant terrible.

Shortly thereafter, Kirk's *Enterprise* tracked down a Romulan vessel that had attacked Starfleet outposts along the Romulan Neutral Zone. Engaging the ship, Kirk guessed that its actions were a test of Federation resolve. Despite the fact that the Romulans enjoyed a cloaking device and superior weaponry, Kirk outmaneuvered the commander of the Romulan vessel and forced him to self-destruct as an alternative to surrender.

On another occasion, Kirk was split into two distinct personalities by a transporter malfunction. With the help of his chief engineer, Montgomery Scott, Kirk arranged for his two halves to be rejoined.

In 2267, Kirk found himself at odds with his first officer when Spock hijacked the *Enterprise* and took it to Talos IV against the express dictates of Starfleet's General Order 7. It was only when the *Enterprise* arrived at its destination that Spock's plan was revealed—the transport of former *Enterprise* Captain Christopher Pike, crippled in a recent accident, to an environment where he could live out his life in happiness.

Kirk encountered Trelane, an illogical but extremely powerful alien, in the middle of the *Enterprise*'s original five-year mission. Although Trelane appeared to be an adult humanoid fascinated with Earth's history, Kirk recognized that there was more to the being than met the eye. His suspicions were confirmed when Trelane's parents intervened—and Trelane himself was exposed as an alien child.

On the planet Cestus III, the super-advanced Metrons pitted Kirk against a representative of the merciless, lizardlike species known as the Gorn in a one-on-one competition for survival—in which the loser's crew would be destroyed. Using his wits against the Gorn's brawn, the captain defeated his opponent, but refused to kill him. Impressed, the Metrons allowed both crews to live.

The captain also encountered a being who called himself

Apollo, a member of a band of space travelers who lived on Mount Olympus, on old Earth. Though Apollo declared the *Enterprise* crew to be his children, Kirk and his officers refused to stay and worship him—and destroyed Apollo's temple, the source of his amazing powers.

Kirk made one of his greatest enemies when the *Enterprise* discovered a sleeper vessel from the late twentieth century. Its crew turned out to be a group of eugenically created and cryogenically preserved supermen. Their leader, a magnetic but ultimately contemptuous individual named Kahn, tried to take over the ship. However, Kirk defeated Kahn and dropped him off on a virgin world, where he could put his superhuman abilities to the test.

Then again, not all of Kirk's challenges were quite so adversarial. Some of them were a good deal more complex.

At one point, the gravitational forces of a black star hurled the *Enterprise* back in time to the twentieth century, where it was sighted by a pilot named John Christopher. So as to leave the time line intact, Kirk beamed Christopher aboard the *Enterprise*. However, when Spock pointed out that Christopher's son would become an important space explorer, Kirk returned the pilot to Earth.

In 2267, Kirk came upon two worlds engaged in a war in which randomly selected casualties, who willingly sacrificed their lives in antimatter chambers to prevent the resumption of a real conflict. Kirk destroyed the computers on one of the combatant-worlds, thereby forcing the two worlds to engage in a bloody fight or seek peace.

When Spock entered the ponn farr, the Vulcan mating cycle, Kirk was forced to return his first officer to his native planet. However, through a series of machinations, Kirk wound up not as a visitor to a marriage ceremony, but as a participant in a deadly combat—pitted against the inhumanly strong Spock. Only an injection by Dr. McCoy allowed Kirk to escape his dilemma by appearing dead and thereby ending the combat.

By 2267, Kirk had earned an impressive list of commendations from Starfleet, including not only the Palm Leaf of Axanar, but the Grankite Order of Tactics (Class of Excellence) and the Preantares Ribbon of Commendation (Classes First and Second). Kirk's awards for valor included the Medal of Honor, the Silver Palm with Cluster, the Starfleet Citation for Conspicuous Gallantry, and the Kragite Order of Heroism.

In 2268, Kirk and two of his officers were abducted by a group of advanced beings called the Providers and forced to fight as gladiators for the Providers' amusement. To save his people and his ship, Kirk wagered their freedom on his ability to defeat three of the Providers' best thralls—a feat he then carried off.

Soon after, Kirk took the *Enterprise* into Romulan space and feigned a nervous breakdown due to overwork. Spock denounced his captain and gave the appearance that he had killed Kirk, thereby attaining his way into the trust of a female Romulan commander.

However, it was all part of a scheme to gain possession of the Romulans' cloaking device, the efficacy of which Kirk had experienced firsthand a couple of years earlier. In disguise, the captain beamed aboard the Romulan flagship, stole the device, and escaped.

Kirk was known to violate Starfleet directives when he saw no viable alternative. In 2268, for instance, the Klingons armed one component of a planet's population—the Hill People—with firearms, thereby endangering another component of the population. In violation of the Prime Directive, the captain reluctantly restored the balance of power by arming the endangered tribespeople as well.

His Romances

Kirk was notably unsuccessful in maintaining long-term liaisons with the opposite sex. Although he was romantically involved with a great many women during his life, his intense passion for his career always seemed to interfere with his relationships.

In 2252, Kirk dated a woman named Ruth. Not much is known about her, though she seemed to occupy Kirk's thoughts for years afterward. Later on, while still attending the Academy, Kirk spent a year or so with a woman named Janice Lester. Some fifteen years later, Lester would attempt to switch bodies with her old flame in a bizarre attempt to realize her dream of becoming a starship captain.

A few years prior to his command of the *Enterprise,* Kirk became involved with a scientist, Dr. Carol Marcus. The two had a child, David Marcus, but Kirk and Carol did not remain together because their careers took them in different directions.

Other significant romances in Kirk's life included Janet Wallace, an endocrinologist who later saved his life from an aging virus; Areel Shaw, who, ironically, prosecuted Kirk years later in the case of Ben Finney's apparent death; and Miramanee, a beautiful primitive woman Kirk married in 2268 after he was struck with amnesia on a landing party mission. Miramanee became pregnant with Kirk's child, but both she and her unborn baby were killed in a local power struggle.

Kirk fell in love with a woman named Antonia after his first retirement from Starfleet, and for the rest of his life regretted not having proposed to her. However, Kirk's most tragic romantic involvement was with American social worker Edith Keeler, whom he met when he traveled into the 1930s through the Guardian of Forever. As it turned out, Keeler's existence was a focal point in time, and Kirk was forced to watch her die to prevent a terrible change in the established time line.

Kirk was not involved with the upbringing of his son, David Marcus, at the request of the boy's mother, Carol Marcus. In fact, Kirk had no contact with his son until 2285, when Carol and David were both working on Project Genesis and Kirk helped rescue the two from Kahn's vengeance. Later, Kirk and his son were able to become friends. Tragically, David was murdered shortly thereafter on the Genesis Planet by a Klingon officer named Kruge, who sought to steal the secret of Genesis.

His Later Career

Following the return of the *Enterprise* from its five-year mission in 2269, Kirk accepted a promotion to admiral and became chief of Starfleet operations, while the *Enterprise* underwent an extensive refit. At the time, Kirk recommended Will Decker to replace him as *Enterprise* captain.

However, when V'ger—a highly destructive mechanical life-form—approached Earth in 2271, Kirk accepted a grade reduction back to captain in order to reassume command of the *Enterprise* and deal with the threat. In the end, he defused the problem, thanks to the willingness of Decker and a Deltan female named Ilia to merge themselves with the V'ger entity.

Kirk's first retirement from Starfleet took place some time thereafter. Nonetheless, unable to ignore the siren call of duty, he returned to Starfleet in 2284 and became a staff instructor with the rank of admiral at Starfleet Academy.

Before long, however, Kirk found himself dissatisfied with ground assignment. He returned to active duty in 2285 when Khan Noonien Singh hijacked the starship *Reliant* and stole the Genesis Device, a revolutionary terraforming tool. Commander Spock, Kirk's close friend, was killed in the effort to retrieve the device.

Upon learning that Spock's katra—or personal essence—had survived the incident, Kirk hijacked the *Enterprise* to the Genesis Planet to recover Spock's body and take it to Vulcan. There, on the planet of his birth, Spock was brought back to life, his body and katra reunited.

In the course of retrieving Spock, Kirk was forced to destroy the *Enterprise,* to prevent the ship's capture by Klingons. Later, in 2285, he was charged with nine violations of Starfleet regulations in connection with the hijacking of the *Enterprise.*

All but one charge was dropped. Kirk was found guilty of that one remaining charge—disobeying a superior officer.

However, the Federation Council was so grateful that Kirk had saved Earth from the devastating effects of an alien probe, it commuted his sentence and granted him the captaincy of a second starship named *Enterprise,* known colloquially as the *Enterprise-A.*

Kirk was an intensely motivated individual who loved the outdoors. His greatest accomplishment in that regard was free-climbing the sheer El Capitan mountain face in Yosemite National Park on Earth.

The captain was an accomplished equestrian as well. He kept a horse at a mountain cabin that he owned during his first retirement. Another companion at his mountain cabin was Butler, his Great Dane. He sold the cabin some time after his return to Starfleet.

Kirk's bitterness over his son's murder by Kruge colored his feelings about the Klingons for years after. He therefore opposed the peace initiative of Klingon chancellor Gorkon in 2293. Nonetheless, Starfleet appointed him the Federation's "olive branch" and assigned him the duty of escorting Gorkon to Earth.

During that mission, Kirk—along with his friend and fellow officer, Dr. McCoy—was arrested and wrongfully convicted of the murder of Gorkon. It later turned out that Gorkon had been killed by Federation and Klingon forces conspiring to block his initiatives. Escaping from Rura Penthe, a cold and deadly Klingon prison-planet, Kirk played a pivotal role in saving the historic Khitomer peace conference from further attacks. He retired from Starfleet a second time about three months after the Khitomer conference.

Shortly after his second retirement, Kirk was an honored guest at the launch of the Excelsior-class starship *Enterprise-B* in 2293. When the vessel ran into trouble on its maiden voyage, Kirk was believed dead.

However, it was later learned that he had actually disappeared into a unique temporal anomaly called the nexus. Kirk remained in the anomaly until 2371, when he was contacted and roused from his "paradise" by twenty-fourth-century *Enterprise-D* captain, Jean-Luc Picard.

Working alongside Picard, Kirk emerged from the nexus to help save the inhabitants of the Veridian system from the machinations of a deranged El-Aurian scientist, Tolian Soran. However, Kirk's heroic effort cost him nothing less than his life. Throughout his illustrious career, he had cheated death at every turn, until, at last, he could cheat her no more.

James T. Kirk is buried on a mountaintop on the planet called Veridian III. Fueled by a burning curiosity to see "what's out there" and armed with an unparalleled resourcefulness, Kirk will long be remembered for going boldly where no one had gone before.

Captain Hikaru Sulu

Sulu began his career in Starfleet under the command of Captain James T. Kirk on the original *Starship Enterprise*. Sulu, born in San Francisco on Earth was initially assigned as a physicist in 2265 but later transferred to the helm.

Sulu assumed command of the *Starship Excelsior* in 2290, and subsequently conducted a three-year scientific mission of cataloging gaseous planetary anomalies in the Beta Quadrant. Sulu and the Excelsior played a pivotal role in the historic Khitomer peace conference of 2293 by helping to protect the conference against Federation and Klingon forces seeking to disrupt the peace process.

Sulu demonstrated his loyalty and courage when he risked his ship and his career by violating Starfleet orders and attempting a rescue of his former shipmates James T. Kirk and Leonard McCoy. During the attempted rescue, Sulu narrowly escaped a Klingon patrol commanded by Captain Kang in the Azure Nebula. Sulu never entered the incident into his official log.

Sulu had a wide range of hobbies, including botany and fencing. The latter interest surfaced when Sulu suffered the effects of the Psi 2000 virus in 2266, and Sulu threatened everyone in sight with a foil. Old style handguns were another of his hobbies.

Hikaru Sulu had a daughter, Demora Sulu, born in 2271.

—Adapted from *The Star Trek Encyclopedia* by Michael and Denise Okuda

Look for STAR TREK Fiction from Pocket Books

Star Trek: The Next Generation®

Star Trek: Deep Space Nine®

Star Trek®: Voyager™

Flashback • Diane Carey
The Black Shore • Greg Cox
Mosaic • Jeri Taylor

#1 *Caretaker* • L. A. Graf
#2 *The Escape* • Dean W. Smith & Kristine K. Rusch
#3 *Ragnarok* • Nathan Archer
#4 *Violations* • Susan Wright
#5 *Incident at Arbuk* • John Greggory Betancourt
#6 *The Murdered Sun* • Christie Golden
#7 *Ghost of a Chance* • Mark A. Garland & Charles G. McGraw
#8 *Cybersong* • S. N. Lewitt
#9 *Invasion #4: The Final Fury* • Dafydd ab Hugh
#10 *Bless the Beasts* • Karen Haber
#11 *The Garden* • Melissa Scott
#12 *Chrysalis* • David Niall Wilson
#13 *The Black Shore* • Greg Cox
#14 *Marooned* • Christie Golden
#15 *Echoes* • Dean W. Smith & Kristine K. Rusch

Star Trek®: New Frontier

#1 *House of Cards* • Peter David
#2 *Into the Void* • Peter David
#3 *The Two-Front War* • Peter David
#4 *End Game* • Peter David
#5 *Martyr* • Peter David
#6 *Fire on High* • Peter David

Star Trek®: Day of Honor

Book One: *Ancient Blood* • Diane Carey
Book Two: *Armageddon Sky* • L. A. Graf
Book Three: *Her Klingon Soul* • Michael Jan Friedman
Book Four: *Treaty's Law* • Dean W. Smith & Kristine K. Rusch

Star Trek®: The Captain's Table